The Courage of Horses

Pegasus Equestrian Center Series: Book 4

Diana Vincent

This is a work of fiction. Names, characters, places, and incidents are the product of the author's imagination. Any resemblance to real events or persons is purely coincidental.

Cover design: Kimberly Killion
www.hotdamndesigns.com

Cover photograph: Dee Dee Murry
www.deedeemurry.com

ISBN-13:978-1512297195
ISBN-10:1512297194

DEDICATION

Dedicated to my ever faithful husband Dom, and to all the readers who wrote asking for more. You have given me the courage to keep on writing.

My horse, share with me
Your fleet legs, your strength, your speed
Your heart of valor.

Also by Diana Vincent
The Girl Who Loves Horses, Pegasus Equestrian Center Series: Book 1
The Boy Who Loves Horses, Pegasus Equestrian Center Series: Book 2
For the Love of Horses, Pegasus Equestrian Center Series: Book 3

CONTENTS

1 U.S. DRESSAGE FINALS

Blind repetition and drill are the enemies of feeling riding. They create dullness and disobedience instead of cooperation, freedom and willingness to work. - Klaus Balkenhol

"Calm down please, Ms. Barringer. I'm sure we can adjust stabling. I have notified the owner and he is on his way here now." The grounds official spoke calmly to the young woman standing in front of him with hands on her hips and a defiant expression on her face.

Lisa Barringer, the grounds official, and his assistant, all turned their heads when a hoof banged loudly against the wall between two stalls, followed by a horse's squeal of alarm. The head of a large, dark bay pushed against the grate of his stall, his teeth bared and ears laid flat. Next to him, a chestnut gelding backed into the corner of his own stall, his legs trembling. He had dared to step forward to the hay rack at the front of his stall. But every time he neared his feed, the neighboring horse threatened him.

"You see? I want that beast relocated now!" Lisa demanded. "He is terrorizing my horse. I don't think Volantis has had one bite to eat since he's been stabled here."

The grounds official coughed behind his fist. He did not want to remind the woman that she had only moved her horse to this barn a few hours ago, after insisting the previous barn was too drafty. Nor did he suggest she simply move the hay out of the rack and to the back corner of the stall. The woman's eyes blazed and there were red splotches of anger on her cheeks. She was obviously not in a receptive mood to suggestions.

At that moment, a figure emerged into the light at the entrance of the barn. The assistant recognized the young man and raised a hand in relief. He nudged the official to let him know the owner had arrived.

Sensing the group had been in a heated discussion in front of his horse's stall, the young man's stomach knotted in dread. *What has Oberon done now?*

"Ah, Mr. Girard, thank you so much for coming right away," the official greeted as soon as River Girard reached the group.

"No problem," River replied and looked quizzically at each face, trying to discern the trouble. But no explanation was needed when the chestnut again gingerly approached his hay, only to be driven back by the intimidating head of Oberon threatening again with banging his hoof and bared teeth. "Oh," River said in comprehension.

"Your horse is a monster!" Lisa turned on River now, her voice rising. "You shouldn't be allowed to have such a dangerous animal in public places…oh, it's you!" Her tone immediately softened when she recognized River. "You own this horse?"

"I do," he admitted.

"Oh…well, but…." Her anger dissipating, she extended her hand and her expression softened into a smile. "I'm sorry, I'm Lisa Barringer."

"River Girard," he replied with a half-smile and shook the proffered hand. "Nice to meet you."

"You're the rider everyone is talking about. You blew everyone away in that Prix St. Georges test. You are the most phenomenal rider I have ever seen." She cocked her head toward Oberon and asked, "Is this the horse you rode in that test?"

River nodded, wondering what she was talking about.

"You are like this big mystery," Lisa went on. "Nobody knows where you come from. You just sort of appeared out of nowhere. You haven't competed in any of the big events nationwide or in Europe, have you?"

"No, just in my region."

"And you haven't been to any of the social events happening around here either."

"No," River admitted, still feeling baffled over what she was talking about. Nor did he want to explain how he felt shy and uncomfortable in a room full of strangers. He had avoided all the parties and even the award ceremonies here at the U.S. dressage finals.

"Didn't you ride a grand prix test as well?"

"Yeah, on my other horse," River said, indicating the horse across the aisle from Oberon.

She looked over at the stall where Pendragon, also a bay, placidly chewed his hay, unconcerned by all the commotion. "You should have won," Lisa stated. "That was the most correctly performed test I have ever witnessed."

"Thank you, but the first and second place horses did very well," River said humbly.

Lisa laughed. "They were nice. I guess it's the age old question of which should earn more points, brilliance or correctness."

"I think in a freestyle brilliance is probably more important, as long as the horse is mostly correct."

The official coughed again to interrupt and bring the attention back to the issue. "What is it you would like me to do?" he asked, sensing Lisa might have changed her mind.

"Well …" She looked pleadingly at River.

"I can move him," River offered. It was obvious the two horses needed separation, and since it was Oberon causing the trouble, it was only fair that he be the one to move.

"I believe there are some vacant stalls in the shed rows," the assistant suggested. "I could locate one."

"Thank you, please do," the official said, and then turned to River. "Do you have a groom or someone who could lead your horse out until we assign a new stall?"

"No problem, I'll take him out. Do you think you could find two stalls near each other so I can keep both my horses in the same barn?" River asked.

"Certainly," the official replied. He nodded to Lisa and then left to expedite the relocation.

"I am sorry to cause all this trouble," Lisa said. "It's just…"

"I guess it's my horse causing the trouble, not you," River interjected. "I don't want to see your horse traumatized either." He picked up Oberon's halter and stepped into his stall. He wisely held back mentioning the fact her horse was too stupid to realize Oberon could not get to him. Oberon started to shift away but River moved into his shoulder, adeptly placed the halter, and led him out.

"I could help you move your tack," Lisa called after him as he led Oberon toward the exit doors."

"Thanks, it's okay," he said over his shoulder, but continued to the exit. Outside, he walked with Oberon along the horse path while he waited for his new barn assignment.

"Why do you have to be such a bully?" he asked, partly annoyed and partly amused. Oberon was smart, and whenever he could get the advantage, he took it. It became a game to him when he had figured out he could intimidate the gelding in the next stall. River did not approve of his bad manners, but he couldn't help but derive some humor in the bay's trick. And at least his aggression had been toward another horse and not a human. A few months ago at another show, Oberon had nipped at a person who had foolishly stuck a hand in his stall, trying to pet him.

Twenty minutes later, the assistant located River and gave him the new stall assignment. River settled Oberon and then went back for Pendragon. He noticed Lisa still inside her horse's stall, encouraging him to eat. She looked up and smiled as River walked his second horse out. To his surprise, she left her own horse and came up to him.

"I really am sorry," she apologized again. "I hate to disrupt your evening."

"It's not that much trouble," he assured her.

"I am going to help you move your stuff."

He shrugged but didn't object as she walked with him to the new barn.

"Has your horse always been so difficult?" Lisa asked conversationally.

"Yeah, actually worse when I first got him. A friend gave him to me as a last resort. Her father was going to have him put down because he was too dangerous."

"Really?" She sounded shocked. "He obviously is very talented."

"Yeah, I think it's his talent that got him in trouble. He figured out how big and strong he is."

"But you saved him?"

River laughed softly. "Yeah, I guess. I spent months trying to teach him basic ground manners and I wasn't sure I would ever dare try to ride him. Fortunately, I got some help from an old cowboy friend."

"Obviously you did try to ride him."

"I did, and once I started riding him it seemed like we got along much better. I never intended to compete on him though."

They reached the new barn, and River settled Pendragon in the stall next to Oberon. Lisa insisted on helping with the rest of his equipment, and they were able to move everything in one trip.

"Don't pick on anyone else, okay?" River said, tossing in what was left of Oberon's dinner hay. The official had judiciously managed to get an end stall so that Oberon only had Pendragon for a neighbor and a storage bay across the aisle. Oberon gazed out at him with what River thought was a sulking expression before he dropped his head to eat.

He looked into Pendragon's stall, satisfied the gelding had settled back to his own dinner hay in spite of the move. He checked both stall latches and then left the barn.

Lisa waited for him outside. "Are you going to the competitors' dinner tonight?" she asked.

"No, I need to be up early to check on the horses."

"Don't you have a groom to help you?"

"No, it's best if I handle Oberon, and my other horse is no trouble."

"Well, have you had dinner yet?"

"I was just headed out to eat when the guy called me."

"The least I can do is treat you to dinner. I really appreciate you going to all this trouble," Lisa offered.

"It's fine, you don't have to," he said.

"But I want to, okay?"

She's nice, River thought. *There's nothing wrong with going out to dinner as a friend.* The fact that his girlfriend Sierra, had not come to be with him for the finals made it easier for him to accept. He was a little annoyed with Sierra right now. "Okay," he said with a smile.

They walked to one of the restaurants on the horse park grounds, and after being promptly seated, they placed their orders.

"Why didn't you want to compete on Oberon?" Lisa resumed their previous conversation while they waited for their food.

"Maybe being entered in too many competitions at a young age had a lot to do with souring his temperament. I just wanted to ride him for my own pleasure and spare him that stress. He's a lot of fun to ride because he has great natural movement."

"He certainly is a splendid mover. But obviously you did decide to enter him in shows."

"He's one of those horses who likes to show off. I started to notice how he gave me so much more whenever he had an audience. He's very proud."

"Yeah, I know what you're saying. I've known some horses who really perk up at a show."

"Me too, but nothing quite like Oberon. It's funny, but he's the one who chose dressage."

"What do you mean?" Lisa asked.

"I knew he had been shown as a jumper before I got him, so one day I decided to see how well he could jump. We're really more of an eventing stable. I started with some very low cavalletti, something any horse could do." River smiled as he recalled the memory. "It was as if I had asked him to jump the moon or something. His ears went back, he got choppy, and he hit every single pole. I swear, his whole body sagged, like I had deflated him. I tried again a couple months later, taking him on an outside course just to see if it made a difference. He wanted to refuse or run out at every jump. He very clearly told me he does not like to jump."

"You're kidding! Okay, I know you're not. He really is quite opinionated, isn't he?"

"Yes, he is."

The food arrived. They ate hungrily in silence until the initial pangs of hunger had been assuaged. Then River asked, "What about Volantis? Has he always been so timid?"

Lisa laughed (*a very pleasant laugh*, River thought). "Yeah, even as a foal…" and she spent a good part of getting through the entrée to tell River stories of her own horse.

They had dessert, and then reluctantly, for he was really enjoying exchanging stories with Lisa about different horses they had known, he said, "I really do need to get to bed, but this has been fun." He reached for the check.

"No, no," Lisa said, placing her hand on top of his to prevent him taking the bill. "I invited you, remember? It's my thanks for being so willing to move Oberon."

He argued, but ultimately let her pay the bill. They rose and made their way outside.

"What time is your class tomorrow?" Lisa asked.

"Nine-twenty."

"Which horse are you riding?"

"The mean one," he said, his mouth twitching in a sly smile.

"What test?"

"The Prix St. Georges freestyle."

"That should be amazing; I'll have to watch. I don't ride until after one."

"Well, uh...." He held out his hand, feeling a little awkward now that it was time to go their separate ways. "Thanks for dinner."

"It was my pleasure, really," she insisted. She clasped his hand briefly, not a handshake but more of a quick holding of hands. She smiled, turned and walked away.

He watched her disappear from his view, thinking to himself, *Yeah, really nice girl. Pretty too.*

"Here's your coffee. Are you warm enough?" Leanne McCall asked, handing her father an insulated mug with a lid. Without waiting for his answer, she tucked the fleece blanket in tighter around his lap and legs where he sat in his wheelchair.

"I'm fine, sit down, dear," Jack McCall assured his daughter. "Here comes the first entry."

Father and daughter watched together the first three competitors in the Prix St. Georges freestyle. They complimented and criticized each horse and rider, usually in agreement.

"This is the one," Jack said, referring to the show schedule in his lap. He shifted up a little straighter in anticipation.

"Number two-sixty, Oberon; owned and ridden by River Girard of Pegasus Equestrian Center, Washington State," came over the PA system.

Jack and Leanne did not speak during the performance, mesmerized by the perfection of movement of the talented bay horse, and not wanting to distract each other with talking. The horse flowed through the test, appearing to execute the movements as if they were his own ideas, his rider merely a silent partner, or rather an appendage of the horse's body.

The spectators exploded into applause at the final salute.

"Now that is what I call classical dressage," Jack stated as the bay left the ring.

"River Girard goes on the list?" Leanne asked.

"Top of the list," Jack replied.

Textbooks, lab workbooks, and folders stuffed with notes surrounded Sierra Landsing, where she had settled into the most comfortable easy chair in her apartment. She had been studying nonstop all weekend, taking breaks only to go to the bathroom or get snacks. Tomorrow, Monday, the grueling week of midterm exams began.

The chime of her cell phone interrupted the very difficult concept she had been trying to memorize. Annoyed, she grabbed her phone, but recognizing the caller, her annoyance immediately was replaced by a sudden onset of guilt. *Oh no, I forgot to watch!*

"Hi, River. How did it go today?" Sierra asked.

"Fine, we're home," he answered, sounding tired.

"You're home already?"

"I rode my last class in the morning. We left a few hours after that."

"So, how did you do?"

"You didn't watch?" It almost sounded accusatory.

"Not yet, I've been studying nonstop. I kind of lost track of time." She did not want to admit she had completely forgotten. "But I'm really looking forward to watching all the videos right after my last exam. It will be my reward," she explained.

River said nothing, and she sensed he was still upset that she hadn't flown to Kentucky to be with him. And since she hadn't even taken the time to watch....

When River had qualified to compete in the dressage finals, she had been so proud and encouraged him to go. He had agreed, probably because his boss Tess Holmes, and Mrs. Galensburg, Pendragon's owner, had insisted. It meant flying to Lexington, Kentucky and staying for the entire first week of November. River had asked her to come with him. He had made arrangements for his assignments and to miss classes with his professors at the nearby university where he was enrolled. He did not understand why she couldn't do the same. At first, she thought she could fly down late Friday night and at least be with him for the last two days on the weekend. But when she checked her schedule and discovered it was the week before midterms, she could not spare the time away from studying. River never could understand her need to maintain top grades, and not just because she needed them to maintain her scholarship. She was in her last year of getting her bachelor's degree in biology, her chosen pre-veterinary major. Getting into the veterinarian program was highly competitive. She *had* to be at the top.

"Please, River, just tell me how you did?" She pleaded into the silence.

"We scored eighty-six."

"Wow, awesome; and...?"

"We took first place."

"Oh my," she exclaimed. "River, I am so proud of you and Oberon."

"I'm going to bed, I'm really tired," he said in the same dull voice. "I'll let you get back to studying."

"River, wait …" but he had hung up. Sierra shook her head in exasperation and tossed her phone back into her bag. "His feelings are hurt," she muttered aloud, shuffling through the notes on her lap.

Are we drifting apart? The bitter thought entered her mind. River and she had been going together since high school. Their relationship had lasted so far, even though they only had school breaks and summers together. But this championship seemed to have put a rift between them. He had wanted her support at the show. She wanted his support of her dream of becoming a veterinarian.

Christmas break was a month and a half away. *I'll make it up to him when we are together again*, she resolved. With a tired sigh, she picked up her notes and went back to studying.

"You going to stay here?" River asked his dog Storm, after hanging up with Sierra. He did intend to go to bed as he had told her. But first, he wanted to make his habitual last check on the horses in the stable.

Storm cocked an ear and thumped her tail, but did not get up from the comfortable rug where she lay.

Getting old. It was not a new observation. River bent down to pet her head before he stepped outside. Storm no longer had the energy to follow him everywhere, especially at the end of the day.

River made the rounds, checking on each horse for signs of discomfort; colic, injury, or some other ailment. He especially wanted to be sure Oberon and Pendragon were well and comfortable after the stress of traveling by plane from Kentucky back to Washington, and then another two-hour trailer ride home.

Everyone appeared well. He lingered a few moments when a horse whickered at him in recognition, seeking attention. A few horses still nibbled on the last remnants of hay. Most stood with a back leg bent in rest and their heads lowered in sleep. Both Oberon and Pendragon appeared sound asleep, Oberon already lying down. Sierra's horse Fiel, the old pony Muffin, and his own filly Ysbryd, also lay comfortably nestled in the shavings. Satisfied, River stopped last at the stall of Corazón, his favorite. The black gelding raised his head and whickered a low, almost soundless, rumble. River stepped inside and stood close to his warmth, stroking his neck.

"I missed you," he murmured as the black nuzzled at him.

In a much better mood, River returned to his room above the lounge. As he undressed for bed he considered calling Sierra again and apologize for being curt with her. But it was already after ten, and if she wasn't still studying, she had probably gone to bed herself.

The phone call came twenty-four hours later than Tess Holmes expected, and the delay chewed on her nerves, leaving her frazzled. "Hello, Mrs. Galensburg," she greeted.

"Good evening, Tess," replied Frances Galensburg, Pendragon's owner. "I assume you watched the live-streaming."

"Of course, Pendragon did very well." *Here it comes....* Tess expected now to hear a tirade of complaints and demands of why Pendragon only came in third and did not win at the dressage finals.

"Pendragon does not have the talent I had hoped for when I purchased him. Your boy rode him to the best of his ability, but Pendragon simply cannot compete at that level."

Tess almost dropped her phone, not quite believing the words coming from that woman's mouth.

"I've learned quite a bit over these years, and I believe Pendragon has reached his peak. I would like to make an offer to purchase the other horse your boy rode, Oberon. Now that is a horse with the scope to go all the way to gold in the Olympics."

"You want to buy Oberon?" Tess asked, her voice cracking in dismay. Now she clutched the phone to keep it from slipping from her nervous hands.

"Are you hard of hearing?"

"But..."

"I'm offering two-hundred and fifty thousand; plus I will donate Pendragon to your stable. He should make a fine school horse."

"That is a very generous offer," Tess gasped. "But River is the owner and...."

"I realize River is the owner, so present him my offer. I will talk to you later in the week." With that, Frances Galensburg hung up.

The call had come just as Tess was getting into bed. She collapsed back against her pillows, still clutching her phone. How was she ever going to present this offer to River in a way to convince him to accept? She was surprised Mrs. Galensburg actually used River's name. After all the years of River riding for that woman, she still referred to him as 'your boy'. *River is twenty-one, for heaven's sake!*

Many changes had occurred at her stable, Pegasus Equestrian Center, in the three years since River and Sierra had graduated from high school. The physical improvements to the property she owed to Mrs. Galensburg. When her previous partner wanted out of the business, Tess did not have the means to buy him out or take over full payments for what was still owed on the property. She had already been turned down from two lenders when Frances Galensburg, who somehow had found out she was in search of a loan, offered to buy out her partner and take over the lien on the property. Apparently it appealed to her to be part owner of a stable.

So far, this partnership had worked out very well. Mrs. Galensburg wanted to improve and expand the facility, and it seemed she had an unlimited amount of liquid assets to spend on what to her was probably a hobby. Ten more stalls had been added in a new row barn, increasing the capacity from twenty to thirty horses. She bought an adjoining parcel of land which gave them room for several more turn-out pastures as well as a field to grow their own hay. It added additional acreage for the cross-country jumping course and many more practice obstacles had been built, including a full pond with jumps in and out of the water for all levels of eventing. The indoor arena lights were replaced with high-quality lighting as bright as full sun, extending the hours in a day for training and for boarders to ride. An additional outdoor dressage arena had been built with mirrors, outdoor lights, and attractive landscaping.

Mrs. Galensburg had also insisted, "Your boy needs his own space." She took on the project of remodeling the upper floor above the lounge from just a bedroom for River, to a full one-bedroom apartment. He no longer had to share the downstairs bathroom, kitchen area, and living space with boarders.

Pegasus Equestrian Center (now owned jointly by Mrs. Frances Galensburg and Teresa Holmes), had the reputation as the stable where horses received the best possible care, and although the most expensive in the area, always had its stalls filled and a waiting list.

Those were the physical changes. When Tess had offered River the position of her apprentice trainer, she had for a short period of time thought she might actually teach him. It had been humbling to realize that suddenly, more and more owners wanted to send their horses to Pegasus as the success of horses trained by River increased way beyond the reputation Tess had earned. She had not fully appreciated the extent of his natural gift that went beyond his years of experience. The year after River graduated from high school, she promoted him to assistant trainer, but in truth, he was the primary trainer of all the horses sent to Pegasus.

During the months of school, there were too many horses for River to train totally by himself. Tess rode some of the training sessions but told River to recruit his own apprentice trainer. Kate Ramsey, a long-time student at Pegasus, was thrilled to be offered the position that included a small salary. River also recruited a few students to help out with conditioning rides in exchange for reduced lesson fees. That helped Pegasus keep all the horses on their rigid conditioning schedules and gave the students a chance to ride horses other than their own (not to mention it was considered a high honor for River to ask a student to ride).

Everyone wanted lessons from River. Tess looked forward to his graduation, for she planned to turn nearly all the lessons over to River then. She didn't really enjoy teaching. She had simply always offered lessons as a way to make money. She planned eventually to only teach some of the more advanced jumping lessons and fill in for River when needed.

With River now doing most of the training, Tess, after many years of riding solely as her business, began to ride again for the joy of it. She took over Meridian as her own competition horse. She had bought him as a potential Olympic prospect for River and he had ridden him all the way to advanced level in combined training. But when River began eventing his own horse Corazón, it soon became obvious that horse had much more potential. Tess then hoped Corazón would be the horse to take River to the Olympics.

It could have happened. She still wanted to cry out her frustration over the fact that River competed Corazón to advanced level, winning a regional championship, but refused to campaign him beyond the local region.

"It is way too much stress for Corazón," River claimed. "He can handle the courses, but I don't intend to submit him to all that long-distance traveling. Strange places, strange stables, too much excitement.... Cory doesn't need that, and neither do I."

Nothing Tess could think of to argue with him, changed his mind.

Now, he most likely had a second chance, not in eventing but in dressage, with his horse Oberon. Mrs. Galensburg knew it, and it had always been her dream to own an Olympic contestant. *What will it take to persuade River to sell Oberon?*

2 TODD AND MEGAN

Inflexion is so often misunderstood. It should be realized that it is the inside leg, and not the inside hand that creates inflexion. - Udo Burger, *The Way To Perfect Horsemanship*

"Todd, let go of the inside rein." It was the third time in the lesson River had said that. "Use your leg to bend her, outside leg behind the girth; inside pushing into your outside rein." *What didn't Todd get about releasing the inside rein?* River was feeling very frustrated having to repeat the same instruction over and over. He could partially understand why some trainers yelled at students. He had observed shouting and even swearing at riders at a few clinics he had attended. Personally, he believed it didn't help the student understand and actually contributed to the rider becoming nervous and tense, which then affected the horse. But right now, he felt like yelling at Todd, *I'm going to cut off your inside hand*, but he held his tongue.

At least for the moment, Todd did release the inside hand, and Fala, the black Arabian mare he rode in this flat lesson, responded with a slight straightening of her body instead of hollowing and bending with her neck only. But it wasn't enough, nor enough for Todd to realize a change from the softening of the aid. Fala was already too tight in her neck, and the moment she felt the release of pressure pulling her head to the inside, she turned away and headed off the circle, her trot short and choppy.

"See what happens?" Todd cried out. "I can't keep her on the circle."

River had asked Todd to ride Fala in a three-loop serpentine, straightening her in the center and then changing her bend by a slight shift of weight, legs, and steadying with the new outside rein. But Todd consistently arrived at the center of the loop with Fala's head and neck lifting as he tried to straighten her, and then he pulled on the inside rein to change the bend.

"Take a break. Give her a long rein and let her stretch. Stay on a big circle, rising trot."

Todd released his hold, allowing Fala to take several lengths of rein as she stretched her neck forward and down.

"Good," River said when the mare snorted, releasing tension. Fala, one of the school horses, had been used in a jumping lesson yesterday, and sometimes Tess overused a horse when she was trying to get a point across to a student. Perhaps Fala was a little sore or just plain tired today. He hadn't noticed any signs of lameness, but he believed horses were stoic, and the soreness could be there even without visible signs. He was relieved to see her trotting now with rhythmical, forward moving strides and probably nothing physically wrong with her.

The problem could just be Todd, a fifteen-year old teenager. River had started giving him lessons at the age of eleven. But once Todd had gained enough skill to ride out on trails, it was all he wanted to do. Then he wanted to learn to jump. Tess started giving him lessons over fences but insisted he continue flat lessons as well.

River believed Todd tried, but he also knew he was bored with riding on the flat and didn't understand the importance of basic dressage exercises. Two years ago, Tess let Todd ride Fala at junior beginner novice level, and again last year at junior novice level. In spite of only fair dressage scores, he managed to qualify for the end of year championship at each level. He placed sixth at beginner novice, but did not place at novice level. Each time, his poor dressage scores kept him from placing in the top ribbons or placing at all.

In spite of that, Todd still considered the dressage test just something he needed to get through in order to ride the much more exciting cross-country and stadium jumping. River believed Todd genuinely loved horses, so he continued to give him lessons with the hope that someday Todd would 'get' the amazing experience of communicating with a horse with seat, legs, and soft hands, and have the horse 'answer back' with correct movement.

As he watched Todd trot the mare on a long rein, both horse and rider now appearing relaxed, he tried to think of how he could teach him these things. *Back on a lunge line?* He knew Todd would object to that. There were quite a few teenage girls boarding and taking lessons at Pegasus now, and he knew Todd would feel humiliated if they saw him having a lunge lesson. *Well, so what?* Since he taught most of those girls, they could all benefit from a few lunge lessons. Maybe he could arrange a group lesson and have them lunge each other.

"Okay, Todd, leave the reins that length. Sit…legs on…think walk, just squeeze…no, no, don't pull, go back to trot," River called out his instructions and corrected Todd who wanted to use the reins to transition down to walk. "Try again. Sit deep, legs on…good." This time Fala came down to walk, but River suspected it was more she had anticipated the transition, so he asked Todd to repeat several times, walk-to-trot-to-walk, coaching him to use seat and legs and just squeezes with the reins. Finally, it seemed Todd successfully aided Fala and she made the transitions without falling onto the forehand. "Do you feel the difference?" This was key, that Todd could feel when it was correct.

"I think so," Todd answered.

"Good, right now she is straight and although she is not 'on the bit', she is moving with good energy. Try to keep that feel and see if you can move her off the rail. Just leg-yield to the quarter line. No, don't pick up the reins, legs…legs!"

The lesson ended with Todd managing to move Fala from the rail to quarter line and back with his legs, both at walk and trot. Although Fala wasn't always straight and lost impulsion, she did keep her head lowered in a relaxed position, and at least Todd had managed to aid primarily with his legs.

"That's good. We'll quit with that," River said. "Todd, practice that on your own. Even riding the trails, try to use your legs first for transitions, and try to move your horse from one side of the trail to the other with just legs. You've got to get the legs working before you pick up the contact."

"I'll try," Todd promised.

The cell phone rang just as Gwen Marshall pulled into the stable yard at Pegasus Equestrian Center.

"Telephone, I answer?" Megan, the little girl Gwen babysat on weekdays, called out from her car seat in the back.

"No, darling, not now," Gwen said, glancing at the caller I.D. on the screen. She sometimes allowed the precocious three-year-old to answer when the call was from Megan's mother or a friend that knew Megan…but not this call. "Here comes Todd. He'll take you to see the horses." She watched the long-limbed teenage boy coming out of the stable, slinging a backpack over one shoulder. A girl in the entryway called something to him that made him laugh. His hazel eyes sparkled, and wearing a lopsided grin exposing slightly buck teeth, he reached the car.

"Hi, Mom," he greeted as he opened the front passenger door and tossed in his backpack.

"Hello, Todd, take me to the horses, please," Megan demanded, speaking her words crisp and concise.

Todd peered into the car's back seat. "Hi, Megan."

Gwen requested, "Todd, take Megan to visit the horses. I need to make a phone call while you do that."

"Sure," Todd agreed. "Come on, Megan," he beckoned as he opened the back door and unbuckled her from her car seat.

"Unca River, I want to see Unca River," Megan declared as she scrambled out and began to skip toward the stable.

"Don't run," Todd reminded, following after her.

Gwen watched them from her car window a few moments. Then with a deep breath, she picked up her phone and returned the call.

"Hello, Gwen," Peggy Steinberg answered. "How are you?"

"Fine, how are you?" Gwen answered, her heart fluttering in dread of bad news.

"I'm okay, very busy…. I called because I heard from Linda's case worker. It's been two years."

"Yes, I know. I have the date marked on my calendar." Gwen shuddered involuntarily. Linda Grant, a bipolar drug addict, had lost custody of her son Todd when he was seven. He went back to her six months later after she completed a drug rehab program and stayed clean according to terms of a court contract she had signed. But only two months later, she abandoned her son to run off with an old boyfriend, a known drug dealer. Gwen and John Marshall had fostered Todd since the age of eight, and wanted to adopt him. But Linda periodically went through drug rehab and made contracts to regain custody of her son. The courts had been reluctant to finalize the adoption since Linda showed attempts to clean up her life. But two years ago she had been arrested again. "This is the last time we contract with you," the judge on the case at that time had warned. The conditions of her contract required her to again complete rehab, hold down a job, and she would not be allowed to see Todd unless she could keep these conditions and remain clean for two years. Then she would be allowed visitation and the judge would reconsider another contract.

"She has apparently been clean and taking her prescribed medications. She actually has a job and has been working for six months. She is requesting a visit."

"When?" Gwen asked.

"Over Christmas break. She figures he won't have school or anything that should prevent the visit. She is only allowed three hours. She wants to take him out to lunch."

"What if Todd doesn't want to see her?" Anguish filled Gwen's heart as she watched Todd catch up to Megan and take hold of her hand. He ruffled her mop of curly black hair and she could see Megan's shoulders rising in laughter. What a difference this handsome, confident teenager was from the very frightened, timid little boy with an abysmal stuttering problem that had come to them so many years ago. Todd had flourished under their protective and loving care. She had homeschooled him the first few years while he attended sessions with a child psychologist and speech therapist. She had not wanted him to have to deal with the teasing and bullying from other kids along with the deep trauma from his mother.

A few years ago, The Marshalls had also fostered River for six weeks while he recovered from an injury and before becoming an emancipated minor. They had discovered then, through River's dog Storm, that Todd related well to animals. They let Todd adopt a dog from the animal shelter. Knowing a helpless, living creature depended on him for all its physical and emotional needs had helped Todd gain a sense of self-worth and purpose. River also introduced Todd to horses and it had been impressive at how much he overcame his timidity and gained confidence after several months of riding lessons.

By the time Todd was middle school age, he had control of his stuttering and he seemed as well-adjusted and mature as kids his age with normal backgrounds. They enrolled him in public school and marveled at his success. Now in high school, Todd was popular among his peers, earned average to above average grades, and demonstrated artistic talent.

"Gwen, I would encourage you to facilitate this meeting, even if Todd is reluctant. You don't want it to seem as if you tried to create barriers between Todd and his mother."

"I should feel guilty for wishing Linda would go back on drugs and fail her probation, but it would be easier all around that way. Todd doesn't want to see her. We've talked about it and I know that's how he feels."

"Nevertheless, talk to him. They have requested his break schedule, so please email me some possible dates as soon as you have a chance."

"Very well," Gwen agreed in resignation.

"I'll be in touch, and don't worry. She has a long way to go before the courts are ready to even consider custody. Todd could turn eighteen before anything happens."

"Where is Unca River?" Megan asked, looking around as they entered the stable. In her mind, River should always be here with the horses.

"I don't know, he's around somewhere. Come on, there are horses in the crossties you can pet." Todd led her around the corner, where he had just left two of his friends getting their horses ready for a ride.

"Shammie! Firefly!" Megan exclaimed, catching sight of a chestnut mare and a bay gelding.

"That's right," Todd said. It amazed him how this little girl remembered the names of every horse stabled at Pegasus and could tell them all apart.

"Hello there, Megan." The two girls working with the horses both turned and smiled brightly at the little girl.

Megan flashed them each a quick smile, but she really only had eyes for the horses, already reaching out with the flat of one hand towards them.

"This is Mindy and Brooke," Todd informed Megan. "You should say hi to them as well as the horses."

"Hi, Mindy, hi Brooke," Megan said, ducking her head at having to be reminded of her manners. She quickly brightened and asked, "May I pet your horse?"

"Of course you may," Brooke said and came over to squat down at Megan's eye level, followed by Mindy.

"You adorable little pixie," Mindy said and picked her up so that she could reach her horse's neck. "This is Shammie."

"I know Shammie," Megan stated as she began to stroke the neck of the chestnut mare.

What is it with girls and babies? Todd watched, a little amused, a little annoyed, and a little jealous, as the two girls cooed over Megan. They lifted her up so she could pet each of the horses and gave her treats to feed them. He loved Megan, really like a little sister. But at fifteen, Todd was more enamored with the charms of teenage girls than with charming preschoolers, and it was kind of boring to have to take the time to babysit her now.

"Are you guys going to ride on the trail?" he asked, trying to divert the girls back to the purpose of having their horses in the crossties, so he could finish up this visit.

"Thinking about it," Mindy said, returning to Shammie while Brooke held Megan so she could pet Firefly. "Did you ride already?"

"Yeah, had a lesson. My mom's here but Megan wanted to see the horses before we go home."

"She is so adorable, and so smart," Brooke declared, having set Megan down and had returned to saddling Firefly.

"I want to see Muffin," Megan interjected, now that the girls were back to tacking up their horses.

"In a minute," Todd promised. "I rode on the trail yesterday. You might want to stay off the lower branch because it was kind of boggy in the dip after the last hill," he advised.

With a big breath and a grunt, Mindy struggled to buckle the girth of her saddle as her mare blew up her belly with air. She looked back over her shoulder at Todd with a pleading look. "Can you help me tighten my girth?"

"Sure." He went over and managed two more holes up, making it look effortless.

"You are so awesome," Mindy said, looking at him with a flutter of her lashes, and then she giggled.

"Can you help me too?" Brooke asked.

Todd snugged up the girth on Firefly, both girls giggling and eyeing him flirtatiously. He didn't mind. They were both his age and in his sophomore class at Firwood High School. He liked their attention and even suspected Brooke might have a crush on him. He liked both girls, considered them his friends, but he wasn't interested in them except as friends that shared a mutual interest in horses.

Lately, maybe he did go out of his way to hang out with them, for they were both friends with Melody Cannon, and Melody, well.... He had known her since middle school, a girl who lived in his neighborhood. Just another girl until one day last summer he sat in the backseat as his parents drove past her house. Melody stood in her driveway wearing very short shorts and a cropped tank top, hands raised defensively and laughing as a boy who had been rinsing soap off the just-washed car, squirted her with the hose. Sun glinted off her arms and exposed midriff, gilding her skin. The sun's rays played through her chestnut hair, glimmering it with diamonds from the spray of water. Todd had sucked in a breath as his heart jumped unexpectedly and hammered almost painfully. She appeared as a vision of perfection. He had just turned fifteen, his hormones raged, and he was smitten.

Todd usually had no trouble talking to girls. For as long as he could remember hanging out at the stable, girls were always around. With a mutual interest in horses, he never felt shy around them, and that habit had carried over to being around girls in school. Many of his friends were envious of how comfortable Todd seemed to be around the opposite sex. Ever since the eighth grade, Todd had been invited to every important party, and he had asked girls to dance and even kissed a few. As a freshman he even 'went out' with Mia Spelling, for three months, but he had been kind of pushed into that relationship. He hadn't minded for he had been curious to know what it was like having a girlfriend. It had been okay, but Mia had broken up with him when she realized Todd was more interested in horses than her. He had been okay with that as well.

But Melody was different. Whenever Melody passed him in the hall and met his eyes, he found his heart thumping, his throat tightening, and his tongue tied in a tight knot. He always ducked his head and looked away to hide the heat rising from his chest up his neck and into his face. *Is this what it's like to be in love?*

So he found himself hanging out with Mindy and Brooke more often than he used to. Just knowing they hung out in the same crowd as Melody, might somehow bring him closer to Melody.

"Did you hear about Joe and that weird girl Tasha?" Mindy asked, picking up her riding helmet and buckling it on.

"Todd…." Megan whined.

"Just a minute, Megan. No, what happened?"

Both girls, eager to share gossip, told him the story, talking over each other's sentences. They all laughed, and then Todd told them what he had heard in the locker room about Tasha. He really wasn't interested in the gossip, but sometimes if he encouraged them, they also told stories that involved Melody. That was how he learned that she had already broken up with that guy, the first week school had started. So far, although he heard she had gone out on dates with a couple other guys, she hadn't hooked up with anyone as a boyfriend.

"Todd, are you ready?" Gwen stepped around the corner and then looked around in alarm. "Where is Megan?"

All three kids looked around, just now aware the little girl had wandered off.

"Todd, how could you not keep track of her?" Gwen accused as her anxiety escalated when the little girl was nowhere to be found in the immediate vicinity.

"She was just here, Mrs. Marshall. She can't be very far," Brooke said.

All of them spread out through the stable in search of Megan, calling out her name.

"She's not inside here," Todd said after searching inside the tack room and down both aisles between the stalls.

"She's not anywhere around the arena," Brooke announced, returning from searching that area.

"She must have gone outside. I bet she went to the paddocks," Todd said.

"That is so far for a little girl. Oh, Todd, she's only three years old. You have to watch a child that age all the time!" Gwen in her worry couldn't help but chastise Todd again.

"We'll find her, Mom," Todd tried to reassure her, hoping he spoke true. "She will be where the horses are."

"You run on ahead, you're faster," Gwen ordered. They hurried outside and Todd took off at a jog. Gwen followed at a half jog, half fast walk, visualizing scenes of a little girl trampled beneath the feet of a horse or lying unconscious after having been kicked.

When she reached the paddocks and saw Todd staring down the hill with no child in view, her heart sank with the heavy weight of foreboding. "You didn't find her?" she called.

He turned with a stricken expression. "Muffin's not in any of the paddocks. He must have been turned out in one of the pastures."

"Oh, no! She couldn't have tried to go on her own to the pastures. That is so far away!" Gwen searched desperately with her eyes in the vicinity.

"Look!" Todd exclaimed.

She looked in the direction he pointed, and a brief wave of dizziness accompanied her relief. River had just come into view, leading the horse he had ridden on the trail, and also a black-and-white pony. A small figure sat on the pony's back. Gwen started down the hill to meet them, brushing away tears. She stifled a happy sob when Megan waved happily and called to her, "Auntie Gwen, look at me. I ride Muffin!"

"I found her in the pasture with Muffin," River said, lifting Megan off the pony and handing her to Gwen. "She crawled under the fence to get in."

Gwen cuddled and petted the little girl at the same time that she scolded her. "You must never run away on your own, especially without telling someone where you are going."

"But I told Todd I wanted to see Muffin," Megan explained, very confused by the fuss. "I didn't run away. I was here with the horses," she stated indignantly. In her mind, being with a horse was the same as being with a person. She was perfectly safe and protected.

"How did you even know how to find Muffin?" Gwen asked as she smoothed the little girl's mass of black curls. The pastures weren't that far from the stable, but it was a considerable distance for a three-year-old all by herself.

"Unca River took me there once. I knew the way."

"You did?" Gwen looked quizzically at River. As far as she knew, Megan had only been inside the big stable or the paddocks.

"Yeah, once last summer," he answered, smiling when Megan reached out for him to place her back on Muffin as they continued on to the stable yard. He actually didn't worry about Megan running around at the stable. He had been the same way at her age for he had grown up around the race track where his mother worked as a jockey. It didn't surprise him that Megan would remember how to find the pasture with Muffin even though he had only taken her there once.

"But that was months ago!" Gwen frowned quizzically at Megan. "How could you remember that?"

"I just remember," Megan said simply.

3 TWINS

When riding a horse we leave our fear, troubles, and sadness behind on the ground. - Juli Carlson

"We were trying to help Robyn with her make-up, trying to do something nice," Sophie Kinderman said in a whining voice. "Then all of a sudden I hear a thud, and Tina is on the ground. I look behind me, and I see Jodi walking away."

"She is so mean," Tina Stafford sniffed, and wiped her eyes again with her crumpled tissue. "We try to be nice to her, but it's like she goes out of her way to make enemies."

"What is wrong with her anyway? Is she jealous because we didn't pick her? I mean, she could really use some make-up tips," Sophie stated, cocking one hip and holding a hand up with an open palm.

Principal Massey looked behind the two girls standing in front of his desk. Robyn James stood several feet behind them, her eyes wide in bewilderment, looking back and forth between Tina and Sophie. He asked, "Robyn, what happened?"

"I told you…" Sophie spat out.

Massey held up a hand for silence. "I want to hear from Robyn." He smiled encouragingly at the overweight girl dressed in very unfashionable clothes and with smears of make-up on her chubby face. "Robyn?"

"Sophie and Tina wanted to show me how to put on make-up," Robyn said hesitantly. "Then all of a sudden Tina fell down. That's all I know."

"Robyn, you know very well Jodi pushed her down. You were there!" Sophie shouted at her.

"Silence," Massey boomed. "I think I get the picture. Girls, you may go on to your class. Ms. Jonar will give you late passes."

"What are you going to do?" Sophie insisted.

He glowered at her and stood up from behind his desk.

"We're just trying to comply with the 'no bullying' policy," Sophie persisted, her tone reverting back to its whining quality.

"Thank you for coming to me," Massey answered, trying not to sound sarcastic. He stepped around his desk and opened the door to usher the girls out. "Give them late passes," he told the school secretary. He waited for her to write them out and the girls to exit the office before he asked Ms. Jonar to summon Jodi Cannon.

Ten minutes later Ms. Jonar called his extension, "Jodi Cannon is here."

"Send her in," he replied. He flipped open the thick file he had asked the secretary to pull for him, inwardly groaning.

The secretary opened the door and with a tilt of her head, directed the student to enter the office. She rolled her eyes in silent commiseration behind the student's back before shutting the door again.

Massey watched the tall, skinny girl limp into the room, her left leg dragging behind, causing her to list slightly with each step. Her shoulders slumped into her dark, hooded sweatshirt; and if it were allowed, he was sure she would have the hood up, further obscuring her face now hidden by long dark hair falling forward. "Sit down, Miss Cannon," he directed.

Jodi dropped into a chair, still hunched over.

"What happened?" he asked without preamble.

"I shoved Tina. I didn't mean for her to fall down," Jodi mumbled.

"Please, what did you say?" he asked for clarification.

"I shoved Tina."

"Why?"

Jodi shrugged her shoulders, a very irritating gesture he often got from students in trouble.

"You must have had a reason to shove her."

"It was an accident."

"I see." Massey waited but it was soon apparent she was going to offer no other explanation. "Okay, Jodi," he said looking at her with a pointed expression. "Here's what I think happened. Sophie and Tina told Robyn they wanted to help her with her make-up, but what they really wanted to do was make her look ridiculous. You knew they were mocking her and you didn't like that. So you pushed Tina." He waited for her to say something but gave up again. "Am I right?"

"How would I know what they were thinking?"

"Am I right?"

She shrugged again.

"All you have to do is confirm that I am right," he stated. He wasn't surprised when she pressed her lips together and frowned at her hands in her lap.

"Jodi, you are an intelligent girl with lots of potential. I'm on your side, believe me. I don't want to punish you. But you know we have a 'no bullying, no violence' policy at this school. Couldn't you have come up with a less violent way to stop those girls?" He waited again in vain for an answer. "Did you try asking them not to tease Robyn?"

She looked at him with an expression he interpreted as 'yeah, right'.

"All you have to do is confirm that what I believe happened is the truth. Teasing Robyn is a form of bullying and they will be reprimanded. Can you do that?"

Jodi stared back at him in disbelief. *Is he a total idiot?*

Massey took in a deep breath and forced it out through his nose. "Seems to me you just completed a week of detention for…" He drummed his fingers as he looked down at the file. "Cutting class…classes," he amended. He thumbed through the file to pull out the latest grade report. "Your grades are interesting, Miss Cannon."

Jodi sat, unmoving.

"You have a *B* in English, but Ms. Rusinsky remarks you would have an *A* if you turned in all your assignments."

Jodi liked Ms. Rusinsky. She read all the reading assignments, but the written assignments were sometimes just stupid and too much trouble. She didn't expect Mr. Massey or Ms. Rusinsky to understand.

"You also have a *C* in algebra, even though you have *A*s on all your tests, but you never turn in the homework." He raised his eyes in a questioning expression and waited, determined to get an answer.

"Why should I do the homework problems when I already know how to solve them? I've proved that by acing the tests," she stated. Seemed logical to her.

"Should have been easy for you to do the homework then," he commented. He went on with his review of her grades when she returned to staring at her hands. "You have an *A* in gym. That's impressive."

She frowned and swallowed down her rising anger. "It's 'crippled gym'," she said and smiled smugly when he physically cringed at her use of politically incorrect language.

"Modified physical education," he corrected her.

"Modified for disabilities. Gym is a no brainer." She actually liked doing all the exercises the gym coach assigned her - upper body work and core strengthening as well as non-weight-bearing leg exercises.

"Also an *A* in Spanish. Ms. Valdez thinks you have an aptitude for foreign languages."

Looking down at her hands she rolled her eyes. *It's conversational Spanish. If you pay attention in class and learn the dialogues you pass.* Besides, Jodi liked *Señora* Valdez. She taught them Mexican street slang and modified the dialogues to more realistic scenarios. She was a good teacher and her class was fun.

He flipped to the next page. "You are failing history. Why is that?"

She shrugged again. When he stared back at her, waiting, she said, "I didn't do the homework." *Mr. Sullivan is a complete jerk and totally boring. Even if I turned in the assignments he would give a good grade only if you agreed with his views. If he listened to other people's opinions, I might do the assignments.*

Massey sighed and set the grade report down. He referred to notes he had written after a meeting with her parents. "You've been in trouble at home. You lie about doing your homework, won't do your chores...caught smoking...sneaking out at night." He looked up. "Jodi, what is going on?"

"Nothing," she mumbled.

"What was that? Please look up at me when you are talking."

"Nothing," she repeated, meeting his eyes with a steely glare. "What has any of this got to do with shoving Tina?"

Massey gave up. "All right, Jodi. I think your attempt to come to your friend's defense is admirable, but I cannot allow violence for any reason. I'm assigning you to detention for another week. Try using that time to do your homework." When she remained silent he dismissed her with the order, "Get a late pass from Ms. Jonar."

Jodi left the office with anger still smoldering inside. *Unfair ... so unfair!* Mr. Massey was smart enough to figure out Sophie and Tina, yet he expected her to rat on them? Come on! Was he so naïve that he didn't understand that even though those girls had ratted on her, they would find a way to make her pay if she ratted on them?

Robyn wasn't even her friend. She was just a stupid fat girl, too dumb to realize she was the brunt of a joke. But when Jodi walked into the girls' restroom and saw what was going on, she lost control of her temper. Those girls were just evil! Robyn would have been humiliated the moment she walked into the student-filled hallway with her face made up like an eighteenth century French prostitute. Impulsively, Jodi had walked by Sophie and meant to just knock her arm away from Robyn. But she had lost her balance and ended up falling against Tina. She guessed it probably looked like she had shoved her. She really hadn't meant for her to fall down.

And why did Mr. Massey have to bring up her trouble at home, like it was any of his business? Why did her parents always have to complain about her to other people? She had snuck out once and her parents made it sound like she did it all the time.

That one time had turned into a disaster. Jodi shivered as the unpleasant memory invaded her consciousness, even as she tried to push the pleading face of Tasha Smith out of her mind.

Tasha was a loud-mouthed, aggressive girl who wore too much make-up, dyed her hair in garish colors, and wore her clothes too tight for her large size. Nobody at school liked Tasha. Jodi did not like Tasha. But when Tasha began sitting at her table at lunch, Jodi had begrudgingly not moved away. Tasha took that to mean they were friends. Jodi, who considered herself in the lowest social tier at their school, really preferred to be by herself, but she recognized Tasha's pathetic need to not be seen sitting alone. Out of pity, she had tolerated the other girl's presence.

One Friday, Tasha begged Jodi to go with her to a party she had heard about. Jodi had repeatedly refused, not at all interested in crashing a party and wondering why Tasha wanted to go where she wasn't invited.

But then Tasha had casually mentioned with a leering twist of her mouth, "The Crucifiers are going to play there. Live music, Jodi. How often do you get the chance to hear live music?"

Never. In spite of her better judgment, Jodi began to consider the idea at the mention of the local popular rock band, two of its members students at her school.

Kirby Portman played lead guitar in the group. Jodi might not be interested in the usual gossip of the girls her age; their stupid obsessions with what clothes they wore and their ridiculous crushes, hook-ups, and then break-ups every other day. But she did have a normal teenage girl's attraction to sexy guys, especially when Kirby had once said to her, 'you're interesting'. Guys didn't notice her except to tease her. But Kirby had sat next to her a month ago when they both ended up in detention at the same time. He had written down jokes about the room monitor, other kids there, and their school in general, and then passed them to her in tightly folded notes. She knew he had done it because he was bored and nobody he knew was in detention that week, and no other girls at all. But he was funny, and he had laughed at the jokes she had written back to him. Ever since, he winked or smiled at her when they passed each other in the hall, about the only person in school besides Tasha who acknowledged she even existed. She didn't want to like him, for he had a wild reputation – a 'bad boy'. Nevertheless, he was the guy in her most secret fantasies.

It was because of Kirby that Jodi finally relented to Tasha's pleas. She snuck out after midnight with her parents in bed and Melody spending the night at a friend's house. Tasha, a year older even though still a sophomore, could drive, and she picked Jodi up a block away from her house.

They easily crashed the party for there was a constant stream of kids going in and out of the house. No one paid attention to who had actually been invited. Jodi and Tasha had entered a room of claustrophobic closeness with music turned up to maximum volume, just a few decibels higher than the screams and laughter of the partygoers, and the cloying smells of sweat, alcohol, smoke, and vomit.

After the first few minutes, Jodi had enough. Kirby and none of the other members of The Crucifiers were even there, or else they hadn't shown up yet. She tried to get Tasha to leave but Tasha pleaded for just one hour.

In that hour the neighbors called the cops. Many kids were arrested for underage drinking and some for drugs. Jodi passed the breathalyzer test and was not arrested, but a police officer still called her parents to pick her up.

Her parents did not believe that all she had done was taste a beer (which she hadn't liked at all). They were convinced she had been smoking, for her clothes reeked of cigarettes. They took away her phone, her television and movie privileges, and put her on restriction until the end of the quarter. That meant she could not go to the public library and of all the punishments, not being able to check out books or read books on her phone app was the worst.

That was what she got for being kind to Tasha Smith.

That's me, defender and companion of the pathetic and downtrodden, she thought sardonically as she reached her classroom. She pushed open the door and limped in.

Of course, all eyes looked up.

Mr. Sullivan turned away from lecturing, his face folding into an expression of extreme annoyance. Wordlessly he extended his hand for her late pass. Jodi slapped it in his hand and stood at the front of the class while he read her excuse. She swept her eyes around defiantly. She glared back at anyone who dared to meet her eyes. The only eyes she would not look at were those of her twin sister.

"Take your seat," Mr. Sullivan ordered.

Jodi limped over to the only empty desk, behind Todd Marshall.

"That is the advantage of..." Mr. Sullivan droned in his monotone voice.

Todd gazed in adoration at Melody, sitting two seats ahead in the next row. She rested her cheek in one hand while she took notes with the other, scribbling away rapidly, taking down every word their history teacher spoke. Sometimes she tilted her chin up and when she did, her reddish gold hair, pulled back in a ponytail at her neck, moved - a slight wave like a horse's tail...*horse's tail...horse's tail* .... Todd's eyes drooped to half mast, the droning voice lulling him into a dream state.

"Mr. Marshall!"

Todd sat up with a jerk, dropping his pen which rolled onto the floor. He opened his mouth but could form no words, and closed it in futility. He had not heard the question.

"Are you a guppy?" Mr. Sullivan asked, his mouth twisting up at one corner, "or a mute?"

Todd ducked his head in embarrassment. He heard a few sniggers behind him, even from his own friends.

"Very well, Mr. Marshall." The teacher tightened his lips in disgust and then turned his attention to Melody, as usual with her hand raised. "Miss Cannon, can you answer the question?"

"S-s-stupid," the girl behind him muttered. She shifted in her desk so that it bumped against the back of his seat, and then poked him in the back with his pen that she had picked up.

"Quit," he snarled back at her, and snatched his pen that she held over his shoulder. *What is wrong with her?*

How could two girls from the same family, twins even, be so different? The one behind him so annoying, and the other....

Melody...! It used to irritate him when she always knew the answers, outsmarting everyone in class. Now he even wished for the teacher to ask questions because inevitably Melody would be the one to raise her hand, and just to hear the sound of her voice and watch her earnest expression filled him with delight. He found himself choosing desks one row behind and to the side of her, just so he could study her profile. Gazing at Melody helped him endure the boring minutes in class.

But her twin Jodi...that one went out of her way to make herself as unattractive as possible. Her long hair, a muddy brown color, hung around her face, her bangs long enough to hide her eyes. Her thick, dark eyebrows were always drawn together in a permanent scowl, and she glared out beneath them through narrowed lids. She was tall, almost his height, and bony. Fashion-wise, even as a guy, he knew she made poor choices, always wearing oversized dark hoodies with baggy jeans. Maybe she wanted people to despise her, and in his opinion, she was succeeding.

How does she even know I used to have a stuttering problem? Todd hadn't been around any of these kids when his stuttering had been at its worst, and by middle school, when his foster mother no longer home-schooled him, his stuttering was hardly noticeable. None of his classmates seemed to find it unusual the few times he did relapse. Even normal kids would stutter over words when they were nervous. It was a mystery to him that Jodi could sense how deeply embarrassed he was when he did stutter or find himself speechless. *What have I ever done to her anyway?*

Todd believed he had the best life with the Marshalls. They were the kindest, most wonderful people in the world. He had taken their last name and he called them 'Mom' and 'Dad', for that was how he thought of them now, even if they hadn't been able to legally adopt him. He hardly thought about his birth mother anymore.

But when he did, it was usually after contact with her, and it tore Todd apart inside. He loved his mother. He hated his mother. He was terrified of his mother. His early years had been a torment of never knowing what mood she would wake up in – paranoid and abusive, or tender and loving. She shifted from depression to where he feared she would never get out of bed, to bouts of manic activity that filled him equally with joy or fear. One moment she would hug and cuddle him, singing songs of endearment. Then suddenly she would act as if he were a demon, beating him with a broom, whipping him with a belt, and worst of all….

His mind had blanked out 'the worst of all'. But whatever it had been, it had caused nightmares every night for the first year he had lived with the Marshalls. He awoke screaming, filled with terror of a suffocating darkness, but when Gwen Marshall rushed in to comfort him, he could never remember any details of the horrifying dream.

He wished he had been born to the Marshalls and the life he had now had always been his life. Then he wouldn't feel guilty about wanting to stay with the Marshalls and never see his mother again.

Living with the Marshalls, he was a normal kid with a normal teenager's life. He was in the upper social strata of his sophomore class.

Only the super jocks were more popular than he and his group of friends - the artists, musicians, and politically inclined. In middle school, Todd had gained fame as an artist and photographer that stayed with him in high school. He was sought out for every school project from pep rally signs, prom decorations, to the year book.

But next to the Marshalls, the best thing in his life now were the horses!

At last the bell rang. Todd leaned down, zipped open his backpack and fumbled around in the main compartment to find his notebook so he could stash today's notes. Behind him, Jodi pushed heavily against the back of his seat as she got up. His knee knocked against his backpack and it tipped over, spilling out the contents. He turned his head to glare at Jodi but she was bent over, picking up his things. "Leave it," he snapped. The last thing he wanted was that girl touching any of his stuff.

She stood and dropped a folder with papers sticking out the edges onto his desk. She kept one, gazing at it and wrinkled her nose as if she smelled something bad.

"Jodi, why do you have to be such a brat?" Melody cried out, coming up to Todd's desk.

Jodi ignored her. She let the paper flutter down from her hand onto Todd's desk, and then limped out the door.

"I'm so sorry," Melody said with a sigh, watching her sister disappear.

"It's okay," Todd said, busying himself with straightening his papers.

She turned to him with a sweet smile. He felt the heat rise in his face as his mouth turned up in an uncontrollably foolish grin. "Uh, hi," he managed to say.

"Hi," she said with a friendly laugh. When he continued to gape at her, his tongue twisted in a speech-prohibitive knot, she said, "Mr. Sullivan is a jerk. He shouldn't put you on the spot like he did today. It's not your fault he's so boring hardly anyone can stay awake."

He nodded in agreement but it occurred to him that she never fell asleep in class. *Tell her that; tell her how smart she is.* His tongue remained stuck and his mind numb.

"I just wanted you to know…oh, can I see?" She tipped her head over the last paper Jodi had dropped on his desk. For an art assignment, he had sketched a horse in the moonlight in shades of black, gray, and white; intended to demonstrate principles of chiaroscuro.

The heat in his neck and face deepened, but he turned his paper to allow her to view his drawing. "It's my art homework."

"It's incredible!" she stated in a sincere tone as she studied the sketch. She held it up to her face at eye level, then an arm's span away and tilted her head. "It really has a magical feeling with that moonbeam lighting up the horse. You are so talented," she praised as she handed it back.

"Thanks," he replied meekly. *Think of something witty, intelligent, impressive…say anything….* But his mind was empty of everything except the vision of her angelic face.

"So, um…do you think…?"

"Melody, come on," a girl called from the doorway, interrupting whatever Melody was about to say.

"I'll talk to you later," Melody said and left him to join her friend without a backward glance.

Todd sat frozen, watching her disappear from view before he could even stand. *What was she about to ask me? Should I have asked her like what she was doing after school or something like that?* But the opportunity was lost. Anyway, usually when anyone praised his artwork is was because they were about to ask him to help on a project. She probably just needed something like that.

4 THE DUN MARE

What is riding all about? Legs, legs, legs! Legs are the anchor of the rider.
– George H. Morris

The school bus belched a gust of exhaust as it pulled away to merge back onto the highway. Todd waved goodbye to a friend making faces at him from the rear window, and laughing, he broke into a jog up the lane flanked by the sign for Pegasus Equestrian Center. As he passed the outdoor arena with a few jumps set up and the large stable came into view, he inhaled deeply. The smells of grass and hay, shavings and manure, and the horses, filled up his airways. The tightness in his shoulders from the tense aura of school melted away and his soul filled with contentment.

After stowing his school things and changing into riding clothes, Todd checked the bulletin board for his assignment. His spirits took a downward turn when he read next to his name: *Tucker - walk briskly, include many hills, at least forty-five minutes.* He did not look forward to the boring ride on the placid, warmblood gelding sent to Pegasus for re-conditioning. In fact, it would involve a lot of work for Todd. He would have to constantly push the gelding to keep up a brisk pace rather than plod along dragging his feet and looking for something to nibble on. But as River often said, 'every horse has something to teach you'.

"But I don't know what you can teach me," Todd grumbled to himself as he filled his pockets with carrots and then headed outside to find Tucker. He had once tried to get the lazy gelding to trot on a level section of trail, just to see if a short stretch at a faster pace would perk him up. He believed it worked, for Tucker raised his head, pointed his ears forward, and stepped into trot with unexpected energy. The trail just then came to a junction, and unfortunately for Todd, River at that moment rode toward him from the cross trail, catching him trotting on the horse he was supposed to only walk.

"What are you doing?" River called out, keeping his voice low, but the anger evident.

"I just wanted to see if a few trot steps would liven him up," Todd defended himself. "You trot him in the arena so I didn't think it would hurt."

"I trot him for only five minutes a session on totally level ground and in very soft footing." River had brought his horse to a halt in front of Todd and now faced him head on, his expression tight. "He's recovering from an injury and this uneven ground could easily cause him to misstep and re-injure his tendon."

"I'm sorry, I didn't know…he's just so hard to keep moving."

"If you can't follow instructions…"

"I can! It won't ever happen again," Todd promised. River had scowled at him but then passed him by, returning to the stable in the other direction. "It was just a few trot steps," Todd grumbled to himself in his own defense. It really didn't seem that big a deal.

The unpleasant memory returned to him every time he was assigned Tucker. "I guess I did learn something from you," he grumbled again to himself as he stepped outside and headed toward the paddocks. "River gets mad about little things."

In the lane between rows of white-boarded paddocks, he caught sight of River talking to Tess. It didn't look like a congenial conversation. *A new horse*, he realized, not recognizing the dun-colored horse inside the paddock, its nose deep in a pile of hay. "Hi," he greeted, coming up to join them. "Who is this?"

"Hey, Todd," River greeted him in a neutral voice, but Todd detected the underlying irritation.

Tess grasped at her short hair in frustration and shook her head. "See me in my office when you have a moment," she ordered, and then huffed away, not even acknowledging Todd's greeting. Since Todd was one of the non-paying riders, he knew Tess didn't feel like she needed to make the effort to be polite when she was angry. He half-smiled, more amused than annoyed by her rudeness, and stepped into her place beside River to look at the new horse.

"This is Dune," River said. "They're culling their stock at Meadowood and they were going to send her to auction."

"You bought her?" Todd asked, cringing at the thought of the horse in front of him at the stock auction. She was good-sized in height, maybe sixteen-one or sixteen-two hands. Her hipbones protruded from her thick, dirty winter coat. Even so, she had a bulging hay-belly below a sharp-looking backbone and prominent withers. Her head was overlarge with small ears and her mane looked like she had rubbed it to a frizzy mat along her thin neck. A thick scar blemished her coat on the near side just below the stifle. *Old, scarred, and ugly!* No one would bid on this horse except meat-buyers, and his heart filled with pity.

"Yeah, for five hundred dollars plus I agreed to give a clinic for their pony club. I remember this mare, last year at a one-day event. She's not put together very well, but I was impressed with how she handled the cross-country course. She's bold and jumps efficiently, and she had a green rider. I watched this mare actually adjust herself whenever her rider got out of balance, which was a lot of the time. She's smart and she's kind."

Todd listened, trying to see what River saw in the disproportionate, raw-boned mare. All he could see was neglect. She had buckskin coloring with four long black stockings and a frizzy, thin black tail in as poor shape as her black mane. The yellowish color of her coat was dull and not just because her winter coat had not been clipped. He suspected poor nutrition and probably wormy. She lifted her head and Todd gasped when he saw the empty, puckered right eye socket. "She's blind!"

"No," River disagreed. "She sees well enough in her one eye."

"What happened?" Todd asked, more pity filling his heart.

"She was in a trailer accident about six months ago. Something lacerated her eye and gave her that scar. But she had no broken bones and no other serious injuries. They sent her to a farm where she was turned out in a field to recover from her wounds. Then her owner quit paying the board. She had grass and water at the farm but nothing else and I guess they forgot about her. When someone saw her in the field she was in this condition. The grass was gone and she was surviving on the few weeds that still grew. They wanted Meadowood to take her back, but their trainer didn't want her. Dr. Patterson was asked to see her before they sent her to the auction and he told me about her."

"What are you going to do with her?" Todd asked with a half-smile. He guessed Tess wasn't too happy about River bringing this neglected mare in deplorable condition to Pegasus.

"We need another school horse. Morris and Fala are both getting on and I really don't want either of them doing much jumping anymore. I think this mare has the temperament and the heart to be a school master. Dr. Patterson says there's really nothing wrong with her except neglect. She's only twelve."

They stood together watching the mare hungrily consuming the hay. Every few minutes she raised her head, chewing happily and blinking her one good eye looking back at them. Todd totally agreed with River that she deserved a chance, but not because he saw any potential in her. He simply had a soft heart for all animals, especially neglected ones.

"I was worried about loading her in a trailer after what happened to her. But when I picked her up this morning, she walked right in. Didn't even blink her one eye," River said with a wry smile. "I think she's about as level-headed as a horse can get."

"Yeah," Todd mused. They watched her a few more minutes. Todd tried to imagine the mare under saddle and could only visualize her staggering around as if drunk.

"Think you could help me out with her?" River asked.

"Sure, what do you want me to do?"

"We'll let her have a couple days to settle in. Dr. Patterson got her up-to-date with her vaccinations and floated her teeth this morning. I'll worm her later tonight. Can you take her into the crossties when you have time and start working on her coat? We'll need to clip her but she needs cleaning up a bit first."

"Yeah, no problem."

"I'll start riding her in a few days just to be sure she still minds her manners, and then you can take her on trails. We'll get her into some kind of condition by spring, and then we'll see what she can do."

"I can do that," Todd agreed, but his heart sank. She was another out of condition horse that needed a lot of slow walking on the trail to build up her muscles. It would be weeks before he would even be allowed to trot on her.

"Spend the time getting to know her," River said. "If you want to ride training level, she just may be your competition horse next season." With those words he walked away.

Todd had tried not to sound unwilling to ride this mare, but he guessed River had detected the disappointment in his tone when he agreed to help. He knew River was annoyed with him lately, for Todd had complained a few times how boring it was riding on the flat and just walking on the trails.

"Not everyone is a horse whisperer like you," Todd mumbled to himself. He believed he loved horses just as much as River, but he had to admit, he didn't have the same deep connection. He idolized River and his abilities, envied him even. He had just wanted to be honest when he complained to River about being bored, and didn't know why that should make him mad. *What's wrong with just saying how I feel?*

The mare snorted, pulled a mouthful of hay and chewed in contentment. "You're about the ugliest horse I've ever seen," he said in a sympathetic tone. She flicked her ears and watched him from her one good eye and he thought her expression said, *so what?*

The Dun mare thrived in her new home. With just three days of good food and care she began to trot off when first turned out in the mornings, kicking up her heels in a good buck to express her joy to be outside and free to move.

"Where are you getting all this energy?" River wondered in amusement, watching her on the third morning. "I guess it's time to start you back in work."

Later that day, River brought Dune into the crossties to tack her up for her first ride at Pegasus. Her coat was still dull, but Todd had done his job, and she obviously had been vigorously brushed. River took his time grooming her, checking out her manners and noting her attitude. She stood calmly in the crossties with her head lowered and ears to the side, as if half asleep. "Nothing much upsets you, does it?" He liked how relaxed she was in this new environment and with him, a relative stranger, working around her.

River tried a few saddles and different pads until he was satisfied the saddle would not cause any pressure or interfere with her movement. Through all the fitting, Dune remained placidly half asleep. He selected a plain snaffle bridle and was pleased when she lowered her head and opened her mouth to accept the bit. So far, her manners were perfect.

"Okay *mujer, vamanos.*" He led her to the indoor arena and walked her once around the perimeter in each direction to allow her to get her first look. She followed quietly along at his shoulder and only flicked her ears at the horse Tess was working in the arena. It was as if she understood it was time to do her job and not socialize.

"*Bien*," River complimented the mare. He led her to the mounting block, patted her neck, and mounted. She stood without flinching or stepping away as he settled his weight in the saddle. He picked up the reins but left them loose as he touched her sides to move her onto the rail at a walk. She stepped out willingly and energetically.

River spent the first ten minutes walking her around and testing her responses; how sensitive she was to his legs and shifts of weight. When he first touched her with one leg to see if she would move away, she jolted up her head and picked up the trot.

"No, no," he murmured, and sat deep, giving her the chance to come back to the walk before he used reins. She took a few more trot steps until she figured out what he wanted, and came back to walk.

It was evident she had never been taught to move off of a leg, and that her only response to any leg aid was to speed up. River spent this first session teaching her to move away from his leg, and that supporting legs combined with his weight meant, 'slow down'. The mare was smart and seemed eager to please. By the end of twenty minutes, she had learned to move from walk to trot and back to walk off his leg and weight aids, and to yield to leg pressure. River was able to ride her in a series of figure-eights both at walk and trot, totally off his leg aids. He quit with that, wanting to keep her first workouts short until her condition improved.

The next few sessions River spent reinforcing that she understood the leg aids. So far, he had kept the reins loose, using only a leading rein to help her understand moving off the leg. Then he was ready to try her with rein contact. He gently gathered up the reins to feel her mouth. At the first shortening of the reins, she thrust her head up with her neck hollowed. River recognized the action as defensive. With her poor conformation, it was not natural for her to round her frame under the weight of a rider. Her previous trainers had tried to force her into a round frame by a tight hold on her mouth to pull her head down. But that only resulted in her stiffening her neck and sucking back, making her actually more hollow. It was a common mistake often made by inexperienced trainers.

"No wonder your neck looks like it's been put on upside down," River said. The muscle at the bottom of Dune's neck was much more developed than her topline muscle.

The rest of the session River spent with small increments of taking up the rein and giving every time Dune did not hollow her neck, and especially when she started to reach forward to the bit. He wanted her to learn to seek the contact for communication, and not to react to contact in defense.

By the end of her first two weeks, she understood weight and leg aids to increase and to slow down. By habit, she still tended to jerk up her head at the first touch of reins, but she was learning to drop back down and seek out the contact when the hands connected to her bit remained soft and reassuring. She worked honestly, trying to figure out what River wanted, her attention never distracted by other activity around her. It was time to test her manners outside.

The next Saturday he asked Todd, "Do you want to ride Felicity on the trail?"

"Yeah, of course!" Todd answered, his face lighting up.

Tess had let Todd ride Felicity, a young chestnut mare, in his last two jumping lessons. Since then, Todd had decided the mare was his favorite horse to ride at Pegasus. He was hoping he might be assigned some of her conditioning rides on the trail. He figured today River intended to check out how he handled her before approving the assignment.

River had two reasons for allowing Todd to ride Felicity. First, as Todd suspected, he wanted to observe firsthand how well Todd handled her out in the open. Felicity was an energetic mare that tended to easily startle. She needed a confident rider that could quickly calm her nerves to prevent her from bolting. Todd was at the age where he wanted to ride spirited horses that liked to act up. River wanted to see if Todd rode the mare to calm her down or if he encouraged her to spook and run, giving him the excuse to gallop. He knew Todd wanted to ride Felicity as his eventing horse in the upcoming season, but River wasn't sure it was a good match.

Second, he wanted to see how Dune would react around a spooky horse. He believed she would remain as calm as she had in the arena, but he wanted to know for sure.

It was mid-November and the time of year when they eased up on the work schedules of each horse, especially those in competition last season. The winter months were the time to let any overstrained muscles heal, and the time to work the horses without stress. Each horse had a light schedule of two to three days of arena work and then three to four days of trail work, mostly at a walk, but small bouts of trotting or galloping were allowed.

Felicity had not been out on the trail for three days, and had not been worked at all yesterday. She already demonstrated high spirits, jigging and pulling at the bridle reins as Todd led her down to the field. She acted like a race horse being led to the starting gate. Todd laughed at her antics.

Dune walked along placidly at River's shoulder, a flick of her ears her only reaction to Felicity.

River waited for Todd to mount first. In spite of her energy spilling over, Felicity stood properly at the block as she had been trained. But once Todd moved her off, she immediately broke into a trot. He hauled her back and turned her in a circle while he waited for River to mount.

"Easy on her mouth," River admonished.

"Okay." Todd loosened his hold but kept her in a small circle until River mounted and moved Dune away from the block.

"You lead, but keep her at a walk," River said.

For the first part of the trail, Todd managed to keep Felicity at a walk, although River noticed he relied too much on the reins when she jigged or startled. When River coached Todd in his flat lessons, he guided him through the work, assuring that Todd did not hold too much with the reins. But it seemed Todd had developed a bad habit out in the open, especially since he was usually alone when he rode on the trail. River repeatedly called out to him, "Use your seat. Let go of her mouth."

They reached a level stretch of trail, a good place to trot or canter for it ended with a slight uphill. Without realizing it, Todd had begun to rely on that uphill section to slow any horse he was riding that was going too fast. "Can we trot here?" He glanced over his shoulder to ask River, one horse length behind him.

"Okay, trot only," River said.

Felicity jumped forward, eager to gallop. Again, Todd shortened the reins and held tight to bring her down to trot. At least he loosened his grip once she settled into a rhythmic trot. River noticed Felicity increasing her speed; getting faster but not lengthening her stride. He called out instructions to Todd, trying to get the boy to ride with his seat and legs, stay off the mare's mouth, and make her work her muscles from her hind end.

They approached the hill. With the confidence of knowing the mare would slow down, Todd sat deep with legs supporting her sides to bring Felicity to walk, and did not pull back on the reins.

"Good, that's how you should ride her all the time," River said, bringing Dune alongside. "The way you ride in the arena is the same as out here."

Todd nodded. "I guess it's easy to forget when we get moving outside," he admitted.

"You cannot ride her in an event unless you can control her without hauling on her mouth," River stated.

"Okay, I've got all winter to practice." Todd would try, for he wanted River's approval. But in his heart, he believed he could already handle Felicity. Hadn't he kept her from bolting today?

They finished the ride and led the horses back toward the stable. "You are one fine lady," River said, stroking Dune's neck. She had proved herself as steady outside as she had in the arena, never once reacting to Felicity's many antics. But when he had asked her for trot, she had instantly responded and moved out with a surprisingly buoyant stride. She had the energy to match Felicity. She was just better able to contain it.

He planned to continue to work her in the arena two or three days a week, and have Todd start walking her out on trails on alternate days for conditioning. There was nothing to compare with asking a horse to walk out with long strides and to walk up and down hills with lowered neck, to build up their chest, shoulders, and hind end muscles.

"Looks like Megan's here," Todd said as they crested the hill and he could see Gwen at the top watching a small girl coming toward them.

A wide smile spread across River's face as he raised his hand in greeting. The child waved back and skipped a few steps, her crown of curly black hair blowing in the breeze, until she remembered she should not run around horses, and she slowed down.

"Unca River, Unca River," she called out when they were in range of her voice. He crouched down and held his arms open for her.

"Hey, little princess," he greeted, taking her up and giving her a hug, loving the feel of her small arms circling his neck as she hugged him back and kissed his cheek.

"Unca River, oh I love you," she affirmed in her child's uninhibited enthusiasm. She reached out to pet the neck of Dune. "Pretty horsey!" She held her arms out in a clear gesture that she wanted up on the mare's back. "Ride please?" she asked.

River had worked enough with the mare now to feel confident she was safe, and he swung Megan up onto her back. The little girl immediately sat up straight and let her legs hang down, already having had lessons on Muffin. Her face lit up in delight as River led her onward.

"Look, Todd, I ride a big horsey!" she exclaimed, looking down at him from Dune's back. Then she leaned down to hug Dune around her neck, placing her cheek on top of her frizzled mane.

"You sure are," Todd laughed.

5 TATTOO

The secret of success lies in maintaining determined forward movement, which obliges the horse to swing his legs powerfully and to make long, bounding strides. - Udo Burger, *The Way To Perfect Horsemanship*

"Please, please, please, please, Mrs. Stevick," Sheryl Andrews pleaded, her hands folded in over-dramatized supplication and giving each 'please' a different emphasis. "Melody and I have called our moms and it's okay with them if it's okay with you."

Please, please, please, Jodi, in the front seat next to Mary Stevick's mother, mimicked sarcastically in her head. How she despised the three empty-headed, cheer-leading bimbos in the back seat, and right now that included her twin sister.

"You said you wanted to look at the table linens on sale at Macy's," Mary reminded her mother, "and the mall is on the way home." Mary, Sheryl, and Melody had plotted all week to coerce one of their mothers into taking them to the mall after school, and today, Friday, was the last chance to find outfits for the Fall Frolic dance Saturday night. They were desperate! But of the three mothers who rotated driving the girls back and forth to school, Mrs. Stevick was the most likely to give in.

"Not exactly on the way if I want to avoid Pacific Avenue," Mary's mother stated, but she had already relented. She saw no harm in letting the girls have an hour or two to shop and she actually did want to look for a tablecloth and napkins for Thanksgiving dinner. She turned right at the next corner and the three girls in the back seat squealed in delight. "Quiet down," she ordered, but she smiled as she caught sight of their eager, happy faces in her rearview mirror.

The three in the back talked excitedly, running over each other's sentences as they discussed a strategic shopping plan. Jodi stared out the window in hostile silence. The thought of having to trail around the mall after those three became too much. "Can you drop me off here?" She suddenly whipped her head toward Mrs. Stevick. "I can catch the bus home."

"You know I can't do that, Jodi," Mrs. Stevick replied in a stern voice. "I believe you are on restriction, aren't you?" She glanced to the side, but Jodi had already turned to stare back out the window. *What a relief my own daughter doesn't get into trouble like this one.* She didn't know what Jodi had done this time, but Cora Mae Cannon had specifically said that no matter what story Jodi might tell, that she did not have permission to do anything but stay with the carpool group. *I do pity Cora Mae, but at least she has Melody. What a jewel! I am so happy that Mary has a friend like Melody.* As she drove toward the mall, she thought about the odd contrast between the Cannon twins. They were not identical, but still, no two girls could be more opposite. Where Jodi was tall and bony, Melody was normal height and had developed very womanly curves. Jodi had mousy brown, stringy hair and Melody had bright reddish-gold wavy hair. Both girls had blue eyes, but Jodi's were darker and cold, whereas Melody's eyes were as bright as the sky, open and friendly. And those were just the physical differences.

She pulled into the mall parking lot and found a space. "Meet me at the entrance into Macy's in two hours," she directed.

"I'll stay here," Jodi said, slumping deep into the seat and slamming her head back with eyes closed.

"No, Jodi, it's not safe. You go with the others. Isn't there something you'd like to shop for?" Mrs. Stevick asked, trying to sound kind and keep the annoyance from her voice. She found it hard to like this girl with her withdrawn, cold attitude.

Jodi blew out between her lips in resignation and got out of the car. Mrs. Stevick wanted to call out to the three girls already skipping toward the entrance to 'wait for Jodi'. Instead, she watched in pity as Jodi trailed behind, her left leg slightly dragging. When the girls reached the entrance, Mrs. Stevick saw Melody stop the others to wait. *Such a sweet girl,* she thought, *always looking out for her sister.*

Jodi trailed after the three girls into the first store, and the next, becoming more and more disgusted listening to them discuss fashion and gossiping. When Sheryl looked over her shoulder at Jodi with an annoyed expression and then pulled Melody behind a rack of jackets, she knew they were going to talk about her.

"Why does she have to go everywhere we go?" Sheryl asked in a harsh whisper.

"How else is she going to get home?" Melody answered, annoyed. *Obviously.* She wasn't any happier than her friends to have her twin sister trailing behind while they shopped. But what was she supposed to do?

"I guess," Sheryl agreed in resignation. "Oo la la, what do you think of this?" She pulled a short, faux leopard print jacket from the rack and held it up to her chest.

Jodi wanted to tell her, 'it looks fake, cheap, and you'd look like a hooker in it,' but she held her tongue. She knew the others would scorn any opinion she might offer. *Enough of this.* "I'm going to the book store," Jodi informed her sister.

Melody looked up but didn't reply, her attention focused on Sheryl now trying on the jacket. Mary never even looked her way.

Jodi limped back out to the mall aisle, her left foot and ankle aching from keeping up with the quick pace of the other girls. She still had well over an hour of time to kill, and knowing those girls as well as Mrs. Stevick, she probably had twice that much time.

It's bad enough I got detention, but for my parents to add on more restriction as well, is so unfair. I didn't even deserve it in the first place, she grumbled to herself. At least Sophie and Tina also got a week of detention. She found that out when Sophie shoved her in the hallway and hissed at her, "You rat. You better watch your back!" Mr. Massey had apparently decided to punish them as well, even though Jodi had not told him anything. She didn't even bother trying to defend herself to Sophie, for that girl always looked for someone to blame for her troubles.

Half way to the book store something in a display window caught her eye. *What is this?* A life-size molded horse stood just inside the open door of a new, recently opened shop. A saddle with the sales tag attached had been placed on the horse. In the shop's display window a hay bale had been arranged with various items of bright colored stable equipment - buckets in several shapes and sizes, grooming brushes, and colorful horse halters with matching lead ropes draped over the hay bale. *A tack store – wow!* Jodi went inside.

The smell of new leather filled her lungs as she walked along a wall hung with bridles in various shades of browns and black and different styles and sizes. She fingered the different parts, curious as to how they fit on a horse and the purpose of each piece. Then she studied a rack of bits, amazed at all the different possibilities; some in silver-colored metal, others gold-colored, and some with rubber or plastic parts in black, yellow, or white. Some of the mouth pieces were solid and others were jointed or even had pieces that rolled.

She moved to an area with rows of saddles stacked on racks and ran her fingers over the various models. She imagined what it must feel like to sit on one of these on a real horse.

Then she found a rack of magazines next to a shelf of books on horses, the subjects ranging from stable care, breeding, to all types of riding and training. She picked up a magazine at random, and flipped through its pages, enthralled by the photos of magnificent horses.

"Do they fit?" she overheard a woman's voice coming from the boot section, just on the other side of the book shelf.

"Yeah, these are great. They're not exactly like River's, but they are waterproof and the foot looks like it will easily fit in a stirrup."

I recognize that voice! She peered over the top of her magazine, and saw Todd Marshall with his foster mother, scrutinizing a pair of boots on his feet.

"Good, but try on that other pair just to be sure," Todd's mother advised.

He mustn't see me here! She quickly thrust the magazine back on the rack and retreated to the mall aisle.

Her mind flashed back to a few days ago. *He probably thinks I bumped his desk on purpose.* In truth, she had lost her balance, something that often happened when she had been sitting still for a while. She did not mean to knock his backpack over.

But she had teased him about his stuttering. *Why do I like to humiliate him about that?* She really didn't know. Years ago she had overheard her mother talking to a neighbor when the Marshalls had first taken Todd in. They spoke in hushed tones how he had an extreme stuttering problem and was emotionally disturbed, and how brave of the Marshalls to foster him. When she actually met Todd in middle school, it had become her secret, a weapon to make someone else feel the way she did when people teased her about her leg.

The thing was though, she liked Todd. He had never teased her about her limp and she had never seen him act mean to anyone. But at the same time, she resented him. It just wasn't fair he got to live with the Marshalls and they let him ride horses. He might be nice and she thought he was kind of cute, but at the same time she sometimes felt so overcome with envy that without thinking, her mouth mocked his stuttering. It eased some of her sense of injustice to watch his humiliated reaction. But moments later, she always felt ashamed, and that is what she felt now. She imagined if he had caught sight of her looking longingly at all the equestrian equipment he would have thought, 'what right does that girl have to been in this shop?' She did not want him to ever know how much she envied him.

Deep in these thoughts as she shuffled toward the book store, she paid no attention when a voice called out, "Hey you." When the voice called again, "Hey, Jodi," she stopped and looked back. Tasha Smith leaned in the doorway of a body piercing and tattoo parlor, smirking at her. "I'm getting a tattoo. Want to watch?"

Jodi stared at her. Jodi had avoided Tasha ever since they had crashed that party.

"Hey, I told you I'm sorry about what happened," Tasha said.

Jodi relented. "It wasn't your fault. You couldn't have known the party would get busted." Jodi never did blame Tasha for what happened, but it had been a good excuse to avoid her. Truthfully, she was tired of hearing Tasha talk about the boys she had been out with, trying to give the impression she was a wild and crazy girl just out for a good time. The sad thing, in Jodi's opinion, was that Tasha desperately wanted a boyfriend – a real boyfriend, not just a guy taking advantage of her. But that was all Tasha got. She would go up to a guy that interested her, and often managed to get him to meet her somewhere. But it was never a date, never taking Tasha to a school dance or football game. And none of the boys that Tasha said she had been out with, would acknowledge her in the halls. Jodi wanted to tell her not to be so easy, but she didn't think Tasha would listen to her.

Tasha had no other friends, and Jodi really did feel sorry for her. It was actually a little self-serving to know somebody more pathetic than herself. Even so, she did not want to re-establish a friendship with her now.

Nevertheless, when Tasha said, "So, come on," Jodi thought to herself, *I am really bored and I've got nothing better to do.* "Okay," she said.

Tasha shifted lazily and with a cock of her head, stepped inside the shop. Jodi followed, even though her parents had forbidden her to have anything to do with Tasha, and if Melody or the others should happen to see them together…but whatever. One thing about already being on restriction and most of your privileges taken away, there wasn't much left to lose.

"Nancy back yet?" Tasha directed the question to a guy bent over a counter filling small bottles of ink from larger containers.

"Not yet."

"Do you know Jake?" Tasha asked Jodi. "He goes to our school. His cousin owns this shop and he's learning the business."

Jodi shook her head.

Jake looked over his shoulder, nodded at Tasha and gave Jodi a cursory glance before turning back to his task.

"What are you doing?" Tasha asked, moving in behind Jake and pressing her chest against him as she looked around his shoulder.

"Careful, baby," Jake said, as she bumped his arm. They talked together in low voices accented by giggles from Tasha, ignoring Jodi's presence.

She likes him, Jodi noted. Yeah, definitely Tasha's type - black hair slicked back in a ponytail, mustache and small goatee, a pierced ear and eyebrow, black jeans with a studded belt, and motorcycle boots. He wore a tank top and his exposed arms, neck, and top of his chest were covered in intricate, colorful tattoos, a living advertisement for the shop. As she studied him, she thought she may have seen him around school, but if so, he must always wear long sleeves for she would have remembered those tattooed arms. He had to be a senior, for he really looked too old to still be in high school, and he was definitely too old for Tasha. He wasn't very good looking, with big ears that stuck out, close-set eyes, and pocked complexion. But it was the image that attracted Tasha, and maybe because he wasn't all that hot, Tasha thought she might have a chance.

Jodi looked around, fascinated. The shop walls were plastered with posters, some of them life-size, of models proudly exposing most of their skin with intricate tattoos and unusual piercings. Stacks of magazines and three-ring binders covered the surface of a table. Two folding metal chairs allowed clients to sit and browse through the countless designs to make their choice. Music played from ceiling mounted speakers. It surprised Jodi that the song playing was a rather mellow folk-rock piece that she recognized from an indie band. She would have thought they would play harder rock - metal or rap, or something like that.

A door opened in the back of the shop behind a screen and someone entered, coughing a harsh, lung-wracking cough. "Come on back," a raspy voice called.

"Here goes," Tasha said. She patted Jake on the rear and then tugged at the back of his shirt. Jodi thought he seemed a little annoyed as he pulled his shirt from her fingers. Then he led the way to the back of the shop behind the screen.

A scrawny, middle-aged woman with magenta-dyed hair and wearing an ink-stained smock stood at a metal rolling stand arrayed with various pieces of equipment.

"You can sit there." Tasha indicated a straight chair near the wall. Tasha sat down in what looked like a dentist's chair and pulled off her sweater.

"Wow!" Jodi exclaimed at the sight of Tasha's bared skin. An almost completed dragon tattoo in multiple colors spread its wings across the width of her belly. Its tail curled up between her breasts and its fiery mouth aimed suggestively down below.

The woman frowned at Jodi as she pulled on a pair of black vinyl gloves.

"She's thinking about getting a tattoo," Tasha explained giving Jodi a wink. "She wants to see what's involved first."

The woman snorted but apparently the explanation satisfied her.

Jake also pulled on gloves and then he stepped up to Tasha and wiped an area on her skin with a gauze pad along the back scales of the dragon, and then set to work with the tattooing gun. Nancy stood over his shoulder, directing the work and occasionally taking the instrument from his hand to demonstrate or help him out.

Jodi stared, fascinated. She flinched as the instrument hummed to life with a low buzzing sound like a low-speed dentist drill.

"Nancy started this two months ago," Tasha explained, sitting calmly and apparently not at all bothered by what must be a needle going in and out of her skin. "Jake is learning how to add color to the scales."

"Doesn't it hurt?" Jodi asked, wide-eyed. A shiver ran down her spine every time Jake paused in his work and then started up the instrument again.

"Not too bad. You get used to it," Tasha replied nonchalantly. "It's taken three sessions so far, but this is the last. He's just finishing the last accent colors." She chatted on, explaining the process as Jake and Nancy worked, and the minutes flew by.

"That's it," Nancy stated. She stepped back to survey the design while Jake wiped down the area he had just inked. Nancy pulled off her gloves and dropped them on the tray. "Clean up," she ordered and left through the back door.

Jake also stepped back to admire his work. Then he ejected the needle from the gun into a needle disposal container and pulled off his gloves. "Go take a look," he said to Tasha.

Tasha hopped off the chair and went over to a full-length mirror to survey the final results. "Awesome," she breathed out as she turned at different angles to see all aspects of the finished dragon.

"It's amazing," Jodi agreed, and actually felt relieved the process was over.

"Nancy's the best," Tasha stated. "Jake is really lucky to learn from her. But she can't go longer than fifteen minutes without a smoke." She laughed, cocking her head toward the back door where Nancy had exited. "Jake, I love it!"

Jake leaned against the counter with a look of pride on his face. Then to Jodi's surprise, he turned to her and asked, "You want a tattoo?"

"What? No way," Jodi said with a laugh.

"Why not?" he asked, eyeing her with a predatory look.

"Uh…." she stared back at him, feeling uncomfortable.

"I seen you around school. You're…" He snapped his fingers, frowning, obviously trying to come up with a name.

"Jodi," she stated to help him out.

"Right, you're Melody Cannon's sister."

Jodi wasn't surprised that he knew her sister's name but not hers. Everybody knew her sister.

"What's wrong with your leg anyway?" he asked, looking down at her foot and then back up to meet her eyes. His own face wore a neutral expression.

Jodi stiffened and the color drained from her face, shocked that he dared ask the question. Nobody ever asked her why she limped, although she knew others talked about it, either in pity or making fun. She heard the whispers behind her back, had been hearing them all her life. She would never forget being called 'Gimpy Jodi' in fourth grade. Back then, she would punch anyone who said it to her face, even the boys, and she had earned the reputation of a tough girl and a freak. Naturally she was in trouble all the time. When she started middle school, Jodi held back from physical violence, not wanting to earn the same reputation in a new school. Plus, the boys were bigger and stronger than in grade school.

But she wanted to use violence right now. Ire bubbled within her stomach, threatening to erupt. She pressed her lips tight and narrowed her eyes. She wanted to slap him.

"Hey, hey," Jake said in a placating tone and holding his hands up defensively. He took two long strides and knelt down in front of her, still looking into her face. "Don't ever be ashamed of what makes you different," he said in a surprisingly gentle tone. Tenderly he put his hands around her left ankle and began to lightly massage it through the leg of her jeans. "Everybody has flaws, and you know the best way to deal with them?" His eyes held her own like a magnetic force.

She shook her head. The earnestness of his tone and actions without any hint of mocking her, had softened her anger, and allowed space for the grief over her leg that she normally suppressed, to seep in. Usually any attention to her leg caused her to feel utterly humiliated, but his soothing hold on her ankle, treating it with such gentle care, for the first time in her life eased some of the disgust she felt toward her own body part.

"Flaunt them!" he told her. When he started to push up the leg of her jeans, she tried to pull away but he held on firmly until she ceased to resist. "Relax, I'm not putting a move on you," he said as he placed her leg on his bent knee, and exposed her ankle by pushing up the hem of her jeans and pulling down her sock. "You know what I think?" He cocked his head side-to-side, looking at her bared flesh. He noted how her left foot twisted unnaturally, the ankle misshapen. He traced a design with his finger on the top of her ankle. "I'd put a tattoo right here, and I'd be proud to show it to the world."

She gasped.

"What happened? An accident?"

She shook her head and finally found her tongue, answering in a hoarse voice, "Birth defect."

He nodded as if he understood all the pain and humiliation she had known in her short life; as if he could fathom the years of agony she had spent in physical therapy so that she at least no longer had to wear a leg brace.

"Yeah," Jake continued, "I could put a set of wings here, or a Chinese character, like for strength or freedom. Something like that, you know? Those are really popular now. Look, I'll do it for free, my gift to you."

"What about the Chinese character for cripple?" she said bitterly.

"No, not even as a joke." Jake gave her ankle a gentle squeeze. "Tattoos are spiritual, don't you know that?"

She shook her head. For some reason, she found herself fighting back tears.

"They are like magic," he continued in a mesmerizing tone. "Put wings or a symbol that means something to you underneath your skin and you will be amazed how it will change you."

Jodi did not believe him. But she did not feel like he was making fun of her or pitying her. It gave her a sense of worth she rarely experienced.

"Don't I have to get my parents' permission?" She asked in a weak voice.

"I'm not charging you anything. This is just between friends. I think I can trust you to never tell where you got it," Jake said in a conspiratorial tone. He set her foot on the floor and stood up. "What do you think, Tasha? Think I can trust her?"

"Yeah, she won't tell," Tasha said. She had been watching the interaction in the mirror but now turned around. The pleased look on her face over her tattoo had been replaced by a different expression that included a grim set to her mouth.

Jodi did not see the look on Tasha's face or she might have changed her mind. But the situation felt surreal to her, like she was on the verge of something important changing in her life. She glanced from the corner of her eye at Jake.

Does all he really want out of this is a little experience? Jodi felt suspicious. Nothing was really for free. What price would she eventually have to pay? But then again, what did she really have to lose…a reputation, friends? She didn't have those things anyway. She looked down at her foot in its aberrant outward angle. How she hated that foot! But, at least she could walk. Her ankle often ached when she became tired, but it didn't hurt her constantly. She remembered some of the other kids in physical therapy that were so much worse off, paralyzed or only able to walk with crutches.

She came to a decision. No, she had never thought about a tattoo for herself. But at the beginning of school Melody had begged for a tattoo. Mary had been allowed to get one over the summer and both Melody and Sheryl wanted one as well. Both sets of parents had firmly said 'no', and eventually Melody and Sheryl gave up. The thought of showing off a tattoo to Melody and her friends and for once, seeing envy rather than pity from them, was the final convincing factor. "Is there a symbol for 'courage'?" she asked weakly.

Twenty-five minutes later, for it did not take long for Jake to ink in the few black lines, Jodi stared at her ankle. "It's beautiful," she breathed out.

Jake finished up by gently dabbing the area with a moistened gauze and then covered it with a dry bandage. "Keep it covered for a couple hours," he instructed. "Wash it tonight before you go to bed and every day with soap and water. Just use your hand, not a washcloth, and it's best to let it air dry. Don't use your towel to dry it. It'll ooze for a couple days, that's normal. When it starts to dry and flake, put just a little of this cream on. It's got cocoa butter or something like that in it. It'll take a couple weeks, maybe three, to completely heal. Okay?"

"Okay," she accepted the tube of cream he handed to her. "Thank you," she said in a husky voice.

He patted her knee where she sat in the dentist chair. "What do you think, Tasha?" He looked over at the chair where Tasha now sat, their positions switched. "Not bad for free hand, huh?"

Tasha's dark demeanor brightened with his attention back on her. "I think you have the talent to be as good as Nancy," she answered.

Jake got up and went over to Tasha and whispered something in her ear that made her blush and giggle. She still had not put on her sweater, and he brushed his finger across the top of her breast where it bulged from her bra.

"Thank you," Jodi said again. "Uh, guess I'll see you at school," she said to Tasha.

"Later," Tasha answered, but her attention was now on Jake and Jodi left the shop unnoticed.

It hurts, oh yeah, but Jodi welcomed the sting as she made her way to Macy's. The sting overpowered the ache of her ankle, a good distraction. Sometimes, when she walked very slowly and really concentrated, she could walk without limping, but most of the time she felt it took too much effort. But now she walked straight and even, her shoulders back and head high. *I have a tattoo!*

"Thank heavens," Mrs. Stevick cried out as Jodi approached.

"Where have you been?" Melody shouted angrily. "We've been looking everywhere for you!"

"Just walking around," Jodi answered, surprised at how late it was for she didn't think she had been in the shop that long.

"I was just about to call security," Mrs. Stevick said. She patted herself over her heart, as if preventing an attack. "Do you have any idea how worried I've been? What would your mother think if…." She continued her tirade as they left the mall. Jodi hung her head as if in shame, but she smiled down at her feet.

"You are in so much trouble," Melody hissed at Jodi as they walked back to the car. "Why do you have to be like you are?" she asked in exasperation.

Yeah, why do I have to be like I am? Jodi wondered, but feeling the sting of her tattoo, she said to herself, *I don't know, but it's okay to be like I am.*

6 PUNISHMENT

Riding: the dialogue between two bodies and two souls aimed at establishing perfect harmony between them. – Waldemar Seunig

Jodi did not get in trouble that night. Mrs. Stevick never said anything to Cora Mae Cannon, primarily because she didn't want Cora Mae to think she had been irresponsible. She hoped to down play how worried she had been when she feared Jodi had run away. Nor did Melody tattle on her sister, for as much as she threatened Jodi, she really didn't like to see her punished. She had always felt protective of her twin.

But on Monday, the week of Thanksgiving, Jodi did get in trouble.

Apparently Tasha assumed the tattoo experience meant Jodi was no longer mad at her, and she sat down at Jodi's table at lunch time. Jodi resigned herself to the company. She half-listened to Tasha talk about what she had done with Jake over the weekend. When the bell rang, Jodi gratefully gathered her things and stood up to escape.

Tasha followed her. As they passed near the table where Melody and her friends were just getting up, Tasha called out, "Hey, Melody, what do you think of Jodi's tattoo?"

Jodi froze in her steps and narrowed her eyes at Tasha. *She wants to get me in trouble!*

"What are you talking about?" Melody frowned at Tasha, surprised she would dare even speak to her.

"I asked what you think of Jodi's new tattoo."

"Shut up," Jodi growled at Tasha in a low voice.

Melody looked at her sister quizzically. "What is she talking about?"

"Nothing," Jodi shot back and started to limp away.

But Tasha stayed behind to tell the story. Melody, her face waning of color, ran to catch up to Jodi, and pushed her into the nearest chair.

Flaunt your flaws, Jodi recalled Jake's words. Defiantly, she pulled up her pant leg and pushed down her sock. She held her leg up proudly for Melody and her friends rushing up behind her to see.

It actually turned out to be one of the best moments she had ever had at school. She became the center of attention, but not because anyone was making fun of her. Girls crowded around, exclaiming excitedly and appreciatively over her tattoo. Many even sounded envious.

She caught Melody's eye and mouthed, 'don't tell'.

When Melody and her friends had seen enough and started milling away to their classes, Melody said to her sister, "I won't tell and I'll ask my friends not to say anything, but you know chances are this is going to get back to Mom and Dad." She smiled and asked, "How did you ever get the nerve to get a tattoo?"

Jodi shrugged, but she smiled back at her sister.

When Melody left and Jodi saw Tasha standing nearby with a sneer on her face, Jodi glared back at her. "Thanks a lot," she said angrily, and then limped away. Tasha had wanted to get her in trouble, but as to why, Jodi did not know, nor did she care. She planned to have nothing more to do with her.

Throughout that day, many kids came up to Jodi, asking to see her tattoo, especially boys. What a glorious feeling to have others interested in her for something good rather than making fun of her.

Best of all, Kirby Portman actually waited for her after one of her classes and without preamble demanded, "Let me see it." She had lifted up her pant leg and he bent down to examine her ankle, tracing the design with a finger. "I like it," he said very seriously. "It's different." Then he looked up, straight into her eyes. "You're different."

She decided whatever punishment her parents dealt out would be worth this one day, especially because, *Kirby thinks I'm interesting, and he thinks I'm different!* The way he said it, she thought he meant 'different' in a good way.

Of course, her parents found out. She knew Melody never told, but suspected any one of her friends told their parents and that's how her parents probably found out.

The phone call came while they were at dinner. Afterwards, she was summoned into her father's study.

"Sit down, young lady," Martin Cannon ordered from behind his desk. He watched his daughter enter with shuffling steps and slumped posture. He pressed his lips firmly together as she plopped down on the narrow sofa at the far end opposite her mother and leaned over her lap, letting her dark hair fall around her face to obscure it from view. He waited, hoping for some sign of remorse, but Jodi held her closed posture as still as a statue, as stubborn as ever. "I want an explanation, Jodi," he demanded.

Jodi shrugged, a gesture that always grated down his spine, a gesture he interpreted as complete disrespect.

Martin slammed the palm of his hand onto the surface of his desk. He shifted his position to sit straighter, more commanding. Raising his voice, he declared, "I cannot understand you at all. What in the world were you thinking?" He paused, waiting for an answer that did not come. "Do you purposely try to do whatever you think your mother and I will most disapprove of?" Jodi shrugged again. He fought back the desire to jump up, grab her by the shoulders and shake her soundly to rattle some sense into her dense skull. "Well?"

Jodi looked up, trying to feel fearless, trying to tap into the magic on her ankle. But all she felt was the usual self-loathing whenever in trouble and the feeling that her father despised her. "It was just for fun," she offered as an explanation.

"Fun!" her father thundered. "Fun!"

"Martin, don't shout," Cora Mae said, flinching. She turned to look at Jodi pleadingly. "What is fun about scarring and abusing your body?" she asked.

Jodi looked away. At least her mother didn't hate her, but every time Jodi got in trouble, her mother acted like she did it deliberately to hurt her parents. "It's a design and it's beautiful," she mumbled.

Her father snorted in disgust. "I want the person's name who did this, when, and where. This is child abuse. How old is this friend? What did you have to do to get him to agree?"

"Nothing," Jodi snapped back. "I did this myself. Someone left the ink gun in the girls' locker room, and I just borrowed it," she lied.

"How would you even know how to give yourself a tattoo?" Cora Mae asked incredulously, always baffled by this daughter's behavior.

"The internet, of course," she stated in an 'obviously' tone. "I watched a couple YouTube videos. It's easy."

"This is more than I can deal with, Cora Mae," Martin said to his wife.

"Oh, Jodi, why can't you be more like your sister? You have a perfect model of how to behave and you seem to choose to do everything opposite," Cora Mae said pleadingly, her face drawn into a look of pain, as if she were fighting down nausea.

The last time Jodi had been in serious trouble, the night she had snuck out to go to that party, Martin had suggested sending Jodi away to a special school for difficult teens. He had brought the idea up again when he and Cora Mae talked before their daughter arrived. Cora Mae had no idea how to deal with her youngest twin's behavior, but to send her away? She could not agree to that. In anguish, she clutched her hands against her stomach *Please, no, Martin,* she silently pleaded.

"Time and again you have defied our rules...."

"When did you make a rule about tattoos?" Jodi knew that question would increase her father's ire, nevertheless, she let the question slip out.

"That's it!" Martin stood up, his face red with rage.

Jodi cowered into the corner of the sofa. Her father had never hit her before but maybe she had pushed a little too far this time.

"Your mother and I have talked about a boarding school, a place that is strong on discipline and will set you on the right path. We can't seem to influence you, so maybe it's time to turn the task over to experts."

Every word sliced into Jodi's chest. *Sending me away?* It was what she had always feared; placement in an institution...the cripple...out of sight, out of mind, out of shameful view.

"Martin...."

"No, Cora Mae, I give up." He turned back to Jodi. "Go to your room."

Jodi fled, as fast as her left leg allowed her to move, determined not to cry in front of her parents.

Two days later, Cora Mae pushed a shopping cart down the produce aisle, listlessly selecting the items on her grocery list. She did not agree with her husband's decision to send Jodi away, but she had no idea what else to do. She felt she had dismally failed as a mother. Her one comfort was that Melody was such a joy, the perfect daughter.

She had always treated both girls the same. They had the same privileges, the same allowance, they received equal gifts for their birthday and Christmas. Of course the ballet lessons, summer soccer league, and last summer, cheerleading camp for Melody, were all things Jodi simply could not do. Maybe she should have tried harder to find something to compensate. Well, they had offered Jodi piano lessons, art camp - those kinds of activities, but nothing seemed to interest her.

"Hello, Cora Mae."

Startled out of her thoughts, Cora Mae looked up in surprise. One of her neighbors stood in front of the apple bin and Cora Mae had accidentally bumped into her cart. "Oh, I didn't see you there. Hi, Gwen," she greeted. "How are you?"

"Fine, how are you and Martin and the twins?" Gwen Marshall asked.

"They're fine. How are you and John, and let's see, you still have a foster child, don't you?" Cora Mae asked politely, but not really interested.

"Yes, we still have Todd. We're all fine." Gwen did not point out that Todd had been living with the Marshalls for almost seven years. "Hmm, these apples are not very appealing. Wasn't a very good year for apples," she said conversationally, holding up a sickly specimen.

"No," Cora Mae said absently. "No, not at all." Her voice choked on her last words. Something about the pathetic looking apple seemed to parallel Jodi, and she felt overcome with despair.

"Cora Mae, something is wrong," Gwen said gently, noting the stricken expression on her neighbor's face.

Cora Mae gripped the handle of her shopping cart, feeling suddenly faint. She looked down into her basket, the last items she needed for Thanksgiving dinner (*maybe the last meal we have together as a family*), and gulped in air to keep from bursting into tears in public. She felt a light hand on her shoulder.

"What is it?" Gwen asked softly. "Can I help you?"

Regaining control, Cora Mae looked up with a weak smile, and read genuine concern in the other woman's face. *This woman has been taking in foster children for years*, it occurred to her. *She must have some kind of training in child behavior or psychology or something. Maybe she can help.* "Gwen, I don't know what to do," she admitted.

"Come on," Gwen said. "Let's go get a coffee at the Starbuck's up front, and you can tell me everything."

Cora Mae agreed. The two women parked their carts, ordered lattes, and sat down at a table. Cora Mae told Gwen about her daughter's tattooing, and other misbehaviors that had landed her in trouble.

"I don't know what to do," she finished her story after telling Gwen of Martin's decision. "I don't want to send my daughter away. But we have tried everything - restriction, taking away privileges, withholding allowance. Nothing daunts her. She is such a handful...." Cora Mae sighed as if her problem child weighed down heavily on her shoulders. "I can't understand how two girls, and twins at that, can be so opposite. They are not identical, but still...if only Jodi could be more like her sister."

Gwen swirled the remnants of her coffee as Cora Mae talked. She did not want to say out loud, *that's part of the problem, Jodi is always compared to Melody.* She had known the Cannons since they had moved to her neighborhood when their girls were in the fourth grade. Her oldest daughter had even babysat for them a few times. She knew Jodi had some kind of physical disability but it had never seemed that bad or obvious to her. Jodi walked with a limp, that was all. But where Melody readily fit in with other girls her age, Jodi did not seem to be able to get along. She had been known to get into actual fights when she had been younger, and the gossip now was she was going wild, hanging out with a bad crowd and completely undisciplined.

"It's not like Jodi doesn't have the same abilities. Actually, she always scores higher than Melody on those aptitude tests they give in school. That has always surprised Martin and me, because Melody gets much better grades."

"Umhmm," Gwen mumbled to indicate she was listening.

"Gwen, you've had a lot of experience with all kinds of children. What would you do?" Cora Mae asked bluntly.

Stay out of it, Gwen warned herself. *You've listened to her and that's enough*. Without even knowing Jodi, she could surmise much of the problem here. Always in the shadow of her sister who fit the ideal of the perfect child to her parents, Jodi had given up trying to please them. But Gwen had a soft heart for all children, and especially for those in trouble. Against her better judgment, she decided to give a little advice. "One thing I have tried is giving a reward rather than punishment. Sometimes when you take everything away from a child, they figure they have nothing more to lose. Therefore they do whatever they want. Try offering her something she really wants, with the agreement she will meet certain behaviors in order to keep it."

"What?" Cora Mae raised her eyes incredulously.

"It's just a suggestion. You might try it once and if it doesn't work, what have you really lost other than giving your child something?"

"Hmm…. I don't know…. I can't see Martin agreeing…." Cora Mae picked up her hardly touched latte and took a swallow. She closed her eyes, thinking. "Does it really work?"

"It has a few times, not always. But like I say, it might be worth a try."

Cora Mae took a few more sips, and then pushed away from the table. "Thank you, Gwen, I will certainly think about that. Well, I better get back to the shopping."

Both women returned to their carts, said the obligatory 'say hello to your husband', and then parted down different aisles.

Perhaps Martin also had second thoughts about sending his daughter away, for after two nights of discussions, he agreed to Cora Mae's suggestion. The day after Thanksgiving, after a dinner of leftovers, Martin called Jodi again into his study.

Jodi entered the room. Her father sat at his usual spot behind his desk and her mother on the sofa, a repeat of several nights ago. She slumped over to her corner of the couch, expecting to hear what school, where, and when she was being sent away.

"Jodi, we have punished you over and over, and nothing seems to have any effect on you," Martin began. "I have been doing some research, and I think I have found a suitable school. It's in Utah, and it is conducted in a military tradition."

Jodi's heart plummeted. A military school was her worst fear. *How is a cripple supposed to survive in the army?*

"But your mother and I have decided to give you one last chance. We've talked this over, and since punishment doesn't daunt you, we're going to try a different approach. Mark my words, this is against my better judgment, but we have decided to try making a contract with you. We will give you something you want now, something very special. You will then adhere to our rules in order to keep it. If you break the contract, not only will you lose whatever it is you decide you want, but we will again consider a special school."

"What are you talking about?" Jodi pushed her hair away from the side of her face and looked up, sure she had misunderstood the words.

"What would you like, dear?" her mother asked. "Maybe that computer program for editing photography? You seemed interested in that last summer."

Jodi did not remember ever being interested in photography. It had probably been Melody who wanted the program. But a new computer, maybe one with a touch screen and…. "Anything I want?" She still did not quite believe what her parents were offering.

"Yes, Jodi, within reason of course."

Jodi looked from her mother to her father. Both sat expectantly, waiting to hear what might interest her enough to keep her in line. "Wow," she murmured under her breath. Suddenly, she thought of the one thing she had always wanted and pleaded for as a child, but had long ago given up hope. There was no way they would even consider it! Perhaps to test their sincerity, she boldly said, "A horse."

"A horse?" Martin wrinkled his brow.

"Sweetie, you know you wouldn't be able to ride a horse. I mean, your leg and all…." Cora Mae said.

"Why couldn't I ride a horse? I'd be sitting down, not walking."

"You don't know anything about horses. We don't know anything about horses. Now think of something realistic," Martin ordered. *Why does she have to be so difficult? Why is she asking for the impossible?*

It had been years since Jodi had asked for a horse, but suddenly, it was the most important thing in the world to her. Ever since her tattoo, Jodi had felt something change inside her, and she actually began to hope. She could not think of anything else she really wanted, other than acceptance, respect…love. But those were things you couldn't ask for. "What about this?" she suggested. "What about riding lessons to see if I could even ride?"

"Now listen here…" Martin raised his voice in frustration.

"Why not, Martin?" Cora Mae interjected. "You know that boy living with the Marshalls, I believe Gwen told me once he takes riding lessons. I could talk to her."

"Cora Mae, do not encourage her in something that is bound to end in failure and disappointment," Martin admonished his wife. "What about her balance problem? It's not just her leg."

"Please, let me try," Jodi asked in a small voice, looking up to meet her father's eyes.

Martin studied his daughter. For once her face was not hidden by her hair, and she looked at him with an open expression, her eyes wide with hope. For the first time in years, he noted the resemblance between Jodi and Melody. *They really do look alike. What a difference an attitude makes.* He was astonished to have just noticed that. His heart softened. He loved both his daughters, but it was Melody he cherished. If it were Melody asking him…. He dropped his eyes to study his hands folded on his desk. "All right, riding lessons," he agreed, raising his eyes again to Jodi. "But the lessons last only as long as you keep the rules. You come home after school and you help your mother with the few chores she asks of you. You do your homework and you bring your grades up to an acceptable level. You do not leave this house without permission. Can you agree to that?"

"Really? You'll give me riding lessons?" Jodi sat up, a rare smile spreading across her face. "I can agree."

7 A NEW STUDENT

Withhold judgment amid the less-than-perfect rides and remember the serenity of horses munching hay. Do not compare yourself to others, for there will always be those who do a perfect canter pirouette and those who fall. Be content with the level where you are and the horse you are riding, for it is all as it should be; you will ascend precisely at the right moment. Do not distress when you experience setbacks, for they often unlock doors to greater ability and understanding. Be gentle with yourself, do not underestimate your horse, and above all, ride with joy. – Lynn Wolf

"The boss wants to talk to you," Manuel, the stable manager informed River, speaking in Spanish.

"*Gracias.*" River had just stepped out of his truck, having returned from school. He debated whether to go up to his room above the lounge and change into riding clothes, or just meet Tess and get it over with now. He decided to step into the office. It was a day early for their usual once-a-month meeting to review the business of the stable, but sometimes she asked to meet earlier if something had come up she needed to talk to him about.

"Manuel said you wanted to talk to me?"

Sitting in front of her computer, Tess frowned to acknowledge his presence, finished typing her sentence and then turned away from the computer to face him. "Sit down," she commanded.

River hooked the leg of the chair opposite Tess and sat down, folding his arms defensively. Discussions with Tess didn't always go well, for they had many differing views on the care and training of horses.

Tess and River had come to somewhat of a truce now that he did most of the training. She had reconciled herself to the fact he was probably right most of the time when it came to training the horses. Most of their disagreements now came about because Tess was far more ambitious than River. Her priorities were to develop horses and riders who would compete and win in combined training events or in dressage, enhancing the reputation of the stable. River's priorities were always the horses, what was best for them.

"Read this." Tess pulled a letter from a folder and handed it across the desk. "Well?" she asked when River finished reading and raised his eyes to meet hers. She didn't like the frown on his face where she had hoped to see a smile of delight.

"What is this?"

"It is obviously your chance to ride in the Olympics in two years." When River continued to stare at her as if that didn't explain anything, she continued, "Jack McCall was in Kentucky for the finals. He saw you ride...oh, for heaven's sake, River, he was very impressed. He has been coaching riders for the past fifteen years, preparing them to compete internationally and specifically in the Olympics. He has four available slots and he has been sending out invitations to all the riders he is interested in recruiting. You know who he is, don't you?"

"Uh..." River thought the name sounded familiar but he really didn't know. He always remembered impressive horses he had seen. He didn't always remember the riders.

Tess sighed in resignation and then explained. "Jack McCall was one of the top international competitors in dressage. He has won a gold and a bronze medal in two past Olympic events. Now he devotes his career to helping promising riders … go to his website." Tess clicked on a link and turned her computer screen to face River. "Read his mission statement."

Leaning forward, River scanned the brief paragraph:

The mission of Jack McCall Dressage in conjunction with Stone Valley Farm, is to promote the art of classical dressage as the most appropriate method of training horses of any breed or quality, to reach their highest potential athletic ability in any equestrian discipline, while maintaining their health and happiness; and to exhibit to the world the significance of horses in contributing to the humanities and by their example, improving humankind.

"That's a mouthful," he commented, after the several minutes it took to read the words and absorb the meaning. The statement seemed rather pompous, but River did like what he perceived as its intent.

"Training under Jack is almost a guarantee of making the U.S. Equestrian Team and riding in the Olympics."

"I don't want…"

"River," Tess raised her voice to interrupt. "This is a business. This is your livelihood. If you think you can make a living doing only the things you want to do, then you will go broke. You have to keep your name and reputation out there. It's because you've won the regional championship so many times and you rode in the national finals that we have a waiting list for training and lesson slots."

"So, if we do well with the horses I train and people make progress from our lessons, I think we are succeeding."

"Yes, but to have an Olympian associated with our stable will guarantee a lasting prestigious reputation. We'll draw riders from out-of-state, and they will pay top fees."

River tightened his jaw and clamped his teeth for a few minutes, fighting down the urge to explode at Tess and storm away. How many times did they have to have this conversation? It wasn't that he was opposed to the Olympics. But for him, it would mean traveling around the country and then internationally to compete at that level. It had been hard enough to go to Kentucky and stay there for a week. That was the longest he ever wanted to be away from his own horses. He could just imagine the high pressure to win. Pressure like that could outweigh the joy of riding a grand prix level dressage horse. He could imagine how stressful it was for horses to travel so often, stabled in unfamiliar barns, around horses and people that were strangers. He just didn't want to subject any of his horses to that level of stress. He had given in to the pressure from Tess and Mrs. Galensburg when he qualified for the national dressage finals. Wasn't that enough?

Swallowing down his antagonistic feelings, he said, "We make enough. We already charge higher fees than any other stable in this area. Tess, I've told you this before. I don't care about money. I understand we have to make enough to be able to take care of our horses properly, but the way I see it, we are making enough to do that. We make a profit above yours and my salary, and you tell me Mrs. Galensburg is satisfied with her investment. If we ever get in financial trouble, as I've told you many times, you can make budget by cutting into my salary."

Tess pressed with her hands on the surface of her desk in frustration. She could never understand why River didn't want to be an Olympic rider. Wasn't that every equestrian's dream? She knew all of the students currently riding at Pegasus would be thrilled at such an opportunity. It had been her own dream when she was an amateur rider, and she had come so close. She wanted to scream at him, *you blind idiot!* But both she and River were learning to control their tempers around each other. She took in a deep breath and lowered her voice to almost a whisper. "Please, River, I am begging you. You know the reason Mrs. Galensburg bought Pendragon was her dream of owning an Olympic horse, and because of how well he has done, she was willing to become our financial backer. And, by the way, she called me again about buying Oberon…just listen," she insisted when River opened his mouth to protest. "We've talked about this before. You know very well it would be in name only, and that is all she wants, her name announced at the Olympic Games as the owner. All decisions regarding what you do with him would still be yours to make. She doesn't even care if you win a medal. She just wants to see her horse in the Olympics. We are so close. She has done so much for us financially, especially for you." She watched him furrow his brow and twist his hands together. "Is it really that important for you to have his ownership papers?"

With a deep sigh River answered, "I just don't want to worry about something happening like with her finances or something and all of a sudden she up and sells him."

"I told her that, and she faxed me over a copy of a proposal for a contract. It specifically states you retain all rights to his training and competitions. It also gives you first right to buy him back in case she did need to sell him."

"Yeah, and what if she wants more money for him than I can afford?"

Tess glared at him. She shoved the copy of the contract she had just pulled out of another folder at him. "Look it over. Have Delia Evans look it over. Isn't she some kind of property lawyer? It should be within her specialty."

"Okay."

"And think about Jack's offer. It would be good for you."

"Okay." He looked up at the ceiling in resignation.

Tess picked up Jack McCall's letter reverently and placed it back in its folder. Then she picked up another folder and handed it across the desk, getting down to the business of the stable. "Julia Salinger is late with the board again and has not paid for the last two weeks of lessons. I have sent her an eviction notice."

"Uh huh," River said absentmindedly as he opened the folder with the training and lesson schedules for the month inside. He hadn't thought much of Julia as a horsewoman - too interested in getting her horse quickly into competitions regardless of what was best for him. He wouldn't miss her at all.

"I've added a new student into her lesson slot. She's lucky, because none of the four students ahead of her on the waiting list could take a lesson at Julia's time. She's apparently someone your friend Gwen Marshall knows, because when the girl's mother called, she said Gwen had recommended Pegasus to her."

River nodded to indicate he was listening as he looked over the calendar. "She ever ridden?" he asked, hoping to hear 'no'. He actually liked starting new students that had never ridden, because they didn't have bad habits they needed to overcome.

"No, and I'm not so sure she can ride. Her mother says she has some physical disabilities and even her mother is doubtful. But apparently the girl is set on learning to ride. See what you think when she arrives today. I told the girl's mother that if you think it is unsafe to put her on a horse, then we won't be able to give her lessons. I may be able to juggle a weekend student to accommodate someone on the waiting list to fill that slot."

"Okay," River agreed. He stood, picking up the schedule to post on the tack room bulletin board. "Anything else?"

"No, just think about Jack McCall's offer," Tess said to his retreating back.

River did not think about Jack McCall or the Olympics anymore that day. He had two horses to ride before the first student arrived for a lesson. Years ago, taking instructions from his friend João Mateus, he had developed the habit of focusing all his attention on the horse he was riding. He would never forget the first time his teacher scolded him for inattention.

"What are you thinking of, River? Is your mind on the pizza you are having for dinner? Are you thinking about what you are going to wear to school tomorrow?"

"Huh?" River actually had been thinking about what might be in the oven that had smelled so good, the aroma wafting out when he arrived for his lesson and stood at João's door. He was hungry, and João always invited him to stay for dinner after they had finished with riding and caring for the horse. His mind had drifted from Duerme, the little bay horse he was riding in the lesson.

"Tsk, tsk, tsk," João chided. "Duerme certainly knows you are not thinking about him. He is drifting out and his attention is back in the field. Don't you feel how he is crooked?"

Now that João mentioned it, River did feel how the bay's shoulder had dropped to the inside and he was ever so slightly shifting himself toward the exit of the arena.

"Why should he listen to you when you are not paying attention to him? A horse knows, River. They deserve our attention if we expect them to understand what we ask of them. Do you agree?"

When River turned his attention back to Duerme, the bay straightened, reached for his bit, and brought his hindquarters deeper underneath, ready to work. It had impressed him that day, and he never forgot.

A light rain never prevented riders taking horses out on the trails at Pegasus. There were plenty of rain ponchos available and rain sheets for the horses' backs. But the downpour happening right now was more than even the most intrepid rider cared to endure. Todd held his backpack over his head as he ran from the school bus to the shelter of the stable, grumbling to himself that he would probably have to ride inside today.

Before he reached the tack room, he passed River leading a horse out from the cross ties. "Hey, Todd," River greeted. "Can you do me a favor?"

"Sure."

"A new student is arriving probably in the next twenty minutes. I want to get a short ride on Oberon and I'm running out of time. Can you bring in Morris and show her how to groom and tack up?"

"Yeah, no problem."

"The last name is Cannon," River said over his shoulder as he led his horse toward the indoor arena. "Tess didn't write down her first name."

Todd froze, watching the tail end of the bay disappear around the corner. *Cannon? Melody Cannon?* His heart sped up as his imagination ran wild with images of Melody arriving at the stable, looking up at him with adoring eyes as he showed her how to groom a horse, touching her leg as he adjusted the stirrups for her.... *Is that what she wanted to ask me the other day? About riding lessons? Have Mindy and Brooke convinced her to try riding?*

His mind in a cloud, Todd stepped into the tack room, stowed his backpack, and changed into his riding clothes. In the small restroom, he surveyed his image critically in the full-length mirror. Immediately he noted a stain above the knee of his riding breeches, the place where he had rested a horse's muddy fetlock yesterday while he picked dirt out of the hoof. He dampened a paper towel and sponged at the stain without much success, wishing he had remembered to take them home yesterday to get washed. He straightened his jacket, making sure the collar lay flat, and even raked his fingers through his rain-damp hair. He frowned at his image, and then left to bring in Morris.

"Turn off the engine, Mom," Jodi said. Her mother had just pulled into the stable yard, but she sat behind the wheel with the engine idling, as if ready to back out and drive away.

"Are you sure about this?" Cora Mae asked, looking out through the rhythmic pattern of the windshield wipers, trying to find a reason to turn around.

"I'm sure." *No, I'm not sure. I'm so scared I won't be able to do this, but I have to try....*

With a deep sigh, Cora Mae clicked off the wipers and lights, turned off the engine, and pulled out the key. "I just don't want you to be disappointed, baby."

"I have to try, Mom." Jodi pushed open the car door and stepped out, pulling up her hood against the rain.

"I don't see anybody around," Cora Mae said, getting out hesitantly and looking around.

"It's raining, Mom. They are probably inside the stable." Jodi led the way, concentrating so as to hide her limp. She did not want her mother to notice how nervous she felt. Nor did she want the riding instructor to see her walk in limping and say 'no way'.

Inside the stable they first came to three empty crosstie bays. Lights shone into the aisle from behind the bays, so they continued on around the corner and came up to the rail of an indoor arena.

Jodi drew in a sharp breath at the sight of a horse and rider working in the arena. She had often admired horses on television and movies and in photos and paintings, but none of those images came close to the magnificence of a horse in real life. The overhead lights gleamed off his mahogany coat, highlighting the definition of his muscles as he moved. He arched his neck so that his black mane fell in a graceful wave, and he carried his thick black tail proudly. She heard his breath exhaled in rhythm with his motion. He moved in a stride so light that he looked almost as if he floated on air, his hooves barely touching the ground as he pushed off again. Even so, as he passed near, she could feel the vibrations of his massive weight beneath her feet. The smell of him filled her nostrils, a pungent, living scent. The look in his large dark eye mesmerized her. It was a look of concentration, and she could tell he somehow had a connection with his rider, although she could not detect how they communicated. But the eye also held for her a promise of strength, flight, and freedom.

"Are you okay? Are you afraid?" her mother asked, feeling the trembling in her daughter at her side.

"He is the most beautiful sight I have ever seen," Jodi breathed out.

"Yes, he is quite lovely," her mother agreed, but Jodi heard no awe in her mother's voice.

She doesn't see what I see, or feel what I feel, Jodi realized.

The rider, aware of their presence, transitioned the horse to a walk and moved him over to the rail where they stood. "Hello," he greeted. "Are you here for a lesson?"

"Yes, we are. I'm Cora Mae Cannon and this is my daughter Jodi. I believe she has a lesson arranged for three-forty-five. We're a little early," Cora Mae answered.

The rider nodded in acknowledgement. "I'm River," he introduced himself. "I'm almost done here. Someone is bringing in the horse for your lesson. If you go back to the crossties, he should be there soon and he'll help you get started."

"Thank you," Cora Mae replied. "Let's go, Jodi."

Jodi gazed up into the face of the rider and her heart filled with adoration. He looked so natural astride his horse's strong back, like he fit perfectly and belonged there. His voice was soft and kind. She noticed how he stroked his horse's neck while he talked. She thought he was the handsomest man she had ever seen.

Her mother took her arm, and Jodi allowed her to guide her along as they retraced their steps.

Someone had brought a horse into a crosstie bay and was undoing the buckles of a very wet and muddy blanket on the horse's back.

Is this the horse I will ride? Jodi slowly approached the stocky bay horse standing patiently, blinking the rain from his long eyelashes. As soon as the blanket had been removed from his back, he shook himself all over, spraying rain from his exposed wet neck and mane.

Cora Mae uttered a weak squeal and stepped back out of the way, but Jodi smiled in delight. She wanted to reach out to touch the horse's soft nose, but she felt too timid.

The boy hoisted the wet blanket over the rail of the crosstie bay. He then turned to acknowledge their presence. Catching sight of Jodi, his eyes widened in surprise, but Jodi thought she also detected his mouth turn down in disappointment.

"Hi," Jodi greeted, surprised to see Todd, even though she knew he rode here.

"Jodi," he said in a choked voice, "you're here for a riding lesson?"

"Yeah, what's wrong with that?" she came back defensively. His entire attitude was as if he had been let down. It occurred to her, *he must have expected Melody! It doesn't matter*, she told herself, wishing it didn't always sting to know everyone liked her twin best.

"Can you even ride? I mean…." he dropped his head, embarrassed. He didn't mean to point out her leg, for he had no idea if it would prevent her from riding. He had just blurted it out without thinking.

"I don't know, Todd," she answered defiantly.

"Well, step over here and I'll show you what to do." When Jodi walked straight forward, he said in a tone as if she should know better, "Don't walk straight at a horse you don't know. That is very threatening. Walk toward the shoulder."

"Oh," Jodi said meekly, but she obeyed and shifted her approach. She could see the horse's large eye following her.

"This is Morrison," Todd said. "We call him Morris. He's one of the school horses."

"Can I pet him?"

"Sure, start on his neck," Todd said matter-of-fact, trying to dissipate the tension between them. He watched her tentatively use her fingers to touch Morris's neck, and jerk her hand away when Morris quivered his skin at the touch so soft it felt like a fly.

"He's so big!" Jodi remarked.

"You can start brushing him." Todd handed her a dandy brush and showed her how to press slightly and with short, quick strokes to groom the hair. "This brush is for the really dirty parts," he explained. Then he handed her a body brush to finish off the neck and legs and to use on the parts of his coat that had been clipped and covered with the blanket. "This is a softer brush and you don't want to use anything stiffer than this where the hair has been clipped."

Jodi listened carefully to everything Todd said. Her awe of being around a real horse and her eagerness to do everything correct, reminded Todd how he had felt when he first was introduced to a horse. This was a very different Jodi from the girl he knew at school. Her enthrallment was contagious, and he found himself having fun showing her what to do.

They had Morrison groomed and Todd was showing Jodi how to place the pad and saddle on his back and move it into position, when River returned from the arena and led his horse into an empty crosstie bay.

"Hi, River. Morris is almost ready," Todd said.

River nodded, scanning his eyes quickly over the little bay to be sure all was well. He trusted Todd to do things correctly, but he still always checked over any horse before putting him to work. "I just need to finish up with Oberon and put him away. Go ahead and take Morris into the arena and walk him around."

"Sure," Todd agreed. He showed Jodi how to fasten the girth, and then put on the bridle. "You can lead him." He pulled the reins over the bay's head and guided her hands where to take hold in order to lead a horse.

Jodi stepped forward and felt a thrill of delight as Morris actually followed behind her. *I'm leading a horse!*

As they walked along the rail of the arena Todd explained, "Most horses hold their breath when you first tighten the girth. It helps to hand walk them a little and get them to relax before tightening up the last hole or two."

"Oh," Jodi said. The jitteriness of her stomach had settled down while getting Morris ready, but now that the moment of actually getting on his back loomed closer, the trembling inside erupted again. She had not realized how massive a horse actually was. How would she ever get on his back? What if River, came out now and saw her limp? What if he said, "Sorry, you can't ride with a leg like that?" Her mother had stayed behind to talk to River. What was she telling him?

She shivered when she heard the gate to the arena open.

"Good enough," Todd said. He stepped over to the side of Morris and snugged up the girth. Then he pulled the stirrups down on the leathers. "Okay, lead him over to River and he'll get you mounted up."

"Thanks for your help, Todd," Jodi said. She gulped in a deep mouthful of air and then led Morris to where River leaned against the arena wall, watching her. Her mother stood next to him, a very anxious expression on her face and her mouth moving, saying something to River.

"You see how the foot turns out?" Jodi overheard her mother explaining. "I don't see how she can fit it in a stirrup."

Silently, River waited until Jodi brought Morris up near the mounting block. Then he stepped forward from the wall and approached them. Morris stretched his muzzle toward him and nickered softly, recognizing a friend. Jodi noted how River reached out to pat the bay's neck and run his hand down his shoulder. Then he met Jodi's eyes, and he said to her in a low voice, "You don't need stirrups to ride. Are you ready to give it a try?"

She swallowed, and nodded her head.

"Good for you. Okay, step up on the mounting block and face the saddle...hand here." He placed her left hand on the pommel. "And here." He guided her right hand to the cantle. "It might be easier for you to mount from the off side, but let's see if you can do it the traditional way. Try to place your left foot in the stirrup." He held the stirrup iron while Jodi tried to thrust the toe of her left boot into the opening. She could place her foot there, but the angle moved her leg too far away from the horse's side.

"I think you can learn to mount from this side," River said calmly, "but for now let's make it easier. Stay there."

Jodi complied, standing still on the top step of the mounting block while River led Morris forward and brought him back around so that she could mount from the right side. He helped her again to place her hands and then held the stirrup iron. From this side, Jodi was able to place her foot and then swing her left leg over so she could sit in the saddle.

And then she was sitting on a horse - a living, breathing, enormous animal! She looked down, and dizziness assailed her, for the ground was so far below. She clutched at the front of the saddle, feeling like she needed to hold on to keep herself from falling.

"You okay?" River asked, noting her tight grip and tense posture.

She nodded slightly, afraid to move her body. "Where's the horn?" she asked.

"There is no horn, this isn't a western saddle. And even in a western saddle you don't use the horn."

"What do I hold on to?"

She's scared, River observed. "You're not going to fall," he said in the same soothing tone he used with frightened horses. *She's more than just scared, she's petrified!* "You don't need to hold on to anything. Sit there and just get used to how he feels. When you feel steady enough, let go with your hands and rest them on your thighs." River waited patiently, watching as Jodi's hands at last relaxed from the grip she had on the front of the saddle. Then, tentatively she let go with one hand and set it on her thigh. A few moments later, she let go with the other hand.

"Good," he continued in his quiet, reassuring voice. "You don't ride by holding on, you ride with your balance. And you don't ride with your feet either," he added, guessing she was worried about that. "Now, I'm going to lead Morris away from the block. Try your best to keep your hands on your legs. Take a handful of your pants if you feel you need to grab onto something. Are you ready?"

She took several moments, breathing shallowly before she finally gave a brief nod of her head. He led Morrison away from the mounting block at a slow walk. He heard her gasp and her eyes widened at the movement beneath her. She stiffened again and in spite of his instructions, grabbed the front of the saddle. *What is wrong with her? This is only a slow walk.* He had never experienced anyone so terrorized the first time on a horse. "You're not going to fall," he reassured her again.

Jodi's legs banged against Morrison's flanks and he laid his ears back, but obediently followed River, although a few times he held back, not understanding the signals from his rider. River brought him to a halt. *This is not working.* "Are you scared?" he asked Jodi.

She nodded. "My foot fell out of the stirrup."

He looked back. Her left leg frantically tried to find the stirrup iron, resulting in her bumping annoyingly at Morrison's belly.

River was not very insightful where people were concerned, but he sensed something very broken about Jodi. He had also recognized right away her adoration of horses, for he knew a kindred spirit when he met one. She might be afraid of horses, but that didn't mean she loved them any less. *How can I help her?* The girl's mother had told him something about her disability also affected her balance. It had prevented her from even being able to master riding a bicycle. He had only half listened, preferring to judge for himself the probability of the girl being able to ride. But maybe her mother was right and it might not be possible. Nevertheless, he wasn't ready to give up as long as Jodi was willing to try.

"Hold your leg still," he directed. "Let's forget about stirrups. You don't need them." He waited for her to still her leg. "Are you afraid you are going to fall off?"

"Sort of," she replied meekly.

"Do you want to get off?" He waited, watching her decide.

Jodi swallowed hard and shook her head. "No, I don't want to get off."

"Okay, trust me, I won't let you fall," he spoke soothingly. "Now, pull your other foot out of the stirrup." With her legs free, he then crossed the stirrup leathers over Morris's neck so they would not bump his sides. "I start beginners without stirrups anyway but I usually let them keep them for the first lesson. But I think you are better off without them right away."

Jodi was not so sure about that, but she nodded her consent.

With Morrison standing obediently at the halt, River tried to get Jodi to relax by coaching her through some warm-up stretches - rolling her head and shoulders, swinging her legs back and forth, and twisting at the waist. When she finally let go of the pommel and could keep her hands on her waist while she did the exercises, he asked if she was ready for him to lead off again.

"I think so," she said, with a timid smile.

"Let's go, Morris." River led the little bay at a very slow walk. This time, although at the first sense of motion Jodi grabbed the saddle, after a few strides she found the courage to put her hands back on her thighs. When River glanced back at her she smiled happily.

It was a very slow lesson with not much happening to any observer. But for Jodi, by the end of the thirty minutes River thought enough for the first time, she had been able to sit on a horse's back without holding on, and was beginning to feel like she could safely move her body. As frightening as it had been at first, she now marveled at the feel of a horse moving beneath her and began to anticipate how his body, at least at the walk, swung side to side between her legs. It was the most amazing sensation!

After the lesson, River helped her untack and let her groom Morris again. She figured she probably took much longer than necessary to brush his coat. But she loved being near his warmth and loved his smell. Even the sounds he made - a snort, a shifting of his feet, swish of his tail, the gurgle of his stomach - were fascinating to listen to. What a pleasure to feed him carrot bits, to feel his velvety lips pick them delicately off the palm of her hand, and watch him crunch in pleasure, blinking his eyes, and then nuzzle at her for more.

As they drove away from the stable, Jodi was surprised to see tears on her mother's cheeks. "What's the matter?" she asked fearfully. *Does she think I can't do this?*

Cora Mae glanced at her daughter, her eyes shining. "This is the happiest I have seen you in a long time," she admitted.

Jodi felt her own eyes pool with tears. "Oh, Mom!"

Some time ago Sierra discovered the benefits of combining stretches and light physical exercise with studying. Now she stood next to the kitchen counter with her lecture notes spread out where she could read them. Balancing on one leg, the other bent at the knee, and both arms outstretched, she recited out loud the physiological process of the sodium-potassium pump involved in muscle contraction.

Her phone rang. She considered letting it go to voice mail but glancing over to where it sat near her notes on the counter she saw the call was from River. Dropping out of her pose, she picked up. Her heart fluttered with apprehension. Ever since the championship, River never called her. They still talked two or three times a week, but it was always Sierra who initiated the call. If he was calling now, it could be because of bad news, and her first thought was something happened to one of the horses. *Is Fiel okay?*

"Hi, River," she greeted.

"Hi."

"How are you? Is everything okay?"

"Yeah, everything's fine. How are you?"

"I'm fine," she breathed out in relief. "I was afraid you were calling to tell me something happened to Fiel."

"No, he's fine, why would you think that?"

"River, you never call me anymore. I always call you."

"Oh…well, I never know when you are studying. I figure you'll call when you have the time."

He's still mad about Kentucky, Sierra determined. "I've told you, River, it's only around midterms and finals that I don't have time to talk for very long."

"Do you have time now?"

"Yes, of course. What's up?"

He told her about the offer from Jack McCall.

"A chance to ride in the Olympics? Are you crazy? Why wouldn't you jump at the chance?" she responded, very excited about the news. "River, I am so proud of you."

"It would mean weeks, actually probably months away from Pegasus. What would I do with my own horses?"

"Really, River, you would take Oberon with you. You already told me I could ride Corazón this summer. And Todd and I can take care of Ysbryd. They'll be okay."

"What about us? I might have to be away a lot during the summer. I don't want to lose that time with you."

"Maybe I could come with you and be your groom. I won't have to study during the summer."

He argued with her a little longer, but most of his excuses had to do with missing her and the horses at Pegasus.

"Just think about it. Jack McCall is a great rider and I think his philosophy of riding is very much like yours. You might actually learn something from him. You're good, River, but you don't know everything," she challenged.

"I know that," he answered, and she detected annoyance in his tone. That could actually be a good thing, she thought to herself, because it meant she might be getting through to him.

"I think you should do it," she stated.

"Maybe…I am thinking about it."

"How's everything else? Are Del and Fiel doing okay?"

"They're fine."

They talked a while longer, mostly River answering Sierra's questions about the horses at Pegasus.

"Thanks for calling," Sierra said when she was satisfied the horses were all fine and she had heard the other news of Pegasus. "Please don't always wait for me to call you. I love you so much, River. It hurts to think you are mad at me."

"I'm not mad. I love you too."

"You'll call me?"

"I will."

"Just a few more weeks and I'll be home. I can't wait to see you. I wish you could hold me right now."

"I'm counting the days until you are home and in my arms again."

Sierra smiled happily after they hung up. Not that they had actually been fighting, but River and she had made up!

8 WINTER BREAK

To many, the words love, hope, and dreams are synonymous with horses. -
Oliver Wendell Holmes

Jodi's life changed.

The first morning after her riding lesson, Jodi lay in her bed thinking back over the marvelous experience. *Yes, to ride a horse, even just to be around horses. This is worth any bargain, any contract…anything!*

She got ready for school without her mother's usual knock on her door with orders of 'get up'! In school, when her mind began to wander in boredom, she forced herself to pay attention. She went to all her teachers and asked what she could do to bring up her grade. That very day she began the make-up work. She wolfed down her lunch standing up, and then spent the rest of her lunch hour in the library to work on the assignments. That also solved the problem of avoiding Tasha.

"You made your bed this morning," her mother commented, smiling, when Jodi came home from school.

"Do you want me to help cook dinner or something?"

Cora Mae's heart ached in joy. "No, sweetie, but thank you for offering. How about if you set the table at five-thirty. That would be helpful."

"Okay."

The amazing thing, it wasn't that hard to force herself to finish her homework. All she had to do was think about Morris's lovely eyes, the feel of his warm body, and how it felt when he moved beneath her seat. For Morris or any horse, she could do it. And chores were even easier than homework, because they were mindless and she could think about horses.

It wasn't that she morphed into an identical twin of her sister. She was still the quiet one, not interested in gossip, fashion, or parties. Dinner was still dominated by Melody's chatter about her day or her father complaining about his work. But instead of slinking off to her bedroom after dinner, she stayed without being told to help clear the table, load the dishwasher, and tidy the kitchen. It wasn't even that bad, because both her mother and Melody seemed happy to have her helping out.

Jodi felt happy nearly all the time. And it had been a long time since happiness dominated her mood.

All her life, Jodi's emotions had risen incomprehensibly at the sight of a horse. Something about their majestic beauty stirred a place deep within her that yearned for freedom, strength, speed…to conquer something she couldn't explain. Even so, she never imagined the actual experience of being around a horse and sitting astride its back, would be so incredible. Riding lessons became the focus of her life. She knew her progress was very slow, but at least she was making some progress. She still had not ridden any faster than a walk, but she no longer felt dizzy when first mounting up, or terrorized when the horse moved.

In her second lesson, River led Morrison, staying near his shoulder so if Jodi lost her balance he could put a steadying hand on her leg. He again directed her through a series of stretches to get her to relax. Then he said, "Close your eyes."

"I can't!" Jodi had gasped.

River led Morrison a few mores steps, then halted. He stepped back, petting the bay on his shoulder. "Trust me," he said in a low, quiet voice. "I'm not going to let you fall. Nothing bad is going to happen."

"Okay," she squeaked.

"Hold onto the strap. Can you do that?"

"Yes," Jodi answered. She had been riding with her hands on her waist, but now she reached forward to grab the leather strap River had hooked to the front dee-rings of the saddle, a strap she could grab whenever she felt like she was losing her balance.

"Close your eyes," he told her again.

Jodi sucked in a breath and squeezed her eyes tight. She immediately felt dizzy and her eyes flew open. River said nothing, just waited. She tried again. This time she managed to keep her eyes squeezed shut as the dizziness assailed her, and within moments it passed.

"How do you feel now?" River asked when he observed her shallow, rapid breathing calm to a normal breath.

"Okay," she replied hoarsely.

"How does Morris feel beneath you?"

"Uh…what do you mean?"

"Is he relaxed or is he nervous?"

How should I know that? But then she realized that yes, she could tell. Morris was very relaxed, bored even. He rested one rear leg for she noted his hips had shifted to an unevenness beneath her seat. He must have turned his head to River for she could feel a hollowness on the inside of his body. With a wide grin she answered, "He's relaxed."

"Good, yes he is. Now, tell me where each of his legs are. Is he standing square?"

"No, he is resting his right back leg." It amazed her that without her vision, she could answer each question River asked about where Morris held his legs, his shoulders, his neck, his belly, and even his ears, although that was a guess when she said they were probably flopped to the sides.

"I'm going to lead him forward again, and as he starts to move try to keep your eyes closed and you tell me which leg he is moving and tell me when it lands."

She made no mistakes, for with her eyes closed it seemed very easy to feel which leg Morris moved, for it wasn't just a leg that moved, but his hips, belly, and shoulders. And by concentrating on how the horse moved, she totally forgot her terror.

"You are doing great," River praised. "You can open your eyes."

Jodi obeyed and a grin lit up her face. She couldn't help but laugh. "That was amazing!"

River led her around and asked her again to tell him what leg Morris moved. It surprised her how hard she had to concentrate with her eyes open to answer the questions that had been easy with her eyes closed.

"We need to get there thirty minutes before my lesson so I can help get the horse ready," she told her mother on the day of her next lesson. She didn't want to miss out on leading Morris in, grooming, and tacking him up. The ground work was almost as much fun as riding.

When she arrived for her third lesson, she was allowed to bring Morris in by herself and groom him. "Just let me check things over before you take him out," Todd said. When he returned to the crossties and checked the placement of the saddle and fit of the bridle, he smiled at her. "You're a fast learner. You don't really need my help anymore getting him ready."

"Thanks," Jodi said and smiled back, for she no longer had that feeling from Todd that he helped her begrudgingly. His smile and friendliness seemed genuine.

The lesson began in the same manner with River leading her on Morrison while she performed the warm-up stretches. Then he put Morrison on a lunge line so that he walked out on a circle around River in the center. Jodi was essentially on her own on the horse's back.

"I have control if necessary but Morris never shies. You are going to talk to him and tell him what you want him to do," River said.

He then coached her through the use of her weight and legs to get Morris to move forward, to move in on the circle, back out on the circle, and to halt.

This is incredible! Jodi had always thought riding a horse involved kicking to go faster and pulling back on reins to slow down. She had no idea how sensitive a horse was to just its rider's seat and position and slight pressure of the legs. This was the language used to talk to a horse!

She begged her parents for more lessons, hoping for at least two times a week and maybe three.

"If your grades are improved by the end of the quarter, we will consider it," her father promised. Jodi noticed that he answered her plea with a twinkle in his eye, the same look he got on his face when Melody asked him for something.

Finally, school let out the week before Christmas for winter break. Jodi waited anxiously for the mail every day. Three days into the holiday, the grade reports arrived.

"Oh, Jodi, oh my goodness," Cora Mae exclaimed. She sat at the kitchen table opening the mail that Jodi had just brought in. Her mother looked up with tears in her eyes. Jodi felt like her heart crashed into her stomach. *I failed!*

Her mother pushed up from her chair and hugged Jodi tightly, smoothing down her hair. Then she handed her daughter the grade report.

"I did it!" Jodi exclaimed. She had brought her grades up from *D*s and *C*s to *A*s and *B*s. History, the class she had been failing, she had brought up to a *C*.

As promised, her parents arranged for one additional lesson a week.

Standing on the landing of a set of stairs leading down to baggage claim, River had a view of the carousel where he expected to meet Sierra. He hated the airport during the holidays. The crowd was already thick, pushing and shoving at the edge of the carousel, and the belt hadn't even started to move yet. How was he ever supposed to find a petite young woman who barely came to five feet three inches, in this mass of frantic people? He stared down at the tops of heads, searching for one in the most perfect shade of honey brown, and hoped she didn't wear a hat.

"Looking for a date, big boy?" a sweet voice said behind him.

His heart jumped and he turned to look into the mischievous, large brown eyes of the most beautiful woman in the world (in his opinion). A smattering of freckles crossed her shapely nose and her sweet face was framed by soft, waving brown hair. Her lovely mouth quirked in a teasing grin.

He swept her into his arms and lifted her off her feet as he hugged her tightly. "Sierra!"

She laughed in delight, and then as he set her down and not caring about the people around them, they kissed with a passion of making up for months apart.

When the kiss ended, Sierra did not let him go. She pushed his thick black hair away from his face, ran her finger over his brows and down his high cheekbones, and brought it to rest over his mouth that she had just kissed. She gazed lovingly into his beautiful, dark eyes, and then she kissed him again.

There really was no point in hurrying down to the carousel, so they waited on the stair landing for the crowd to thin; kissing, gazing at each other, and laughing.

By the time they made it out of the terminal and River drove them away in his truck, they were ready to talk about the days ahead.

"I promised your mother to bring you over for dinner tonight, as soon as you're settled," River said.

"I know, she's been texting me, and I called her as soon as the plane landed. She still hasn't found anyone to trade shifts with her so she can get Christmas off. I keep telling her it doesn't matter because we will have other days."

"Yeah, and the Marshalls are giving a big party this year. Your mom is invited, of course."

"Oh, it's so good to be home!" Sierra exclaimed, stretching out her arms and then dropping her hand onto River's leg. "I can't wait to see the horses. Think we'll have time for a ride before going to my mom's?"

"Sure, I think so."

For the remainder of the ride home, Sierra asked for details about every horse she knew at Pegasus, beginning with her own horse Fiel, a gray Lusitano gelding. Last year she agreed to lease him to Delia Evans, a woman who had been taking lessons on Fiel while Sierra was away at school. Del had fallen in love with the sweet-natured gelding and offered to buy him.

"Let her have him, Sierra," River had encouraged. "It's a good match. You want to event, and you know Fiel's conformation is better for dressage than jumping. Besides, Del will always keep him here at Pegasus. You'll be able to see him and she said you can ride him anytime you want."

Sierra had to agree it was an ideal match, but she couldn't bring herself to sell him. Then Delia offered to lease him, and that Sierra could agree to. Delia found the well-trained Lusitano the perfect school master to teach her dressage under River's coaching. With his calm nature and perfect manners, Delia also felt confident to ride him on her own, both in the arena and out on the trails. Fiel was now eighteen years old, and at the level Del was riding, she would keep him active but not over-stressed, and most likely he would stay sound well into his old age.

When Sierra came home for breaks and the summer, she was able to spend time with Fiel and she would still ride him once in a while. But there were other horses for her to ride at Pegasus, and even to compete in combined training events, so she left most of the riding of Fiel to Del.

At school, Sierra had started taking lessons at a stable near the university, just to be able to ride. The instructor offered to let her come and ride on her own whenever she wanted, for there were plenty of horses that needed exercising and Sierra had the skill to ride them properly. So at least she was able to ride two to three days a week while at school, a needed break from her heavy study schedule and riding also helped reduce her stress.

"How's that new mare working out, Dune? She sound's so sweet," Sierra asked, after hearing about River's three horses - Oberon, Corazón, and Ysbryd, the school horses - Fala, Morrison, and Muffin, and then the horses she had known in training - Pendragon, Felicity, Prospector, and a few others.

"She's great. You'll love her. In fact, you could ride her today if you want to try her out. You can't ride Fiel because Del already rode him this morning, but she told me you can have him the rest of the week. She's going out of town for a few days anyway."

"I'd love to try her," Sierra agreed. "Ahh," she sighed and said again, "It is so good to be home and you close enough for me to touch." Impulsively, she leaned over and kissed his cheek. She loved how she could make him smile whenever she did that. "No more exams, no more papers to write, no more studying for two weeks!"

"You did okay on your finals?" River asked.

"I don't have my official grades yet, but most of the profs posted exam results before I left. I'm pretty sure I still have a four-point-o. How about you?"

"I passed," River said flatly.

"What's wrong?" Sierra knew him well enough that he wasn't telling her something.

With a confessional sigh, he admitted, "I barely passed Quantitative Analysis. I got a D-minus."

"Whoa, must have been a tough class. But a D is still passing, right?"

"Yes, and I'm really glad because the class is required for my major and I don't think I could struggle through it again."

"Didn't you ask Laila to help you?" Sierra asked, referring to Megan's mother, a friend of River's who had tutored him through high school.

"No, I didn't want to hear her scold me." *You have no idea how that woman tortured me to get through my first year,* he thought to himself in amusement. He had never confessed to Sierra how Laila had pestered him to complete assignments, looked over all his work before turning it in, and quizzed him relentlessly before exams. He was grateful now, because it got him through the basic courses needed for a degree and enabled him to transfer from community college to the university in one year rather than two. "I just never got caught up after not going to class for a week while I was at the finals in Lexington. She was the one teacher who didn't really want to work with me to miss class." He flashed her a smile. "And I did pass. I don't have to get top grades like you do."

She smiled back but River thought he detected hesitancy in that smile, like she wanted to say something else, or that she was disappointed in him. He couldn't help that. He didn't like school the way she did and never would have gone to college except for her encouragement. Nor did he want her to be ashamed of him. He could imagine how it would feel when she made it all the way through college and veterinary school if he only had a high school diploma.

Surprisingly, once he transferred to the university, he actually liked most of his classes. He was in a rural land management program and he had learned a lot of practical stuff, like optimizing the use of the acreage at Pegasus – which grasses were hardiest for this region, rotation of pasture turn-out, irrigation, and growing their own nutritious hay. He had taken an organic gardening class last spring, and found he really enjoyed planting seeds or greenhouse starts, watching them grow as he watered and weeded, and then harvesting. Manuel's wife Rosa had been thrilled with the fresh produce, and she had taken over his garden when the class ended. The professor for the animal husbandry classes had allowed him to concentrate on horses for his assignments. He had learned useful information on horse health, physiology, nutrition, and other practical knowledge that he could actually use.

"Just two more quarters, and I graduate!" Sierra said triumphantly, and tactfully said no more about his poor grade.

"I'll pick you up in exactly two hours," Gwen Marshall promised as she walked with Todd toward the restaurant where the arrangement had been made for Todd to meet with his mother.

He nodded, his hands in his jacket pockets nervously picking at the lining. The level of his anxiety had twisted his tongue, and he had not spoken one word during the ride over.

"It will be okay," Gwen tried to reassure him. "Her case worker will be there the whole time."

Just before they went in the entrance, Todd stopped and gave Gwen a tight hug. She hugged him back, her throat tightening. *Let him go*, she silently pleaded with the woman she had never met. *He is doing so well. He is happy. For his sake, let him go.*

Todd had wanted to refuse this visit. He wanted to forget his real mother. But she still had a tether connected to his heart. What tore him up inside was the desire for his mother to stay clean and straighten up her life, but equally the desire for her to fail. Then he could stay with the Marshalls forever. It was the hope of her failure that tormented him with guilt.

Todd released his arms from his foster mother, and setting his jaw, pushed open the restaurant doors. Inside the foyer, the subdued lighting obscured his vision from seeing anyone inside.

"Todd!"

He heard her tremulous voice call his name, and as his eyes adjusted to the dim light, he made out the slight figure of his mother standing up from a bench.

"Hello, Todd," Mrs. Miller, the case worker, stood and came forward to guide Todd to stand in front of his mother.

"Hello, Mother," he greeted, and awkwardly gave her a very brief hug.

"My baby," she whispered hoarsely, and touched his cheek with her fingers, peering into his face to assure herself it was really him.

"I will pick him up in two hours," Gwen Marshall stated. Mrs. Miller nodded and turned away, dismissing her.

"Goodbye, Todd," Gwen said and turned quickly away. She did not once let her eyes meet those of Linda, for she did not think she could control the look of pity and abhorrence on her face.

The hostess escorted them to a table and handed out menus. They sat stiffly through the recital of today's specials and then the hostess hastily retreated, sensing the awkwardness in these guests.

"Todd, you are looking very well," Mrs. Miller tried to start the conversation. "You have grown so tall. He is quite handsome, don't you think?" she turned to Linda.

Linda had not taken her eyes from Todd. She smiled with closed lips, and nodded in agreement. "He is beautiful," she said.

The waitress arrived to fill their water glasses and take drink orders. Todd ordered a lemonade and then ducked his head to study the menu, reading the items without comprehension, his insides numb and his skin prickling. He did not want to look at his mother. She seemed so frail, her clothes hanging on her frame as if there was no flesh to support them. He knew she was only thirty-two. She had been a teenager when she got pregnant with him. But her dry, sunken face looked the same age as his foster mother who was twenty years older.

"Order anything you want. It doesn't matter how expensive. I have a job now, you know," Linda stated proudly.

"Uh…" He tried to think of something to say, but the way she stared at him made him nervous. He looked back down at the menu. "Uh, what is your job?" he asked keeping his eyes down.

"I'm a housekeeper at Pinewood Care Center. It's a hospital and it's very important to clean properly. I had special training."

"Oh, um, g-good."

"Don't stutter, Todd," Linda said.

Todd flinched reflexively.

"Linda, remember what we talked about," Mrs. Miller warned.

They ordered, and somehow they got through the meal. Todd forced himself to chew and swallow food he could not taste, and then to fight his nausea to keep it down. He could not relax.

It seemed his mother could not relax either after having reprimanded him about stuttering. She knew she was on trial. She looked to Mrs. Miller to guide the questions, to keep the conversation safe. They mostly talked about Todd's school.

When the plates were cleared away, Linda shyly opened her purse and produced a gift-wrapped square box. "Here, Todd, for Christmas."

He accepted the gift, wishing she wouldn't bother.

"Open it now."

"You don't want me to wait for Christmas?"

"No, I want to see your face." She tilted her face and looked up at him sideways, almost a flirtatious gesture.

He carefully unwrapped the present and opened the box. Inside was a wide, shiny green plastic band inset with a watch face. The band was decorated with yellow smiley faces. He had seen watches like these at the mall at one of the kiosks in the center aisle, a place that sold cheap, garish fashion accessories. "Thank you," he said, trying to sound pleased and forced a smile. He took the watch out and slipped it on his wrist. Another item he would add to the box of gifts she had given him, all equally inappropriate.

Linda giggled. "It looks good on you."

"Thanks, I can't wait to wear it to school," he lied.

There was nothing more to say or do. They had only taken up one hour of the allotted time.

"Todd, don't you think you could eat dessert, a growing boy like you?" Mrs. Miller encouraged.

The last thing he wanted was to try to choke down more food, but it was better than sitting there with his mother staring forlornly at him with nothing to say, and her case worker next to her with a stern, thin-lipped expression. He acquiesced and ordered a piece of apple pie. Waiting for it to come and then forcing it down, took another twenty minutes. They retreated to the foyer to wait awkwardly for Gwen to return.

Fortunately, Gwen came twenty minutes early. Todd again gave his mother a brief hug.

She hugged him back, squeezing as tight as she could. "I love you, Todd," she said in a choked voice.

"Yeah, me too." He could not make himself say the actual words. "Thanks again for the watch." He stepped away from his mother and pushed his way through the restaurant door, so very, very glad that Gwen followed protectively behind him.

Winter break passed in a flurry of riding horses, holiday parties, opening Christmas presents, and then the last weekend arrived.

Brown mud, the color of caramel, spray-painted the belly of Prospector, a five-year-old gray thoroughbred gelding, and splattered River's boots as they trotted through a deep puddle in the middle of the trail. "*Bien, hombre*," River murmured with a quick pat beneath the gray's damp mane, praising him for plunging into the cloudy water without hesitation. Prospector shook his head and snorted as if to say, 'no big deal'.

"Whoa-ho!" Sierra, riding behind him on Felicity, cried out as the mare suddenly balked at the puddle. Sierra pressed her legs against Felicity's sides as soon as she felt the hesitation beneath her. The mare responded by hurdling over the puddle rather than step in it. Her feet landed just short of the far edge, and a fan-like spray of brown mud and water splashed up to drench the mare to her flanks.

Aware of the commotion behind, River came to a halt, moving Prospector's hindquarters around with his leg. "What happened, Sierra?" he asked as she brought the mare alongside.

Laughing, she replied, "She stopped at the puddle. What is her problem? I thought Felicity had gotten over her fear of water." Sierra stroked the mare's slick neck affectionately. "Silly girl!"

Often, River knew exactly why a horse reacted the way it did. But sometimes, like now, he could only guess. "I'm not sure, but I think she is a little mad at you. You haven't been here to ride her and she's telling you that she's losing her confidence without you."

Sierra laughed again. "Really, River?" she smirked at him as she tucked strands of loose hair back up beneath her helmet. "Are you teasing me?" She liked the softness she saw at this moment in his dark eyes. He seldom joked, especially about horses. Maybe he was trying to lighten the mood to ease the upcoming time of saying goodbye.

"Maybe," he said with a slight shrug. "Or maybe she's coming into heat."

"Probably that," she retorted, wrinkling her nose. "Canter to the bend?"

"Sure, you lead this time."

Felicity eagerly picked up the canter at Sierra's signal, her spirits bolstered by her excited jump across the water. Both horses moved out energetically, enjoying the fresh winter air.

The first drops of rain fell unnoticed, easy to ignore when wearing a rain poncho and riding helmet. But when the drops increased to streams, the two riders didn't hold back when both horses asked to gallop. It was a short stretch to the end of the trail and to a covered shed, a recent addition to the grounds. It had been intended to provide shelter both from rain and sun for spectators watching horses on the outside jumping course. But riders had taken to leaving rain sheets and coolers to cover their horses when leading them back to the stable.

Laughing at their soaked condition, Sierra and River dismounted at the edge of the field, and led the horses underneath the shed cover.

"I think for once I'm going to be glad to go back to Sacramento, just to dry out," Sierra exclaimed. She stepped back to Felicity's side and loosened the saddle girth. As she turned around, she found River had stepped in behind her. He pulled her against his chest, holding her tightly, and then having removed his riding helmet, reached up to unbuckle hers and pull it back off her head. Then he leaned in to kiss her long and deep.

"I hate that I won't be able to kiss you for another three months," he said as he released her, looking deep into her eyes.

"I know, me too," she said in a choked voice. "I love you so much, River."

"I love you more than anything." He kissed her again. When one of the horses stomped a hoof and snorted, he let her go.

They threw waterproof coolers over the horses' backs and led them back up to the stable.

"I'm missing you already," Pam Landsing said, standing at the curb of the departure drop-off area at the airport. River always picked Sierra up when she flew home from school, but they both found it easier to say goodbye at the stable. Consequently, it was always Sierra's mother who drove her back to the airport at the end of each break.

"I know," Sierra agreed. She gave her mother an extra tight hug and a kiss on her cheek, before pulling up the handle of her bag and heading inside the airport. She turned only once to wave, her mother still watching at the curb until her daughter was out of sight.

How lucky I am, Sierra kept thinking as she checked her luggage, made her way through airport security, and then to her departure gate. Her father had died in a car accident before she was born, so her mother had been a single mom raising her. *My wonderful mother, always a comfort, always ready to listen to me, supporting me in all my dreams.* When she heard stories about other kids' parents, and especially what she knew of Todd's mother, and the fact that River lost his mother at the age of eight, she never took for granted her own good fortune to have a great mom.

After boarding the plane, Sierra dozed the short flight to Sacramento, thinking about River, her mother, the horses…. Tomorrow when classes resumed for winter quarter, she would have to forcefully push these thoughts aside and concentrate on studying. Since she had been in an advanced placement program in high school earning college credits, and had taken on-line courses each summer, she was going to graduate early, in just three years, with a degree in biology this spring. She had just recently been accepted into the veterinary medicine program, conditional on her graduating. *Then four years of veterinary school….* She fell asleep trying to hold onto the feeling of being held in River's arms.

The announcement to bring seat backs up and tray tables stowed, woke Sierra. A quarter hour later, she made her way off the plane and moved with the crowds, many of them also returning students, to baggage claim.

"It's Sierra, isn't it?" a pleasant male voice said at her elbow.

Hearing her name, she turned and being a friendly girl, smiled in confusion at the somewhat familiar face. It wasn't unusual to run into classmates on the last day of break at the airport.

"I'm Sean Casey. We had microbiology together last year," he added, seeing the unsure expression on her face.

Her smiled broadened. "Oh, right, you're the guy who always made paramecium jokes."

"And you always sat up front, underneath Dr. Werner's nose." He laughed with a teasing twinkle in his eyes.

"I've always been a front row girl," Sierra said, with a smirk and shrug of her shoulders.

"Have you always been the smartest girl in class, too?"

"Always," she replied, not interested in downplaying her brains.

"Hmm, I like that in a girl," he said, having fallen into step beside her.

Is he flirting with me? Sierra wondered, glancing at him from the corner of her eye. She only remembered him from class because he had such a quick wit, certainly not appreciated by their very serious professor. She was surprised he remembered her, for that class had been a year ago. She supposed many would consider him good looking, but since she compared everyone now to River, she found his easy smile, sky-blue eyes, and walnut-brown hair attractive, but not even close to the sexiness of River's dark and what she thought of as 'sensuous' features.

But she remembered Sean as a nice enough guy, and she didn't mind him walking with her to the baggage carousel, so she rewarded him by laughing rather than acting offended at his comment.

"Do you live on campus?" he asked conversationally as they watched luggage drop off a chute and circle slowly in front of them.

"Nearby, I live in one of the student housing apartments."

"How's that working out for you?"

"Fine, I'm in a two-bedroom, and my roommate goes out a lot. So actually, it works out very well for me. Gives me lots of quiet study time. What about you?"

"I couldn't get into student housing, but I have an apartment not too far away. How are you getting back?"

"The shuttle," Sierra answered, and then pushed her way forward as she spied her bag approaching.

"This one?" Sean had stepped in behind her, and as she reached for her bag, he swept it easily off the moving belt.

"Yeah, thanks. Careful, it's heavy."

"What have you got in here? Workout weights?" He grinned as he set the large bag down on its wheels and pulled up the handle.

"Riding boots and a helmet," she answered, embarrassed about the size of her bag, especially since all the luggage he seemed to have was his backpack.

"Ah, let me guess. You're a pre-vet student." He creased his brow as if concentrating on the solution to a difficult problem.

Laughing, she admitted that she was. "What's your major?"

"Would you believe it actually is microbiology?" he said, his eyes twinkling.

"No, I don't believe that. Not the way you disrespect a paramecium."

"I have nothing against those poor little one-celled critters, but it's actually viruses I'm more interested in. Working on the proverbial cancer cure, that's my life goal," he said jokingly, but Sierra detected a serious undertone.

"You really are majoring in microbiology," she stated.

"Yep, microbes; love those little can't even see 'em devils," he confirmed. "So…" They had moved away from the carousel crowd, heading to the exit doors. "Can I give you a ride back to your apartment? I have my car here."

"Uh," She hadn't expected him to offer her a ride, and caught by surprise, wasn't quite sure if she should accept. She really didn't know him.

He held his hands out as if balancing a scale. "Let's see - crowded, stuffy, smelly bus or…" He looked with disgust at one hand, and then switched his gaze with an expression of delight to his other hand. "…a comfortable, temperature-regulated, fabulous stereo system or brilliant conversationalist chauffeur-driven Kia." He raised his eyebrows with a hopeful, pleading expression.

With a mock frown as if thinking hard, Sierra hesitated. Then she bumped her fist against the hand representing his car. "You win, I'll take this one."

9 DUNE AND OBERON

You must never punish the horse. Teach yourself to elicit his happy cooperation to achieve the harmony and beauty of dressage. A horse who submits out of fear loses his beauty and spirit. – Reiner Klimke

It hadn't rained for several days which left the outside arena footing soft but without mud puddles, a good day to try Dune outside for the first time. River rode the mare along the rail, warming her up. He had been working with her for almost two months now and he was impressed with how quickly she was getting into shape. Her hay belly had trimmed away and she had notably firmed up her back, neck, and chest muscles.

The mare snorted, and stretched her nose toward the ground. "What do you think?" River murmured to her, amused at how she evaluated this new working space. She walked out with long strides as if happy to be out in the open air and moving. "*Bien,*" River said, "let's see how you feel today."

He pressed softly with his legs, sitting deeper in the saddle; a half-halt with legs and seat to let her know it was time to work. He squeezed the reins, still loose. Dune immediately popped her head up, feeling the pressure on the reins through her mouth. "No, *calma,*" River soothed, easing the pressure. He held her sides firm between his legs as he squeezed the reins again, and immediately released the pressure when she lowered her head. "*Bien*," he whispered. He continued to coax her into lowering her head into the bridle, combining hands, seat, and leg aids. When she remained soft in his hands, he kept his light contact, and increased pressure with his legs. He rejoiced when Dune kept her head lowered into the bit as she picked up the trot. "*Bien, muchacha!*" he praised. He moved her into a figure eight, holding gentle but steady pressure on the outside rein and guiding her just with legs and weight. She kept her head lowered into his hands, and he rejoiced when he felt her back rounding beneath him as she moved forward energetically and rhythmically. "*Gracias!*"

When he first started working with Dune, he realized she had never learned that the bit should be soft in her mouth, a way for her rider to speak to her and for her to answer back. He understood with her conformation that it had not been easy for her to carry a rider and work in a balanced frame. Her trainers and riders before him had probably tried to force her into roundness with too much reliance on the reins. She had developed the very defensive habit of tightening her neck and hollowing her back to relieve herself of the constant and probably painful hold on her mouth.

"She doesn't ever score very well in the dressage test," the trainer at Meadowood had told him. "But she consistently jumps clean both cross-country and stadium, and she is very steady under our green riders. She often places in the ribbons in spite of her poor dressage scores."

At the age of twelve, the mare had years of developing her defensive habit, and it would take many months of work to help her overcome her stiff responses and to trust the hands of her rider. River started her re-training by encouraging her to move out rhythmically with a loose rein, and even though she was working on the forehand, his first goal was to keep her in a steady rhythm and moving forward energetically without feeling inhibited. Eventually he hoped she would get over her habitual defense of stiffening her neck whenever he touched the reins. Now, she was starting to respond to his hands, even though she still reacted with stiffness at his first touch.

She had also been very cold in her sides and didn't seem to understand leg aids. Again, he knew her previous training had involved jerking her around with reins rather than working her off the legs. Having carried many green riders, she had learned to accept a lot of banging of legs against her sides that didn't mean anything.

The mare was very willing however, and learned quickly. She already moved readily off his legs after the weeks of working with her on a loose rein. Now, he wanted to maintain her promptness to his leg aids as he tried to encourage her into self-carriage and to work off the hind end rather than the forehand.

Work on the trails also helped. In spite of thinking her boring to ride, Todd followed River's instructions exactly (not daring to do anything different), and he had done well with the mare. Todd had pushed her to walk out in long, energetic strides, keeping the reins loose to encourage her to stretch her neck forward, especially climbing hills. River believed asking a horse to climb uphill with a lowered neck helped develop the muscles necessary for a round frame. The past two weeks he had instructed Todd to start trotting her for short distances and to include small hills at the trot, requiring her to maintain a steady rhythm in spite of the variation in terrain. When Todd reported that Dune handled the trot work with ease, River believed she was ready to jump again.

After her warm-up and some trot and canter exercises, Dune had settled into a balanced frame, relaxed but energetic. River liked it when she snorted in rhythm with her canter strides. Now, with her balanced and responsive, he was ready to test her jumping skill.

Earlier, he had set up a course of six jumps and a line of low cavalletti. He directed her now toward the cavalletti line at a trot. She pricked her ears and he felt her push off even more from her hind end as she approached the first rail. Keeping her rhythm, she trotted the line of six cavalletti as if it was an exercise they did every day. "*Que bien!*" River exclaimed. He circled around and trotted her down the line one more time, and then reversed and took the line from the opposite direction.

He had asked Enrique, one of the stable hands, to help out with setting jumps. He saw him at the rail now.

"She good," Enrique commented as River rode up to him.

"She's very good," River agreed. "Can you take out the next to last pole and raise the height of the last one?" he asked in Spanish. Enrique quickly made the changes.

River started Dune again down the line in trot and let her negotiate her approach to the last raised pole. She trotted on, jumped clean and efficiently, and then cantered on rhythmically and balanced.

"Bien," River praised her and brought her to walk and allowed her to stretch. "Take out one more pole and increase the distances to a canter stride," he called out to Enrique.

The next approach they took at the canter. River kept his contact light, allowing Dune to negotiate the rails on her own. Dune pricked her ears as they approached the line and River felt her shorten her stride just before the first rail. She jumped efficiently, lifting her knees and hocks just enough to clear the low obstacle, and then took each successive jump in a steady rhythm. He reversed their approach and marveled at how the mare adjusted her balance again to jump the line.

"Smart girl," he praised her. He was ready now to take her around the course. The jumps were all simple oxers no higher than two and a half feet and with even strides in between, nothing tricky today. Dune again proved her ability to handle a course and took each obstacle well in stride and without hesitation. He praised her lavishly. As she didn't seem at all tired but actually energized by the activity, he asked Enrique to raise the last three jumps to two feet nine inches. The increased height did not trouble Dune at all as she sailed over each obstacle. He liked the feel of her rounded back as she jumped, and that she jumped efficiently, raising her legs just enough to clear. He then asked Enrique to move two of the jumps together with two strides in between. He didn't interfere with her, and thrilled when she adjusted her stride for the shorter distance. *She may only have one eye, but it is very good!* He finished off the session by asking Enrique to raise the next to last jump to three feet. Dune cleared the course again. *This mare is a gem!* It amazed him that the trainer at Meadowood did not want to keep her. He would have thought a barn that gave lessons and sponsored a pony club would treasure a steady, school master like Dune.

"That's enough!" He gave the reins and allowed Dune to stretch her neck as he cooled her out in a walk.

"I really have to run this errand and I might be late picking you up," Cora Mae said, the day she dropped Jodi off for her riding lesson the first week of January.

"It's fine, Mom, don't worry. It will give me time to hang out with the horses," Jodi assured her.

That day changed the routine for Jodi. After her lesson and she had put Morris away, she limped slowly along the lane, stopping at each paddock to gaze at the horse inside. It thrilled her when many of the horses sauntered over to the fence, hoping she might have a treat. She went back to the arena and watched River giving the next student a lesson. When Todd returned from his assigned trail ride, he graciously let her help him untack and groom his horse.

She had already made friends with Manuel and Enrique. They had been delighted when she had tried to speak to them in Spanish. Now, as they began to bring horses in for the evening, she asked if she could help. Manuel let her bring in Morrison and two other horses with quiet manners.

Gwen Marshall arrived to pick up Todd even before Jodi's mother came. "Why don't you call your mother and tell her I'll give you a ride home?" Gwen suggested. Jodi took her up on the offer, and her mother was happy not to have to pick her up.

"I wish I could just hang out every day, even when I don't have a lesson," Jodi had said on the way home.

"Why don't you take the same bus that Todd takes after school?" Mrs. Marshall suggested. "I certainly don't mind giving you a ride home."

Jodi looked quickly at Todd, to see how he reacted to the suggestion. To her amazement, he turned to her from where he sat in the front seat. "Yeah, Jodi, I can show you which bus to take and which stop is near the stable."

"River won't mind if I'm hanging around?" she asked.

"Nah, he won't mind at all. And Tess won't even notice you," he said.

Her parents didn't mind as long as she continued her good behavior and made sure she finished her homework. In fact, this arrangement meant Cora Mae would no longer have to drive Jodi to her lessons.

From that day on, Jodi spent almost every afternoon at the stable, and weekends when she could get a ride with Todd. If she didn't have a lesson that day, she watched others ride, or she walked around visiting the horses in the paddocks. She lured them over to the fence with carrots so she could pet their noses. She didn't care that she was a misfit at school and had no friends. She didn't care that her parents loved Melody the best. She didn't care about her crippled leg. She didn't care because the horses didn't care.

There were two horses she eventually visited more than any of the others, attracted to them for reasons she didn't bother to analyze. The first was Oberon, the beautiful mahogany bay horse she had seen River riding in the arena the day she came for her first lesson. The second was Dune, the dun mare.

Oberon – first it was his incredible beauty that drew her attention, the magnificent head and proud carriage of his neck, and the graceful but powerful way he moved when he sometimes galloped and bucked in his paddock. It caused her to suck in her breath and drew her to his paddock fence to watch in awe. Oberon was the one horse she had never been able to entice over to her with carrots. It was as if approaching her for a treat was beneath his dignity, and she believed he looked down his nose with scorn when the neighboring horses came up to her so willingly. Not only his beauty, but his aloofness attracted her. She could sense the unwillingness in him to befriend anyone until they proved their worth.

"What is it about that horse?" she had mused out loud one day as she walked alongside Todd on his way to bring in his assigned ride.

"Who, Oberon?" Todd asked, and when she nodded, he laughed. "He's River's horse. He's a rogue."

"What does that mean?"

"I was pretty young when he first came here," Todd related, "but I remember how dangerous he was then. He tried to bite or kick anyone who came close to him, even River. I guess he had been abused at his previous home and they were going to put him down. River was his last chance."

"He doesn't do that now, does he? I've seen Enrique leading him in for the night."

"No, he minds his manners now, but it took River a long time to teach him those manners. You've probably noticed River is pretty amazing with horses and he eventually got through to Oberon. Well, you've seen River riding him. They won the national Prix St. Georges championship last season."

"Wow!" Jodi knew very little about dressage and had no idea what he meant by Prix St. Georges, but she wasn't surprised to hear that Oberon and River had won some kind of championship. She idolized River as if he were a sports hero or movie star, and she watched him ride every chance she could with a fan's devotion.

She became more intrigued with the big bay gelding, and one day, steeled her nerves and decided to enter his paddock. His pride would not allow him to come to her, but maybe he would appreciate it if she brought a carrot to him. She opened the gate and stepped inside, watching him askance and noting how he kept his eye on her. She moved toward his shoulder as Todd had instructed with an unfamiliar horse, talking to him in a low, soft voice.

He stood his ground with head up suspiciously, but he did not back away, or more importantly, did not turn his hind end to her threateningly. She came up close enough to extend her hand with a piece of carrot. Her heart jumped with joy when he actually condescended to lower his head and carefully lift the carrot off her palm. She grinned from ear-to-ear with a sense of accomplishment. But when she reached out to pet his neck, he shot his head up and side-stepped away. She did not try again to touch him that day.

It became a challenge to her. How long would it take before he would allow her to stroke his silky neck? For several days, she simply approached him and offered the carrot. On the fifth day, she tried to touch him with just the tips of her fingers, but he flipped up his head and stepped away again. The next day, after he took the carrot, she asked, "May I touch you?" She slowly raised her hand, showing him her fingers held softly. She waited while he eyed her. Then he actually lowered his head. She gently stroked down the curve of his neck muscle, just once. "Thank you," she whispered in a voice thickened with emotion. That was enough for the first touch.

It had been two weeks since that first physical encounter with Oberon. Now she could enter his paddock, give him his carrot, and he would stand patiently and allow her to stroke his neck, shoulder, and even the side of his face. It thrilled her!

The dun mare had been much easier to make a friend. She readily came to the paddock fence even before Jodi held out her carrot. Dune liked people and enjoyed their company. Jodi didn't know if she was allowed to enter the paddock of a horse not assigned to her for a lesson, but much sooner than she had dared with Oberon, she started going inside to pet Dune and even hug her around her neck. The mare seemed to like the contact, and even nuzzled her head against Jodi's chest. To Jodi, it was like maternal affection, and she took more comfort from Dune than she ever had from her own mother.

Compared to Oberon, Dune was ugly. Even to Jodi's uneducated eye, she could see the lack of balance in the mare's proportions. Her knees and hocks were large and knobby, and one hock turned out more than the other. Her coat color was dull and never held the shine of Oberon's rich mahogany color. Dune did not have a thick, full mane and tail like Oberon, but rather hers were thin and scraggly. The puckery flesh around her empty eye socket was unsightly and repulsive. But her manners were sweet, her one eye gentle and kind, and Jodi sensed in her a very generous heart.

Oberon and Dune were opposites, and Jodi loved them both dearly.

Jodi had been taking lessons for over two months. River kept her on a lunge line and she still had never held reins in her hands. But for the past few lessons, she was actually trotting a few steps. Since she didn't use stirrups, she couldn't post (at least not until her legs and balance were stronger. River had told her it is possible to post without stirrups). She had to clutch both the strap and often the front edge of the saddle with all her strength to keep the bouncy motion from tipping her off Morrison's back. But each lesson, she managed a few more strides of trot, and even better, a few strides where she could actually keep her seat square in the saddle. She knew her progress was extremely slow, but the fact she no longer felt dizzy or terrorized by the movement of the horse beneath her, was amazing to her.

Once, she overheard Tess say to River, "We are not a therapeutic riding facility. Why don't you send her down to Second Chance?" She had held her breath anxiously, waiting for River's response.

"She pays attention. She is learning and she likes her lessons," River had answered in an acerbic tone. "What is your problem? She pays her lesson fees and on time. I'd rather teach Jodi than those students who think they know everything."

Jodi did not catch all of Tess's snarled reply, but she heard enough to know that Tess must think Jodi's presence marred the reputation of Pegasus.

That night, Jodi looked up 'Second Chance' on the internet. She learned it was a farm that rescued animals but also gave lessons to disabled children and adults on horseback. They participated in a national therapeutic riding program and even held horse shows, the ultimate goal, the Paralympics. She actually felt hurt that her parents hadn't discovered this program for her, rather than all the physical therapy she had undergone. But at the same time, she was glad, because otherwise she wouldn't be at Pegasus.

One afternoon, Jodi was in Dune's paddock, when she heard, "You like her?"

Jodi gasped, and quickly stepped away from the mare. "Uh, sorry," she apologized. River stood at the paddock gate. *How long has he been there watching? Am I in trouble?*

To Jodi's surprise, he unlatched the gate and entered the paddock. Dune whickered low and stepped toward him, obviously recognizing someone she liked very much. It actually made Jodi feel just a twinge of betrayal and jealously that Dune might prefer him. But just as those feelings came upon her, they vanished when Dune turned her head and looked back as if to say, 'aren't you coming?'

"Hey, *bella doña*," River murmured to the mare as she came up to him and gently touched his chest with her nose. He reached up to stroke her neck affectionately.

"I just gave her a carrot," Jodi explained, hoping it excused her presence inside the paddock.

River smiled at her and Jodi thought her heart would explode. "It's okay to give her carrots," he reassured her.

"Oh," she replied and tried on a weak smile. "I do like her," she added. "I like her a lot."

River nodded and began to scratch Dune beneath her jaw, a place he had discovered she liked to get scratched, and spoke softly to her in Spanish. In the same quiet voice he said, "She's not the most beautiful horse but she's got a good mind and heart. Nobody here can see that yet…except maybe for you." He smiled at Jodi again, and she felt as if the explosion of her heart overflowed into a million shards, each one pricking her with painful points of hope. Hope of what...that River thought she was worth talking to...that he didn't think she was a crippled freak...that he might actually like her? "She'll surprise everybody though," he added and she thought he sounded defensive.

"Yeah, I bet she will," Jodi agreed. "She's so sweet and she seems very wise, I mean like she knows things. She..." Jodi bit her lip, suddenly embarrassed at her own chattiness.

River nodded his head in agreement. "*Luego, prima.*" He gave Dune a final pat and stepped away. To Jodi he said, "It's okay to visit the horses, but most of them here belong to boarders so you probably shouldn't go into their paddocks unless it's okay with the owner. But the Pegasus horses and my horses you can visit whenever you like." He did not sound at all angry, maybe even a bit amused. But then he added, "Except for Oberon. He can be mean sometimes."

Jodi gaped back at him. In spite of his friendliness she still had expected to get reprimanded. But he was actually giving her permission! Perhaps because of that, she suddenly did not want to hold back any secrets from him...well, no secrets regarding the horses. "Uh, really?" She found her voice and confessed, "I have gone into his paddock. He lets me pet him." It didn't sound like much, but she believed River would know it had taken time and patience for that to happen.

"What?" His eyes widened in surprise and his expression changed to one of alarm.

"I'm sorry. I didn't know...I mean, I thought it would be...." Her color deepened and her heart beat in horror at the thought she had just lost his faith in her. *I should have kept my mouth shut!*

"He lets you pet him?" River asked, still looking surprised but in a softer tone.

Jodi nodded, shrinking back away from him and up against the solid side of Dune. The mare seemed to sense Jodi's need of support, and she stood firm.

Suddenly River laughed. Jodi had never heard him laugh before, and the sound was like a balm, assuaging her panicked emotions. "Hmm, maybe you better show me."

Meekly, Jodi gave Dune a goodbye pat, and then followed River out of the paddock and down the lane. When they could see Oberon's paddock, River stopped. "He'll know I'm here so I'll stay back and watch how you approach him."

It seemed different to enter the gate, knowing someone watched. But at the expectant look in the big bay's eye, Jodi pushed away the strangeness, and quietly approached Oberon. He no longer eyed her in hostility, and although she wouldn't call him exactly welcoming, they seemed to have come to terms of agreement. She gave him treats, and he bestowed upon her the privilege of touching him. She extended her palm now with the bit of carrot from her pocket, and then slid her hand down the graceful arc of his neck while he chewed his treat.

Oberon looked up and she knew River had entered the paddock and came up behind her. "Well done," he said quietly. Oberon lowered his head to allow River to give his forehead a quick pat between his eyes. Jodi thought it was a gesture of mutual respect. "What do you think of him?" River asked.

"He is very proud," she answered. She knew River was not looking for comments on his physical beauty. "He wants to be the one making decisions."

"He's not just proud, he's totally arrogant," River said, sounding amused. "You're right. He wants to be the boss. This guy has excellent breeding and he is very talented. Unfortunately, he got a bad start in his training and Oberon learned he is bigger and stronger than humans."

"He behaves for you," Jodi stated, thinking of all the times she had watched the harmony between them when River rode the big bay.

"I had to learn how to ask him in a way that convinced him doing what I wanted was the easiest way; kind of make him think it was his choice."

"Oh yeah?"

"I had help from a friend. We had to make him uncomfortable every time he showed hostile behavior. Nothing that actually hurt him, just annoying enough for him to decide it was easier to be nice."

"Hunh," she thought about that, fascinated, and wished she could have observed that training. "Todd said you won a championship on him."

"Yeah," River answered with a laugh. "I never intended to show him, thinking he had enough of that in his early life. But he loves an audience, and nothing like a competition to let him show off."

"Yeah, I can see that," she agreed, thinking back to the proud bearing whenever she had watched River ride him.

"I don't know how you managed it, but he tolerates you. You can keep visiting him, but don't ever let him push you. Let me know if he even lays his ears back at you."

"Thank you, I will. Thank you."

Sierra dropped her phone into her bag, having just hung up from the third conversation this evening. She sat up a little straighter, pushing her back into the pillows she had arranged on the sofa, her feet stretched out on the seat cushions. She opened the textbook on her lap, intent now on reading the chapter assigned for her first class in the morning. But her mind kept drifting from the description of cell physiology back to her phone calls.

The first had been River. Their time together over winter break seemed to have mended whatever resentful feelings he had harbored because she had not joined him at the championship. However, the last two times he had called went to her voice mail. The first time happened because she had turned her phone off as usual during classes, and had forgotten to turn it back on. The second time, she had been in the library and didn't pick up because she didn't want to talk out loud. Both times she had called him back later the same day.

But tonight when he called and she answered, she detected just a hint of sarcasm when he said, "Amazing, you're actually there."

"I'm usually always here, River. I'm either in class, the library, or I'm here studying," she had replied defensively.

He seemed okay after that. They talked a few more minutes and then River said, "I better let you get back to studying." He never used to end their calls like that. Sierra wasn't sure if it was because he worried she didn't have time for him or if he was trying to be considerate of her need to study. Lately she often thought to herself, *if our relationship can just hang together until I get through school, then we'll be okay.*

She had finished two slow pages of her text when she received the next call from Sean Casey.

Ever since the night he had given her a ride home from the airport, he had been calling. When he dropped her off that night he had asked, "Can I call you sometime?"

Surprised, she had stumbled over her answer, "Uh no, I mean, I have a boyfriend."

"Okay, I think I knew that. But what about if I call you just as a friend?"

"I don't think so, Sean," she had answered with a smile, trying to be polite and not seem ungrateful for the ride.

"Why not? Can't a guy and a gal be just friends?" he persisted.

"Of course, but…"

"It's okay. I guess I can be pretty obnoxious."

"No, no you're not," she quickly assured him. "It's just…"

He held up his hands in surrender. "I promise, just friends. Hey, I really enjoyed talking with you tonight and I just thought it would be fun to get together for coffee sometime, or even help each other study. Nothing more than that."

The ride home that evening from the airport had been fun. He was intelligent and funny and she couldn't remember when she had laughed so hard at some of his comments. Although they had only shared the one class, they had similar curricula and they knew a lot of the same professors. They really had a lot in common to talk about.

And what was wrong with having a friend who just happened to also be a guy? She could use a study partner. In the end, she had relented and given him her number.

But so far, she hadn't quite decided to actually meet him for coffee or accept any of his dinner invitations, even though he called her two or three times a week.

It was the same tonight. He asked if she had dinner already, and when she said yes, tried to convince her to take a break from studying and meet him for a late coffee in two hours. She turned down all his offers, but she also didn't say she had to go right away. They talked on the phone for almost twenty minutes.

"If you change your mind and need a break, just call," he said just before they hung up.

After talking to Sean, Sierra's emotions were a jumble of pleasure, excitement, and guilt mixed in. *If he is just a friend, then there is nothing wrong with me talking to him,* she assured herself. But she found she could not concentrate on reading her chapter, so the third call she made herself, to her best friend currently attending Duke University on the east coast.

"I hope it's not too late," she said after Allison picked up and greeted her with her usual enthusiasm. "I know you are three hours ahead."

"Of course not, it's just a little after ten. You know I rarely get to bed before midnight."

"Good, I mean, that's what I thought." Sierra asked how things were going before bringing up the reason she had called. Then she told Allison about Sean, wanting her friend's opinion.

"Of course men and women can be just friends. But if you thought of Sean as 'just a friend', I don't think you would feel guilty about talking to him. I think you're attracted to him."

That was not the answer Sierra wanted to hear, because she feared it was true. "Allison, I feel awful. I love River so much. How can I be attracted to another man?"

She heard Allison laugh softly over the phone. "Oh, Sierra, you never cease to surprise me with your innocence. Do you think humans are by nature monogamous?"

"Yeah, of course. Well, yes…don't you?"

"We make the choice to be monogamous, and it is in some people's natures much more than others. But even when we choose, it is still very human to be attracted to others besides the one you have chosen."

"I don't know if I believe that," Sierra replied.

"Whatever, Sierra," Allison said mockingly. "Hmm, you are so in love with River that you don't notice attractive men around you?"

"Of course I notice, but that doesn't mean I'm interested in them."

"Listen, girlfriend. You and River have been going together since high school. You really haven't had much experience with the opposite sex, you know. River just might be the one for you, but I think you owe it to yourself to go out with this Sean guy. It won't take long for you to figure out if you can just be friends with him, or if the attraction is strong enough for you to reconsider your relationship with River. Isn't River the one always telling you to go out with other guys, so you will be sure about him?"

This really wasn't the answer Sierra had wanted to hear. It was true that River a few times had told her she should go out with another guy if he interested her. But that had been several years ago, before she first left for school and before…well, her relationship with River was much more intimate now. He had not made that suggestion in a long time.

"Just think about it. I really don't think meeting him for coffee is that big a deal."

"I don't know…so, what about you and Rob?" Sierra changed the subject, and after Allison filled her in on the details of her latest boyfriend, they said goodbye.

She managed to read one more page of her text, but when she realized she had no idea what she had just read, she gave up. She thought for a few minutes, and then made a decision. "We're just friends," she said out loud. "Meeting him for coffee is no big deal." Then she picked up her phone and called Sean.

10 JACK MCCALL

There cannot be competitive, specialized dressage riding without first simply becoming a good rider. - Charles de Kunffy

"I don't think that girl should hang around here when she isn't taking a lesson," Tess said as River stepped into her office.

"Who are you talking about?" River scowled at her as he hooked the chair opposite her desk and sat down.

"You know who I mean, that crippled girl. What if she gets hurt and her parents sue?"

"Isn't that why you have everyone sign a release?"

"People still sue," she snapped back at him.

"I don't think she is going to get hurt. She's got good sense around horses, better than most, and a lot better than some of the boarders here," River defended Jodi. "And she's not crippled."

"Whatever," Tess sighed and gave up, not wanting to push River. She opened her notebook of training schedules and they spent the next half hour discussing the students and the progress of each horse.

Before River got up to leave Tess said, "By the way, I got a call this morning from Jack McCall. He's giving a clinic at a stable near Sacramento in a couple weeks. He was hoping you and a few other candidates on the west coast might be able to ride for him while he's there. It would save you having to travel to his farm in Virginia. It would be a Friday before the weekend of his clinic and then he would fit riders in between clinic rides on Saturday and Sunday." She watched triumphantly as River's expression perked up with interest when she mentioned Sacramento. When he didn't say anything she persisted, "Come on, River. Why not at least go and meet Jack? You'll probably like him and you might even learn something. And of course, you could spend time with Sierra."

"Okay, I'll go."

Tess internally cheered in victory. She sincerely believed if she could just get River together with Jack, he would be more willing to consider the chance to ride under him. "I'll take care of the arrangements for your flight and rental car. They have a guest house at the center where they are putting up riders." She handed him a paper with the dates she had written down and the address and description of the stable.

"I'll miss the cross-country clinic," River reminded her with a sly look, noting the dates.

"I know, too bad," she smirked back. Tess gave a cross-country jumping clinic every year to herald the eventing season, traditionally the first weekend of March. For years, River started the clinic out by riding a demonstration course. He didn't complain anymore, but she knew he would prefer not to be involved. "I was thinking maybe Kate could do the demonstration ride. What do you think?"

"Sure, she can do it. I was going to have Todd ride Dune in the clinic. He's been riding her on the trail and I had him take a few jumps on her in his last lesson. They get along well and I think she's going to be perfect for him to compete if he goes training level this season."

Tess frowned at the mention of the horse she considered a nag, but quickly smoothed her brow and nodded. She certainly didn't want to say anything antagonistic now that River had agreed to meet Jack McCall.

They talked a few more minutes about the clinic, and then River left, his spirits lifting at the thought of being with Sierra in just a short time.

Over the next two weeks, River debated whether he should tell Sierra he was coming or just surprise her. In the end, he opted for surprise, imagining how her eyes would open wide and light up, and then how she would fling herself into his arms.

He could not consciously let himself believe that he wanted to catch her unprepared, for he trusted Sierra. But even after years of going together and her constant avowals of her love, a part of him still doubted his worthiness of her – she was so much smarter, more beautiful, purer in her soul. If he was honest with himself, he had to admit he felt jealous and suspicious every time he called her but only got her voicemail.

Friday morning River flew to Sacramento, rented a car at the airport, and drove to Claremont Equestrian Center. He stopped at the ostentatious gated entrance and gave his name. Wide iron gates swung open and River drove up a long paved drive, noting the fine breeding of the horses he passed in the front paddocks.

A woman stepped out the main door of the expansive guest house and waved him toward the parking area.

"Welcome, Mr. Girard. I'm Darlene Edwards, the Events Coordinator. Please come in," the woman greeted after River had parked and approached her. "Please call me Darlene. How was your flight? Most of the others have already arrived…" Darlene chattered on, asking questions for which she did not pause for answers. She led him inside and up a short staircase to a hall of guest rooms, opening the door of the one prepared for him. "Jack will meet you in the Sycamore Arena at one o'clock. A groom will bring the horse Jack wants you to ride to the arena." She looked at her watch. "It's just eleven-thirty. There are drinks and snacks in the salon if you didn't get a chance to eat." She gave him directions to the salon and with a parting, "contact me if you need anything at all," she left.

A laminated map of the center sat on top of the bureau. River noted the location of the Sycamore Arena, within a few minutes' walk from the guest house. He had enough time to eat something and have it settle before riding. He set down his overnight bag, changed into riding clothes, and exited the room.

The salon was not difficult to find, even if Darlene had not provided directions. All he had to do was head toward the buzz of many conversations peppered with laughter and the smell of food. He stopped at the entrance and almost turned away. Several people milled about the buffet table, filling plates and drink glasses, some dressed in riding clothes. He did not like crowds and was shy of meeting strangers. He surveyed the room and watched the activity a few moments before discovering a place against a wall where he could lean unobtrusively. He moved along the edge of the crowd to a buffet table, selected some fruit, a muffin, and a bottle of water and then retreated to his chosen spot. He planned to eat and then walk around outside until time to go to the arena.

"I'm not surprised to see you here." A young woman in a black tee and dark gray riding breeches approached River, a warm smile on her face. "You probably don't remember me. I'm Lisa Barringer. We met at the finals."

"I remember you." River shook her outstretched hand and smiled in return. "We had dinner one night. It's nice to see you." He was genuinely relieved to actually know someone in this crowd, someone he liked.

"You are here by invitation from Jack, right?" she asked.

"Yes, are you?"

"Yes, to my total amazement. I didn't think I was anywhere near the level of a rider that he would consider," she said.

"But you qualified for the finals."

"Lots of people make it to the finals, but that doesn't guarantee you have what Jack is looking for. I'm just thrilled to even try out. But anyone who has seen you ride would know why you are here."

He frowned, not quite sure how to respond to her compliment.

"Don't be modest," she said good-humoredly. "You do know you are an exceptional rider, don't you?"

He laughed, embarrassed, and shrugged his shoulders. He felt flattered by the compliment and the attention. She smiled at him, not appearing as if she intended to go away and poised and confident that he wouldn't mind her hanging out with him again. *She is very pretty.* He liked her eyes that were not quite blue and not quite green. When she smiled, dimples complimented the corners of her well-shaped mouth. "Are all these people here trying out for Jack?"

"No, I think there are only four of us. The other people are spouses or friends of candidates and I think a few clinic riders who came early just to watch the try-outs, or rather to hear Jack's comments. You know, I really appreciate not having to go to Virginia to try out. It's very nice of the center to accommodate him."

"Yeah, I don't even know if I would have come if it meant flying to Virginia," River said.

"Really, you wouldn't have?" Lisa asked, not quite believing anyone would not jump at the chance to ride with Jack.

He shrugged again. "Maybe. I don't know."

She shook her head smiling, and then asked, "How is that naughty horse of yours?"

"He's fine…still naughty. How's that chestnut. Getting enough to eat?"

"Oh yes," she laughed. "Even at home he is bottom of the pecking order, but we make sure none of the others bully him. He is so sweet, so willing…" Lisa chattered on about her horse.

She's nice! River had forgotten about Lisa after returning home last year, but now he recalled how much he had enjoyed having dinner with her that time. He liked listening to her talking about her horse with the same affection as a mother for a child.

During a pause in their conversation he said, "I was going to walk around and check out the grounds before going to the arena. Have you been here before?"

"No, but if you don't mind, I'll walk with you," she offered.

"Yeah, sure," he agreed for he had hoped she would want to come with him. They set down their plates and went outside.

The equestrian center spread over rolling hills greening up in the early California spring. Stepping out from the guest house, they had a view of multiple fenced pastures and paddocks interspersed with several large outdoor arenas. Two smaller indoor arenas each sat between long stables of large, light-filled box stalls. The owner's massive castle-like mansion topped the estate, the only other building on higher ground than the guest house. The center hosted many horse shows and clinics and obviously could accommodate events of large numbers of attendees, both human and equine.

River enjoyed the walk, noting to himself how the facility compared to Pegasus. He took pride in the fact that although this center was much more grandiose, Pegasus could equal it in the accommodations for horses and riders. He was thinking he could even write a paper critiquing this place for one of his classes.

Lisa and he strolled around, discussing the beautiful grounds and the fine horses. He was enjoying himself, in fact so much that he was surprised when she said, "Look at the time! We better head on over to the arena."

Jack McCall arrived just a few minutes after Lisa and River, rolling himself onto the observation deck in an electric wheelchair and settling himself in a strategic location to observe all of the arena. He was welcomed by the observers who had gathered on the platform - the friends of the candidates and those who had arrived early for the clinic. They settled into chairs around him.

"You didn't know he was paralyzed?" Lisa asked, noting the startled look on River's face. When he shook his head she explained, "He was in a very bad car accident quite a few years ago that left him a paraplegic."

"He can't ride?" River asked.

"No, not really."

Jack picked up a microphone, tested the sound, and then addressed the candidates. Lisa and River joined the two other riders standing near the deck in front of Jack. "Welcome, and thank you so much for coming." Jack introduced each of the riders, where they were from, and some of their accomplishments to the observers. Then he gave his instructions as two grooms led in two saddled horses. "You don't know the horses you are going to ride today. I want to see how you get to know the horse and how you decide to school him. Please ride as if I am not here."

Everyone laughed, as if anyone could forget that Jack was watching.

"Mark Church, please take the bay gelding. River Girard, I'd like you to ride the gray mare." He instructed the other two riders, Lisa and Colleen Kreisner, to join him on the deck for the first round.

This is Misty," the groom holding the gray mare said, as River walked up.

"Thank you," River replied, taking the reins the groom handed off. *This feels strange.* He had never walked up to an unknown horse, mounted, and just started riding. Even when he tried out a new horse, he watched someone else ride it first, and if he could, he liked to observe the horse in its paddock and then while being led, groomed, and tacked up. He studied this mare now, mid-sized with good bone, perhaps a little under muscled. He noted her soft eye looking back at him, perhaps apprehensively? He extended his hand slowly, then stroked her neck and shoulder on both sides, allowing her to study him as well and to familiarize herself with his scent. He murmured softly, to accustom her to the sound of his voice. He took the time to check her tack; the fit of the saddle, the snugness of the girth, and then the type of bridle and bit, noting a plain snaffle with a flash cavesson.

"You have good manners," he said to her softly, for she did not move away from his inspection, and only laid her ears slightly back when he checked her girth. River mounted up, softly settling his seat in the saddle and feeling for how the mare responded to his weight. "You're not green," he spoke softly to her. She had not stiffened her back or raised her head at the addition of his weight, so he knew she was used to carrying a rider. As soon as he was in the saddle, she began to step away from the mounting block, an action that most horses wanted to do. He noted her quick response to his weight and legs asking her to stop.

"How is the stirrup length?" asked the groom.

"Maybe down one hole?" River answered, checking where his calves fit against the rib cage of the mare. The groom came over and efficiently adjusted the stirrup length. River liked that the mare did not fidget during the process. "Okay, *amiga*, shall we walk?" He moved her away from the block to the perimeter of the arena to warm up, joining the other rider.

The afternoon flew by. River rode two horses, first Misty and then after Lisa and Colleen rode, he was assigned a young black stallion. In between rides, he watched along with the other spectators, listening to Jack's comments. He agreed with practically everything Jack noted and what Jack said he might do differently to school the horse. The other three riders all had talent and experience, rising stars in the dressage world. River was impressed watching them ride, but he especially appreciated they were all committed horsemen and horsewomen. They wanted to ride in a manner best for the horse, not only to maximize the horse's talent but also for its well-being and happiness. They were ambitious and hoped to someday ride in the Olympics or World Equestrian Games, but River's impression was they would not jeopardize a horse's well-being in order to win. These were people he enjoyed being around and he knew he could work with them on a team.

River had found Misty responsive to his aids, moving off his legs and accepting the bit, but her movements were not as fluid as he liked, and she tended to lean on his hands. He suspected she had been ridden by someone used to holding on to her mouth to hold her in a proper frame, rather than working with the mare to carry her own weight and move freely in self-carriage. He didn't try any upper level exercises even though he suspected she had been trained in them. He spent the session with her in basic suppling exercises, transitioning her within the gaits and using many circles, figure eights, and serpentines. Even though he probably would never ride her again, out of habit he was already thinking about a training schedule for her to build up her hind end muscles and top line and loosen up her joints so that she would be able to carry herself with more impulsion and elasticity in her body.

The stallion, River determined, was much greener in his training than the gray mare. He also had a hotter temperament and his attention easily distracted by all the activity around him. He needed a different approach and River spent the first part of the session working him in an active trot on a longer rein but with a lot of supporting leg, encouraging him to stretch and lower his head to release tension. He liked the young horse's energy, but wanted to re-direct it into productive work rather than jumping at every movement or noise from the shadows and outside the arena. This was a horse who would work at his best with a consistent rider that would not react by snatching the bit every time the stallion raised his head, but rather would use legs to keep him moving forward. This horse needed to trust that his rider would not hurt him and would keep him safe.

"Very well done, all of you," Jack said after the last two riders dismounted and joined him on the deck and he had excused the other observers. "Tomorrow I'll have each of you ride one horse you worked with today to see how you progress, and then one of the horses you didn't ride today. The clinic starts at nine fifteen so I will ask Lisa and Colleen to ride at eight thirty. River and Mark, you will ride at eleven forty-five, right before lunch. River and Lisa, your second ride will be right after lunch and Colleen and Mark, at the end of the clinic at six. That way you each have the chance to observer each other. Oh yes, I am also evaluating you on your observations and comments as you watch each other ride, and the riders in the clinic tomorrow. My goals for the riders who work with me include of course schooling horses to the best of their abilities and maybe bring home an Olympic medal." He paused while everyone laughed. "But I also expect you to pass on your knowledge to other riders. I want you to be top trainers and riding instructors. Any questions?"

"When will we know if we've made the team or not?" Colleen asked the question she believed the others were as anxious as her to know.

"I know you'd like an answer by the end of this weekend, but I have two more sets of candidates coming to my farm in Virginia this month. As you know, I can only take on four riders, and to be fair, I have to evaluate all the candidates. But I promise you will know soon after I have watched the last group.

"When is the last group?" Mark asked.

"Third week of March, and I will let each of you know personally one way or the other." When no one had any more questions Jack announced, "Dinner is hosted for us tonight and we will meet in the guest house dining room at seven. That's in about an hour and a half. Is that enough time?" They all nodded and Jack said, "See you all then," as he turned his chair around to roll away.

"Phew, that was grueling," Colleen said as they left the arena as a group. "I ride six horses a day at home but I am more exhausted riding just two knowing Jack was watching."

"Lead me to the bar," Mark said as a joke and they all laughed.

At the guest house they split up to their rooms to rest and clean up before dinner.

In his own room, River began undressing to take a shower, with his thoughts now turning to Sierra. He still wanted to surprise her, but it would also be fun to bring her to this dinner. Mark had brought his wife and Colleen had invited a friend from her stable. Darlene said it was fine if he wanted to invite a guest. The equestrian center was not that far from the university. He had time to pick her up. But when he placed the call, it went to voicemail. He tossed the phone on the bed, swallowing down his annoyance and the old suspicions. *It's a Friday night. Has she gone out with someone?* He pushed away the thought, *on a date*, from his mind.

After taking a shower, River checked his phone. He had not left Sierra a message, but she would still know he had called. Hoping she might have called him back while he was in the shower, he checked his own voicemail, but there was nothing. Disappointed and pushing away his jealous feelings, he left his room.

Downstairs, a few people sat in the salon, most sipping a cocktail or glass of wine, and conversing amicably. River considered joining them, but he was too shy to enter a group uninvited.

"River, we're in here," Mark called out. "Come have a drink."

"Hey, River, come join us," someone else invited.

"Thank you," he replied, surprised by the invitation. He entered the room and saw Lisa gesturing to an empty space on the sofa where she sat.

River was even more surprised when everyone started complimenting him on his riding today.

"You know Jack will select you," Colleen stated with conviction.

"I don't know that," River said. "All of you are great riders." He made the statement sincerely. They all deserved to be here, although he thought Colleen was probably the weakest of the four of them.

"You are the only one Jack had nothing to correct," Lisa said.

When River's expression looked as if he didn't quite understand, Lisa added, "He had nothing but good to say about you."

They heard voices in the foyer, and the group merged into the dining room where Jack now sat in a chair at the table. It seemed natural that River sat down next to Lisa.

The conversation centered on horses and with encouragement, Jack told stories of horses he had known in the past, especially his Olympic champion Good Mileage. River enjoyed the stories and felt at ease with Lisa beside him. *I'm having a good time*, he realized, and looked forward to telling Sierra about this day.

After dinner, some of the guests excused themselves to go up to their rooms while the remainder gravitated to the salon for more conversation.

"You going to your room?" Lisa asked as River stood up from the table.

"Actually, I have a friend at the university and I'm going to drive over there now." He was surprised at Lisa's expression – *disappointed?* It occurred to him a little guiltily, that all through the evening he had not once mentioned he had a girlfriend close by. *Why did I say friend instead of girlfriend?*

"Well, I'll see you in the morning then," Lisa said.

"Yes, good night." They walked out of the dining room and Lisa headed to the stairs.

"A few moments, River?" Jack asked. He beckoned to River at the doorway of a small private den.

"Sure," River answered, and followed Jack as he wheeled himself back into the room.

"Please, close the door and then have a seat." Jack settled his chair near a small table with a tray of stemmed glasses and a bottle of red wine. "Wine?" Jack asked, lifting the bottle.

"No, thank you," River declined the offer as he sat in the chair Jack waved him toward.

Jack nodded, poured himself a small glass, and then settled back in his chair. "You don't drink, do you? Why is that?"

River gave him a wry smile as he answered, "I come from a family of alcoholics and drug addicts. I'm afraid to start. I'm saving my alcoholism for when I can no longer ride."

Jack laughed heartily and lifted his glass toward River in a small salute. "Good for you. However, don't think your life is ended when you can no longer ride."

"I didn't mean…uh…." River's color deepened, but then he blurted out, "How can you stand no longer riding?" At the look of amusement on Jack's face, River fumbled for words. "I mean, I shouldn't have…."

Jack nodded, and took a sip of his wine. "For many months after my accident I was in a deep depression. I think if I physically could have managed suicide I might have tried. But my wife and my two daughters watched over me very closely, and they did not allow it." He chuckled softly as he continued, "My wife is an angel for what she has endured for my sake. When my daughter Katie came to me for advice on a horse she was training at that time, and pleaded with me to watch her ride, I refused. But she persisted and eventually I surrendered. The first time to enter the arena, rolling in on wheels rather than astride a horse…well, that was the hardest moment for me. To smell the horses and hear them snort and blow; to even feel the vibrations as they trotted by…. But, I watched Katie ride. I advised her on how to correct her seat and how to use her aids, and the horse she rode transformed before my eyes from an over-bent, tense animal, to one of fluid and relaxed muscular beauty. I was awed on how a few simple changes Katie made under my coaching could transform her horse so dramatically. I continued to coach Katie and my other daughter Leanne, and then others came to me. I had purpose again. Now my life is dedicated to improving horses through classical training. And yes, it still sometimes overwhelms me with sadness that I no longer ride, but I can control my despair in those moments. My heart is gladdened by the beauty of a well-trained, happy animal and its great courage. I believe I get my courage to go on by the example of horses. I have seen so many horses endure all degrees of mistakes and cruelty, and still they give their best."

River listened intently, trying to imagine if he could live his life as this man now chose. He felt humbled, and his respect for Jack intensified.

"I do not know or care what your religious or spiritual beliefs are, but I am telling you, there are divine forces working in this universe. There is a purpose to life on this planet. All life forms each have a unique purpose and many are gifted. You, River, are the most gifted rider I have seen in quite a while. Whether it has come naturally to you or whether you have worked hard in your short life, this doesn't matter. You have a harmony with horses that most riders will never achieve. Many will have moments, I had such moments. But you have that harmony all the time. So, what is your purpose, River? What are you doing with your gift to leave this planet a better place?" Jack sipped his wine and waited patiently, allowing River time to absorb his words.

After several long minutes of thinking, River answered, "My purpose is to train horses to the best of their abilities, but in such a way that it is a joy for them."

"That is very likely a large part of your purpose since you have been given such a gift. But what about the purpose of each horse? Is it enough that it reaches its highest potential?"

Again, River sat in silence, thinking of an answer that would sound credible. But he shrugged and said, "I guess I've never really thought about whether or not a horse has a purpose."

"Throughout history," Jack began, leaning back to rest his head, "the purpose of the horse insofar as its usefulness to mankind, has been obvious. But what about now? Humans no longer need the horse for transportation, to plow a field, or to carry them into battle. Have horses outlived their usefulness?"

"No," River answered definitively. He might not have the words to explain what he felt, but he was sure horses were still very important to mankind.

"I know you have reservations about riding in the Olympics if you were to make the team, or so your boss has told me. And River, with that bay horse you rode Prix St. Georges, I am very confident you could make the team. So, ask yourself, what is the purpose of the Olympics?"

"It's just a sport," River answered.

"It is sport, and of course it is heavily commercialized through greed to make a fast dollar. The Olympics have devolved into an economic and political miasma. But at the same time, it is the place for the very best in all sports to shine. And in the equestrian events especially, it is a venue for all the world to witness the majesty of a well-trained grand prix equine athlete. Even people who are not especially attracted to horses cannot help but gaze in awe at a grand prix freestyle.

"River, I believe this is the purpose of horses. It is to remind humans of beauty, to stir their emotions at the joyful example of a harmonious partnership. Not just in the Olympics, but showing your horse in competitions allows his magnificence to shine out to the world. Horses are living art. And more than ever, in a world filled with violence predominating the media both in the news and entertainment, humans need this example.

"You really didn't need to come for this evaluation. I have wanted you on my team ever since I saw you ride at the finals. You were my first choice then, and watching you ride today, you are still number one." Jack laughed and raised his glass again. "Your boss tells me it took quite a bit of persuasion to get you to come. It's rare I have to beg a rider to try out."

"It's not..."

Jack laughed again. "No pressure, but how about thinking about joining my team more in terms of the universe rather than just yourself?"

With a slow nod of his head, River said pensively, "I never thought about horses like that." He laughed softly. "I will think about it and no matter what I decide, it would be an honor to ride for you."

"Thank you, River. I don't know that I could teach you much, but everyone benefits from eyes watching their horse from the ground. And I think I could help you learn to use the curb rein. I noticed at the championship you just held that rein, and it does have a purpose."

"I think you could teach me a lot," River admitted. They talked a short while longer about horses and training. Then River excused himself, anxious now to be with Sierra, not only to hold and kiss her but to share with her the things Jack had said.

He felt good, very glad in fact that he had agreed to come. He liked Jack very much. He was a man he could respect and he knew he would enjoy working with him. They shared an equal love of horses and Jack's approach to training was in accord with River's views. Jack reminded him a lot of his old friend João.

Maybe Sierra could come with him tomorrow since he didn't think she had classes on Saturday. He would love for her to meet Jack McCall and he thought she would enjoy auditing the clinic.

In the rental car, he smiled to himself as he entered the address of her apartment into the GPS system, thinking how she always teased him about his technological ineptitude. He made one stop. Passing a strip mall with an open-air flower shop, it occurred to him, *flowers, I should get her flowers.* The shop had a nice selection and he chose a bouquet in colors he knew Sierra liked. He wanted to be a better boyfriend to her, more romantic. Flowers weren't very original but still….

The GPS guided him to the entrance of Sierra's apartment, but River had to drive two blocks away to find a parking spot. Then, with flowers in hand, he quickly walked back to the door of her apartment number and rang the bell.

"Coming," a voice from inside called out. Several minutes later, a girl flung open the door, dressed to go out with purse over her shoulder. "What took you so long?" she asked, then, "oh, sorry, I was expecting someone. May I help you?" She eyed River up and down, the corners of her mouth smirking up, and then she exclaimed, "Ooh, flowers!"

"Is Sierra here?" he asked, taken aback. He forgot she had a roommate.

"No, she's out with…oh wait, who are you?"

"Sorry I'm late, Kelly," another girl called out, just then coming up behind River.

"I'm just leaving," Kelly, Sierra's roommate said, stepping out the door and pulling it shut behind her. "Sierra should be home anytime." She hurried off to join her friend without a backward glance.

River stared at the closed door, his heart sinking. *I should have called first. She can be anywhere, at the library studying, out with friends like her roommate….* He didn't know whether to just wait on her doorstep or go back to his car. He realized now the surprise idea had really been stupid. Fumbling for his phone to try and call her again, he began to retrace his steps back to the street.

A car pulled up to the curb in front of the sidewalk leading to Sierra's apartment. Its engine silenced and a young man got out from behind the wheel, hurrying around to open the passenger door. Before he could, the door opened and Sierra stepped out.

Sierra?

In shock, River watched the man pull Sierra into his arms and kiss her.

11 A SURPRISE

Four things are greater than all things are -
Women and Horses and Power and War. - Rudyard Kipling, *The Ballad of the King's Jest*

"Wow, I can't believe it's almost nine. Sean, you promised to have me home by now," Sierra cried out in dismay. As usual, when she agreed to let Sean take her out for a coffee break or to study together, she lost track of time. Talking with him seemed to help her relax and she always enjoyed their conversations. He was so funny, very intelligent, and he was interested in everything, even when she went on and on about horses. She was glad she had decided to allow this friendship to happen, *and we are just friends*, she always assured herself. "I have to be at the animal shelter at six!"

"Right, sorry, I forgot. It's too easy to forget about everything else when I'm with you, Sierra," Sean said as his excuse.

She rolled her eyes, for even though he had agreed to her terms, 'just as friends', he always said things to let her know he was ready for a different relationship whenever she might change her mind.

They made their way out of the near-empty coffee shop, Sean guiding her with his hand at the small of her back. That was something he had only started doing the last two times out together. It was a 'gentlemanly' gesture, and Sierra did not protest.

"What is it you do at the shelter?" he asked once they were settled in his car and he pulled out of the parking lot.

"Clean pens, walk the dogs, feed and help with wound care and giving medications," she rattled off.

"Aren't you already accepted into the vet program? Why do you have to keep on volunteering?"

"They really need the help. I can't just stop because I don't need any more volunteer hours. And I like working there. The hardest part is not bringing a rescue dog or cat home with me."

"Hmm, I see. Hey, why don't you rescue me and bring me home?" he asked with a leering sideways look.

"You don't need rescuing," she said firmly.

The coffee shop was only five minutes by car from her apartment. Sean parked the car at the curb, and hurried around to open Sierra's door before she could get all the way out. He placed his hand under her elbow to help her up, (as if she needed it).

"Thanks," she began, ready to say good night.

Sean suddenly grabbed her by the shoulders and pulled her close. Before she could protest, he leaned down and kissed her full on the mouth. His lips were warm and soft, and his breath caressed her face as he kept his mouth lingering on hers, not insisting, but by his stillness leaving the decision up to her – to pull away or return his kiss.

For a moment Sierra closed her eyes, and mostly out of curiosity allowed herself to feel the sensation of kissing someone she liked a lot, someone who was not River. But only a brief fraction of a moment, and then she pulled away.

"Sierra?"

The familiar voice triggered her eyes to fly open. She looked around Sean's shoulders and saw River, a startled and very hurt expression on his face.

"Sierra, what's going on?" River asked in a choked voice.

"River, what are you doing here?" Sierra pushed against Sean's chest and abruptly stepped away, her eyes opening wide in shock.

"I wanted to surprise you," River answered, struggling to speak as his eyes bored into hers and noted the distressed look on her face. He read that expression as guilt, the look of a criminal caught in the act. The flowers in his hand felt hot and sticky. His fingers opened, releasing the stems. As they hit the pavement petals broke off and scattered at his feet. He felt his chest ripping apart as his heart exploded within. He spun away and fled.

"River," Sierra had taken a step toward him, reaching out. She broke into a run. "River, stop…River!"

After pounding full out for many blocks, the lack of oxygen burning his lungs forced River to eventually stop and lean over his knees, gasping for air. When he regained his breath, he stood and looked around. He didn't know where he was but it didn't matter. He walked aimlessly through unfamiliar streets, trying to blot out the image of Sierra kissing that man. While running, he had been able to blank out all thoughts except making it to the next corner and forcing his feet to keep moving. But his legs ached and his exhausted body did not want to move any faster. He could no longer avoid the thoughts flooding his mind. *I trusted her…I love her…how could she do this to me?* Anger moved in. Anger temporarily eased slightly the acute pain in his heart.

"Sean, let me go, please!" Sierra pushed at the hand that forced her to stop running.

"You can't catch him, he's already out of sight. Sierra, stop!"

She gave up. Her lungs begged her to stop and it was true she had lost sight of River several blocks ago. She fell sobbing against Sean.

He supported her wordlessly, waiting for the deluge of tears to subside. As much as he wanted to cradle her close and comfort her with caresses and kisses he knew now was not the time.

When her sobs ended in sniffles and gulps, Sierra pushed away and started walking back in the direction of her apartment. Sean walked at her side. "That was your boyfriend," he stated, to start the conversation that needed to happen.

Sierra nodded, and after blowing her nose said in a whimper, "I had no idea he was coming here."

"That's obvious." They walked a block, the silence between them interrupted only by Sierra's sniffles. Sean's heart thumped with a mixture of foreboding and anticipation. He was sorry to have caused Sierra so much distress, but one thing he was definitely not sorry about was kissing her. And if that resulted in her boyfriend breaking up with her, well, possibly…maybe? "Sierra, I am so sorry." When she did not acknowledge having heard, he continued, "I guess I should apologize for kissing you."

"Yes," she stated coldly.

"Okay, I'm going to be totally honest with you. It hurts me to see how upset you are. It is my fault and I am very sorry to be the cause. But I can't say I'm sorry for kissing you because I have wanted to do that ever since I met up with you at the airport that day."

"Don't, please," she said, not looking at him.

"I'm not sorry, Sierra." He stopped her with a hand on her arm, and turned her to face him.

"Don't do this now," she whispered hoarsely. "I may have just lost the man I love because of that kiss." She pulled away from him and walked ahead with faster steps, trying to leave him behind.

When they came up to the front of her apartment, Sean offered, "Do you know where he's staying? I will drive you there if you want to find him."

"Of course I don't know where he's staying. I didn't know he was coming," she snapped back at him angrily. "Just go home, Sean. I don't want your help."

"I want to help," he said softly. "Even if it means helping you get your boyfriend back. I want you to be happy."

She shook her head, turned her back and opened her apartment door with her key. "Good bye, Sean." She went inside and shut the door softly behind her without looking back.

"You look terrible," Lisa commented the next morning on the way to the arena. "What's wrong?"

"Nothing," River replied curtly. "I didn't sleep well."

In spite of aimlessly walking around, River eventually found his rental car and drove back to the equestrian center. Some people were still up in the salon, but he quickly made his way upstairs, pretending not to have heard his name called out. In bed, he flung himself from side to side, tangling within the sheets, as he yearned for the obliterating balm of sleep. He fought tears, but eventually he allowed them to flow and cried silently into his pillow. He slept after that, but only a little over an hour. The rest of the night passed in sleepless, long hours of agony.

Lisa sensed he did not want to talk and tactfully kept silent.

Thank goodness for the horses. River was able to maintain an outward semblance of nothing wrong as he rode the black stallion again and then a chestnut gelding. Studying the other riders and their horses helped him maintain his composure. Jack excused them at the end of the day, thanking them again for coming. They were all invited to stay over and observe the clinic riders again on Sunday, and if they wished to ride, a horse would be provided. Dinner was again hosted.

"Thanks for inviting me," River said, going up to Jack in a pause between people wanting to ask Jack questions. "If your offer still stands, I would like to accept it."

Jack actually clapped his hands together and smiled broadly. "Wonderful, fantastic. Welcome to my team." He reached out and they shook hands.

"I still have one more year of college," River said.

"That's okay, many of the team members through the years have been college students. I can work with your schedule. You're not taking summer classes, are you?"

"No," River assured him.

"Great, it will not be a problem at all. Are you staying over tonight?"

"No, I'm actually going to leave now."

"You're not staying for dinner?"

"No, I appreciate all that you and the center have done to make us comfortable, but I want to get home tonight."

"Something wrong?" Jack asked. He detected a certain despondency and a lack of enthusiasm in River that he didn't understand. Usually riders learning they had been accepted on his team exhibited exhilaration and gratitude.

"No, I just want to get home and back to my own horses...thanks."

"Very well then. I'll be sending out the training schedule at the end of the month when I have the other three riders selected."

"Okay, I look forward to it." River backed away as others came up to talk to Jack. He returned to his room, took a quick shower, and packed up his bag. He found Darlene downstairs and thanked her for her hospitality.

"There is a young woman waiting for you outside," Darlene informed him. "She did not want to come in."

Sierra!

In the parking area, he saw Sierra pacing, waiting for him. His heart quickened in gladness as if it had forgotten the recent blow. He wanted to rush over to take her in his arms. His eyes drank in her sad face. Oh, how he wanted to kiss the downward corners of her mouth. But then the image of that mouth kissing another man swooshed in and his heart sank in despair. He slowed his steps and dropped his eyes. Reaching his car, he opened the back door and tossed in his bag, still not looking at her.

"River."

"How did you know where to find me?" he asked accusingly, and slammed the back door. He turned and leaned against it with folded arms and stared at his feet.

"I called Tess."

"How did you get past the gate here?"

"I gave your name and said I was your friend. River, it doesn't matter how I got here. I've been calling you all night and day. You have to talk to me."

"I don't have to."

She reached out to take his arm but he snatched it away. He knew he was acting like a petulant child, but he couldn't help it. He was so very, excruciatingly, painfully wounded.

"Why are you assuming the worst? Why won't you let me explain what you saw?" she pleaded.

"All I know is I saw you kissing that guy. What is there to explain?" he replied in a snarly tone.

"What there is to explain is that it never happened before. I didn't know that was going to happen and he caught me by surprise. He kissed me, River, I did not kiss him." She watched him furrow his brow as he studied his shoes. "I thought Sean was just a friend. I go out for coffee with him once in a while and we study together. I've told him about you many times, so he was way out of line with what he did."

"How come you never told me about this friend?" he asked accusingly.

"He isn't a secret. And I have mentioned that I've been going out to study with a friend sometimes."

"You just didn't mention he was a guy."

"No, I didn't." *Because I was afraid you might get jealous and I figured you would never need to know,* she thought to herself. Her frustration was culminating in anger after her own tear-filled, sleepless night and trying to reach him by phone. Her tone intensified as she said, "Why are you acting like this? What is wrong with you?"

He jerked his head up and at last met her eyes, his own flashing in defensive anger to guard exposing his raw heart. "What is wrong with me is I caught my girlfriend kissing another man," he snapped back, raising his own voice.

"I told you, he kissed me. I did not kiss him back."

"It sure looked like you kissed him back."

They were both talking in loud, hostile voices. Sierra turned away from him and took in several deep breaths to calm her rising anger and still her shaking fingers. She hadn't expected him to be this stubborn. It made her so angry that River didn't even want to hear her explanation. And worse, now that he had, he did not trust her enough to believe her.

When she felt she could speak in a normal voice, she turned back and asked, "Don't you trust me?"

"I used to trust you," he retorted, his jaw tight and eyes narrowed.

That is just too much! How dare he! Sierra pulled off the ring he had given her and threw it at him. Perhaps if she hadn't been so tired and gone through so much suffering to find him and talk to him, she might have thought better of the impulsive and immature action. But to not be trusted…well, that was just the last straw. She turned and fled to where she had parked the car she had borrowed from a friend, and she drove away without looking back.

River watched the car until out of sight, his mouth hanging open in shock. *Why did she give up so easily?* "I shouldn't have said that," he spoke to himself out loud, for he certainly did not mean it. *Of course I trust her.* He had actually been about to apologize when she reacted by throwing the ring at him. *She broke up with me!*

Then jealous suspicions rushed back in. *Was she just waiting for an excuse to break up?* He felt dizzy as he bent over and picked up the ring which had nestled in between two pieces of gravel.

12 THE DITCH

A schooled horse is the best teacher. - Advanced Techniques of Dressage, The official Instruction Handbook of the German National Equestrian Federation

"By the way, Todd," Melody said, stopping by his desk at the end of history on Friday.

"Hi, Melody," he greeted. He felt his mouth widening and ducked his head, using the excuse of gathering his notes to hide his foolish grin.

"I've been wanting to thank you for quite a while now."

"Thank me for what?" he asked, his curiosity piqued. He couldn't think of anything he had done for Melody to earn her gratitude.

"For how nice you have been to my sister. It's like she's a different person since she's been taking riding lessons. She talks about you all the time...you and some guy named River, and how much you are both helping her. You've been a good friend to her."

"You don't need to thank me," he assured her, looking up and still grinning like an idiot at receiving this gratitude from Melody. "Jodi is a different person around the horses and I do think of her as a friend."

"She doesn't really have any friends, so it means a lot." Melody smiled sweetly, looking sideways at him through her lashes.

He continued to gape at her, his mind a blank. He could think of nothing else to say, so merely nodded, still grinning.

"So, Brooke asked me if I wanted to watch some kind of clinic at your stable this Saturday. I guess she and Mindy are riding. Jodi's planning on going to watch, and she asked me to come too. She and I haven't really done anything together for a long time, so I thought it might be fun. Are you going to be there?"

"Uh, yeah, I'll be riding," he finally found his tongue to answer. At the same time his nervous fingers abruptly sent his notes scattering onto the floor. Embarrassed, he quickly bent over to retrieve them.

Melody knelt down to help and her fingers brushed against his as they gathered the papers.

Did she do that on purpose? He wondered, hoping. The fleeting contact of her soft, warm fingers delighted him and the blue-green color on her nails intrigued him. As they both stood up and she handed him the papers she had picked up, she laughed. *A friendly laugh,* he wanted to believe, *not a laugh making fun.*

"I guess I'll see you tomorrow then," she said.

He nodded, grinning, speechless, and then watched her walk away.

The remainder of the day, Todd sat through what seemed to be extra-long, agonizingly boring classes, annoyed that his teachers expected him to pay attention. His mind could not hold onto any thoughts except those of tomorrow's clinic. He had already been looking forward to this clinic, his first time to actually participate. Two years ago when he had enough experience jumping to participate, there had not been room. Last year, he had the flu and his mother wouldn't let him out of the house. Tomorrow, not only did he get to ride, but the thought of Melody watching intensified his excitement.

Visions of galloping over the cross-country course, brilliantly clearing each jump with Melody watching awestruck, filled his mind. Alternately, he imagined disaster where his horse refused, or even worse, falling off and landing in mud, humiliated with Melody standing nearby laughing.

But one image troubled him the most. He visualized the field of riders on their beautiful, well-bred horses, and then pictured himself on Dune. How degrading to be mounted on an old nag among the elite of equines. *If only I could ride Felicity….*

It bothered him that he felt ashamed of Dune, for he did like the mare and was beginning to recognize what River appreciated about her. His last lesson riding Dune had been one of the best lessons in quite a while. He had obediently been practicing on his trail rides using more leg and lightening his hands as River had told him. Then in his lesson he had found Dune amazingly responsive to his legs. He had been so proud when River had praised him over and over on how well he was communicating with Dune. Then River let him take Dune over a jumping course including two jumps over three feet, the highest he had ever jumped. How exciting it had been to ride the bold mare who obviously enjoyed jumping and knew what she was doing!

"You get along well with her," River said as Todd began cooling down. "I think she'll be good for you to ride in the clinic."

"You want me to ride Dune?" Todd tried to hide his reactive disappointment.

Apparently River detected that reaction for he frowned and folded his arms. "You could ride Fala but you'll have to stay on the novice course. I don't want her jumping at any higher level. If you want to ride training level it will have to be Dune." When Todd's face still bore a sunken expression, he added, "Todd, she's very capable. She could easily take you to intermediate level."

"Um…what about Felicity?" Todd asked. River had let him ride Felicity a few more times on the trail when River had been able to ride along on a horse with a calm temperament. Tess had also given him a few more jumping lessons on the mare. He thought that meant Tess and River both believed he could handle her.

"No, Todd, she needs a very confident rider and you don't have the experience yet to manage her on an outside course," River said with finality.

"Okay, I'll ride Dune," he said in resignation. When River's frown did not smooth out and he set his mouth firmly before turning to walk away, Todd knew River was disappointed in him. Regret filled him that he hadn't been able to muster up outward enthusiasm over Dune because he very much wanted River's approval. But it didn't change the fact he believed he could handle Felicity, and that's who he wanted to ride.

The thought of Melody seeing him on Dune continued to plague his thoughts. River had said he could ride Fala, and Fala was a very attractive black Arabian. But then he would only be able to take the novice jumps. *What will Melody think when other riders, including Brooke and Mindy, are taking much more challenging jumps and I only get to take the easy ones?* Besides, if he rode Fala he knew River would be mad at him about that, even though he said he could ride Fala instead of Dune. Throughout the day he debated with himself, *Dune and River's approval but embarrassed in front of Melody? Fala, so I won't be embarrassed, but River disappointed and Melody thinking I'm not as good a rider as Brooke or Mindy?* At the end he always concluded, *if only I could ride Felicity.*

River would be gone all weekend, having left this morning to try out for Jack McCall. *Maybe I could ask Tess...*it became a nagging idea. Tess didn't pay that much attention to Todd and she just might say yes if he asked to ride Felicity. Then he would be riding with Tess's permission and she could tell River how well he did on Felicity and what a good match they were. He was confident that would become evident if he rode her in the clinic.

Early Saturday morning, Gwen Marshall dropped Todd off at the stable. Riders who didn't board at Pegasus were already pulling in with horse trailers and unloading their mounts. Inside the stable,

Brooke and Mindy groomed their horses in the crossties, chatting with their usual animation. He greeted them cheerfully, and before he lost his nerve, went back outside to find Tess.

He found her listening to the mother of one of the riders who trailered in, diplomatically nodding her head as the mother essentially told Tess how to coach her daughter. He waited with growing anxiety for the conversation to end. Finally, the mother seemed satisfied and went over to the trailer to help her daughter get her horse ready. With a sigh of relief, Tess turned away.

"Uh, Tess." He stepped alongside her. "Do you think I could ride Felicity today?"

She looked at him with an expression as if trying to remember something about him. "Who did River want you to ride?" she asked.

"Dune, but he's not here and I was going to ask him if I could ride Felicity instead."

"I don't care, ride who you want," Tess replied distractedly, her thoughts obviously elsewhere.

"Okay, thanks," he said and quickly retreated back into the stable before she could change her mind, his heart thumping with excitement. He found Felicity in her stall, pacing and tossing her head impatiently. Manuel and Enrique were starting to lead the horses that weren't being used in the clinic out to paddocks or pastures for the day. Many of the horses, anxious to get out of their stalls and worried they might be forgotten, acted up waiting their turn. It didn't concern Todd that Felicity was already excited. He led her out to the one empty crosstie bay and began to groom her.

"You're riding Felicity today?" Brooke asked.

"Yeah, this is going to be fun. You rode last year in the clinic, didn't you?" Todd asked, wanting to move the conversation away from the fact he was riding Felicity.

Brooke, with Mindy chiming in, chattered on about last year's clinic and what they expected today.

Candace, one of the adult borders, rounded the corner leading her mare Moonshadow, and eyed the full crosstie bays.

"Hi," Mindy greeted. "We'll be out of here in just a sec." The two girls bridled their horses and led them away.

Candace led her horse into the vacated bay next to Todd. They greeted each other in a friendly manner, but Todd was relieved when Candace kept her attention on getting her horse ready and he didn't have to keep up a conversation.

Felicity was more fidgety than usual, sensing the heightened activity and aware of strange horses outside in the stable yard. She shifted her feet, pawed with a foreleg, and tossed her head impatiently as Todd groomed and tacked her up.

"She's quite excited today," Candace commented as Felicity emitted a high, ear-shattering neigh.

"Yeah, all the strange horses around. Well, see you down at the field," he said to Candace as he finished with Felicity's bridle and led her away.

"Hey, settle down," Todd coaxed as Felicity pranced alongside him on the way down the hill, frequently trotting in front of him, raising her head and huffing in loud, short snorts. She held her tail high and a few times kicked out, tugging at the bridle reins. This was the most high-strung he had ever seen her. A small shiver of apprehension ran down his spine. *Maybe she is more than I can handle.* She had never been this excited when he rode her in a lesson or on the trails. He swallowed down his fear for it was too late now to change horses, and he believed (hoped) she would settle down after he warmed her up. Most of the riders were already mounted and beginning to warm up along the perimeter of the field.

A handful of spectators had gathered under the shed with folding chairs and blankets, and some with thermoses of hot drinks. He saw Jodi, her tall head standing out, and he looked for Melody. He spied her next to her twin, looking adorable in a faux fur jacket with a matching hat and colorful scarf and mittens. Even from this distance he noted the rosiness of her cheeks in the fresh morning air.

At the mounting block, Felicity would not stand still, constantly shifting away or stepping forward. Todd was just about to try and mount her from the ground when Jodi and Melody approached.

"Hi, Todd," Melody sang out cheerfully. The tone of her voice startled Felicity, and she spun away from where Todd had stepped up to her shoulder, forcing him to stumble backwards to keep his balance.

"You're riding Felicity?" Jodi asked, her eyes wide in surprise.

"Yeah…hey, do you think you could hold her head while I mount? She is really excited with all these strange horses here."

"Sure," Jodi agreed.

Todd led Felicity back to the mounting block and then Jodi held her head, trying to soothe her with soft words. He stepped onto the block and swung his leg over, having to practically leap onto Felicity's back as she moved her hindquarters away.

"River said you could ride Felicity?" Jodi asked. When Todd ignored her question she stated as if suddenly realizing, "River doesn't know."

"Tess said I could ride her," Todd replied defensively, quickly gathering the reins into a tight hold. Then for a brief moment, he met Jodi's eyes with a pleading expression. "Don't tell River. Let me tell him."

"Tess!" Jodi snorted. "You're an idiot, Todd."

Maybe, but he was committed now, and he moved Felicity away from the block, hoping once he got her trotting around the field he would regain control.

But Felicity did not want to trot. She jigged and swirled her head, crow-hopped and fought to gallop. He gave in, hoping the faster gait would deplete some of her energy and settle her down. She did not settle down. She wanted to race with the other horses and his arms ached trying to hold her in. This was more than he had bargained for. She had never been this unruly on his trail rides!

"Riders, over to me," Tess called out through a megaphone. She stood at the edge of the field, watching the riders warming up.

As the other horses came down to a trot and walk, Felicity at last responded to Todd's hard pull on the reins and abruptly slowed down. He noticed Tess eyeing the mare with a look of disapproval as they joined the others. He didn't blame her, for Felicity's coat was already slick with sweat and her sides were heaving from her exertion. A few of the other horses had broken a sweat and also seemed in heightened spirits. But none were drenched and blowing to the extent of Felicity. Todd felt ashamed. At least Tess didn't say anything and turned her attention to the group.

"River is in California with Jack McCall," Tess announced. "If you don't know who Jack is, he has coached many riders to qualify for the Olympic team." The riders and spectators appropriately exclaimed over the news that River might ride in the Olympics. Then Tess continued, "River usually starts the clinic with a demonstration ride, but today Kate Ramsey will ride the first course." She then pointed out the obstacles for the first round and Kate moved her horse Jubilee, onto the course.

One by one, the others took the same obstacles after Kate. By the time it was Todd's turn, he felt as if Felicity had finally calmed down, and he breathed out in relief as he moved her forward. She readily picked up the canter as he circled before the first jump, an easy round log. She sailed over, but on landing, she unexpectedly bolted, pulling at the reins, and she rushed over the remaining jumps, her head high as Todd fought for control. He did manage to keep her on the correct course, but he knew he never had control and was only able to bring her down to a trot by making a tight circle after the last jump.

"You are letting her rush," Tess commented when he rejoined the group. "She can manage at these low heights, but when you start getting over three feet, she needs more length to her stride, especially when you ride a combination. She'll need her hind end impulsion and she can't do it with her neck in the sky. You need to be the one in control. It looked to me as if Felicity set the pace on that round."

Todd nodded. It was true, she was more than he could manage today. This was different than Felicity shying at something on the trail and trying to bolt. He had enjoyed her high spirits then, for he had always been able to calm her. But she was not calming down today. This was a different feeling, this tight, pent-up energy, and her excitement seemed to be escalating. She was in control and he admitted to himself, he was scared.

"This time I want you to follow each other in a line and keep three horse lengths in between. This will help you learn to set the pace and adjust your horse's stride. You're going to take a circular course of six jumps, starting with the log, then the coop, the ditch, the rail fence, and finish with the barrels." Tess gestured with her hand in a circular wave, pointing out the jumps. "Beginner novice and novice riders, take the lowest sections of the obstacles and jump the ditch at the narrow end. The rest of you, follow Kate. If you can't rate your horse and he crowds the horse in front of you, I want you to pull out and circle back to the end of the line. Stay safe! Kate, you lead out."

Todd found himself in the middle of the line and struggled to keep Felicity three horse lengths behind the one in front. After the first jump when she landed with a buck, pulling the reins from his hands and he out of balance over her neck, she was rapidly closing the distance between her and the horse ahead. He barely had time to sit back and with a hard jerk, pulled her head to the side and out of the line. He could hear Tess yelling through her megaphone, "Todd, circle!" He managed to get Felicity to the back of the line but now they were way behind the others and Felicity took off at a mad gallop to catch up.

"Slow her down! Don't let her rush!" He heard Tess yelling at him.

I'm trying! He clutched at the reins, his heart racing in terror and tried to steer Felicity straight on to the coop. Everything River had taught him about how to manage a runaway horse fled his mind along with his fleeing mare. He had stiffened his back and leaned over her neck rather than sitting deep with his weight back in the saddle. He gripped the reins in a persistent tight hold, rather than giving and taking or even resorting to a pulley rein and getting her to yield on a circle.

Felicity jumped the coop in a wide arc, and again Todd found himself thrown onto her neck. His hands had frozen on the reins in terror with fistfuls of her mane as well. He could not stop Felicity careening after the other horses, her ears laid flat. Her focused attention was to 'catch up'. Todd's focused attention was to 'not fall off'. All thoughts of showing off in front of Melody had long vanished.

The ditch loomed ahead, a dark crevasse with stakes at each end to mark its location. He had jumped this same ditch on Fala and he knew Felicity had jumped it many times. Even though he was supposedly not doing the novice course, he tried to steer her to the narrow end of the ditch. But Felicity saw no reason to go over the ditch at all, and she resisted by veering to the other end, intending to cut across the field to reach the herd. Todd managed to jerk one rein, trying to steer her back in line to the ditch and stay on course. Felicity twisted her neck up and swung her hindquarters away from the rein at the same time Todd pressed with his heels. She leapt forward in a twisting motion, but out of balance. Her foot caught at the edge of the ditch. She stumbled forward to her knees, throwing Todd off and to the side. His head hit against the sturdy side stake with a resounding whack and his body slipped, tipping his head down into the ditch. Pain seared up his back. Darkness descended. In his mind he cried out, *don't shut me in!*, just before everything went black.

"Todd, you have a visitor," Gwen announced, tapping on Todd's bedroom door.

Todd made a sound, but did not turn his gaze away from his window where he had been staring forlornly at a tree in the backyard, studying each one of the new buds as if he could make them blossom with his will. His dog Brownie, curled at his side with his head on Todd's lap.

His door opened and Gwen asked, "It's Jodi; can she come in?"

Todd turned his gaze from the window, moving slowly so as not to increase the throbbing of his head. He frowned as Jodi limped into the room.

"Hey, Todd," she greeted hesitantly, unsure of her reception. She looked briefly over her shoulder when Gwen softly closed the door and waited until she heard retreating footsteps before trying again. "How's it going?"

"Hey," he greeted from where he lay propped against pillows on his bed.

She looked down at her fingers, twisting them together. "I heard you have a concussion."

"A mild one," Todd answered.

"Even wearing your helmet?"

"Yeah, they said it would have been worse without it. The impact still rattled my brains." He tried to smile, twisting up one corner of his mouth. "You want to sit down?"

"Okay," she agreed and looking around, finally sat down on the one chair, pulling it away from his desk to face him.

"How's Felicity?" Todd asked. All he remembered of yesterday was being carried away on a stretcher by paramedics, his body strapped down to a hard board so that he could not move. He knew he had been unconscious for only a few minutes, but he could only remember a blur of people around him, the arrival of paramedics and then his foster parents talking with a doctor in the emergency room. He hadn't paid attention to his head at that time, for his left arm burst with pain every time he tried to move it even a slight bit or something jolted his body. X-rays and a CT-scan were done before he was finally given pain medicine. After that, he remained in a groggy fog while the doctor explained that he had a mild concussion and a sprained wrist. Someone placed his arm in a sling with an ice pack, and soon after, his parents took him home. Then in the middle of last night he awoke with an excruciating headache and a throbbing arm.

He didn't call out for pain medicine but accepted the pain as his punishment, hoping pain might assuage some of his overwhelming remorse.

"Tess had the vet come look at her because she was limping when someone finally caught her, but she's okay. The vet says she may have strained a shoulder muscle. He recommended hand-walking her for a few days and three days of bute. I went there this morning and helped Enrique walk her. She's not even limping anymore.

"That's good," Todd said. "Is River back?"

"I heard he got back late last night, but I haven't seen him."

Todd shuddered, dreading River's reaction when he heard about Felicity. He only hoped he could somehow convey to River how sorry he was. "He's going to be so mad," he stated.

"Probably," Jodi agreed. She reached over to pet Brownie who thumped his tail in appreciation. They remained in silence, both visualizing an angry River. Eventually Jodi asked, "Are you going to school tomorrow?"

"No, the doctors say I have to be on bed rest for at least three days and I probably shouldn't go to school for a week or even longer. I'm only allowed up to the bathroom. My head feels like it's going to explode whenever I get up anyway."

"I'm sorry, Todd," Jodi said with genuine sympathy.

He smiled and suddenly he saw for the first time that Jodi had beautiful eyes, and wondered why he had never noticed before. *She always hides behind her hair, that's why*, he remarked to himself. "I'm an idiot," he said, ducking his head and hoping she hadn't noticed him staring at her eyes. His own hand absentmindedly scratched behind Brownie's ears.

"Yeah, you are."

He half smiled but kept his eyes on Brownie. "You don't have to agree with me."

She laughed and any tension between them eased. "Well, I just wanted to see how you are. I told your mom I'll pick up your assignments this week."

"Thanks," Todd said appreciatively.

"I guess I better get going." Jodi stood and moved to the door.

"Thanks," Todd repeated. Jodi turned the door knob but before she opened the door, he called out, "Jodi..." She looked back over her shoulder. "I'm not very good company right now, sorry. I really don't feel very good. But you're a really good friend. Thanks for coming."

Jodi smiled and then opened the door. "See you tomorrow." She walked out and closed the door quietly behind her.

A good friend. Todd wondered just when Jodi had changed from an annoying classmate to someone he actually liked to hang out with. "Pretty eyes and a nice smile, too. Don't you think so, Brownie?"

Brownie thumped his tail in agreement.

13 LIGHT AIDS

They say princes learn no art truly, but the art of horsemanship. The reason is, the brave beast is no flatterer. He will throw a prince as soon as his groom. - Ben Jonson

"Good morning," Tess greeted as River walked into her office Monday morning. She held her breath, studying his face for some evidence the trip had been successful. Her heart sank as she noted the shadows under his eyes and defeated expression.

"I'll go," he said, knowing that was what she wanted to hear. He looked down at his feet and then back up to meet her eyes.

"With Jack? Oh my, oh, River, that is so wonderful!" Her face lit up at his news. But when his did not change she asked, "What happened?"

"I like Jack McCall. He offered me one of the spots. I think I can learn some things from him."

"This makes me so happy. You can imagine how pleased Mrs. Galensburg will be!"

River nodded and turned to leave.

"Wait, River...."

He paused at the door.

"What's wrong?"

"Sierra broke up with me," he stated flatly, and opened the door.

"What? River, come back here…River!" She thought he was going to ignore her, but after a moment he pulled the door closed and turned to face her.

"Tess, I don't want to talk about it. She is just way beyond me in her life. She has so much more going for her and we probably should have broken up when she first went away to school."

"No…River…"

"I don't want to be here this summer when she comes home. That's why I'm willing to go with Jack, so you should be glad."

"No, I'm not glad about this…I know how much…River, please come in and sit down."

He shook his head. "I can't talk about this, okay Tess?" He looked at her with a pleading expression, and then he turned and fled the office.

Her heart erupted into pieces. Her stomach churned nauseatingly with shock and anger. *You little witch! What did you do to him? What happened?* Tess and Sierra had never been on a standing that could be called friendship, but over the past few years they had developed a tolerance for each other primarily because they both loved River. For Tess, he was the closest she had to a son.

He didn't give me a chance to tell him about Felicity. She knew no one had dared tell him last night.

Tess wasn't surprised when thirty minutes later River stormed back in. "Why didn't you tell me about Felicity?" he demanded.

"You left before I had a chance," she answered him calmly. "Sit down, River."

"I don't have time," he snapped back, and remained standing with his arms folded in irritation and his expression tight with anger.

"It was an accident. Felicity was very excited and Todd lost control. She was going too fast and she slipped at the ditch and stumbled. Todd fell off and hit his head against the post."

"Why was he even riding her?"

169

"He asked me if he could. He was doing fine with her in his jumping lessons, so I thought he could handle her."

"You know very well she gets over excited around other horses. It's one thing for Todd to ride her in a lesson or on the trail with me along, and totally different at a clinic or show."

"All right, River, it was a mistake. I'm sorry you weren't here to supervise Todd. Felicity is going to be fine."

River clenched his jaw to keep from shouting. *There's no point in even trying to talk to her.* He glowered at her and then turned to go.

"Todd has a mild concussion but he is going to be okay," Tess said to his retreating back, pointedly reminding him he had not asked about Todd. She noted his back stiffen but other than that, he did not acknowledge he had even heard.

Jodi was truly sorry Todd had been hurt, but his injury also meant he wasn't going to the stable and his mother was not picking him up. *If I can't be around the horses more than just my twice a week lessons, I'll go crazy*, she determined, after just two days of going straight home after school (and carpooling again with Melody and her ditzy friends).

"You know, that stable isn't too far out of my way," her father said Tuesday night. "I could pick you up on my way home."

"Really? You could?" Jodi responded, her heart leaping at this incredibly welcome offer.

"You'd be getting home much later, so as long as you keep your grades up and do your chores...." He glanced at his wife and they gave each other a conspiratorial look.

"I will...I can!" Jodi promised. At the pleased look on her father's face, it suddenly occurred to her, *maybe he really does love me!* That was an assumption she had not made in a long time.

On the next day that she had a lesson scheduled, Jodi headed as usual to bring in Morrison, when River intercepted her.

"Would you like to ride Dune today?"

"Dune?" Jodi's eyes widened in delight as a smile spread across her face.

River actually smiled back. "Yes, bring her in and groom her and I'll show you what tack to use."

"Okay!" Jodi's heart soared at the thought of riding one of her favorite horses. She gave the mare two extra carrot bits when greeting her. "I get to ride you today," she said as Dune crunched happily on the treats.

Dune placed her nose on Jodi's arm, and Jodi interpreted the gesture to mean, 'yes, I know, dear. Isn't it great?'.

She brushed the mare's tawny coat of all dirt and loose hairs. Like all the horses this time of year, the mare was shedding in handfuls. She picked out her feet, combed her thin mane and tail and then used a damp cloth to wipe her face and clean the crustiness from her nostrils. She stepped back to survey her work. There was actually a shine to Dune's sides, for the months of good feed and supplements and steady, progressive exercise had brought health to her coat and a more balanced appearance with the development of muscles.

"You are beautiful!" Jodi exclaimed.

Dune lowered her head and snorted.

"Don't argue with me," Jodi said with a soft laugh. "Your beautiful soul is shining through."

"She does have a beautiful soul," River said, coming out of the tack room carrying a saddle and pad.

Startled, Jodi turned and smiled at River. A very warm feeling spread from her core outward. River understood what she meant. They certainly shared a perception of what was inside a horse.

With River's help, they soon had Dune tacked up and ready for the lesson. In the arena, Jodi mounted and at River's instructions, began to walk the mare on a loose rein.

"Get to know how she feels and how she is different from Morris," he said. He waited for her to walk the perimeter in both directions before asking her to bring the mare to the center. "What do you think of her?"

"She's taller than Morris, but thinner in the sides. I like where the calves of my legs fit against her. I like how she walks with big steps without me having to kick at her all the time like with Morris."

"Yeah, I think she's a better fit for you," River said. He had actually been thinking about putting her up on Dune before he left for Sacramento, but then used her for Todd's lesson instead. Well, Todd wouldn't be riding her now. Already River noticed how Jodi's long legs came against Dune's sides in a position where she could use her calves effectively. "You don't mind the extra height?" Morris was only fourteen-two hands, just barely taller than a pony. Dune, at sixteen hands was six inches taller at the withers.

"When I first got on her I did feel a little dizzy," Jodi admitted. "But I just concentrated on how she felt. I even closed my eyes, because I already know her so well I knew she'd be okay. And that helped. I already feel as comfortable on her now as on Morris."

"Good, let's get started then." River attached the lunge line and sent Dune out on a circle at a walk. Jodi began her stretching exercises, the usual start of each lesson to relax and loosen her muscles. Next River asked her to try walk-halt-walk transitions. Since Jodi still had not used reins other than long and loose, she had to ask for the transitions with her seat and legs.

"She is amazing!" Jodi exclaimed, for with just a straightening of her back and holding legs against Dune's sides, the mare came to a square halt with her head in a neutral position. With a mere lightening of her seat and increased leg pressure, Dune stepped forward in her energetic walk.

"You are both amazing," River said, happy with the responsiveness of the mare and with Jodi's light aids. "Now, try some walk to trot and back to walk transitions."

These transitions had been a struggle for Jodi on Morrison, for the lazy old horse had dead sides from so many students banging against him with their heels, trying to get more energy out of him. Morris was great for beginners with his quiet manners and tolerance of unsteady riders, but it also meant he was unresponsive to light aids.

Jodi had not always been able to get Morris to trot. Often River had to help out by stepping toward the little bay's hind end or flicking the lunge whip.

As much as Jodi trusted Dune, she still felt apprehensive about trying to trot on her. Nevertheless, as the sweet mare walked with long strides, her head bobbing in rhythm, Jodi squeezed with her legs, and whispered, "trot." Dune obediently stepped up into a swinging, forward moving trot.

"Whoa!" Jodi cried out in alarm, grasping at the front strap. She had not expected such a prompt response or such energy in the trot. Feeling her rider losing her balance, Dune returned to the walk. "Wow, I did not expect that!" Jodi exclaimed.

"Yeah, not as much work as Morris, huh?" River acknowledged. "You know how quick she is and how she feels now, so try it again. Start out holding on if you want."

"Sorry, lady," Jodi whispered. "You did everything perfect. I think I'm ready for you this time. Shall we try again?" Jodi took in a deep breath and let it out as she engaged her core muscles in preparation, and touched the mare with her legs. Dune answered with the upward transition. Jodi concentrated on pushing her breath in and out with each contraction of her abdominal muscles in rhythm with the mare's big trot.

"Good," River called out.

For two circles, Jodi rode in rhythm with Dune's motion, but then fatigue overcame her. Jodi began to bounce out of balance, her seat catching air. But what a pleasant surprise when Dune gently transitioned to walk as she felt her rider no longer moving with her. "Wow, thank you," Jodi breathed out gratefully.

The remainder of the lesson Jodi practiced the walk-trot-walk transitions in both directions. She lost all trepidation, for every time she tired and began to lose the rhythm, Dune took care of her by transitioning down to walk. As fear no longer tapped into her energy, Jodi could actually ride longer before she tired.

Just before the end of the lesson, River asked her to try and post. Even without stirrups, Jodi managed a full circle, for Dune's energetic trot helped her rise out of the saddle.

"Well done, both of you," River complimented, "That's good for today."

Over the next few weeks, they repeated the same exercises. Jodi became more comfortable and confident on Dune, and able to trot without fatigue for as long as River requested. Then River said, "I think it's time for you to try stirrups." He walked over to where Jodi had brought Dune to halt and helped her maneuver both feet into the stirrups. Her left foot twisted out so that her heel was at right angles to Dune's belly.

"Let's just see how this works. You can use the back of your leg, but I'd like to see you try to move your leg so it's a little more parallel with her side. Don't force it, but just stretch a bit gradually. I bet in time you'll develop a better leg position."

After riding so long without stirrups, Jodi found them awkward and uncomfortable. But gradually she got used to them and found they certainly made it easy to post the trot, and provided some security when she lost her balance. She still rode much of her lesson without stirrups, but River said he wanted her comfortable in them before going on the trails.

"I'm going on the trail?" Jodi asked in amazement. It had never occurred to her that with her slow progress and disability that she would ever ride anywhere but in the security of an arena.

"Do you want to?"

"Yes, of course. Do you think I can?"

"I think Dune will keep you safe."

A few lessons later, River opened the gate of the outdoor arena and told her to walk Dune out. She obeyed, and he walked alongside as she turned the mare to cross the stable yard.

"Are you okay?" River asked.

"I don't know why, but I feel a little dizzy," Jodi confessed. "I think it's just psychological…being out in the open like this."

"You let me know if you don't think you can handle this," River said casually, apparently not concerned she felt dizzy.

His confidence helped. The vertigo passed and soon they walked through the lane and then started descending the hill. "Oh my," Jodi cried out fearfully and clutched at the front strap on the saddle. She had never ridden on uneven ground, and going downhill, she felt as if she was going to slip forward over Dune's head. But River placed a steadying hand on her leg and said nothing. In a few minutes, when Jodi didn't fall, her panic subsided. She relaxed her grip, sat up straight, and regained her balance. Dune had slowed her pace when she felt her rider tipping forward, but now she stepped out again with good energy.

"Well done," River praised.

They walked around the field, going up and down the shallow hills so Jodi could become accustomed to keeping her balance on uneven terrain.

A few days later, River took her out on the trail, walking alongside on foot the first time. "While I'm gone this summer, you can ride Dune on the trails like this. When you feel confident, you can even try a little trot on the flat stretches. When I return next fall, we'll see if you're ready to start cantering."

Jodi loved Dune with an intensity that sometimes hurt, and she was very, very happy.

During his convalescence, Jodi dutifully visited Todd every evening, walking the two blocks between their houses to bring him his assignments and tell him about the horses. She avoided mentioning River, for she sensed what Todd wanted to hear was that River had forgiven him and wanted him to come back. But that was news she could not give.

"River's been really gloomy lately," Jodi told him when Todd asked if River had said anything. "Manuel told me that he and Sierra broke up."

"What? Are you sure about that?"

"I think it's true because I overheard Tess saying something to that lady who leases Fiel."

"Wow, that's hard to believe. They've been going together almost as long as I've known them. What happened?"

"I don't know, I just heard they broke up, and everyone's kind of avoiding River. He's okay giving lessons and when he's riding, but otherwise, he doesn't want to talk to anyone."

This is going to make it extra hard to apologize. Todd felt bad for both River and Sierra, and wondered what could have gone wrong between two people who always seemed to get along so well and loved each other. But worse, he knew River was not going to be in a forgiving mood.

His closest friends at school called him a few times, offering sympathy and to update him on the latest gossip. A few came to visit, but didn't stay long when it was obvious Todd did not feel well. Even Melody stopped by once, but not alone, coming with Mindy and Brooke. The girls were full of sympathy over the accident, and gave no indication they thought it was his fault.

The most faithful visitor was Jodi. She came every evening and after telling him about the horses, often stayed to work on homework with him. He found himself looking forward to her visits and enjoying them. His other friends just made him tired.

The one person Todd wanted to see the most never came.

Twice he tried to reach River by phone to apologize, but only got his voicemail. He left apologetic messages that he hoped River would accept. But River never called him back.

It took two weeks before Todd did not feel dizzy when he first got up from a supine position and for his head not to throb. Gwen kept him home one additional week to be sure he was back to normal. Then he returned to school, a little behind in his work for it had been hard to do homework with a constant headache, even with Jodi's help.

"When you are caught up with your assignments, you can go to the stable," Gwen told him.

As much as Todd longed to be around the horses, he dreaded going to Pegasus. He knew he had to face River and apologize, but he was afraid. He felt such a fool. How stupid he had been and so over confident, thinking he was an accomplished rider. *I know nothing.*

Two more weeks and Todd had caught up with his school work. He no longer had an excuse not to face River. When he brought his progress report home on Friday, Gwen offered to drive him to the stable the next day. But Saturday morning, Todd woke up with a stomach ache and said he didn't feel well enough to go. He thought both his parents gave him a strange look.

Sunday, he woke again with a stomach ache, but by mid-morning, he accepted that it was caused by his nerves, and agreed to go when Gwen offered to drive him to the stable.

A horse whinnied as Todd stepped out of the car. The familiar smells of the stable wafted in and he sucked in a deep, pleasurable breath. It had been over a month since his accident. How he had missed this place! He walked in through the main stable doors to the crossties, hoping he might find River there.

"Todd, how nice to see you!" Kate greeted him. She had just finished placing the saddle on Jubilee's back, getting ready for a ride.

"Hi Kate."

"How are you feeling? Are you ready to start riding again?" she asked in a friendly manner.

"Not quite yet, but soon, I hope. Do you know where River is?"

"He's working with his filly in the round pen."

"Thanks." Todd gave Jubilee a pat and walked outside. From Kate's friendly greeting he guessed she didn't realize he was in trouble with River. Jodi knew, and probably Tess, and his parents knew he needed to apologize but they didn't know the reason why.

In the round pen, Todd saw Ysbryd, a four-year-old bay thoroughbred filly, cantering rhythmically at the end of the lunge line around River who stood facing away. Todd stopped at the gate and watched. He would let River see him first.

River turned with the filly, but when he faced the gate, he gave no indication he saw Todd. Using voice commands, he brought Ysbryd to trot, then back to canter a few times before he brought her all the way down to walk and halt. Then he reversed her direction, working her through walk, trot, to canter the other way, ignoring Todd. Finally the session ended. River brought the filly to halt, praised her lavishly and fed her carrot bits. Then he led her toward the gate.

He will have to speak to me now.

River glared at Todd as he opened the gate to lead Ysbryd out. He said nothing and did not stop.

"River, please," Todd called out to his back and then picked up his pace to catch up and walk alongside River. "I'm so sorry. I was stupid. I'm so ashamed," he blurted out.

At last, River halted. He turned to face Todd and finally spoke. But the words he said pierced Todd's heart as painfully as if he had actually shot an arrow. "I can't trust you, Todd. I cannot work with someone I can't trust."

Gwen did not know what Todd had done wrong, but she knew he had been upset about something more than just getting injured in the accident. He had told her he needed to apologize to River, and that she should wait for him in case things didn't go well.

When she saw Todd returning to the car with uncontrolled tears running down his face, she knew whatever Todd had done, River had not accepted his apology. *What could a fifteen-year-old do that was so unforgivable?*

"Todd?" she asked as he got into the car. She waited, allowing him to wipe the dampness away and get his face under control. He blew his nose and gave her a stricken look. "What happened?"

The story came out. Todd confessed how he had chosen to ride Felicity, even though he knew River had said 'no'. He even confessed how he had wanted to show off in front of Melody. "Yeah, I'm sure she thinks I'm really hot stuff now," he ended sardonically.

"That's it? River is mad at you for riding a horse he didn't want you to ride?"

Todd nodded.

"He can't forgive you for that?"

"Mom, you don't understand. River cares more about horses than people. Felicity could have been seriously hurt."

Frowning, Gwen studied Todd, a picture of dejection with his hunched shoulders and wiping his eyes and nose. Then she looked out the window and around the stable, trying to make sense of this. *Why is riding a forbidden horse an unforgiveable crime? Does River truly care for horses more than people?* She had known River ever since she and John had fostered him. She believed him to be a decent, caring young man. He had been like a big brother to Todd. She knew Todd looked up to River and that his approval was very important to him. River must know that as well. She could understand him being angry and that he might want Todd to have some punishment for his mistake, but Todd had already suffered a concussion and humiliation and he was obviously filled with remorse. How could River be so cold and hard?

"D-d-do you think you could talk to River?" Todd looked over at her pleadingly through reddened eyes. "Tell him how sorry I am?"

I could talk to River, she thought to herself, *use my influence for I know River thinks he owes John and me.* But she wanted River to truly forgive Todd, not because she asked him to. In some ways, this might even be a good lesson for Todd in facing the consequences of his actions. So she said, "Todd, do you really think that is the answer? I think you and River need to work this out between you. Maybe he just needs more time. I heard he broke up with Sierra and I'm sure that does not have him in the most forgiving of moods."

"That was a month ago."

"Not very long to recover from a broken heart. Now this is the first chance you've had to face him. Why don't you wait a couple weeks, and try again?"

"Two weeks? No horses for two weeks?" That seemed an eternity, especially since it had already been so long since he had touched a horse.

Every morning, Todd woke with a sick feeling in his stomach. *No horses....* How could he stand it? How much he had lost with his stupid, impulsive action! *What a way to impress a girl,* he scolded himself. At least Melody didn't reject him, but he was no farther along in any kind of a relationship with her. *But worst of all, no horses!*

On Monday after their history class, he caught up to Jodi and asked, "How are things at the stable?"

"Good," Jodi answered, surprised Todd had sought her out. Although he said hello to her when he saw her at school, and used to sit with her on the bus back when they both went to the stable together, they certainly were not in the same crowd. In fact, Jodi gave him a lot of credit for even acknowledging her in front of his friends. She could imagine they gave him grief about that.

Jodi's status at school had not changed. She had impressed all of her teachers with the improvement in her schoolwork, and may have risen in esteem in their eyes. But with her classmates, she was still just a crippled wierdo – an outcast.

"I tried to apologize to River yesterday. He is so mad at me. He kicked me out." It hadn't been Todd's intention to tell Jodi what happened, but for some reason, he found her sympathetic expression encouraging as she listened to him.

"Oh, Todd, I am so sorry." Now that Jodi had access to horses, she could not imagine life without them.

"I guess I deserve it," he said.

"No, you shouldn't have ridden Felicity, but I don't think you deserve banishment," she commiserated.

"Thanks, I don't know. How are your lessons going?"

"I'm riding Dune now," Jodi said, her face lighting up as she described to Todd her last few lessons.

The mention of Dune filled his heart with a heavy weight that settled achingly into his stomach. But he eagerly listened to Jodi talk about her lesson, vicariously sharing her experience.

"Do you want me to say anything to River?" Jodi offered.

"No, thanks. I don't think it will help. My mom told me to wait a couple weeks and try again."

"I guess he's not handling breaking up with his girlfriend very well. Even Manuel says River is so gloomy he doesn't like to be around him. The only time he looks happy is when he's working with a horse."

"Well, they were together for a long time. I'm sorry about that, too."

"Todd, come on. I'm starving," one of Todd's friends that he normally ate with in the cafeteria called out to him.

"Thanks, Jodi, it helps to hear about horses. I'll talk to you later."

"Bye." Jodi watched him join his friend with her heart aching in sympathy. How horrible to be banished from Pegasus!

It got to be routine for Todd to wait for Jodi after history to ask her about the horses. One day he said, "Hey, if you ever want someone to eat lunch with…well, I'll eat with you."

"Todd, that is very sweet. You're a good friend." Jodi was deeply touched. She understood much by the fact he said, 'I'll eat lunch with you', rather than, 'you can eat lunch with me'. He could not invite her to sit with him and his friends, for they would not accept her at their table. Yet his invitation indicated Todd's willingness to jeapardize his social status to eat with her. "But I take advantage of lunch to work on homework. It gives me more time at the stable." She definitely did not want to cause a rift between Todd and his friends, not when he didn't have access to horses to compensate.

"Okay, but anytime…."

"Thanks." She gave him a warm smile before she turned toward the library. She stopped once and looked back as Todd headed over to his friends. She noted the dissapproving looks on their faces. *Yep, there is no way his friends would accept me sitting at their table.*

Weeks passed, spring break passed, and in a month school would be out for the summer.

Hearing the news of Pegasus from Jodi, Todd did not feel encouraged that River had softened at all toward him. Several times his mother offered to drive him to the stable to talk to River, but he refused. He could not face that rejection again.

"Should I talk to River, or you talk to him?" Gwen asked her husband one night.

"No," John said after a few minutes of thinking it over. "I think River is being way too harsh, but I believe he has to want Todd to come back, and not do it out of obligation to us. Maybe we should find another place for Todd to take lessons."

The thought of riding someplace other than Pegasus caused another heavy stab of remorse to settle deep within Todd. But after thinking about it for a day, he decided it was better than not being around horses at all. He knew about Meadowood as another stable that gave lessons and suggested there.

14 MEADOWOOD

Dressage riding is not push-button riding, but putting the horse in a position physically and mentally that he will find it easy to do the movements. - Jane Kidd, *Practical Dressage*

"Are you looking for Virginia?" asked a little girl of perhaps nine or ten, in baggy riding breeches and pony-motif sweatshirt.

"Yes," Gwen replied. She and Todd stood in the stable yard at Meadowood, looking around.

"She's in the third stall over there." The girl pointed toward a row of stalls adjacent to a covered riding arena.

Just then a middle-aged woman with weather-beaten skin, brown hair pulled tightly back, and wearing riding breeches and muck boots strode forth and greeted, "Hi, you're Todd Marshall?"

"That's right, I'm supposed to have a lesson at three-thirty," Todd replied. "This is my mom, Gwen Marshall."

"Nice to meet you. I'm Virginia Maxwell. Welcome to Meadowood." She extended her hand to both of them. "Sarah," she turned to the little girl. "Can you take Todd to Willow and show him where the brushes are kept? If you'll come with me, Gwen, we can get the paperwork out of the way."

"Follow me," Sarah beckoned to Todd and led him toward the row of stalls. "Are you going to take lessons here?"

"Yeah," Todd replied, meekly following the little girl. As he looked around, he couldn't help comparing what he saw to Pegasus. Meadowood appeared to be a much lower scale place, a row of stalls by the covered arena and one other shed row of stalls. Beyond the stalls he could see some horses in two pens, and a large outdoor arena with some jumps and muddy footing from the spring rains.

"I just had my lesson. I've been riding for a year. I love riding. I can't wait to have a horse of my own," Sarah chatted. Apparently she did not expect Todd to comment. "Here's Willow." She stopped in front of a stall with a bay gelding inside. "The brushes are in the tack room. I'll show you." She led him to the end of the stalls and into a large room, really not much more than a shed, with racks of saddles, a row of bridles hanging from hooks, several buckets with grooming supplies, a pile of horse blankets in a corner, and various other pieces of tack and equipment. Sarah picked up one of the buckets and handed it to Todd.

"Where do I take Willow to groom him?" Todd asked.

"In the stall," Sarah answered. "Here are the boots." She led him to a low shelf filled with pairs of splint boots and bell boots. She handed him a set of the splint boots in a large size.

"Thanks." Todd returned to the stall with the bay horse inside tied to a ring attached to the back wall of the stall. "Hey there," he spoke softly to the horse as he entered.

The bay turned his head to watch Todd approach. When the boy didn't offer him a treat he lowered his head and stood patiently as Todd came up, stroked his neck, and began to groom him.

"Here you go," Virginia said, coming up to the stall about ten minutes later, carrying a saddle, pad, and bridle. "Good, you've got his splint boots on." She entered the stall and helped Todd tack up Willow. "Your Mom says you've ridden before. I can see you know how to groom and tack up a horse. How long have you been riding?"

"About four years."

"Great, what have you done?" She handed the reins to Todd and then led the way out of the stall to the arena.

"I've been doing combined training. I competed the past two seasons at beginner novice and then novice level."

"Uh huh, where were you taking lessons?"

"At Pegasus Equestrian Center," he said, dreading having to explain why he no longer trained there.

"Pegasus, that's a great place. Why aren't you still riding there?"

"Um," Todd looked ahead at the approaching arena. He knew this question would come up and he didn't want to lie. He swallowed and admitted, "I had a falling out with the instructor."

"I see," Virginia said. "With River or Tess?"

"Um, River."

Todd could feel her eyes on him, boring into the back of his head through his riding helmet. *She's going to ask what happened.*

Finally, Virginia unlocked her eyes and merely commented, "Umhmm, well, I've heard he can be difficult, especially lately."

They reached the arena and Virginia opened the gate for Todd to lead Willow inside. "Willow is twenty-two now," she said. "He still goes quite nicely and I usually start students on him because he's safe, until I have a chance to evaluate how well you ride. Do you mind?"

"No, he's fine," Todd said. He led Willow to the mounting block, checked the girth, and then settled into the saddle.

"How's the stirrup length?" Virginia asked, eyeing him from the front as Todd moved Willow away from the block.

"Feels good for flat work," Todd said, pushing his heels down, then standing in the stirrups to let his weight sink back down into proper position in the saddle. *And it feels so good to be back on a horse!*

"Yes, looks good. Go ahead and walk on a long rein, both directions. You're warming up and getting to know each other."

It took a lot of leg to keep Willow walking forward. Todd figured this horse was a lot like Morris, a bit on the lazy side and dead-sided from many beginner riders. He concentrated on what River had taught him. Use leg, ease up and give Willow a chance to respond. If no response, more leg, if no response, a cluck or tap with the whip. Ease up as soon as he picks up the pace. Repeat, repeat, repeat.

"Good, Todd," Virginia said. "Okay, rising trot, go right onto a twenty-meter circle at this end."

Again, Todd used legs, then a touch of the whip to get the old horse into a lumbering trot.

"More leg," Virginia called, just as Todd put legs on and pushed. He applied legs, eased up when Willow increased his stride, pressed again as Willow flagged in his steps and touched with the whip. Willow stepped up into a swinging rhythm, realizing his rider knew what he was doing and there was no getting off easy in this lesson.

"Good, keep that pace - one-two, one-two," Virginia called out.

It took a lot of leg to keep Willow trotting at a steady rhythm. Even as the old horse increased the tempo, it still felt lumbering to Todd, more of a quickening without energy. He squeezed the reins, trying to get Willow to lower his head into his hands. The bay did drop his head but he still felt stiff and he could not feel any roundness through his seat. *Hollow!* The word came to him, and he understood the difference now, for the horses he rode at Pegasus knew how to work off their hindquarters into a rounded frame.

"Good, Todd, keep pushing him," Virginia said.

This is not good, Todd thought, and wished the instructor would tell him what he needed to do to get Willow off his forehand.

"More leg…now go large. Push, Todd, push!"

I am pushing, he thought, kicking repeatedly now at Willow's sides just to keep him in a trot that was more than just a slow jog. He tapped him with the whip and Willow picked up his pace for a few strides before slowing down again.

"Good, bring him back onto the circle here. He's very stiff, Todd. Shorten the reins and get him into a rounder frame."

The lesson continued with Virginia directing him through various gymnastic exercises, trying to get the old horse to move out with more impulsion. But Todd had learned enough from River to realize taking hold of the reins and trying to hold Willow's head to make him round did not work. The school horses at Pegasus were all ridden by River a few times a week to keep them responsive to aids. Now on a dead-sided, hard-mouthed horse, Todd realized how lucky he had been to ride good horses under an expert instructor.

"Okay, let's try canter. With this old boy you will need to bend him to the outside to get him to pick up the correct lead. Go ahead from the trot."

It took several attempts to get Willow to canter rather than trot faster. Todd knew bending to the outside was not the best way to ask for the correct lead. River never allowed that in his lessons. But Todd obeyed Virginia's instructions, and finally, with her chasing after Willow with a lunge whip, they got him into a lumbering four-beat canter.

Finally, the forty-five minute lesson ended. Todd was happy to be back on a horse – any horse. But over and over during the lesson, he realized how much he had lost with his falling-out with River.

"I have another horse I think you can handle. He's recovering from an injury but maybe in a month he'll be back in work," Virginia said, watching Todd care for Willow after the lesson. "I'm afraid you're a little too tall for the school ponies."

She really doesn't have a good horse for me to ride, Todd realized. He thanked her anyway, and then went back to the car where Gwen waited. "How did it go?" she asked, trying to sound cheerful. But she noticed Todd's glum expression.

"Okay," he answered, and gave her a weak smile. Inside, his chest ached with hollowness. *I have lost so much, and it's my own fault.*

It was the end of May, only two more weeks before summer vacation. Jodi hummed happily as she brushed Dune, getting her ready for a lesson. She loved how the mare stood with her head low, flicking her ears in pleasure at the sound of Jodi's voice, and occasionally turning her head to glance at her from her one eye. The winter coat had finally shed out, and Jodi followed the grooming brush with her hand, thrilling at the sleek silkiness of neck and sides. "You are beautiful," she interjected several times into her humming. Dune blinked and Jodi interpreted that as agreement.

"I really think your mane is much thicker," Jodi said, working an oily cream into Dune's mane. Jodi, who had never been interested in make-up or beauty products for herself, spent much of her allowance on horse care products to use on Dune – shampoos, mane and tail conditioners, coat enhancers, and special grooming tools to stimulate healthy hair growth. She moved back to the mare's hindquarters and worked the cream into Dune's tail, beginning at the base and using her fingers to spread it all the way to the ends. "All that frizziness is totally grown out." Jodi stepped back, admiring the healthy long tail hairs. She knew that all the horses at Pegasus were virtually worm-free, which reduced the itchiness that caused many horses to rub their tails. Now she admired the lustrous appearance of Dune's black tail that had grown past her hocks. She laughed when Dune swished it just a little back and forth, as if showing it off.

Horse hooves sounded from the stable entrance and Dune lifted her head and whickered in greeting as a woman appeared with Fala, and led her into the crossties.

"Hi, Jodi," she greeted.

"Hi, Brenda, how was your lesson?"

"Fine," Brenda answered, but there was a note of gloom in her tone.

Jodi glanced over and noted the deep crease between Brenda's eyes, and wondered if something bad happened in the lesson. She had heard the mumblings that River was extra critical lately, although she hadn't noticed that in her own lessons. But maybe he had said something? She knew Brenda was one of the students who helped clean stalls a few days a week in exchange for her lessons. She didn't have a horse of her own and Jodi had always felt a certain sense of shared deprivation with her. Instead of turning her attention back to Dune, she asked, "What's wrong then?"

"It was a great lesson, one of the best," Brenda said as she pulled off Fala's tack. "It's the first time I've been able to ride a serpentine almost entirely off my seat and leg. Why is it so hard to give up the inside rein?" She looked over the back of Fala at Jodi. "But when you do, it's amazing! For the first time I made the connection of how turning with the inside rein can cause your horse to get stiff in the shoulder. When I used my inside leg to push her into the outside rein then wow, suddenly Fala rounded her back and moved onto the arc of my figure with her shoulders in front of me!" This time Brenda was able to hold onto her smile.

"Awesome," Jodi said. "I've been working on that as well. Then you just let her get straight in the middle and shift your aids to change the bend…"

The two discussed their lessons, deeply engrossed in their mutual experiences. Then Jodi remembered how unhappy Brenda had seemed and wondered again what went wrong.

Brenda's face clouded again and she said, "My husband applied for a new position in his company and we heard yesterday that he's been accepted. It's a promotion and a very good opportunity for him."

"Uh, congratulations?"

"We have to relocate. I didn't realize the position meant he will have to work out of their corporate headquarters. We have to move to Houston."

"Oh…." *So, she will have to move. Is that such a tragedy?*

"I've taken lessons for years, but until I came here and met River, I really didn't make much progress. This is the best stable. Where am I ever going to find such an opportunity?"

"I see…yeah, I'm sorry, Brenda. I mean…"

"I should be happy for my husband. I am happy." Brenda managed to smile. "Thanks for listening."

"There's got to be other good riding instructors out there," Jodi offered.

"I'm sure there are. I don't deal well with change. Things will probably work out just fine. At least I've learned enough from River to know how to pick a good instructor."

Jodi offered more sympathy as she tacked up Dune and then led her away.

The next morning, Jodi woke up before her alarm. It seemed she rarely needed the alarm anymore since she had so much to look forward to each day. As she pushed the covers off, an idea suddenly came to her.

She had no lesson that day, but as usual, she took the bus after school to Pegasus. She found River working a horse in the outdoor dressage arena, and she settled on a side bench to watch. When he finished, she met him at the exit to walk with him back to the stable.

"I heard Brenda is moving away," she started cautiously.

"Yeah, her husband got transferred," River said. "She's not too happy about moving."

"I don't blame her. I feel bad for her. She's really going to miss you." Jodi gathered up all her hopes and then asked, "Has anyone been hired to take her place cleaning stalls?"

River glanced at her sideways and asked, "Are you interested?"

"Yes, totally!"

"I don't think Tess has hired anyone. I'll check, and if not, you can work with Manuel and if he thinks you can do it, it's okay with me."

"Thank you, thank you so much. I can do it!" Jodi often helped Enrique clean stalls on weekends when she was able to get a ride to the stable early enough. She enjoyed the work and she liked hanging out with Enrique, practicing her Spanish.

When she told Manuel, he laughed. "You already do good cleaning. I tell River."

"Thank you!"

Manuel just laughed again.

The next day River told her she could replace Brenda who would be leaving about the time summer vacation started. She would clean stalls every other weekend, and every Tuesday and Thursday.

As the traditional *Pomp and Circumstance* blared out from the school's orchestra, Sierra exited with her graduating classmates, many of them throwing their caps in the air, whooping and hollering. She caught sight of her mother with her boyfriend Ron, and her best friend Allison, all waiting for her with wide smiles on their faces. Sierra waved her diploma and pushed her way through the milling throng to join them.

"I'm so proud of you," her mother said for probably the one-hundredth time as she hugged Sierra, her eyes wet and shining.

They moved with the crowd, stopping twice at strategic locations for photos of Sierra and her mom, Sierra and Allison, then all three of them, and Sierra holding up her diploma.

"There you are!" Sean pushed through the throngs to reach Sierra. "I want you to meet my sister and my parents."

Not far behind came the rest of the Casey family. They introduced everyone around, and then took more photos; this time Sierra and Sean together.

"I'm starving," Shannon, Sean's teenaged sister exclaimed, having quite enough of congratulations and photo taking. Like most teenagers, her patience quickly ran out when attention was focused on someone other than herself.

Sean tugged playfully on the ends of Shannon's hair, a gesture that annoyed his little sister, at the same time that she loved any attention from her big brother. "Meet you at the restaurant," Sean called as his sister grabbed his hand from her hair but didn't let go, pulling him away.

"Okay," Sierra waved after him and his retreating family. "It's going to take us awhile to get out of here."

"No worries, we'll get there when we all get there!" He waved and then turned as Shannon tugged hard.

"Sierra, wow; so that's Sean!" Allison exclaimed as she walked alongside her best friend following Pam and Ron blazing ahead through the crowd.

"That's Sean," Sierra confirmed.

"You never mentioned that he is so good-looking!"

"I didn't? I must have," Sierra said. Allison knew all about Sierra's break-up with River; had listened empathetically for many nights while Sierra cried over the phone.

"You didn't do anything wrong," Allison assured her over and over. "Sean kissed you; it's not your fault. I totally support you. If River won't believe you, if he doesn't trust you, well, that's no kind of relationship. You did the right thing to break up."

Although her mother didn't agree that Sierra had done nothing wrong, telling her, "You knew Sean was interested in more than just friendship. You should not have kept seeing him. Not only was it behind River's back, but if you had no intention of breaking up with River, then you were just leading Sean on, and that was not fair to Sean." Pam had not said these things to Sierra at first, her own heart breaking every time she listened to Sierra crying over the phone. But eventually, Pam felt it was her maternal duty to express her opinion.

But Pam agreed with Allison that River had over-reacted. The fact that he did not believe Sierra and did not trust her was reason enough to break up. Eventually, both Pam and Allison encouraged Sierra, if she liked Sean at all, to continue the friendship.

"It sounds like Sean's always been open and honest with you, Sierra, about his feelings for you," her mother said. "You really can't blame him for kissing you...he's a guy, after all. And it sounds like you might have given him enough indication that he thought it was time."

Broken-hearted, for two weeks Sierra had ignored all Sean's many phone calls, and fled from him when he waited for her in places where he knew he could find her. Many times she came close to calling River, especially after lying awake thinking back over all the good times they had together, how much she had loved him. But whenever she heard the words in her head, *I used to trust you,* and remembered the look of what she interpreted as disgust on his face, anger rushed in. How he had hurt her! How could he not trust her after so many years together?

The anger was easier to bear than the deep, deep hurt. Eventually, Sierra gave in to the advice of her mother and best friend. The next time Sean waited for her at the door of her last class, she didn't turn away.

They had been going out ever since. She let him kiss her goodnight, but that was all. She was not ready for anything more intimate. She had agreed to meet his family on graduation day, and introduce him to hers.

Sean was staying in Sacramento for the summer quarter, starting to work on his graduate degree. He asked her to stay, but she had said, "Sean, I don't want our relationship based on the rebound. If what we have is worth anything, it will last through being apart all summer. We'll stay in touch and then I'll see you next September."

She liked Sean. She always had a good time with him. But since breaking up with River, she still experienced an underlying feeling of guilt. She was not totally innocent when it came to that kiss. She had been curious. Well, now her curiosity had been satisfied. She liked kissing Sean, but she constantly had to push away comparing his kisses to those from River. That always led to the realization of how much she missed River's kisses.

Graduated – a bachelor's degree! The prestigious event had Sierra high with excitement and a sense of proud accomplishment - one step closer to her goal of becoming a veterinarian. Her spirits soared on the flight home from Sacramento, with her mother and Ron in the seats across the aisle, and Allison next to her. How great it felt to look over at her mother, constantly gazing at her with love and pride. How wonderful to be with her best friend again, catching up on their lives, and encouraging each other in their dreams, their conversation filled with laughter. Tomorrow, she would sleep as long as she wished, and then she would see Fiel!

It wasn't until Sierra at last snuggled down in her own bed her first night at home, that unexpectedly, a rush of tears flooded her eyes. Her high spirits crashed, replaced by an ache-filled vacuum as she mourned the absence of the one person who should have been there for her graduation.

15 SUMMER ACTIVITIES

(In the canter), most people have a tendency to pull back on the inside rein, which may disengage the quarters and this is the very last thing which the horse needs. – Sylvia Loch, *Dressage in Lightness*

"I know you've talked about it. So when are you and Ron getting married?" Sierra asked her mother the next morning. She sat at the kitchen table in the cottage she had lived in since middle school, a very small two-bedroom rental on the same property as the landlords. Both Sierra and her mother loved the small place, nestled within trees and surrounded by farmer's fields, and in walking distance to Pegasus.

Several years ago Pam Landsing had earned her registered nurse's license and had been working in the local hospital ever since. She could now afford a bigger place or even buy her own house. Nevertheless, she continued to rent the cottage, explaining to her daughter, "When you graduate and start veterinary school will be soon enough. I don't want to rush into anything."

Now Sierra wondered if her mother stayed on in the cottage more because she was waiting to marry Ron, a pharmacist she had met while still a nursing student. It made sense for the two of them to buy a house together.

Sitting across from Sierra, Pam looked at her over the rim of her coffee mug. A sly smile slipped onto her face. "We have talked about getting married," Pam admitted.

"I knew it!" Sierra cried out gleefully. "So, what are you waiting for?"

Still smiling, Pam set down her coffee and distractedly moved crumbs around on her breakfast plate. "First of all, I wanted you to be finished with school, just in case there were any hang-ups with your scholarship. I didn't want you suddenly to have two parents with two incomes to affect your chances of getting grants or loans."

"Mom, that's not a very good reason. Did you doubt that I could keep my grades up?"

"Of course not. It wasn't you I worried about as the reason to lose a scholarship. It's more the economy and rules always changing."

"But I've graduated, and I've earned even more scholarships. You don't have to worry about financing my education."

"Perhaps...oh, I am so proud of you," Pam said, now for perhaps the thousandth time.

"So, what's stopping you?"

"We also thought you and River planned to get married after he graduated next year," Pam said very softly. "We didn't want to overshadow that in any way, and also, once you and River were married, your parents' finances wouldn't affect you."

"But we're not getting married," Sierra stated with her mouth in a grim line. "I don't see any reason for you and Ron to wait." She forced a cheerful expression onto her face. "I'd like to see some romance have a happy ending, and who better than my own mother."

"Oh, kitten," Pam sighed. "Well, it was nice meeting Sean, and his family. He seems like a very nice young man. I'm happy you..."

"Mom, Sean is very nice," Sierra interrupted. "He's good-looking, he's smart, he treats me like I'm very special. He's perfect. Everyone thinks he's perfect and I'm so lucky to have him. But the truth is, I think I'm still in love with River. It's only been a few months. Why does everyone think I'm such a shallow person that I can get over someone I've been in love with since high school so easily?" Suddenly, like a teenager broken hearted over her first rejection, the flood of tears that had overcome Sierra last night, poured out again. She fell into her mother's arms and allowed her to comfort and soothe her, just as she had as a little girl.

A child's broken heart always ruptures that of the mother. Pam's heart ached now as it had when Sierra first sobbed over the phone to tell her she had broken up with River. But when Sierra had called a few weeks later, sounding cheerful, and announced she was going out with Sean, Pam had so hoped her daughter was on the way to recovery.

Pam had rejoiced in everything Sierra told her about Sean. She admitted to herself feeling a certain amount of relief over this new boyfriend. Pam liked River, had always liked him, and been glad for how happy Sierra had been with him. But deep inside, she had always had reservations about River, mostly because of his dysfunctional upbringing. Perhaps no parent thinks any person is quite good enough for one's own child. She had always hoped for someone more on Sierra's level of emotional strength and ambition. She thought Sean might be that person.

When Sierra had introduced her to Sean yesterday, Pam's hopes had soared. Here was the kind of young man she had always visualized for her daughter. In the short time she had spent around Sean and his family yesterday, she perceived him to be a good and kind person from a wonderful supportive and loving family. She had watched how he looked at Sierra, how attentive he was to her, and she had felt satisfied.

Time, she thought now as she hugged her daughter. *She needs more time, and if Sean is the right one for Sierra, he'll be patient and give her that time.*

"Maybe I should have stayed in Sacramento," Sierra mumbled to herself as she changed into riding clothes. She hadn't expected her own emotional outburst last night or again this morning. She thought she had pushed her feelings for River far away into the depths of her being. It must have been the familiarity of home that had conjured them back out.

It didn't help that she dreaded going to Pegasus today instead of looking forward to seeing Fiel, the other horses, and her friends as she usually did at the beginning of summer. First, she would have to talk to Tess and find out if she could even keep her horse at Pegasus any longer. She dreaded the meeting, for she and Tess had never been on the best of terms, and only because of River had they come to a tenuous friendship. *She probably hates me now!* She knew River had already left to spend the summer with Jack McCall, so at least she wouldn't have to face him.

The awkward thing, was since Delia Evans leased Fiel and took lessons from River, her horse needed to stay at Pegasus. What would Del do if she had to move Fiel to another stable?

These thoughts troubled her as she drove to Pegasus and parked her truck. She stepped out and breathed in deeply, looking around with her heart bursting with longing at this place she loved so well. Memories flooded her mind of snuggling with River after a day spent around horses, and of the plans they made together. They had planned to get married right after he graduated next year. She would only have three years of veterinary school left and River thought he could find work at a stable around Sacramento so they could be together.

They had planned to return to Pegasus. It was an ideal setting for the very best training stable and home for horses that would fulfill River's dream. Tess had promised when he graduated to make him head trainer, and allow him to buy in as a partner if he wished. Tess had even offered them a portion of the property to build a house. Dr. Patterson had many times offered Sierra an internship with him, implying she could join his practice.

Such beautiful, beautiful, childish, naïve, pipe dreams, she admonished herself. She steeled her nerves to face Tess, and proceeded with heavy steps to the office. She knocked, and opened the door a crack. "Tess?"

"Come in, Sierra," Tess beckoned from behind her desk.

Sierra stepped inside the door and stopped, gauging her reception.

"Sit down," Tess commanded. "Congratulations on finishing your bachelor's. I heard you graduated summa cum laude." she said, unsmiling.

"Thanks," Sierra replied, confused by the compliment. She walked gingerly over to the chair opposite Tess, and sat down.

"What happened?" Tess jumped right to the issue.

"What did River tell you?" Sierra asked in return, not sure where to start.

"He said you broke up with him. He said you are so beyond him and you deserve better."

"What?" Now she really felt confused. "Tess, we broke up because he doesn't trust me." *Did he not tell Tess he caught me kissing another man?*

"So, you are the one who broke up," Tess said it as a statement.

"Yes, well…he made me so angry. Do you know how it feels not to be trusted?"

"Do you really think he doesn't trust you, Sierra?"

"Yes, I asked him and that was his answer."

The expression on Tess's face was enough to inform Sierra that Tess thought she was not thinking very clearly. With a deep breath, Tess said, "Look, it's not my place to get involved in your disagreements, but I really think River is still in love with you. He is very hurt and very unhappy. He probably would not have agreed to train with Jack McCall if you two were still together. It's because you broke up that he was willing to go. He didn't want to be here this summer with you around.

"We both know River does not handle human interactions as well as he does with horses. Like I said, I don't intend to interfere, but

I would like to see the two of you work out this problem and get back together."

Sierra stared back open mouthed, completely baffled. This was not at all what she had expected to hear. Finally she found her tongue and said, "I don't know if we can work it out. He hasn't even tried to call me. What am I supposed to think? I'm not sure he wants to make up."

"He wants to make up," Tess insisted.

This was news to Sierra. She had thought if River really wanted to get back together he would have called, maybe not to apologize, but maybe to see if Sierra would admit she had been in the wrong and maybe forgive her...? "I don't know, Tess. I need to think about this. I guess what I want to know from you is whether or not I should move Fiel?"

"Of course not. This is a business. In fact, are you interested in competing this season?"

A combination of relief and grief swept over Sierra. She would not have to move Fiel. She would even be able to ride other horses at Pegasus. But the grief came over remembering the plans she and River had made for this summer. He was going to let her compete on Corazón for her first time at intermediate level. She wondered now what he had done with Corazón while he was away.

"Yes, I would like to compete," she answered. "What did River do with his own horses?"

"He took Oberon with him, and of course Pendragon. His filly and Corazón he took over to that cowboy friend of his, Ben Jeffers."

"Oh...makes sense."

"You could ride Felicity again if you like. See how the training goes over the next few weeks and you can decide if you are ready to take her intermediate level. If not, I have a few other horses in training that are ready for novice level."

"Okay, that's great."

"Good, I will put you on the training schedule."

"Thanks, um...is anyone taking over River's lessons?"

"I'm still teaching the jumping lessons. I have several dressage instructors lined up to give clinics almost every weekend throughout the summer, and I'm filling in with some flat lessons before shows. I'm happy to say that none of River's students have chosen to leave Pegasus while he is gone. They are all excited for him and looking forward to even better lessons when he returns this fall. I'll schedule you a jumping lesson and you can decide if you want to participate in any of the clinics."

"Okay, that sounds good."

"Check the tack room tomorrow for your rides." Tess turned back to her computer, dismissing Sierra. She waited until the door closed before she lifted her fingers from the keyboard to rest her head in her hands for a few moments.

Tess still did not understand what had caused the rift between Sierra and River, but watching the girl, she believed there was hope that Sierra also was still in love with River. She wanted those two together. She hated to see them both unhappy, especially River. But her reasons were also selfish, she recognized that. If they went ahead with their plans to get married and Sierra joined Tim Patterson's veterinary practice, then she was assured River would stay on at Pegasus...forever.

He can't be interested in that Barringer girl! Tess could remember every word of the nerve-grating conversation a few months ago.

"Hi, I'm trying to reach River Girard. I believe he is a trainer there?" a clear, confident voice had inquired when Tess picked up the phone one day in her office.

"He's schooling a horse right now. May I take a message?"

"Yes, thank you. I'm Lisa Barringer." She spelled out her name for Tess and then gave a phone number. "Please give him my number and ask him to call me when he gets a chance."

"Are you interested in riding lessons?" Tess asked suspiciously. Somehow, she didn't think that was the reason for the call.

"Actually, I wanted to let him know I've also been accepted on Jack Evan's team. We tried out together in Sacramento."

"I see…I'll give him the message."

Tess had hung up and immediately went to her computer to see what she could find out about Lisa Barringer on the web. Well, she found out plenty, mostly about Sunquest Ranch, a breeding and training facility of fine sport horses, owned for several generations by the Barringer family in California. The woman was rich and came from a long line of horse people.

There was plenty about Lisa Barringer as well, articles and photos of her winning prestigious dressage competitions. She had even competed in Europe. What really disturbed Tess however as she looked at the photos, was that Lisa was very beautiful and she obviously could ride well.

If she is interested in River and they get together, what incentive could keep him here? Sunquest Ranch was much larger and grander than Pegasus. Why wouldn't River be just as happy to train horses in that place?

The incentive was Sierra. Tess needed Sierra and River together in order to keep him at Pegasus. She never gave River the message from Lisa.

"This used to be my job."

The voice sounded friendly, and Jodi turned around from mucking her last stall of the day to find a pretty young woman watching her. She looked familiar, and then Jodi remembered having met over last winter break. *Sierra, River's ex-girlfriend.*

"It's Jodi, right?" She had a friendly smile, but Jodi thought there was a certain gloom about her; a sagging of the shoulders, a hollow look in her eyes even when she smiled.

"Yes, you're Sierra?"

"That's right."

It surprised Jodi when Sierra didn't leave, but hung around to ask Jodi about the horses, who she was riding, and for stable news.

She's nice, Jodi realized. Before long, they were grooming horses side-by-side in the crossties getting ready to ride.

They became friends in spite of the difference in their ages. *But we have more in common than girls my age, even my sister*, Jodi realized. Their conversations centered on the horses. Jodi appreciated that Sierra was the only one besides River, who recognized the value of Dune.

"Tess doesn't like her," Jodi explained. "She doesn't even put her on the conditioning schedule. I'm the only one riding her now with River gone, and the fastest I ever go is a slow trot."

"Hmm, well, I have plenty of time. Tess is only assigning me three horses a day. Would you like me to work her a little?"

"Well…" Jodi's first reaction was a possessive 'no', but thinking for a few minutes, she knew it would be good for Dune and she didn't want the mare to lose the conditioning she had gained when River and Todd had been riding her. "Yes, if you don't mind. It would be good for her."

Jodi did not have the skill to participate in any of the weekend clinics, so she had not had any lessons since River left for Virginia. One day, after watching Sierra ride Dune through a series of gymnastic exercises in the arena, she had an idea.

"I miss my lessons with River. He used to put me on the lunge line and I did a bunch of stretches. Then I worked on riding Dune through walk-trot transitions. Do you think you could lunge me on her once in a while so I could practice?"

"Of course, that's a great idea!" Sierra agreed. They started that very day, finishing Dune's work-out by switching riders.

Jodi realized Sierra did not have the eye or the instincts of River, but Sierra was an experienced rider, and she was able to see many things to help Jodi's position or use of aids. With the trail riding and the lunge lessons, Jodi looked forward to having enough skill to ride canter when River returned.

Any horse was better than no horse at all, but oh, how Todd missed Pegasus. How he missed Fala and Felicity. He even missed Tucker, for as lazy as he was, he could be pushed into more energetic gaits much easier than Willow. At least Tucker had the breeding and ability to move well. And Dune - how ashamed he was to have despised Dune just because she was not beautiful. Guilt and grief filled him as he compared riding Dune to Willow, for the mare had always tried hard and given her best. Really, jumping on Dune had been much easier than on Felicity.

He missed the comradery with Brooke and Mindy, and even the adult riders at Pegasus. Most of the students at Meadowood were grade school age or just starting middle school. This summer, Virginia put on a horsemanship day camp. He had watched a group lesson once and it looked like most of these kids were just learning very basic horsemanship. Many of them could barely post. Virginia only had two older students - her daughter Debbie, and Debbie's friend Mary. Both were going to be seniors at his high school but Todd didn't know either of them, and they didn't seem interested in getting to know him. He wasn't making any friends at Meadowood.

Perhaps if he had never had coaching from River or ridden the quality horses at Pegasus, he would enjoy his lessons more at Meadowood. But he did not find himself looking forward to his next lesson with eagerness.

Virginia kept using Willow for his lessons. Her other horse remained unsound, and Todd was too big for the ponies. He did not feel as if he was learning anything. Each lesson consisted of pushing, pushing, pushing Willow, hanging onto his hard mouth and stiff neck, and only getting into canter with the help of the lunge whip wielded by Virginia. But as much as Todd wanted to protest, he held his tongue. He did not ever want to go against his instructor. He liked Virginia. She was very pleasant with a hardy laugh and relaxed manners. But from the first lesson, he realized even more what he had lost in not having River as his coach.

Today, as Todd walked to the row of stalls expecting to find Willow, Sarah poked her head out of the tack room.

"You get to ride Lady Gray today," the little girl announced.

"Who's that?" *A different horse?* Todd's spirits suddenly lifted.

"First stall," Sarah answered, and disappeared back inside the tack room.

A tall, gray mare stood tied to the ring in the first stall. She didn't look old, and she actually looked like she had decent conformation. He spoke soothingly as he walked in to greet her, stroke her neck, and let her get to know his smell. She seemed a little wary at his approach, shifting her weight restlessly, and then pawing at the shavings beneath her feet. "Relax," Todd soothed. "I'll be right back to groom you."

"Lady Gray is Debbie's horse," Sarah told Todd when he went into the tack room to pick up a bucket of grooming supplies.

"Oh yeah? How come I get to ride her?"

"Debbie's gone for two weeks at some camp for school."

Todd returned to the mare's stall and began grooming her, and at last looked forward to today's lesson.

"We might as well take advantage of my daughter's absence," Virginia explained when she arrived with the tack and helped Todd finish getting Lady Gray ready. "She's quite a bit different from Willow, but I think you have enough skill to handle her."

In the arena, Virginia stayed by the mounting block and held the mare's head while Todd mounted. "The important thing with this mare is to be firm. You won't have to push her like you do with Willow, but she has a stubborn streak and she doesn't always want to work correctly."

"Okay," Todd said, gathering the reins and preparing to move the mare off to the rail. He started the lesson as usual, walking the mare in both directions to warm her up. He noticed immediately the tenseness in her, quite the opposite of Willow. She held her neck high, blowing hard at the corner of the arena, and then shied, preparing to spin and bolt. Todd immediately grabbed the reins to shorten them and pulled her head back to the rail. She planted all four feet and blew hard again at whatever frightened her in the corner.

"Kick her forward, Todd. This is a game she likes to play. She's testing you," Virginia called out.

This was the first spirited reaction he had felt in a horse since his accident. It was the type of antic he used to love. But Todd felt himself stiffen defensively, his heart racing. *Sit back, sit deep, supporting legs*, he counseled himself, remembering River's instructions when a horse shied. He forced himself to take deep breaths to settle his heart and calm the trembling inside so it did not transfer to the mare through his seat. He put his legs on to push her forward. She responded with a leap, almost unseating him, but she trotted on past the corner, and he managed to bring her back to a few mincing steps and then to walk.

"Good, you handled that well," Virginia said.

Todd was ready for the mare when they next approached the corner, and forced his own mind to remain calm and kept his legs on. He felt Lady Gray hesitate but she responded to the increased pressure of his legs and moved past the corner at a crooked angle, but at least did not break out of the walk. Todd was able to complete circuits around the perimeter in both directions with the mare no longer paying attention to the corner.

When Virginia asked Todd to pick up the working trot, Lady Gray responded quickly to his legs. What a relief not to have to push to keep her going. In fact, Virginia frequently called out, "Half-halt, that's too fast. She's getting choppy."

Todd's shoulders began to ache as he found himself using a lot of muscle behind his hands to keep the mare from rushing. *This isn't right!* River always said it didn't take strength to ride. You could never out-muscle a horse. *Why doesn't Virginia tell me how to half-halt...just tell me what to do?* Well, she didn't, and Todd searched back to what he could remember from River's coaching. *Half-halts begin with the seat.* Todd tried to apply everything he had learned from River: sit deep with legs on, squeeze with outside rein, don't pull back, play with the bit in her mouth.

On horses trained by River to respond to light aids, it had never been difficult to 'half-halt'. But now, as Todd tried to apply what he could remember, he realized he had not ever mastered a true half-halt. He had to concentrate with each stride to release his grip with his knees and give with his hands before he could engage his core muscles, and then squeeze lightly on the outside rein but just briefly, coaching himself, *don't hold*. To his amazement, it only took a few strides before Lady Gray began to change. She quit her rushing pace and settled into a rhythmical trot. *She is more relaxed because I am more relaxed and not fighting her!* In this moment, perhaps for the first time, Todd began to connect how his tenseness resulted in his horse becoming tense. As he 'loosened' his hold, both with his hands and not resisting with his seat, Lady Gray trotted out with more buoyancy and became light in his hands. She lowered her head and snorted out tension. *Wow!*

The lesson progressed to circles, figure-eights, and serpentines with Todd keeping Lady Gray in a rhythmical working trot. At last, he was enjoying himself.

"Very good, you get along well with her," Virginia said. "Okay, let's try the canter. Bring her onto a twenty-meter circle up at this end and pick it up from trot."

Todd obeyed, but again he relied on his previous lessons with River to ask for canter, for Virginia said nothing. *Inside leg at the girth, outside leg back, support with outside rein*, he coached himself. A smile spread across his face when Lady Gray jumped into canter on the correct lead.

"Fantastic!" Virginia praised. She instructed him to stay on the circle a few more rounds before coming back down to trot. "It's best you get to know her gaits and habits a little more before we have you go large at the canter," she warned. "Reverse, and let's try the canter going left. She doesn't like this lead as well, so be prepared to check her back until she picks up the left lead."

Todd nodded, and changed rein through the circle. He again coached himself through the aids to ask for canter. But in this direction, Lady Gray stiffened her neck and quickened the trot.

"Push her into it," Virginia called out.

Todd used more leg, but the mare only trotted faster, and he knew this was not the way to ask for the transition. He sat deep, slowing her back to working trot, taking deep breaths to relax himself and thus relax the mare. Then he tried again, using a little more force behind his leg aids when he asked for the canter. Lady Gray began to buck.

"Sit back, pull her head up," Virginia shouted.

Todd froze on the mare's back. Suddenly in the corner of his vision, he imagined a ditch looming in front of them. He clung to the front of the saddle, and as she bucked again, he lost hold of the reins as he fell forward and clutched around her neck to stay on. Lady Gray galloped down the arena, coming to a sudden halt in the far corner.

"Are you okay?" Virginia came toward them as fast as she could walk, not wanting to enhance the mare's spook.

Pushing himself upright, Todd nodded. But he didn't feel okay. He had panicked.

"You naughty girl," Virginia said as she came up to them and took one rein to help steady the mare who stood with head high and eyes rolling. "Well, that was unexpected."

Really? Virginia had warned him that Lady Gray did not like to take the left lead. He didn't say it out loud, however.

"I think we'll put her on the lunge line for the left lead and I can help you out, okay?" Virginia began to lead the mare back to the other end of the arena.

"Okay," Todd agreed, but right now what he really wanted to do was get off. Somehow, he was able to hold his terror in check and they finished the lesson on the lunge line. With Virginia in control, she managed to get Lady Gray to take the left lead, but only by keeping after her with the lunge whip until she trotted faster and faster until she had to canter.

"That's enough. We got her to take the left lead so that's a good place to stop." Virginia recognized Todd's fear, so did not ask him to ride off the lunge line, but kept control herself to finish with the mare trotting on a loose rein, stretching her neck.

Next week, Todd many times considered telling his mother he didn't feel well and wanted to skip his lesson. But he also did not want to give up. *I want to ride and somehow I have to get over this fear.* He acted as if all was well as they drove to Meadowood, hoping all he needed was just more time in the saddle to regain his old confidence.

But when Virginia asked him if he wanted to ride Lady Gray again, he replied, "Maybe I should stick with Willow a few more lessons."

"Why am I torturing myself like this?" Sierra murmured to herself as she shut down her laptop.

A few days after Sierra had returned home, Tess had casually handed her a card with a web address on it. "You might want to check out this web site. It has some good dressage tips on it."

"Thanks," Sierra said, puzzled. She had logged onto the site that evening and found it was the web page for Jack McCall's stable. He had posted photos of the four lucky riders selected for his team. Nice photos - close-ups of each one as well as group photos of the team in their riding clothes. There was River's face with a mere trace of a smile, as if the photographer had demanded it of him. His dark eyes looked back at her from her computer screen, his handsome features that she knew so well enhanced by the lighting of the professional photographer. The suppressed aching in her heart suddenly welled up, choking her with sudden anguish as she stared at his face. *I don't want to, but I still love him. I miss him so much!* Almost as painful was the group photo. A beautiful girl stood possessively close to River. Even with the other two riders in the picture, it very much looked like River and the girl were together. *It sure didn't take him long to forget me.* Then she scolded herself, *Well, I guess it didn't take me long to start going out with Sean either.*

Sierra often wondered why Tess had given her the web address. *Is it out of spite that I lost him and she wants to punish me? Or does she know how much I still care and wants me to know what's going on in his life…to try to get him back?* She had no idea.

Nevertheless, against her better judgment and against her will, she logged onto her laptop every night and found herself going to that page. River had been with Jack over a month now. The page featured photos of training sessions and competitions. River consistently earned high scores on Oberon, usually placing first in his classes. He was also doing well with Pendragon and one other horse that belong to Jack's stable - winning, winning, winning! The other riders were often winning or placing with admirable scores, but none as consistently as River. It was obvious the stable thought of him as their star, and his photo was plastered throughout the site.

The closest in points to River was that disgustingly beautiful girl Lisa. Sierra couldn't help clicking on every picture of her and studying her features, her jealousy magnified by how much more attractive Sierra thought Lisa was than herself. There were occasionally photos of social events connected to a big show, and one of the pictures showed River with his arm around Lisa's shoulders. It was a distant shot, but Sierra had increased the magnification, in spite of the distortion, trying to figure out if the expression on River's face was happiness. She just couldn't tell.

Her phone rang, probably Sean calling as he did every night. He was always so much more faithful in calling than River had ever been. She tried to sound happy to hear his voice and they talked as usual about their day. And as usual, Sierra ended the conversation far sooner than Sean would have liked, stating she was tired, needed to get to bed for she was always up early to go ride.

For some reason, tonight before he hung up, Sean said, "I love you, Sierra," and then disconnected.

What? No, don't say that. It's too soon! It's not how I feel. Sierra held the phone away from her face, staring at it as if it was about to sting her. Those words only intensified the painful shards of her broken heart.

"What's wrong?" Todd asked, entering the kitchen the next afternoon. He had just returned from walking Brownie, and found his mother sitting at the table with red eyes and staring ahead at nothing.

"Oh, Todd, I don't know what I can do." She turned her empty gaze to him and then sorrow filled the emptiness in her eyes.

"What?" he asked again, coming up close to her side, wanting to offer comfort.

"I got a call from Peggy Steinberg."

Just the mention of the name of the social worker who had been in charge of his case for years sent iciness through his veins and down his spine. Unscheduled calls or visits were never a good thing. "Wh-what did she say?"

"Your mother has been granted a trial custody period. The judge on her case is going to allow her to have you for the rest of the summer."

"No, I don't want that!" Todd cried out in alarm. "Can't I refuse?"

"No, Peggy said we don't have a choice."

16 ENDINGS

You took me to adventure and to love. We two have shared great joy and great sorrow. And now I stand at the gate of the paddock watching you run in an ecstasy of freedom, knowing you will return to stand quietly, loyally, beside me. — Pam Brown

The apartment Linda Grant rented had two small bedrooms, one bathroom, and a living room with a kitchenette at one end. A sliding glass door led to a small patio off the kitchenette. Walls on each side of the patio separated it from the neighbors to provide privacy for a withered plant in a pot and two webbed folding chairs.

"This is your room," Todd's mother said, opening the door proudly. "I decorated it for you."

"Uh, it's nice," Todd said, stepping into the small bedroom painted a bright aqua blue with a wallpaper border of prancing ponies in pastel colors with a lot of pink. The spread on the twin-sized bed featured a horse head in the middle of a horseshoe with shamrocks at the corners. The furnishings consisted of a chest of drawers, a folding metal chair, and one small closet. The one window had beige drapes that came with the apartment. The drapes were the only soft color in the room and Todd felt barraged by the rest of the bright, childish colors.

"I'll let you get settled and then I'll cook dinner," Linda said, trying to sound cheerful, but Todd noted the nervous tremor in her voice.

The first thing he did was open the closet door and set his riding boots in front. In his room at the Marshalls (at home) a shut closet door didn't bother him, but something about the door here being closed gave him jitters along his spine. He put away his clothes and the few other items he had brought with him - a few books, his electronics, and a photo album. He left his school clothes and most of his other possessions at the Marshalls, hoping to be back 'home' before school started. He also had to leave Brownie behind.

"They don't allow pets at my apartment complex," Linda said regretfully when he had asked if he could at least bring his dog. "But we could get you a fish tank. Would you like that?"

"No, that's okay," Todd said quickly. Maybe Brownie was better off staying at the Marshalls anyway where they would look after him and he had a back yard where he could go outside.

Todd did bring his riding clothes, hoping he would still be able to take his lessons at Meadowood. But that hope was soon dashed as well. His mother did not own a car. Her apartment was in the center of Firwood, and in walking distance of the nursing home where she worked as a housekeeper. There were no buses that went out into the rural areas near Meadowood or Pegasus.

"Why don't you take this time to develop new interests?" his mother suggested. "I think I could get you a bicycle if you wanted."

Again he said, "No, that's okay."

The housekeeper job required that Linda work rotating days including some weekends, from eight to four-thirty in the afternoon. With Linda at work, Todd slept as late as he could, never getting up before eleven and often not until one. Sleep was his best escape for having nothing to do. The Marshalls were not supposed to have contact with him during this trial period, but that did not stop Todd from calling his foster mother whenever Linda was at work. It was so comforting to hear the voice of the woman he now thought of as 'Mom'. But he knew the Marshalls were unable to help him so he always answered Gwen's questions, "I'm fine, everything's okay."

When he did get out of bed he watched television, played electronic games, and mourned for his old life. A few times he went outside to wander the neighborhood streets past several other apartment complexes and strip malls. He found nothing of interest. The strip malls consisted of small convenience stores, hair and nail salons, and Asian take-out food, and one pawn shop. Out of curiosity, he went into the pawn shop once, but the proprietor kept sending him hostile scowls, so he quickly left. He came across one small park with a square of grass, three weathered picnic tables, and a sand lot with kids' playground toys. Except for the rare appearance of a few very young children with a mother or someone watching them in the play lot, he saw no other kids, and none his age. He called a few of his friends but gave that up when it hurt too much to hear about the fun they were having and especially since he had to decline all offers to join them for he had no way to get there.

When Linda came home, always exhausted, she immediately went to her own room to take a nap. "Wake me when you're hungry," she would say before shutting her door.

Todd never woke her up. He fixed himself sandwiches or ate junk food when he got hungry.

On Linda's days off, she often slept even later than Todd. The one thing he did check up on was the number of pills in her prescription med bottles, assuring himself that she took them every day. He had looked up her psych medications on-line, curious as to how they worked. He learned that chronic fatigue was a common side effect. His mother had no energy. She dragged herself out from her room in the afternoon and as cheerfully as she could, asked what he wanted to eat.

"I'm fine, I just ate a sandwich," he would answer.

Sometimes that satisfied her and she would plop down on the sofa and watch television until she was hungry enough to find something to eat herself. But other times she tried to cook, and Todd suffered through either burnt or undercooked meals, lying as he said, "It's good."

Once a week, Mrs. Miller, his mother's case worker, visited. Todd lied to her as well. "Everything's fine."

Todd was miserable.

How he longed for the sight, the smell, the feel of a horse. Even placid old Willow would have lifted his spirits.

One evening when Linda had fallen asleep in front of the television, he called Jodi. He at least needed to hear about the horses.

Jodi actually seemed delighted to hear from him. Talking to her was the first thing to lift his spirits since coming here. Jodi didn't sound like she had things to do and wanted to end the conversation. She answered all his questions about the horses, giving him every detail he wanted.

She really is a very nice person, Todd remarked to himself after they hung up. Jodi was so different from the sullen girl he had known in school, and he was very grateful they had become friends. He started calling her as often as he could when his mother was asleep or not around. Not that his mother would forbid it, but he instinctively knew she would resent him having contact with someone from his old life.

At first, Todd tried to be nice.

"I just want you to be happy," Linda often said, noting his down-turned mouth and bored demeanor.

"I'm happy enough," he lied.

But as the weeks of summer passed in constant boredom, Todd felt himself slipping into a depression to match those he had seen in his mother, thinking, *my summer is wasted and my life is ruined*. He worried, *am I bipolar?* He knew psychological disorders could be hereditary. But he figured he had good reason to feel depressed. This trial custody period was supposed to end on Labor Day and he could return to the Marshalls for school. But what if his mother 'passed' her trial? Would the judge then consider another trial, or worse, declare Linda had proved herself capable of motherhood and force Todd to return to her permanently? *So unfair!*

As much as she wanted to, Gwen could not reassure him. She dared not promise that he would be able to stay in his foster home.

On one of her days off, Linda actually got up before Todd and when he dragged himself out of his room just before noon, she stood expectantly in the kitchen.

"I cooked breakfast," she announced, and set a plate of rubbery scrambled eggs and burnt bacon next to a glass of orange juice on the table.

Todd often woke with an upset stomach these days, and the smell overpowered him with nausea. He was tired of saying the things his mother wanted to hear. "It stinks," he grumbled. "Can I have cereal?"

"Of course," she said, crestfallen as she picked the plate back up. She stood at the sink staring at the food, not knowing what to do with it.

Guilt added to the nausea in his stomach and he said somewhat remorsefully, "I'm just not hungry." He sat down and sipped at the glass of orange juice. But his irritation increased as his mother stood at the sink holding the plate as if she couldn't figure out what to do with it. "Throw it away," he said in disgust.

'Oh." Linda walked to the garbage and threw everything away, including the plate.

"That was really sensible," Todd said sarcastically.

"Now look here, young man," Linda turned from the trash and stormed over to his chair. She grabbed the back of his tee shirt by the neck, twisting it in her fist. "You don't talk to me like that. I am your mother."

At first, Todd reacted by cowering down in his shirt, hunching his shoulders forward and ducking his head protectively. But much had happened in the years since he had last suffered from Linda's temper.

She can't hurt me. He stiffened his back and jerked himself out of her hand, then stood up to face her.

"Yeah, and some mother you are. You don't care about me," he shouted into her face. "You only want custody back so you get your welfare checks." He was screaming now, "I wish you weren't my mother. I wish I had never been born!" He stormed back to his bedroom, slamming the door behind him. He paced in the room, unable to settle his anger. *Don't you dare open my door!* But nothing happened, and eventually he calmed down enough to fall face down on his bed and lie there in his misery. He heard nothing from the other room and had no idea what his mother was doing. He escaped back into sleep.

Several hours later, Todd woke to a soft tapping on his door. "Todd?" Linda called meekly. "Todd, I'm sorry. Please come out."

He lay still.

"Todd, I'm sorry. Please, I'm so sorry."

"Okay," he replied, his voice muffled in his pillow. He didn't know if she heard or not.

"I wanted us to spend the day together. I wanted to fix you breakfast, and then I thought we could go to a movie or something. Please, Todd, come out."

Feeling numb, his anger having drained his energy, Todd got up and opened the door. His mother looked up at him with her eyes red and puffy from crying. She reached up to touch his face, but Todd cringed away.

"I love you, son," she said pleadingly. "What you said is not true."

"Whatever," he answered sullenly, and then pushed past her to slump down on the sofa. He picked up the remote and turned on the T.V.

Her next Friday off, Linda didn't attempt to cook, but she tried again to take Todd out somewhere - to eat or to the movies, or anything he wanted to do.

"How about take me to the stable where I can ride?" he said, knowing it was impossible without a car.

"I can't, you know that. We have to go where we can walk or take a bus."

When he merely rolled his eyes and looked back at the T.V., she snapped at him, "Todd, horses are big, smelly, dangerous animals. I don't like you around horses."

"Yeah, because they make me happy," he snarled back at her. He could not stand to be in the same room with her after that ignorant, spiteful comment. He retreated to his bedroom. Laying back on his bed, he thumbed through the horse magazine he had bought yesterday at the corner convenience store. It was a glossy, commercial journal with articles of very little practical information. But looking at the pictures of the expensive, well-bred, beautiful horses was soothing in a bittersweet way.

He slept, he played games on his phone, he wandered out a few times for a drink of water, a handful of cookies, or to go the bathroom. His mother slept in front of the television, her head fallen back against the cushions and her mouth open, until she finally got up and went into her bedroom, moving around doing whatever. Todd had no idea or cared.

The sun had set an hour ago when he heard his mother talking on the telephone, but could not distinguish the words. Shortly after, she knocked on his door. "Todd," she called. "Todd," she repeated in a more demanding tone. "Since you don't want to spend any time with me, I'm going to the movies with a friend from work."

"Fine," he answered. *Good, just get out of here and leave me alone.*

She didn't leave for another two hours. He heard the front door open and another woman's voice greeted Linda, and he heard them both laughing. Welcoming silence filled the apartment once they had left.

Hunger drove Todd out of his room and to the kitchen where he ate half a bag of chips, peanut butter with a spoon because it seemed they were out of bread, and more cookies. He looked for milk in the refrigerator, and swallowed directly from the carton the few remaining swallows. *Can't even buy decent food*, he grumbled.

He called Jodi, and hearing her describe her day at Pegasus brightened his mood. In just a few weeks, he would be back with the Marshalls, and at least he could return to Meadowood.

"You know, by the time you get back home," Jodi said. It sent a current of warmth through Todd that she referred to the Marshalls as 'home'. "River will be back. You should talk to him again. He can't stay mad at you forever."

"I'll think about it," Todd said.

They said goodbye and Todd, with nothing better to do, went to bed. He never heard his mother come home.

An unfamiliar sound woke Todd the next morning. He lay still and listened, trying to identify the source of that noise. It took many minutes before he realized it came through the wall of his mother's room next to his. *Ah, her alarm clock.* He picked up his cell phone to check the time, noting it was almost nine a.m. *Isn't she supposed to be working today?* He figured she must have gotten up before the alarm and forgot to turn it off. *But certainly she would have heard it even in the kitchen, and gone back to turn it off?*

Todd didn't feel like getting up yet, but the buzzing alarm grated his nerves and prevented him falling back to sleep. With a grunt of irritation, he pushed back his covers and slowly got out of bed. Yawning and stretching, he padded barefoot out to the main room. The shoes his mother had worn lay on the carpet near the sofa where she must have kicked them off, and her purse sat on the kitchen table. *Why didn't she take her purse with her?* At that moment, the ringtone of his mother's phone sounded from inside the purse. Feeling that something was wrong, Todd went to the purse and pulled out the phone. He saw the call was from the nursing home. When the call went to voicemail he noted three other missed calls, all from her workplace. A heavy weight of foreboding filled his stomach, and his heartbeat accelerated, rising into his throat. The buzzing from his mother's room now seemed like an ominous warning.

He did not want to go into her room. He went to the bathroom instead. *Maybe I should call someone first.* He turned around in a circle, but he could think of no one to call besides the Marshalls, and he thought he might get in trouble if he did that right now.

Finally, he mustered all his courage, and went into the bedroom.

Just overslept, was his first thought at sight of his mother lying prone in her bed, her head turned away from the door. He walked over and silenced the alarm. "Mother?" He stood, watching her, and suddenly it occurred to him that she had not taken one single breath while he stood there. "Mother?" he repeated louder. He didn't want to touch her. Turning away, he started to retreat, but then made himself go around to the other side of the bed.

Linda stared at him through half-opened eyes, her skin gray, and strands of saliva at the corner of her mouth and down her chin. She did not blink or move. "M-m-mother?" Then he saw the syringe on the floor next to the bed. "No...n-no...n-n-no!" he groaned. He rushed to the bathroom and vomited up bile and then dry-heaved. When the nausea at last subsided, he washed his face and called 911.

It is good to be home, River thought to himself, not for the first time since returning to Pegasus a week ago at the end of August. He had enjoyed his time with Jack and was grateful for all he had learned. Jack had a discerning eye, and it had amazed River how 'eyes from the ground', had helped River refine his horse's movements to an even more precise level. Jack had also taught him much about working with a horse in-hand, something River had very little experience in except for lunging. The techniques were things he could use here at home. He learned how to use the curb bit of the double bridle, so that he no longer just held the second pair of reins passively.

Jack worked his students hard. Sometimes River rode as many as eight horses a day. They participated in clinics, giving demonstration rides and helping critique the other riders. They constantly had to critique each other. In addition, Jack gave them reading assignments from classical dressage books. In the evenings, Jack lectured or they participated in discussions. Between riding, coaching, and the required reading and studying, River fell asleep almost immediately upon getting into bed each night.

The level of activity had been just what he needed. There was so much that interested him and he was so busy he went almost all day without thinking about Sierra. And when she did encroach on his thoughts, he could push her aside and replace her with thoughts of a horse he had ridden that day.

Or, he could think about Lisa. They had become almost inseparable when their duties were finished each day. He knew she came from a very wealthy family, but he never felt inferior to her as he often had with Sierra. Lisa's background was as rich in a horse-centered lifestyle as that of River's. They mostly talked about horses and he felt very comfortable around her. She didn't even have a college degree.

One evening, as River walked Lisa to her room in the guest quarters and they reached her door, on an impulse River kissed her. She had kissed him back with surprising eagerness. After that, Lisa seemed to expect kissing and perhaps even more in their relationship. *Does she think we are going together now?* River wasn't sure about that and he wasn't sure if it was what he wanted. He had said goodbye to her at the end of the season, promising to stay in touch, and he had said, "See you next year." She had seemed disappointed that he had not suggested getting together over the winter.

It had been a great relief to come home and find most of the horses at Pegasus sound and in the peak of condition. Kate had kept to the training schedules they had discussed together before he had left for Virginia, and she had done a good job. She had evented on Prospector at senior novice level, and had qualified for the upcoming regional championship. Brooke and five other Pegasus students had also qualified, (including Sierra who had competed on Felicity, her first time at senior preliminary level). Corazón and Ysbryd had thrived at

Ben's ranch, full of health and energy when he picked them up to bring them back to Pegasus. Before River left for Virginia, he had introduced Ysbryd to a saddle and bridle, and Ben had continued her round pen work. River could start her training under saddle any time now.

The one exception was Gunsmoke, Tess's old eventing and dressage champion.

"He is not eating well and he is even more stiff in his hocks," Manuel told River.

Not having been here all summer, it was quite a shock to River when he first saw Gunsmoke, and noted how much weight the horse had lost. Still, the old gelding had greeted him with a friendly whicker, and accepted the horse cookie, softer than a carrot, that River fed him for a treat.

"We have a temporary paddock for him on grass that is behind the stable on level ground. It is only a short walk in and out from his stall," Manuel explained. "Miss Tess thought he should stay in his stall but Dr. Patterson said a little bit of exercise and getting out in the open air is good for him."

Now, the work for the day finished and the horses fed, River walked down the stable aisles for a quick check on all the horses before going in for his own supper. The sound of horses contentedly munching on their hay added to River's assurance that everyone was well as he checked each horse in his stall to be sure they were eating. A horse that doesn't eat is a bothered horse.

When River reached Gunsmoke's stall, his heart sank. The old gelding stood with his head hanging very low, and did not raise it until River had entered the stall and came up to him. Checking his feed bin, it did not look like Gunsmoke had eaten any of his senior feed pellets.

"*Que pasa, hombre?*" River murmured, examining the horse all around. Gunsmoke turned his head and placed it against River's chest. "*No tienes hambre?*" River picked up a few of the pellets and offered them out of his hand. Gunsmoke lipped at them, but never opened his mouth enough to try to eat.

"I'll be right back," River said. He hurried to the front of the stable and into the tack room where he had left his phone. He called Dr. Patterson first, and then called Tess.

"I'm on my way," Tess said when River explained how he had found Gunsmoke.

When River returned to the horse's stall, he found him lying down with his head and neck flat and his eyes closed. But as River re-entered the stall, Gunsmoke opened his eyes and slightly raised his nose a few moments before letting it fall back. He was too weak now to hold it up. River sat down in the shavings next to his head, waiting for Tess and the vet to arrive.

Not long after, he heard Tess's car pull into the yard and then she joined him inside the stall.

"Oh, my poor old boy," she cried out softly at sight of him. River moved away so that Tess could sit near Gunsmoke's head. She knelt down and stroked his neck and cheek, ran her fingers through his thin mane, touched his velvety ears. Gunsmoke could only blink his eyes in response. She lifted his head into her lap, and remained there, murmuring her love to him and stroking his face.

River waited by the stall door until he heard Dr. Patterson's van pulling into the stable yard. Only then did he leave to lead the vet back to the sick horse's stall.

The only time Tess moved away from her old horse was to allow the vet to examine him. It didn't take long.

"Tess, we talked about this two weeks ago. He's losing weight, he's nearly blind, and I believe his arthritis is getting more painful for him," Tim Patterson said.

"He's just twenty-nine...no, thirty," Tess said. "Lots of horses live into their thirties."

"And many horses don't." The vet moved away from the horse and placed a hand on Tess's shoulder. "Tess, I believe he is dying," he said gently.

Choking back a sob, Tess asked, "Can you do anything?"

"I don't think he is suffering. He will just slip away."

Tess dropped back down by Gunsmoke and again cradled his heavy head in her lap. "I guess I should feel grateful that I won't have to put him down."

"I wish I saw more horses have a natural passing," Dr. Patterson said, thinking of all the horses he had euthanized in his career, and often simply because the owner could not afford or did not want to pay for medical treatment.

Tess looked over at River. "Thank you for calling me. You go to bed, I'll stay with him."

"We can take shifts," River offered.

"No, I need to stay with him."

River nodded. He understood. "I'll bring you some coffee."

"That would be nice, thank you." She turned to Dr. Patterson. "Thank you, Tim. If there is nothing you can do, you don't have to stay either."

"I actually got another call on my way over here. I'll go deal with that and then I'll come back and check on you," he said.

When she was alone with her horse, Tess allowed her tears to run freely. She murmured to Gunsmoke, thanking him for the years of service he had given her. He had been her eventing horse in her young rider years and for her first adult events. They had been a very successful team and the two of them had actually tried out for the Olympic team twice, although they never made it to the Olympics. She had retired Gunsmoke from eventing after their second attempt and then competed him in dressage. He had made it all the way to grand prix level before she retired him from showing at the age of eighteen. Since then, he had been a wonderful school horse for her more advanced students. She had used him for lessons as recently as a year ago, but his arthritis had reached a point where he could no longer trot without obvious lameness, in spite of all the treatments they had tried.

Gunsmoke no longer tried to open his eyes. His breaths came deep and spaced far apart. "You've had a good life," she said in a choked voice. She laid her own cheek against his as her tears ran down, dampening them both. *I should have spent more time with you.* She regretted now all the days she had been too busy to even stop by his stall. How could she have let herself get so busy that she would let days go by without even taking a few minutes to give her faithful old horse a pat on the neck and a treat? "I am so sorry," she whispered.

Tess stayed with her horse's head on her lap the entire night. Several times during the night, River brought her coffee and water. He covered her shoulders with a wool cooler as the night chilled. He stayed with Tess, listening to her stories of her early years with Gunsmoke. When she had talked herself out, he bedded down himself on a pile of horse blankets in the aisle outside the stall, in case she needed help or anything at all.

Tim Patterson returned a few hours before dawn. He could not leave either, for he had known this horse for years. He stayed in his vehicle where he could doze in the front seat, to give Tess privacy with Gunsmoke, but he wanted to be there at the end to also say goodbye.

As the sun came up, Gunsmoke took his last breath.

Tess stroked Gunsmoke's face and neck for the last time, clipped a lock of his mane, and then slowly made her way back to her car. "River, can you, or else Jodi when she shows up to clean stalls, call and cancel any lessons I have today?"

"Of course," he answered solemnly.

"Find a good place for him in the field."

Tess drove home, took two pain pills from a bottle left over after a dental procedure, and went to bed. She trusted River and Manuel to arrange for a place in the back field to bury Gunsmoke.

The fall term for Sierra didn't start until the end of September. River knew Tess had assigned horses for her to ride, that she had competed on Felicity during the summer, and would continue to ride up until she returned to school. Somehow, the two of them managed to avoid each other. They might catch sight of one another briefly, but both would turn and go the opposite direction in spite of where they originally had intended to go.

But after the loss of Gunsmoke, a sudden longing to talk to Sierra and hold her in his arms, came back to River with an intensity that re-ignited all his feelings for her. Once, as he stepped out of the tack room and saw her leading a horse into the cross ties, he almost continued on to speak to her. Almost…but then the vision of her kissing that man invaded his mind, and his heart ached with the same excruciating intensity as the first sight. He turned back inside the tack room and started cleaning a bridle. When Sierra came in for the tack she needed, he kept his back turned. He thought she hesitated a few moments, but he wasn't sure when he finally heard the door close.

It's over, he told himself angrily.

They never spoke. River flew back with Oberon to Virginia for that region's dressage championship and Sierra returned to school.

River had qualified on three horses for the regional championship in Virginia, but he decided not to take Pendragon. It was enough flying Oberon back and then riding the horse from Stone Valley he had qualified with. Lisa flew back with Volantis, and the other two riders brought their own horses as well. River was flattered how happy Lisa was to be with him again, and he enjoyed hanging out with her in the evenings. They kissed (a lot), but something about seeing Sierra again had sapped away his enthusiasm for kissing Lisa.

"Well done, all of you," Jack said at the end of the championship event. "See you all in Lexington at the finals!"

One more big event this year, then I can rest until next spring! River's own classes for his last year at the university started next week. Elizabeth, one of the team members, was also still a college student. Lisa and John would return to train with Jack in March. River and Elizabeth would return as soon as they finished their last quarter.

On returning home, River settled Oberon in a paddock and then went to find Tess to let her know he was back. He had already called her with the show results but he knew she would want more details of the championship.

Tess looked up as River stepped into the office. "You're back, good. Congratulations."

"Thanks."

"Call your friend Laila," Tess ordered. When he frowned quizzically at her she insisted, "just do it now, we'll talk later."

He shrugged and went next door to the lounge and collapsed on the sofa to make the call, feeling apprehensive. *Did something happen to Megan?*

"Hi," Laila greeted, sounding solemn.

"What's going on?" River asked. "Is Megan okay?"

"She's fine, she's been missing you. River...listen, it's your father."

"My father?" Relief at hearing Megan was fine had lifted the weight of worry, but a different kind of worry replaced it. *They didn't let him out!* His father was serving a four-year sentence for attempted manslaughter. An argument with his father several years ago had resulted in his father shooting River in the back. Since then, River had severed all ties with his father. He threw away unopened the few letters he received in the first year of his father's incarceration. He never went to visit him. The last time he had seen his father, when the police brought him in handcuffs to his hospital bedside, River had refused when his father, in tears, begged for his forgiveness.

"He's in the hospital. You know he has cirrhosis from his alcoholism. He started vomiting blood and he's now in the hospital with acute hepatitis. He's dying, River."

"So? ...good."

"River, you need to go see him. He's been asking for you."

"I don't need to go. Laila, why are you the one telling me this?"

He heard her sigh through the phone. "The prison warden contacted the social worker on the case. Well, long story short is, she knows a social worker in my office and everyone thought it would be best if someone who knew you told you."

"Great, thanks, Laila. All I can say, it's good news."

"River…"

"I'm not going to see him," he interrupted. "I'll come over later. I'd like to see Megan." With that, he hung up.

The lounge door opened and Tess stepped inside. She stood with folded arms and wearing a grim expression.

"You know," River said.

"For your sake, you need to go see him," she said. "You'll regret this the rest of your life if you don't. I've canceled your lessons. You don't have school until Monday. I'm driving you there now, so go get whatever you need because we might stay overnight."

"No!" he refused.

"You heard about Todd's mother dying?"

"So?"

"I've heard from Mrs. Marshall that Todd is suffering horribly from guilt. His last words to his mother were in anger. That young man is miserable with so many regrets. Believe me, the same will happen to you."

"I don't think so."

Tess did not reply, but stood firm in the doorway. River gave in and went upstairs to pack an overnight bag.

The room smelled horrible, the stink of old blood. A prison guard sat next to the bedside. One shackle had been attached around his father's ankle to the bedframe. When he came closer, River almost didn't recognize the man in the bed. His jaundiced skin was the color of mustard. His distended abdomen was outlined by the covers, sticking up like a term pregnancy. But the rest of the man was skeletal, his cheeks sunken above a neck with protruding tendons and engorged neck veins, the exposed wrists merely skin stretched over the bones.

Intravenous fluid dripped in from a bag with tubing threaded through a pump and then to a needle in his vein. Oxygen flowed in through a cannula in his nose. The foley catheter bag hanging from the bed frame contained a small amount of brown-colored urine.

A nurse escorted River into the room. "This is River Girard, the son," she announced to the guard.

River did not hear what else was said. He just found himself suddenly seated in the guard's chair next to the bedside. The nurse left the room, and the guard stood behind him. Tess remained at the doorway.

River sat stiffly in the chair and stared at his father. Perhaps his father sensed someone watching him, for eventually he opened his eyes, the sclera as yellow as his skin.

"River," his father spoke through his cracked, dry lips in a voice as harsh as sandpaper. His hands trembled where they lay on the sheets and he tried to raise the one nearest his son, but he was too weak to hold it up. "Good to see you, boy."

"Hi, Cray," River finally managed to say, addressing his father by his name, for it had never felt right to call him 'Dad'.

Tears pooled in the corner of Cray's eyes. "So much to say to you." He spoke hesitantly for it left him short of breath with the effort and he had to suck in air after just a few words. "I've wronged you, boy.... Both you and your mother...and Tess." He closed his eyes a few minutes, sucked in a deep breath that ended on a sob. "I've been following everything I can about you...all that stuff back in Virginia...probably go to the Olympics.... Son, I'm so proud of you." He managed to turn his head to look River straight on. "You did all that, in spite of me!" He turned his head back.

Many long minutes passed. As River watched his father, pity began to replace some of the anger and hate he bore for this man. Forgotten memories of his first year living with his father, after his jockey mother had been killed in a race, emerged into River's consciousness. That first year had not been too bad. Cray used to take River with him to the track where he trained race horses. River followed him around as Cray worked the horses in his charge. Cray showed him off to his friends and the stable workers, and often put River up on the racehorses. How wonderful it had been when River surprised everyone with how well he could handle the thoroughbreds. His father had been proud of him, frequently ruffling his hair and hugging his shoulders. Cray exuded charm in those days, his alcoholism under control and hardly noticeable. He had a reputation as a capable racehorse trainer.

There had been some good days back then.

Cray's eyes opened and he summoned his strength to turn his head again toward River. "I love you, son. I am so sorry for everything. All I want is for you to forgive me."

River opened his mouth but could not summon the words.

"Please, I beg you…"

"I…I forgive you," River at last said.

It was enough. Tess did not make him stay any longer. They returned home. Two nights later the news came that Cray Blackthorn had died. He had asked for 'no resuscitation', and a few hours after River's visit, he slipped into a coma and never woke up again.

17 PUTTING THE PAST BEHIND

It is of the utmost importance that the rider changes his natural reactions, adapting them to the new situation of sitting on a horse. Only when the rider has trained his reactions will he be able to develop an independent seat. - H.L.M. van Schaik, *Misconceptions and Simple Truths in Dressage*

"This cannot go on," Gwen stated. "It's breaking my heart to watch that boy suffering so."

"I know, Gwen. We both are suffering with him," John agreed. "I don't know how to help him. Counseling isn't doing much good this time."

Husband and wife lay side by side in their bed, going over again the same tough problem – how to help Todd. After Linda's death, he came home to them deeply depressed and filled with remorse. They did not know all that had transpired in the time Todd had been with his mother. All he would say when asked, was, "I killed her."

It was not clear if Linda Grant had committed suicide or had died from an accidental overdose of heroin. The pathology report confirmed heroin in her system as well as an elevated blood alcohol. She had been off of the drug for over two years. If she had taken the same dose as when she last used, that might have been enough to kill her now, especially in combination with drinking.

However, Todd was convinced his mother had committed suicide. He could not forget how they had argued that night, and he had said many unkind things, including that he hated her. He believed her despair drove her to the fatal act. His parents, case worker, and counselor all tried to persuade him to look at the facts more objectively, and that he was not responsible, even if it had been suicide.

Todd got up in the mornings, showered and dressed, ate what was set in front of him, went to school, came home, did homework, ate what was set in front of him, and went to bed. He did everything mechanically as if he were a robot, with no change of expression and no animation. He spoke as few words as possible when anyone asked him questions. His teachers reported that he did his work but never voluntarily participated in class and seemed to have rejected all his former friends. Gwen drove him to his child psychologist, Dr. Statton, twice a week, but so far, Todd was not responding to the therapy. At least he had not reverted back to stuttering, and Dr. Statton did not think he was suicidal.

His nightmares had returned, and often Gwen awoke to hear Todd moaning. She would go to his room to see him wrestling with his covers, and gently wake him up to rescue him from the unknown terror. When awake, he could not recall the content of his dream.

"John, I'm going to call River tomorrow. It's the only thing I can think of. If River would just forgive him and let him come back, maybe being around the horses will help. The only time Todd shows signs of caring about anything is when he takes care of Brownie," Gwen resolved.

"You said he didn't want to go back to that place where he was taking lessons," John reminded her. "What makes you think he would go back to Pegasus?"

"I don't know. But he has always looked up to River, and it hurt him so much when River rejected him. It might be enough if River forgave him and asked him to come back to the stable. Maybe if we can just get him out around the horses he could start to heal."

"I don't put much hope in that, but it's worth a try. Do you want me to call River?"

"No, I'll do it, and if he doesn't respond to me, I'm calling Delia Evans and I'll ask her to talk to him. He still feels obligated to us and I know he believes he still owes Del for her defense of him and Sierra that time a few years ago. It's time to call in some debts," Gwen said in a mock mobster tone, trying to interject a little humor.

The next day, Gwen left several messages for River. He finally called her back when he got home from his morning classes.

After briefly asking how he was doing, she jumped right to what she wanted to say. "I don't believe in interfering with the consequences when someone makes a mistake. When you told Todd you didn't trust him, well, he learned a very hard lesson. But River, he has learned his lesson, and he is so very sorry. I'm pleading with you now to forgive him. You haven't seen him since he came back to us. He is suffering very deeply. Nothing we do helps. I'm desperate now. Please, River, forgive him and ask him back. Be the big brother to him that he has always seen in you."

If Gwen had asked him this even a few weeks ago, River might have considered her request, for he regarded both Gwen and John with high esteem, and would never forget their kindness when he stayed with them to recover after his father had shot him. He believed he owed them much. So he would have considered it for their sake, but not because he truly forgave Todd.

But a deep, cold part of his heart had melted after he forgave his father. It had been a cathartic experience, and he was glad Tess made him go. Perhaps also the recent passing of Gunsmoke gave River some insight into how a death should occur, surrounded by loved ones. How horrible it must have been for Todd to be the one to discover his dead mother.

River cared about Todd, and it had hurt his own feelings to discover the boy had gone against his wishes behind his back. Perhaps his hurt had been compounded by breaking up with Sierra. Was he continuing to punish Todd because of his own hurt?

River did not like self-introspection because it usually revealed his own mistakes and where he was at fault. But he decided it didn't matter all the reasons now, it was time to put it behind him and forgive. Maybe he even needed to ask forgiveness from Todd for his harshness.

"I'll come over to see him when I'm done here today," he said.

"Thank you."

Whatever passed between River and Todd, Gwen never knew. It was enough that after River left, Todd said he wanted to take the bus after school the next day to go to Pegasus.

"Are you going to the stable today?" Todd caught up to Jodi after a class they had together.

"Yeah, I am," she replied, startled. After Todd had returned to the Marshalls, Jodi had called him many times, but he never returned any of the calls. She eventually heard about his mother. *That might make it hard to talk to your friends*, she figured. Plus, she didn't know what she could say, and feeling awkward and helpless, she quit calling. Since school had started, he hadn't sought her out, not even to ask about the horses.

"I just wanted to let you know I'm going there today."

"That's great! Um, I'll see you on the bus then?" A ghost of a smile crossed her face.

"Yeah." He started to walk away but turned back to add, "Jodi, I'm sorry I haven't been a very good friend lately. Thanks for calling me, even when I didn't call you back."

"Sure, no problem." She watched him disappear into the throng of kids, a warm feeling spreading through her that he had broken the silence between them. She had missed him!

Junior year, Jodi was still an outsider at Firwood High School. Still, things were different from last year. Perhaps it was because she was happy, and something about a happy person does not invite ridicule the way an unhappy or insecure person does. No one overtly teased her, (although she still heard the words 'gimp' and 'crip' behind her back), and many kids actually made eye contact with her and smiled. Once, Brooke and Mindy even invited her to eat lunch with them. She politely declined, for she still took advantage of lunch time to work on homework. But it touched her deeply that they thought her worthy enough to invite. She was an outsider, but at least she was not an outcast. She attended all her classes and did her work. It was early in the quarter, but so far she had straight As. She never got in trouble.

Once, near the end of the first week of school, she felt someone grab her upper arm in the hall. "Hey there."

She turned and looked up into the face of Kirby Portman.

"You going to Sheryl Andrew's party this weekend?" he asked.

"No," she replied in confusion.

"Why not? Isn't your sister going?"

"Yeah, Sheryl is one of her best friends."

"Why don't you go?"

She laughed at the idea, still confused as to why he was asking. "First of all, Sheryl didn't invite me. Second, I don't think I'd go even if she had. I can't imagine anything more boring than a party given by Sheryl."

He smirked as if he agreed and leaned his face in to whisper in her ear, "I bet your sister could get you invited. Go to the party," he said in a commanding tone. "I'll be there and I'll take you to another party that will be a lot more fun." Then he moved on, confident she would do as he asked.

Whoa, is Kirby like asking me out? Sort of...maybe? She considered his invitation, tempted. She knew if she asked Melody that her twin would actually be happy to have her go with her to the party. And, Melody would cover for her if she left the party for a little while. She would only agree to go with Kirby if he would bring her back before

Sheryl's party ended. She could probably get away with it. *And Kirby Portman has asked me out – well, almost the same as asked me out!* She thought about it many times, imagined ridiculous scenes of popular kids staring in awe as Kirby walked into a room with his arm around her, the looks of incredulity, even envy. *Maybe he would kiss me!* She had never been kissed by a boy and was intensely curious. *I could do it…but what if…?*

In the end, Jodi decided it just wasn't worth being restricted from the horses. She never went to the party. The following Monday Kirby gave her a very funny look, and he avoided her for a while. But a week later he began to make eye contact with her again and it seemed he went out of his way sometimes to pass her in the hall. Jodi could not figure that out.

Horses were the most important thing in her life. She doubted she would ever be a great rider, but she was already a fine horsewoman. She knew every horse at Pegasus and loved them all. Nothing equaled the pleasure of a horse whinnying at her in recognition and coming up to her. She loved everything she did at the stable - feeding, turning out horses, grooming, even cleaning stalls - almost as much as riding horses. The thing she hated most about school starting up again, was that she could not spend all day at the stable except on holidays and weekends.

She never used to dream about her future other than wondering if she would ever have a boyfriend. But hanging around Sierra over the summer and listening to Sierra talk enthusiastically about her dream to be a veterinarian, inspired Jodi to think positively about her own future. *It has to be something to do with horses,* she was sure of that. She didn't think she wanted to be a veterinarian. She had spent too much time in doctors' offices, clinics, and therapy; being poked, prodded, and tested. She wanted no part of a medical career.

I don't care about riding in horse shows as long as I can just plain ride. But I bet I could learn to train horses. Just watching River schooling horses and many of the other students at Pegasus, she was beginning to recognize correctness in how the horse moved or responded to aids. She found herself thinking of what the rider needed to do to improve.

River never minded if she stood next to him when he gave a lesson. He even asked her sometimes what she thought. *I bet if I could work with someone like River I could learn to give lessons and even train horses from the ground.*

There were many possibilities. Maybe she would like to even breed horses. Her parents had always declared that both their daughters would go to college. Now, Jodi actually looked forward to going to a university and she began to compile a list of schools that offered equine science degrees.

But more immediately, Jodi dreamed of a horse of her own. Melody's and her sixteenth birthday was coming up in a week. She knew Melody, who had taken driver's education over the summer, wanted a car. Jodi asked for a horse.

"Hey," Todd greeted, slipping into the seat Jodi had saved for him on the bus.

"Hi." She smiled as he settled in, trying to think of how to begin a conversation.

Todd set his backpack between his legs on the floor and then laid his head back with his eyes closed, tuning out everything around him.

Jodi kept glancing at him awkwardly. Finally, she steeled her nerves and said, "I'm sorry about your mother." *Maybe I shouldn't have said that*, she thought when Todd's shoulders stiffened and his brow creased between his closed eyes.

Suddenly, his eyes flew open and he ducked his head toward her. "Do you ever hate your parents?"

Whoa, didn't expect that! She thought for a moment before she answered, "Yeah, I guess I have sometimes."

He nodded in accord and leaned his head back, shaking it a little. "My therapist says all children hate their parents sometimes."

"I guess that's probably true."

"But most kids don't mean it…that they hate their parents. Or, they might but they get over it."

"Yeah…." This conversation was making Jodi feel very, very uncomfortable. "Todd…"

"I can't get over feeling like I killed my mother." He made a noise like he was trying to laugh but couldn't quite do it. With his head against the back of the seat he turned to her. "I'm sorry. I shouldn't be laying all this heavy stuff on you."

"It's okay."

"No." He managed to smile. "Jodi, you're…well, I guess I just feel like I can talk to you."

"Really, it's okay." She smiled back.

Now his smile seemed more genuine, reaching his eyes. "You are a good friend. Enough of this morbidness. How's the riding going?"

"Slow, you know, my ankle and all…." Perhaps because Todd had confessed to her his feelings, she found it easy to express her own. "But it's just so fantastic!" Todd's face softened and even his posture became more relaxed as he listened to Jodi tell him enthusiastically about her past few lessons. His interest spurred her on to give him every detail.

"My first lesson after River got back, he was so impressed! He says the trail riding has really improved my seat and he likes my quiet hands. Even my left leg position has gotten better. Todd, I'm cantering now! It is so amazing and Dune, she is the sweetest horse out there. The first few times I kind of started to lose my balance because it's so different from how trot feels, and I panicked a little. She knew, and she slowed and collected herself to make her back rounder and smoother for me. I'm still a little nervous about cantering, but it's getting easier and someday I know I'll think nothing of it, and I bet I'll even canter on the trails."

"I bet you will," Todd agreed.

The bus slowed and both were surprised to see they had already neared their stop. They gathered their things, ready to hop off.

"You can ride Fala," River said, after Todd had changed into riding clothes and sought him out.

"Okay."

"Jodi has her lesson first, so take your time. Bring Fala to the outdoor dressage arena when you have her ready."

"Sounds good." Todd smiled in gratitude. Before he looked for Fala he spent a little time stopping at each paddock and checking out the horse within, especially the ones he remembered. Morrison recognized him and with a welcoming nicker, sauntered to the gate, expecting a carrot. Todd gave him the treat, and then visited the old pony Muffin, Tucker, Sierra's horse Fiel, and then Corazón. Finally he visited Felicity.

"Hey there, I'm sorry…about what happened," he murmured to her, after entering the paddock and she met him for her treat. "Not your fault." He stroked her neck and felt a little bit better when the mare nuzzled at his hand, only concerned about more carrots. *She forgives me.*

After visiting Felicity, he went to find Fala, pleased when the black mare obviously recognized him and trotted up, looking for a carrot. When River told him to get Fala, Todd had felt relief. He had ridden her so many times over the past years and knew her well. He did not want to admit to anyone how afraid he was of falling.

He did take his time grooming the black mare, relishing the pleasure of working around a horse again. Just her nearness seemed a balm for his spirit. He tacked her up and led her out to the arena. He still had plenty of time, so he watched Jodi riding a few minutes before mounting up.

That's Dune? The cream-colored mare Jodi rode did not look at all like the ugly nag he remembered before his exile. This horse's coat gleamed with health and her one eye shone brightly with enthusiasm as Jodi trotted her around. Her upper neck muscle had developed to dominate the shape of her neck, and her hindquarters flexed powerfully as she moved with impressive springiness. *Could another dun horse have come to Pegasus?* Then Jodi circled away from him to the left and he saw the puckered, empty eye socket. *It is Dune!* Amazing how a year of good care and conditioning work and a rider keeping the horse in a correct frame, could change a horse's appearance, almost as if a miracle.

And Jodi, she looks great! When Jodi had modestly told him about her progress, he got the impression she was still a beginner rider. But he watched her ride that mare with hardly any visible evidence of using her hands and very minimal movement of her legs. She rode Dune through all sorts of gymnastic exercises and gait transitions using primarily seat and legs and steady hands. *Like most people, she's overly critical of herself,* he determined. Yeah, he could see where she had difficulty with canter; tipping forward when she lost her balance, and the downward transition to trot quite choppy. But still, she had come a long way since the last time he saw her ride.

It looked like Jodi's lesson was about over and she was cooling the mare down, so Todd mounted up and began walking Fala around in warm-up. He knew River was watching as he gathered the reins and asked Fala to trot.

"Todd," River called him over after watching him make a few walk-trot-walk transitions. "Would you mind if I put you back on the lunge line?"

"No! River, I'll do anything you ask." He was surprised River even asked rather than just insisting.

"Good, I want you to work on using your seat and legs. No hands for a while."

It was humbling to be back on a lunge line with the reins taken away like a rank beginner. He felt his face heating up when Brooke led her horse into the arena to warm up for her own lesson after his, but quickly pushed his embarrassment down. *What do I care what Brooke thinks? I want to ride like River and I'll do whatever it takes.*

River asked him to make transitions from walk to trot and back to walk. "Take your time, Todd. You used to do this but you've forgotten when you started relying on your reins. It's harder when you have to unlearn something," River said patiently when Todd at first could not bring Fala to walk. "Repeat your aids: sit deep, firm up your back, legs soft…try again. You have to figure out just the right amount of bracing your back with the right amount of support from your legs. There…good!"

It took a few tries for Todd to find that balance, but when he finally brought Fala to a walk, then back to trot and walk to halt again with the same balance of aids, it actually became easy. Fortunately, he had a secure seat from his years of riding and his muscle memory remembered how a horse moves beneath him. He didn't have to worry about staying on. He could concentrate completely on refining the aids.

At the end of his lesson, Brooke, who had been watching, said, "That was awesome. River, you promised to put me on the lunge line too. Are we going to do that today?" Todd laughed to himself that he had actually been embarrassed in front of Brooke.

Todd worked it out with River to have two lessons a week and to return to riding one horse a day on the trail for conditioning. He didn't care at all that he was assigned the slower work on the out-of-condition horses. He was back in the good graces of River and Pegasus!

"Do you want one of your lessons with Tess on jumping?" River had asked.

"Later," Todd promptly replied. "I agree with you, I need to get back to the basics."

"Okay, good."

Todd really did believe re-learning the basics was what he needed right now. But deep down, he did not want to admit that he might be afraid of ever jumping again.

Of course Melody wanted an extra special party to celebrate turning sixteen. Jodi didn't even try to talk her out of it. She did try to convince Melody and her parents to just make it Melody's party.

"That is just ridiculous," Melody declared. "We're twins; and that is so special even if we are not identical. This party has to be for both of us." Her parents backed her up.

Their actual birthday came on Thursday. The party would be on the following Saturday. But after school, they still had a small family celebration, going out to a favorite restaurant and then coming home for matching birthday cakes, each twin's favorite.

So far, neither girl had received a present from their parents.

"Dad," Melody whined, watching him eating his cake slowly, savoring every bite, knowing she watched him expectantly. "Is the birthday party all we're getting for a present?"

"Isn't that enough?" he teased. Cora Mae smiled with a knowing expression.

"A person only turns sixteen once. It is one of the most important birthdays of a life," Melody insisted.

"That's why we rented the ballroom and hired a band. Do you think I'm made of money?" His eyes twinkled.

"Melody, it's enough," Jodi said. She knew her parents had spent a lot of money for this party, and Jodi did not expect anything else. She would have preferred the money spent in other ways but had resigned herself to this ritualistic need to acknowledge turning sixteen. So much for getting a horse.

"Okay, I get it," Melody said, hiding her disappointment. But she possessed an agreeable temperament and as she thought about it, she did appreciate how much her parents had done for this party. It certainly was a much grander affair than what either Sheryl or Mary had when they turned sixteen before her. She got up to help her mother clear the plates and put away the leftover cake. "What's this?" she asked. Beneath the cake plate she had just lifted from the table sat a white envelope with her name on it.

"Where'd that come from?" her father asked, feigning surprise.

Jodi had also lifted up the plate holding her cake, preparing to help as well. A similar envelop with her name on it sat beneath the plate.

"Set the cakes down, girls," Cora Mae said, laughing. "Open the envelopes."

Inside each envelope were sixteen one-hundred dollar bills.

Melody screamed in glee. "A car! This is enough money to buy a used car!"

Jodi smiled happily at both her parents. Sixteen hundred dollars was enough money to buy a decent horse, perhaps not well-bred or highly trained, but a good solid horse (like Dune!).

It didn't take long for Melody to find a car (she had been checking Craig's List for months) that she could afford, adding the sixteen hundred to what she already had saved. With her father's guidance, she tried out three used cars and settled on a four-cylinder Dodge Neon.

Like most new drivers with access to a car, Melody wanted to drive everywhere. She offered to drive Jodi and Todd to the stable after school and then pick them up as long as she didn't' have an after school activity or somewhere she wanted to go. Jodi insisted on riding in the back seat, claiming it was more comfortable to be able to stretch her leg out. What she really wanted was for Todd to sit next to Melody, and that perhaps Melody could help cheer up Todd.

Jodi told River she had money now to buy a horse. "But I always hear that buying the horse is the least expensive part. I don't know if I can afford to keep one. Can you maybe write out a list of everything a horse needs and approximately what it costs?"

"Sure," River agreed. He made the list for her and also began to teach her about horse care beyond grooming and riding. "I'll talk to Tess, but as far as I'm concerned, you can board a horse here in exchange for the stall cleaning you do. I may be able to find some other chores around here that could help pay for the other stuff like shoes and vet bills."

"I could actually own a horse!" Jodi exclaimed. "Do you think you could help find a good horse for me, a horse like Dune?"

"I'll try."

Jodi had hoped he would say she could buy Dune. She knew he hadn't paid very much for her. But River didn't offer to sell her, so Jodi settled for hoping he could find her a horse she could love just as much.

The season changed from fall to winter. The horses had their winter coats clipped and now needed to wear blankets when turned out. It rained as often as not, and the rain ponchos and rain sheets hung on the wall outside the tack room for convenience when needed. Most lessons took place in the indoor arena.

Perhaps after watching Tess mourn the loss of Gunsmoke, River wanted to do something for her, a peace offering to let her know he cared. He finally agreed to sell Oberon to Mrs. Galensburg. Really, it made no difference to him in his relationship with his horse, or according to the terms of the sales contract, his control of Oberon's training and competitions. Mrs. Galensburg, pleased with her 'on paper' ownership of Oberon, donated Pendragon to Pegasus. He would make a wonderful schoolmaster for more advanced riders.

River took Oberon to the Dressage Finals in Kentucky that November. Oberon won both the open grand prix and grand prix freestyle classes. When Mrs. Galensburg actually smiled, a smile that reached her eyes, when having her photo taken as Oberon's owner, River was surprised how good it made him feel that he had helped this woman come closer to her dream of owning an Olympic champion. It especially surprised him because he didn't even like the woman.

Lisa and Volantis had moved up to grand prix this year, and they came in second in the open class behind River. The four riders on

Jack's team all rode horses from Stone Valley, and all placed in their classes, many of them taking first.

"I know you're still in school," Lisa said, on the last day of the championship as everyone was packing up to return to their home stables. "What are you doing for your winter break?"

"Looking forward to not studying and having more time to ride," River answered, not looking up from stuffing grooming articles into the corners of a trunk.

"Why don't you give yourself a break from everything? Come spend Christmas at my family's stable," she invited. "We have a trail that takes us right onto a beach. Have you ever ridden on the beach?"

"Yeah, actually I have." River smiled to himself remembering a few summers ago. He and Sierra had trailered horses to a state park on the coast that had beach trails. *What a fun day that had been!* Bitterness that it had all been part of a false sense of eternal love, quickly obscured the sweetness of the memory. He glanced sideways at Lisa. *What does she want from me?* "It is fun."

"So, come on down," she repeated, her smile full of hope.

He turned his face back to the trunk. "Uh...*be nice*, he warned himself. "Thanks, Lisa. I'll think about it, but I probably won't know if I can get away until I talk to my boss."

"Sure, just let me know."

River didn't have much time to think about anything until he had Oberon settled for his flight home with the equine transporter company, and his own plane was finally taxiing for takeoff. He wanted to sleep, but he found his thoughts drifting to Lisa and her invitation.

He liked Lisa...a lot. She was certainly beautiful, easy to be with, nice to hold and kiss, but...*the truth is, she is not Sierra.* His throat suddenly tightened, and he turned to press his face against the cold glass of the window, peering at the ground receding away as the plane began its ascent. *I don't feel at all for Lisa the way I once felt about Sierra...still feel about her?* If he accepted Lisa's invitation, he would not have the chance to catch a glimpse of Sierra when she came home for her winter break. *Why do I want to torture myself? Wouldn't it be better to go away?*

Perhaps in time he could fall in love with Lisa. He was pretty sure she already liked him. In fact, he had been a little annoyed with her possessiveness during the championship, for she assumed they would go everywhere together. Then it occurred to him it would not have annoyed him if it had been Sierra with him (but she wouldn't have come anyway), and the old resentment resurfaced, that Sierra could not take even a little time away from school to be with him. That helped him decide. *I'll go - spend Christmas with Lisa.*

But by the time the plane had landed and he at last drove into the stable yard of Pegasus, he was not so sure.

Over the remaining weeks before the holidays, River vacillated in his decision to visit Lisa. She called him several times for an answer.

"What did your boss say?"

"I haven't asked her yet," River said. "I've been so busy since I got home that I never remember to ask until she has left."

"Can't you just call and ask her?"

"Yeah, but it's better if I ask in person." River knew he was making up excuses. He didn't need Tess's permission if he really wanted to visit Lisa.

Two weeks before Christmas, Laila brought Megan to the stable.

"Muffin, where is Muffin?" Megan cried out the moment she escaped from her mother's car. Since no horses were around, she skipped up to River coming toward her. She held her arms out and he scooped her up.

"She teases me to take her to the horses from the moment I pick her up from Gwen's," Laila explained, joining them. "Since Todd gets a ride home with someone, Gwen hardly ever picks him up anymore so Megan hasn't been to the stable in over a week."

"You should bring her by more often," River encouraged. "I'll bring her home."

"Great," Laila said sarcastically. "You know I'm trying to get her interested in something besides horses."

"Mommy, you go home. I will stay with Unca River," Megan said, nodding her head solemnly to assure her mother this was an excellent plan. River set her down and she reached up for his hand, pulling him toward the paddocks where the pony, in her mind, should be waiting for her.

"It's in her blood," River said with a shrug of his shoulders and giving Laila a smirk. He allowed Megan to pull him along to Muffin's paddock.

Muffin sauntered over, whickering at the little girl he recognized as one who always had treats. Megan fearlessly fed him carrots, cooing at the pony as he delicately lipped each one from her tiny palm. Then River lifted her up onto the pony's back.

"Walk," Megan said in a commanding tone. She sat up with shoulders squared and her little legs pushing against the pony's sides, already learning the correct seat. Obligingly, Muffin walked off.

"Hold on to his mane," Laila cried out.

"She doesn't need to hold on," River assured Megan's nervous mother, "watch." When Muffin walked to the corner of the paddock and stopped, River called out, "Use your legs."

Megan again commanded her pony, "Walk," and with her legs, aided him to turn and walk on a circle.

"I give up," Laila said, laughing. She leaned against the paddock fence next to River, watching her four-year-old daughter riding the pony independently.

"Horses will keep her out of trouble, be glad," River said, reciting what he often overheard from mothers of his teenage students.

"Great," Laila responded sarcastically, but with a smile of amusement. "So, are you coming to the Marshalls' Christmas party?"

"Uh, I kind of forgot about that. When is it?"

"The Saturday after the kids are out of school."

"Sierra will probably go to that."

Laila frowned and narrowed her eyes to study him. "River, when are you going to quit being so stupid and make up with Sierra."

"Wha..?" he started to protest.

Thumping his shoulder Laila persisted. "Are you going to California or not? You could certainly avoid Sierra if you go." She had heard about the invitation one evening when River had come over for help with a school assignment, and Lisa happened to call.

"I haven't decided."

"Not only are you stupid but you can be a jerk as well," Laila stated bluntly. "If you really liked this Lisa you wouldn't hesitate to spend time with her. Since you can't make up your mind, you obviously haven't fallen in love were her." She punched his shoulder again when he tried to say something. "Look, I've seen her photo, she's beautiful. And you obviously have a lot in common since you're both such great horse people. You told me she's very nice. Sounds like she's perfect for you."

"Maybe it's just too soon after Sierra for me to just fall in love with the next girl who comes along," River said bitterly.

"It's been almost a year." Laila grabbed River's shoulders to make him look her in the eye. "Don't string this Lisa along. Don't hurt her. It's unkind."

Dumbfounded, River stared back at his friend. It had never occurred to him that a girl could care about him deeply enough to have her feelings hurt if he didn't return those feelings. He often suspected Sierra did not suffer as he was over their break-up. He hadn't thought he might hurt Lisa.

"Make up your mind," Laila said. As River's surprised look turned into a frown she persisted, "So, another man kissed Sierra. So what? You told me she said he was just a friend. She went to coffee with a friend. So what? She studied with a friend. Let's see, you've never done anything like that?"

"No," he denied.

"Hmm…"

"Are you talking about you helping me study?"

With a snort of derision Laila said, "No, of course not. Sierra knows I help you; she even asked me to. I'm not a secret. I was referring to when you took Lisa to dinner two years ago, remember?

You and Sierra were still together then, but you went out with another woman."

"She invited me, just as a thank you sort of thing," he replied defensively.

Laila cocked her head with a raised eyebrow. "And right away, you told Sierra all about it."

"Okay, I get it. The truth is I do trust Sierra. I think she was telling me the truth about that whole thing. I was jealous and I over-reacted. But she broke up with me because you are right, I am a jerk. She deserves a lot better."

"I see," Laila continued in a sarcastic tone. She folded her arms and nodded her head as if sorting out his words. She called out to her daughter, "Megan, that's enough, sweetie. We need to go."

"Mommy, look!" Megan tried to distract her mother from leaving. She kicked Muffin into a slow jog.

"Megan!" Laila gasped.

"She's fine," River stated calmly.

Laila took a step forward, but when the pony settled back to a walk with Megan giggling happily, she sighed in resignation. She turned to glare at River who watched Megan with a look of amusement. Laila narrowed her eyes and remarked, "So, you and Sierra are fighting about nothing at all. You're back in the 'I'm so inferior', mood. River, you really are an idiot and a jerk."

That night, River called Lisa and told her he couldn't come.

"Your boss won't let you have any time off for Christmas? Not even two days? That seems kind of harsh. All our workers get Christmas Eve and Christmas off and we rotate giving them a week off if they want it." Lisa spoke rapidly and nervously, somehow sensing what was coming.

"It's not my boss, Lisa. Look, I don't know how to say this but…"

"Don't say it," Lisa blurted out. "Just never mind."

River heard a tremor in her voice as if she were about to cry. "Lisa…"

"Goodbye, River. I'll see you next spring at Jack's." She hung up.

18 LEG AIDS AND JUMPING

Riders should be made aware that to take with the inside rein generally causes the very opposite of what they desire. - Sylvia Loch, *The Classical Rider*

Being around horses and riding again did not result in Todd immediately overcoming his depression, but it definitely helped. Gradually, he no longer awoke each morning with a weight in his belly, but with a normal, healthy emptiness, both physical from hunger but also the healthy desire of an adolescent to experience life with all his senses. By the time school started up after the holidays, Todd was hanging out with his old friends. He could joke around and laugh. The drawings he created in art were not as dark as they had been at the beginning of the school year, no longer exuding morbidity.

Access to horses helped, his counseling sessions helped, but perhaps another factor also helped lift his depression. Sitting next to Melody whenever she gave Todd and Jodi a ride, and getting the impression she really enjoyed his company, helped Todd regain a sense of self-worth. If someone like Melody could think of Todd as 'good', well, maybe he wasn't so bad after all.

Shortly after River returned from the dressage finals in November, he started allowing Todd to use reins while still on the lunge line. "Try to remember they are for communication, not control. You control Fala with your seat and legs," he said.

"I'll try," Todd agreed, determined to follow every instruction River gave him. And, he actually was quite impressed and also proud, at the quick responses now of Fala to his seat and leg aids. He gingerly picked up the reins and concentrating hard, began to re-learn how to use reins correctly. River kept him on the lunge line for only two more lessons after that.

The first few lessons off the lunge line had gone well and Todd felt like he was really making progress. He was using his seat and legs for transitions, and using the reins softly for communication and support. Even when River asked him to move Fala onto a twenty-meter circle, reminding him, "Do it with your legs," Todd had been able to accomplish the exercise, and then onto a figure-eight and a serpentine.

After the holidays, River began to ask for more difficult work in Todd's lesson, adding lateral exercises.

"Off your leg, let go of the inside rein. Off your leg, Todd," River called out repeatedly as Todd tried to leg yield Fala off the rail. He thought he could do it when he pulled her to the side using his inside hand and thumping her with his outside leg, but River said, "She's just turning her head and moving off at a diagonal. She's not straight."

Todd just could not get it. It didn't make sense when River said, "Every time you feel like you need the inside rein is probably when you should lighten up on it or even use the outside rein." How could using the outside rein get Fala to move off the rail? When he tried it, all she did was turn her head to the rail. He felt frustrated and confused.

For the first time, since starting lessons again with River, Todd was not looking forward to today's lesson. Feeling dejected and inept, he walked along with Jodi after the two had been dropped off after school.

River met them at the stable entrance. "Todd, I think I'm going to have you ride Penny today."

"Pendragon?" Todd repeated, very surprised.

"Yeah, bring him in. I'll help you with the tack."

A combination of excitement mixed with foreboding at the thought of riding a horse he had never ridden before, caused Todd's heart to quicken, and he gulped in air to quiet down his nerves as he went in search of Pendragon. He thought River must be as frustrated with his inability to ride Fala in lateral work as he was with himself. Feeling confused, he wondered, *Why is he putting me up on Pendragon? It certainly isn't punishment.*

"You'll be fine, right?" Todd asked softly as he led the bay gelding inside. He had never seen Penny misbehave under River, but he had never seen anyone but River ride him; so that didn't reassure him that he could get along as well.

With River's help, they soon had Pendragon ready for the lesson. Todd's nerves had mostly settled to normal when Penny stood sleepily in the crossties and now placidly walked as Todd led him up to the mounting block. *He's bored, nothing around to excite him today*, Todd reassured himself, but also hating that he was having this fearful reaction.

"Penny is very sensitive to leg aids. I want to see if riding a horse with more refined training than Fala will help you get the feel of what I want you to do," River explained walking with Todd to the arena.

"Oh, good idea," Todd agreed. He mounted and River helped him adjust the stirrup length and then told him to ride onto the rail on a loose rein. Pendragon obediently walked off, stretching his neck comfortably.

"He is nice and relaxed but he has no energy. Wake him up, Todd," River said, watching the bay walking with lazy steps. "Just legs," River called out when Todd began to gather the reins.

Todd was fine with Pendragon's laziness, nevertheless, he pressed with his legs. Pendragon flicked his ears and picked up his pace slightly. Todd applied more leg and again got a response as his mount lengthened his stride.

"Better, keep that walk," River said.

After two circuits around in each direction, and finding Pendragon keeping the pace Todd asked for without becoming tense, Todd also began to relax.

Waiting until he detected a softening of Todd's spine and less stiffness in his shoulders, River then said, "You can pick up the reins. Penny has a very soft mouth and doesn't need more than a squeeze with your hands." River studied Todd's hands as he gathered the reins to be sure he did not pull back or hold onto the bay's mouth. Satisfied, he said, "Go rising trot on a big circle. I want him to loosen up a little more before we put him to work. Keep your hands soft."

Todd obeyed, and when River said, "Good, back to walk," he remembered to sit deep using his core muscles and straighten his back with his legs softly on. He dared not use reins and was pleasantly surprised when Pendragon obediently transitioned down to walk from the seat and leg aids alone.

"Very good, Todd. Okay, you are going to work on moving him off your leg. Your hands are good right now - very quiet. Stay soft like that and ride him down the long side. See if you can move him onto the quarter line with just your outside leg and a little weight to the inside."

"I'll try." Todd brought Pendragon around the corner and rode him forward several steps to make sure he was straight. Then he touched with his outside leg and weighted his inside stirrup. To his amazement, Pendragon obediently yielded away from his leg. *Awesome!*

"Squeeze with your outside fingers very gently to keep his head and neck straight, just the slightest flexion to the outside…great, Todd!" River called out when Todd kept Pendragon leg-yielding to the quarter line. "Now go straight a few strides, then just reverse your aids and leg yield back to the rail."

They continued with the leg-yielding exercise a few times in each direction. Then River instructed Todd to do the same at a working trot.

Todd obeyed, again amazed and exhilarated by Pendragon's obedient response. He glanced ahead at the mirror mounted at the end of the arena, and noticed how his horse moved almost with his body parallel to the wall of the arena as he leg-yielded from rail to quarter line and back to rail. He practiced in both directions.

"That was great, Todd. You did all that with your legs, and you may not realize it, but you used your weight in the direction of movement. Could you feel that?"

"I'm not sure," Todd admitted. "I guess I was just too focused on how awesome it is to have a horse actually move off my leg!"

River nodded and smiled. *At last!* "Okay, one more time in each direction, but now I want you to also focus on keeping a little firmer contact with the outside rein to help keep his shoulders straight."

It felt strange to try and use the reins after so often being told to 'let go'. Suddenly, he felt the connection of how the movement he wanted came from his legs, and how just a little squeeze and steady hold on the outside rein kept Pendragon straight. He reached forward with his inside hand to give one quick pat, and he praised the willing horse, "Good boy, thank you."

For his next few lessons, Todd rode Pendragon. River had him progress from leg-yielding to more advanced lateral work — shoulder-in, travers, and renvers. Riding a well-trained horse - a schoolmaster, made so much difference. Pendragon was quick to respond to the lightest of seat and leg aids and steadying hand aids. Todd felt he had learned more in five lessons on Penny than he had in years on Fala and other horses.

He had thought the ability to gallop cross country and jump was the ultimate in horsemanship. Now, getting quick, accurate responses from the lightest of aids seemed even more a thrill. He began to experience the true partnership of horse and rider, rather than just a rider controlling a willing horse. *How ignorant I was...still am.* Todd had come to a crossroads, and with the recognition of how much he needed to learn, he had turned onto the golden path to true horsemanship.

As his lessons progressed, Todd found that Pendragon responded amazingly to even the hint of a leg aid, almost spontaneous with the flexing of Todd's leg muscle, he was that prompt. But he also found Penny did not appreciate it if he held with too much pressure on a rein or held moments too long. Pendragon let him know with a stiffening of his back and slight push against his hands. But that reaction helped Todd refine his aids to approach precision. Todd realized that Pendragon was the master here, furthering his education. When Todd 'asked' correctly, Penny 'answered' with fluid, balanced movements that thrilled Todd with his amazing controlled power. It was a thrill equal to that of jumping!

After a month of lessons on Pendragon, there came a day when River said several times during the lesson, "Well done, Todd," and not much else. It was the first lesson where Todd realized the horse was 'telling' him what he needed to do, and River didn't have to direct his every move.

"How would you like to try passage?" River asked toward the end of a very satisfactory session.

"You mean it?" Todd asked, excited.

"Sure," River answered, and came up alongside where Todd now rode Penny at a collected walk. River took the dressage whip from Todd, and then jogged alongside a few steps as he coached Todd through the aids, reinforcing those aids with a touch of the whip on the bay's rear end. Once Todd was able to use the aids effectively, River backed away.

Riding passage! Todd's throat tightened in an inexplicable reaction to the thrill in his chest as he experienced the incredible, elegant power of Pendragon's back rounding beneath his seat as his hindquarters pushed him up and forward. It truly felt as if they floated.

"Excellent," River called out. "That's enough; bring him back to a working trot, go rising, and give the reins to let him stretch. Praise him!"

"You are magnificent! You are awesome!" Todd murmured to Penny, and stroked the bay's neck on both sides.

When Todd brought Penny to walk and looked over at River with a wide grin, River's own chest swelled with the feeling of an instructor whose pupil has finally learned a difficult lesson. How gratifying that Todd finally understood how much a horse will give with so little required in the asking.

The next lesson, River told Todd to ride Fala.

"Oh, okay," Todd said, trying to hide his disappointment. He had really looked forward to riding Pendragon again, and this almost felt like a demotion.

"Let's see if you can use what you've learned from Penny on a horse not quite as well-trained."

After the weeks on Pendragon, Todd was surprised at how riding Fala was suddenly a different experience. He could feel now when she hollowed her back and neck when he asked her to move into a shoulder-in. But he used the same aids he had learned to refine from riding Pendragon. He pushed more with his inside leg and held steady with his outside hand to get her to move her shoulders off the rail rather than just turning her neck to the inside. At last he could feel her inside hind leg pushing up underneath his seat. Succeeding with Fala was almost as much a thrill as riding Pendragon, for this time it was because he had communicated with her and she understood. Penny had been his trainer. Now he was the trainer.

Tess happened by and stopped to watch the lesson. *Todd is getting that kind of work from Fala?* She was impressed. The lesson came to an end and she called out, "River, is he ready to start jumping again?"

River looked at Todd, leaving it up to him. "What do you think?"

Todd's stomach lurched unexpectedly. He had pushed all thoughts of jumping out of his mind as he became completely absorbed in his new appreciation of dressage work. The thought, *maybe I should just ride dressage,* came to him at the same time as the sudden onset of physical symptoms. Blackness shadowed the edges of his vision...*a narrow crevasse to swallow him up*...and even deeper...*a lid coming down....."Stay in there, naughty boy." Blackness inside a musty, small space...I can't breathe!*

"Todd?" River asked him again.

He shook his head, not to say 'no', but to clear his mind. *I have to do this.* He nodded to River to negate shaking his head. He turned to Tess, "That would be great."

"You're very quiet today," Melody commented as she pulled onto the highway after picking up Jodi and Todd from the stable. She noted him to be deep in thought, more like how he had been months ago. In fact, she had almost forgotten how depressed he had been back then, for lately he laughed and joked with her the entire ride home. She hoped nothing had triggered a relapse today.

"I'm just thinking," he said, pulling himself out of his thoughts.

"What about?" she asked with a brief turn of her head to give him a smile.

"My lesson today. It was so cool...like I've had a breakthrough." He had actually been brooding about jumping, but of course could not say that to Melody. But he could talk about his awesome lesson. He turned slightly to include Jodi, for she would understand his explanation more than Melody. "I rode Fala in my lesson today and after riding Pendragon, I can't believe how easy it was to get her to respond to leg aids."

"Cool," Jodi said, nodding in comprehension. "That's what I've been working on too, on Dune. She is so sweet and she tries so hard. It is so cool when I can move her around with just my legs. The hard part now, when River wants me to take contact with the reins, is trying to figure out just the right amount of pressure."

"Yeah, it's not the same with every horse. Penny tends to over bend with too much hand and I don't always realize it until River says…"

"Come on, you guys," Melody interrupted with a laugh. "What on earth are you two talking about?"

"Oh, sorry," Todd apologized, and he smiled at Melody. His mood had lightened.

Melody was quiet for a few minutes, concentrating on making a left hand turn. Once she pulled onto the new street she began, "By the way, Todd, um…you know I'm having a small party this Saturday night?"

"Oh yeah?"

"I was thinking…actually I was wondering if you want to come." She turned her head briefly to look at him, and then turned back to watch the road, biting on her lower lip.

Whoa, she's nervous about asking me! Todd watched her face, creasing into a frown while she waited for his answer. "Sure, I'll come," he said, and was just as surprised when her face relaxed into a smile of relief, bright with happiness. *Wow!* A year ago, this would have thrilled him beyond belief. But that was before his mother died. That was before his world had turned gray and his feelings numb. Somehow, when he slowly came up from that depression, he didn't feel quite as overcome in Melody's presence. Maybe it was the weeks of being near her calm, empathetic presence that had somehow taken away the awe and mystery of her. But he was still attracted to her and liked her very much. It would be fun to go to her party.

In the back seat, Jodi rolled her eyes.

Todd went to Melody's party. He stood next to her as she moved through her guests, stopping to talk to a group here and there. He danced with her, and toward the end of the evening, somehow Todd found himself in an easy chair with Melody on his lap. They made out. He liked that, but it wasn't quite the thrill he had always imagined kissing Melody would be.

After that, and he was never quite sure how it happened, he and Melody were apparently going together. That meant he walked with her in between classes holding her hand, hanging out with her during the lunch break (she still ate lunch with her group of friends and he ate lunch with his friends), kissing her whenever they said goodbye, and hanging out with her on weekends. It was nice. Many of his friends envied him. But just as kissing Melody was not quite what he had imagined, neither was having Melody as a girlfriend quite as exciting as he thought it would be.

Two weeks went by before Tess got around to fitting Todd into her jumping lesson schedule. When Todd noted it, he again experienced a wave of dizziness and nausea. He swallowed hard, forcing the feelings into submission. *The day after tomorrow.*

"I adjusted the conditioning rides so you can take Fala on the trail today and tomorrow," River said, coming up behind him. "Trot and gallop her a few times. That will be good before you jump her again."

"Great," Todd replied, hoping he didn't sound as nervous as he felt. He agreed with River. Two days out on the trail on Fala should help him regain some confidence. Fala almost never spooked, and with their improved communication in flat work, she should be easy to control out in the open. After all, he used to gallop her up and down hills and had even jumped her cross country.

Even so, he found himself nervous and tense for the jumping lesson two days later. Fala sensed his nervousness. As he warmed her up, he could feel her responses less prompt as if she questioned him, 'what's going on?'.

"Good warm-up," Tess said after twenty minutes of watching Todd ride the exercises. "It's been a while since you've jumped, right?"

"Yes," Todd admitted, bringing Fala to walk in a circle around Tess while he received her instructions.

"Okay, pick up the trot and circle as if you were starting a course, and then go down the cavalletti line, but keep her in trot."

"Right," Todd said. *No problem.* He signaled Fala to trot and then posting, circled as Tess had instructed. He approached the line, the poles barely six inches above the ground. *No problem, no problem…*Todd recited to himself. Nevertheless, Fala's neck stiffened as she raised her head, feeling a wall in his hands instead of a gentle give with her motion. She trotted across the poles, hitting the last three. Todd let out his breath as they finished the line, unaware he had been holding it in.

"That was horrible," Tess shouted. "Do it again and take control of your mount. You didn't help her at all down that line."

Todd circled again. *That wasn't bad, we can do this.* As they approached the line, he focused his eyes beyond the poles, trying to pretend they did not exist and trusting Fala to get him across. But he had to look at the first pole as he felt the mare veer to the side. He reflexively jerked her head back to the line, forgetting to be soft with his aids. He kept his legs on and urged her over the poles. It was choppy, but at least Fala didn't knock any of the poles this time.

"Better, but that was still far from good. Again!" Tess ordered.

It's only trotting. He circled again, more relaxed as his reflexes finally realized they weren't actually jumping. He brought Fala around, and focusing again beyond the last pole but keeping her straight and forward between his legs, trotted Fala across in a steady rhythm.

"Good…again."

Several times he trotted the mare down the line in both directions. His nerves quieted down with the repetition. He could do this.

"Much better. Let her stretch now and give her a walk break," Tess directed.

Relief settled over him as he complied. Even though it was a cold winter day, he could feel sweat clinging clammily in his armpits and across his forehead under his helmet. *But I finished the lesson and it wasn't so bad!*

Then Todd noticed River entering the arena. *(Has he been watching all this time?)* He joined Tess and helped her alter the cavalletti line, removing some of the trot poles and adding a pole to the last in line to make a two-foot cross-rail jump.

"Let's finish with this, Todd," Tess instructed. "Approach at a trot and keep her in trot over the three low poles. Then let her canter on over the cross rails. Go, now," she ordered when Todd brought Fala to a halt and stared at the obstacles.

All his fear came rushing back at sight of the low jump. Fala tossed her head, not liking the tenseness in her rider or the tight hold on her mouth. He swallowed hard and then pressed his legs against Fala's sides. She obediently trotted off but with her head high and stiff. After the three trot poles, Todd clung to her mane as she cantered on over the two strides to the low jump.

"Oh for heaven's sake, what is wrong with you?" Tess cried out. "Do it again and ride her. Don't just sit there like a burr on her back."

He's scared! River stood next to Tess, watching and realized Todd had frozen up on Fala's back. He watched as Todd approached the second time, his eyes wide in terror. But then Todd swallowed hard and cast his eyes beyond the poles. He loosened his grip on the reins and directed Fala again to take the line, but this time he stayed with her motion, moving into two-point position and holding it over the trot poles and the two canter strides to the cross rails. It wasn't perfect but much better than the first time. "Good for you, Todd," River whispered to himself.

"Better. All right, that's enough for today. But you're going to have to do much better than that if you're ever going to jump an entire course. I don't even know if you're ready for the clinic coming up in two weeks."

Todd let the reins slip through his damp palms as Fala gratefully stretched her neck. *I actually jumped!* He knew it had been very sloppy, but the second time around had been much easier. *Of course the first few times are the hardest*, he reassured himself. *The more often I jump, the easier it will get.* He began to hope he might eventually regain his former confidence.

When he dismounted and led Fala toward the stable, River came up alongside. "Are you okay?" he asked.

"Yeah, I'm okay," Todd answered. "I guess you saw how scared I was."

"You did look scared, but you went down the line again anyway. That took courage."

"River, that jump was only two feet. I was really looking forward to riding training level this season, but maybe I need to stay at novice," Todd said. It felt so good to be able to confess his fear to someone, and River seemed genuinely empathetic. *Maybe he really has forgiven me.*

"There is nothing wrong with staying at a level for as many years as it takes. It's supposed to be all about having fun, isn't it?" River said and actually smiled.

Todd laughed and agreed, "Fun, right." He felt good. It felt like he and River were friends again, or like brothers.

"Better…she's moving forward in good rhythm and you're remembering to move your hands forward," Tess said in Todd's next lesson. He had just trotted Fala down the cavalletti line of one-foot poles for the fourth time. "Give her a walk break. I think you're ready to try a short course."

I'm not so sure I'm ready, Todd thought to himself as he brought Fala down to walk. Just the mention of jumping a short course suddenly sent ice down his spine and his stomach turned over with dread. He felt his heart accelerating and the palms of his hands becoming clammy as he watched Tess make changes to the cavalletti line. She adjusted the line as she had for the last lesson, with three poles and two strides to the cross-rails.

"Okay, you'll start down the same line," Tess said, stepping away from the poles and brushing her hands together. "Trot the first three poles, then let her canter on and jump the cross rails. Stay in canter on around to that low vertical, then on to the next oxer, cross the diagonal and take the two verticals in a line."

Eyes up, move hands forward, let her carry me over the jump, Todd coached himself with everything he had learned in the past about jumping. He guided Fala onto a circle, taking in deep breaths to calm his nerves. He had just started feeling good about going over the cavalletti and he really would have liked to finish with that today. But he knew better than to disagree with Tess.

"What are you waiting for? Go now!" Tess ordered.

Without realizing it, Todd had circled twice. He turned the mare now and headed back down the line. He moved up into two-point position and moved his hands forward up Fala's neck as she trotted over the poles. As she picked up the canter approaching the cross-rails, Todd suddenly felt insecure in his seat and he grabbed mane halfway up her neck, the way he had been taught when he first learned to jump. She cleared the two-foot jump and he turned her now to the vertical. It should have been easy. Tess had not set any of these jumps over two and a half feet. But the closer he came to the jump, it seemed he could see the jump standards growing from the corners of his eyes. He felt Fala's stride shorten and her neck stiffen and then she veered to the side in a run-out.

"You did not convince her you wanted to go over that jump," Tess yelled. "Circle and go over it…now!"

Todd brought Fala back around and kept legs on this time. He felt Fala begin to veer away just as Tess yelled, "Straight! Ride her up to that jump!" He yanked the rein to bring her straight on to the low vertical. She came up to it with her gait choppy and uneven and started to refuse, but Todd put his legs on in several successive kicks, and from a near standstill, Fala hopped over.

Somehow he managed to finish the course, clearing the oxer and then the two verticals, although Fala took the top rail down on the first.

"That's your fault," Tess said. "You are not rating her pace and you are not convincing her you mean to go over each jump. Try it again."

The second time around was perhaps a little better, for Todd steered her straight toward each obstacle and kept legs on. But he allowed her to rush and then take short strides and she knocked a low rail down once again, even though it was only at two and a half feet.

"That's enough for Fala today, but you need a lot more practice," Tess said, finally bringing the lesson to an end.

I need more than just practice, Todd thought ruefully to himself. *I need a good dose of lion's courage!*

For his next jumping lesson, Todd figured Tess would drill him again over the same course or at least a similar one of low jumps; since he had not done so well the last time. But his heart lurched and his stomach knotted again when she directed him to take the same course of only five jumps, but she raised each three inches or more. The last of the two verticals was now at three feet.

"Perhaps if we raise the bars so that Fala has to do more than just hop over rails, she'll try a little harder. Your job is to convince her you're serious about wanting to go over."

My job is to convince myself! But he was not able to convince himself he could handle going over three feet. After Fala refused the last vertical for the third time, Todd gave up. He brought her down to walk and rode up to Tess and admitted, "It's not her fault. I just can't do it."

"Then I can't teach you." Tess threw up her hands and walked away.

"It's not your fault," Todd repeated, this time to Fala. He walked her around to cool her down and then took her into the crossties.

As Todd removed the tack and then brushed Fala's coat, stroking her neck after he finished with the brush, his mind whirled in a turmoil. He knew he was in trouble with Tess. She didn't tolerate disobedience in her lessons and she very likely would refuse to ever teach him again. *Do I want to give up jumping? Do I want to give up riding altogether?*

At that moment, Fala turned her head to him with a gentle nuzzle at his shoulder. He knew she wanted a carrot, but it also seemed as if she wanted to remind him how much he loved being around horses. He looked into her gentle eye, and gave her neck another stroke of the brush. Then he retrieved the carrot he had stuck in the grooming box, and broke it into bits to feed her. She crunched happily on the treats and then nuzzled at his chest again.

No, in that moment, Todd knew he could not stand giving up time with horses. He did not want to give up riding either, and with his new appreciation of dressage, it was really only a question of whether or not he ever wanted to jump again.

When he had finished caring for Fala, he made up his mind to find River and talk to him.

Todd met River leading Prospector back from the trail, having finished his ride. He waited at the top of the field and when River caught up to him, he asked, "How was Prospector?"

"Full of himself today," River said, smiling at the dark gray six-year-old thoroughbred. "I think I'm going to take him up to the arena and take him over a few jumps. Tess set up a course for your lesson, didn't she?"

"Yeah, um...River, Tess is mad at me."

River raised his brow in a questioning expression.

"What's wrong with me?" Todd asked after telling River what had happened. "I've turned into a coward just because I had a bad fall. I'd fallen off lots of times before that day, but it didn't mess me up like I am now."

"I don't know, Todd. You never got hurt when you fell before and you were always able to get up and get right back on. Maybe that's the difference."

"Maybe…. You know, I have these dreams of jumping, and sometimes they are the greatest dreams ever where I'm jumping walls as high as a house and it's so cool, almost like flying. But then I have these nightmares where I'm falling into the ditch and a lid is coming down over my head and that's what puts me into a panic. Maybe I'm as crazy as my mother."

"No, you're not crazy," River said with conviction. "You and I both had some very messed up parents, but it's not our fault and we're not crazy. You know, when I was in high school they made me go see a counselor. I hated that at first, but she ended up really helping me a lot. Don't you go to a counselor or something like that?"

"Yeah, I do, a psychiatrist. Dr. Statton is really good. I only go once a month now but my appointment is next week. I guess I can talk to him."

"You do okay riding on the flat and trails, don't you?"

"Yeah, although I find myself tensing up when a horse shies. I never used to be scared like that. In fact I kind of liked it when a horse got all spooky. Now I get spooked more than the horse."

"Hmm, yeah. Okay, you're handling trotting cavalletti. It sounds like Tess has given up on you, but if you want, I can add some cavalletti in your lessons with me. We'll go slow. When you feel ready we can start adding low jumps, maybe just one at a time."

"That would be good, thanks."

19 BREAK AND BREAK-UPS

Far back, far back in our dark soul the horse prances.... The horse, the horse! The symbol of surging potency and power of movement, of action.... – D. H. Lawrence

The annual cross-country clinic was over. Everyone who had attended was very excited about the upcoming season, all planning on competing in combined training.

"Todd, how come you didn't ride in the clinic this year?" Brooke asked.

"I'm taking a break from jumping for a while," he said, trying to sound matter-of-fact. "I'm really getting into dressage lately and I just want to work on that."

Brooke nodded as if she understood, but she had already moved on to telling Todd every detail about her last jumping lesson with Tess and how well her horse Shamrock was jumping now. "Four feet, Todd, we jumped four feet!"

He nodded, only half listening as he finished grooming the horse he had ridden on the trail. He glanced once over at Jodi in the other crosstie bay, grooming Dune. She rolled her eyes and smiled conspiratorially at him.

"You coming to Sheryl's tonight?" Brooke asked after finally having nothing more to say about her lesson.

Todd shrugged. He didn't know yet what Melody wanted to do this Saturday night. She had gone with the cheerleaders to an away basketball game right after school yesterday and he hadn't talked to her since. Last night he stayed home and finished his homework and then just lay in his bed listening to music. He had actually enjoyed his evening.

"You two ready?" Jodi's mother looked around the corner, having arrived to pick up Jodi and Todd.

"Hi, Mom. I wasn't expecting you. Where's Melody?"

"She just got up and has a lot to do. You know she didn't get home last night until after one."

"Okay, we're both almost done."

"Good, I'll wait in the car."

Todd and Jodi finished with their horses and then walked together to her mother's waiting car.

"Todd, you're not taking any more jumping lessons?" Jodi asked tentatively, not sure if Todd wanted to talk about this. She had noticed on the schedule posted in the tack room that Todd's jumping lessons had been scratched out. "What happened?"

"She was asking me to jump Fala over a very easy course and I froze up. The truth is, I'm just plain scared." Jodi knew enough of his history that he found it wasn't hard to confess to her, even though he felt ashamed. He sensed her empathy and knew she would understand and would not judge him.

"Oh…Todd, it's probably just too soon. That was a really bad accident last year."

"Yeah, I'm just messed up. I hate being a coward."

"You are not a coward. You tried. A coward wouldn't even try," she reassured him.

"Thanks." He smiled. It helped having a friend like Jodi that he could confess his shortcomings to without fear of ridicule. *A coward wouldn't even try!* He already felt a little better.

"Sheryl's folks are going out for the evening and it's just her grandmother at home, so we'll all meet at her place. I'll pick you up at eight, and then we'll swing by Mary's house and pick up her and Tom and…"

"Another party? Mel, don't you ever want to hang out with just me?" Todd plopped down on his bed wrapped in a towel, having just finished his shower when Melody called.

"It's not really a party, just all our friends getting together at Sheryl's. We will be hanging out together there."

"Yeah, you and all your friends."

"They're your friends too," Melody insisted.

"All right, yeah, they're our friends. But wouldn't you like to come over to my house and we can watch a movie together? My parents would leave us alone in the family room."

"You want to see a movie? Well…I can ask Mary if she and Tom want to see that comedy that's just been released and then ask Sheryl…"

"No, not go out to a movie and not get together with Mary and Tom, Sheryl and James. I want to be with you, Melody…alone with you." *She just doesn't get it! Why doesn't she like the idea of being alone with me? Does she think I'm going to try and rape her with my parents in the next room? It's not like I've ever tried anything more than just kiss her.*

"Well, I already told Sheryl we would do something this weekend…um…." For once Melody was speechless.

"Maybe James would like to be alone with Sheryl. Maybe Tom would like to be alone with Mary."

He could hear her taking in a deep breath and letting it out as if he had asked her to sacrifice her life or something. "Okay, Todd. How about if you and I get together tomorrow, just the two of us. It would be too difficult to call everybody tonight and cancel meeting at Sheryl's."

"Why can't everybody else meet at Sheryl's and you and me stay at my house?"

"Oh, Todd, you just don't understand. I already promised to pick up Mary and…"

"Okay, okay. We'll go to Sheryl's."

"Good, see you around eight." Melody hung up.

Todd stared at the phone a few moments before setting it back down on his night stand. No, he did not understand. Ever since he and Melody became a couple, it was party after party every weekend and if not a party, going to a school dance or going out as a group for pizza or a movie. Fine, he did like hanging out with their group of friends. But every single weekend night? He couldn't remember when he started feeling bored at these parties, and actually quite disgusted with how many of the kids were covertly drinking or sneaking outside to smoke weed or do other drugs. After what happened with his mother, he had no patience or tolerance for that kind of stuff. At least Melody didn't do any of that. But she sure liked socializing. She did seem okay with kissing him when towards the end of the night all the couples tended to isolate themselves. *But how close could you ever feel when you were making out with your girlfriend on one end of the sofa and her best friend with her boyfriend are on the other end?* He couldn't remember if he and Melody had ever spent an evening alone together or gone out, just the two of them. And, she liked staying out right up to her curfew of one a.m. on Fridays and Saturdays. Which meant he was always too tired to get up early to go to the stable. But it was expected by all his friends that he do what Melody wanted. He glanced at his bedside clock — six-thirty. He already ate a snack when he got home which would tide him over until the party. He fell back on his bed. Maybe he would just close his eyes and sleep until Melody came….

The table Sean had reserved at The Firehouse Restaurant sat in a corner of the patio behind a gentle water fountain, partly obscured from view of most other tables. The temperature of early April was in the low sixties, cool to sit outside, but space heaters warmed the area around the table to very comfortable. Water trickled soothingly in the fountain, and the brick walls, a live tree and other plants all contributed to a very aesthetically charming and romantic atmosphere.

"This is beautiful!" Sierra exclaimed, holding Sean's hand and following the hostess to the reserved corner.

Sean pulled out her chair for her to sit down, and as he helped move it in he leaned over and said, "You're beautiful." *Does she know what I've planned or suspect? Is that why she's wearing the most stunning dress I've ever seen?*

Sierra suspected nothing, but when Sean told her where he had made a reservation for dinner, she looked it up and realized it would be best to not dress casual. She would never have described her dress as stunning - just a plain cream colored tank style that could be dressed up with a scarf and matching short jacket. She was glad she chose to wear a dress, for Sean showed up in dress slacks, an oxford style shirt and tie, and sports jacket. He looked especially handsome tonight, as comfortable in a tie as in tee-shirt and jeans. She smiled as she noticed the young hostess taking frequent sidelong glances at Sean.

This was to be an end-of-quarter, spring break celebration. Finals had been taken. Sierra knew most of her grades and had no worries over the ones not yet posted. She took her last exam yesterday and she was officially on spring break. Since breaking up with River, she had returned home to spend Christmas with her mother, but decided it was easier to stay at school for all other breaks. She planned to sleep as late as she wanted, ride every day at the nearby stable, read a novel, and just rest. Sean also planned to stay (probably because she wasn't leaving) and they could do something more than just study together.

The food at The Firehouse did not disappoint and now Sierra sipped her hot tea that she had ordered with dessert, feeling sated and content.

"Sierra," Sean began. "Do you realize we've been going out together now for a year?"

"We have?" Sierra hadn't really thought about how long they had dated.

The table was small. Sean had been pushing his knees up against Sierra's beneath the table. Now he reached across to take her hand and leaned forward. He cradled her hand gently between his thumb and fingers, tracing the lines of her palm and stroking each finger tenderly. "Yes, a year since I first kissed you and you were mad at me, but then you finally forgave me and…"

"Oh, it's been a year?" Sierra was starting to feel uncomfortable.

"Sierra," Sean said softly and it seemed the tinkling water of the fountain harmonized with his tone. His hand went quiet and he looked up into her eyes. "I love you. Will you marry me?"

No, I'm not ready for this, oh no, no, no! Sierra started to pull her hand away, her eyes widening at his words. Dread rushed in to churn her just eaten dessert.

"Oh." Sean ducked his head to stare at her hand. He did not let it go. This was not the reaction he thought he would receive or what he had hoped for. He had anticipated a smile across her face and that he would hear a 'yes' and those three special words repeated back to him. The startled look on her face swiftly replaced by a frown, seized his heart, squeezing out his hope.

"Sean, I…" *I don't want to hurt him.* "I…"

"I get it." Sean dropped her hand and pulled his own away. "You don't have to say anything."

"I didn't expect this tonight," Sierra spoke barely above a whisper. "You've really taken me by surprise."

Sean looked up to meet her eyes, his own with a glimmer of hope. "You don't have to love me now, Sierra. We're friends. You like me, don't you?"

"Of course, I like you a lot!"

"You haven't thought about us other than as friends, especially since you were still in a relationship when we first started going out. So maybe you've just kept on with your own feelings at bay, sort of out of habit," Sean rattled on in a very hopeful tone, trying to sound logical. "I shouldn't have thrust this on you so soon. I just thought…well it has been a year."

Sierra nodded. She could think of nothing to say.

"Can you forget about tonight?" Sean continued. "Store those words away for now because I do want you to eventually think about how I feel about you. But let's start over in our relationship. Pretend you just met me and are getting to know me, but this time there are no restrictions on your feelings."

"Um, yes, I think I can do that," Sierra replied, dropping her eyes. She said yes because she didn't want to hurt him, but somehow, she didn't think 'starting over' in their relationship would make any difference. This was so different from how it felt when River had proposed to her. She had been overcome with joy, excited, and definitely knew she loved him. Her feelings for Sean had never come close to what she used to feel for River. *Why? Sean is a very nice man - kind, considerate, smart, very handsome. He supports me in my ambitions, encourages me. He is perfect!* But it just didn't feel right, and Sierra knew she was not in love with him. *And I don't think time is going to make any difference.*

After Sean dropped her off, kissing her tenderly goodnight, Sierra changed into grubby clothes and began to clean her apartment. Her roommate had already left and would be gone over spring break, so Sierra had the place to herself. She was much too agitated to go to bed with so much to think about.

"What are you doing?" Melody asked, tapping on Jodi's closed bedroom door.

"Come on in," Jodi answered.

Melody entered and came over to sit on the edge of Jodi's bed where her sister reclined against the headboard, reading a book. "What are you doing?" Melody asked again.

"Reading."

Melody glanced at the book cover. "*The Tempest?* Why are you reading Shakespeare on break?"

"I like Shakespeare," Jodi answered.

"I hate Shakespeare. Don't we have to read that next quarter? Why are you reading it now?"

"I've actually read it before. I'm just re-reading it."

Melody scrunched her face into a look of disbelief that anyone would read Shakespeare by choice. "I don't get why we have to read stuff that isn't even in the kind of English we talk anymore."

"Because if you can figure it out, he's got a lot to say, and the stories are really good," Jodi stated, looking over the top of her book at her twin, and with a sigh, she let it drop down on her lap, realizing Melody wasn't about to leave.

"I guess. Listen, about that party…"

"No," Jodi said emphatically, and picked up her book again. All week, Melody had been trying to get Jodi to agree to go to Sophie Kinderman's party on Saturday night. Every year, Sophie gave a spring break party and only invited the most elite of their school. It was supposed to be the highest honor to get invited. Melody had never been invited, even though most of her friends got invitations.

Jodi didn't know all the social ramifications of Sophie snubbing her sister, but she knew it had something to do with a boy they had both wanted to date freshman year and he had chosen Melody. In Jodi's opinion, she wouldn't ever want to go to a party given by someone she detested, and she knew her sister hated Sophie as much as she did. The girl was mean, a bully, and it was a mystery to Jodi why she was one of the most popular girls at school. Sophie had more social power than even Melody. Yet it apparently was very important for Melody to go.

This year, Sophie had invited Melody but on one condition, that she also bring Jodi. Sophie had a boy cousin their age visiting from out of town over break, and he needed a date. This was the weird part and in Jodi's opinion, very suspicious. Why would Sophie want to fix up her cousin on a blind date with Jodi? That made absolutely no sense and why couldn't Melody understand that?

"Jodi, I'm begging you. It would mean so much to me. Would it be so hard just to go with me to the party? I told you, Sophie showed him your picture and he wants to meet you. If you don't like this Patrick guy at all I promise I will bring you back home."

Jodi shook her head behind her book.

"Sophie sent me his picture." Melody thrust her phone in front of the page Jodi was trying to read.

Whoa, this Patrick guy is hot! Jodi noted when forced to look at the handsome face obscuring her page. She pushed the phone away. "Mel, think about this. Sophie is plotting something. Why would Sophie want to set her cousin up with me? She hates me. And why would this guy need a blind date? Look at him! Why would a guy this good looking want to meet me? Use your head. Something is very wrong here."

"I don't know, Jodi," Melody confessed. "It does seem strange, but the truth is, I want to go to this party because Gill Overstreet is going. He came up to me last week before school was out and he said he'd see me at Sophie's party."

"Gill Overstreet? Hottest senior in school, overall sports star? That Gill Overstreet?" Jodi asked, astounded. She lowered her book and studied her twin.

"Yes." Melody blushed as she answered.

"What about Todd?"

"Todd and I are kind of drifting apart," Melody confessed. "We really don't have anything in common. All he wants to talk about is horses and he never wants to go out anywhere."

"But he goes out with you all the time."

"Yes, but he doesn't like it. I think he wants to break up, and this party is where it could happen."

"God, Melody. Why don't you just break up with him?"

Melody sighed and then collapsed onto her back on the foot of Jodi's bed. "You don't understand. It's just not how to break up. Todd is going with me to the party. If Gill starts making moves on me and I act interested, it will give Todd an excuse to break up with me."

"You're doing this so Todd will break up with you instead of just telling him how you feel? Why does he need an excuse?" Jodi shook her head, perplexed. She did not want any part of this kind of social manipulation.

"It's not like I'm going to break his heart or anything. I know he's bored with me. The last two times I called he didn't even return my call, and he said he was sick when I wanted to go out last weekend."

"That doesn't mean…." Jodi gave up. She had never had a boyfriend. She had never even held a boy's hand or been kissed. Was this really the way break-ups were supposed to happen? She didn't think Todd played these kinds of games. Yet, she sensed Melody was probably right that Todd was losing interest in her. From the back seat, Jodi had watched how they got along and things had definitely cooled since they had first started going out.

"Please, Jodi, I know Sophie is up to something but it doesn't matter. The point is Gill will be there and he will be looking for me. I'll do anything for you if you will just do this one thing. I'll do all your chores forever, I will give you all my allowance. Please…."

The look of desperation on Melody's face finally softened Jodi's resolve. She supposed she could manage one painful evening if it meant this much to her sister. "Okay, I'll go," she said.

Melody squealed, sat up and hugged Jodi and kissed her cheek. "Oh, thank you, thank you. I love you!"

"Just get out and leave me in peace. And you don't have to do my chores or give me your allowance either," Jodi said as Melody skipped to the door. "Just maybe rides to the stable on weekends."

Saturday night, Jodi sat in agony on the lid of the toilet seat as Melody and Sheryl, with Mary watching, worked on her hair and applied make-up.

"Jodi, you have such beautiful eyes. Why do you always hide them behind your hair?" Mary commented as the eyeliner and mascara being skillfully applied brought out the depth and color of Jodi's deep blue eyes.

"Your hair is gorgeous," Sheryl added, lifting up the mass of Jodi's thick, dark hair away from her neck and shoulders and then letting it fall back. The girls had trimmed her bangs and split ends, washed and conditioned her hair and applied some kind of special treatment that brought the dull brown color to a glossy shine.

"Just get finished," Jodi said. She tried not to smile, but when she looked at her reflection, she could not quite believe the face looking back. *Melody and I really do look a little bit alike!* She had never realized how much a hair style and make-up could transform a person.

"Done!" Melody announced, after the last coat of mascara. "Okay, girls - outfits!"

They all squealed in glee, except for Jodi, who just shrugged and shook her head.

When they tried to put her into skin tight jeans and a plunging, sequined top, Jodi drew the line there. "No way! If you want me to come, you better let me wear my own clothes. I am not putting those things on."

At last Melody surrendered, for it was getting late and they needed to get going. Melody and her friends put on their own tight jeans and revealing tops while Jodi dressed in plain black jeans and a black tee. *Good enough,* she thought.

"We'll be back by one!" Melody promised, sticking her head around the corner of the living room. All the girls wore fleece hoodies so that Melody's parents would not see their tops.

"Have fun. Call if you need anything," Cora Mae said, waving them on. Martin looked up and smiled, but turned his attention back to the show they were watching.

Sheryl and Mary left in Sheryl's car, and Jodi and Melody got in Melody's car and headed over to the Marshalls to pick up Todd.

Todd had apparently been watching for them, for he came out the front door as soon as Melody pulled into the driveway, almost twenty minutes later than she had said. Jodi noted he wore everyday jeans and a sweatshirt and she figured he had no more enthusiasm for this party than she did. Jodi got out from the front seat and slid into her usual place in the back when the three of them were together.

"You don't have to move, Jodi," Todd said. But Jodi had already settled herself in the back seat, buckling up her seatbelt, so he got into the front as usual.

The first thing Jodi noticed walking into Sophie's living room, was how different this party was from the one she had crashed her sophomore year with Tasha. Music played in the background, much softer and not interfering with conversations. The lamps had been dimmed to their lowest settings, and many candles placed on tables between chairs, softly illuminated the space. Sophie and her mother had decorated with pots of lush live plants placed in every bare corner of the large living room. A long, narrow side table bore a large punch bowl and platters of tempting snacks.

Kids stood around in groups, everyone dressed in trendy clothes, and most holding a cup of punch or else soda, and many with plates, nibbling at their selection. The conversations were loud, peppered with laughter.

"You guys are late," Sophie came up to them, smiling her hostess smile. "Jodi, I'm so glad you came. Come on, follow me." But it was Melody's wrist that Sophie grabbed as she led them to a group near the fireplace. "Patrick!" she called.

A tall boy turned, and Jodi recognized him from the photo, just as handsome in person. Then Jodi noticed him looking at Melody and his face lit up in a smile. He took a step toward her.

"I want you to meet Jodi," Sophie said. She had dropped Melody's wrist, and now she grabbed Jodi's upper arm and pushed her forward. "Jodi, this is my cousin Patrick."

The smile on Patrick's face changed to a look of confusion as he tore his eyes from Melody to look at Jodi. Instantly, Jodi understood part of Sophie's game. She could just guess what that evil girl had done; probably shown Patrick a picture of Melody, and told him she had a twin sister she would fix him up with. She just neglected to mention they were not identical twins. His disappointment was intensely obvious, and in spite of herself, it crushed Jodi's feelings. *He doesn't like me.*

"Uh, you're Jodi?" he finally managed to say.

She nodded, and her face creased into her defensive scowl to hide her wounded feelings.

He said no more, but turned his attention back to the people in the group he had been talking with.

Jodi turned to find Sophie watching her with her eyes gleaming and a triumphant smile on her face. Melody watched, just beginning to understand. Her eyes widened in comprehension and she gave her sister a sympathetic look. Todd had not followed them but had headed first thing over to the refreshments.

Sorry, Melody mouthed at Jodi. "I better find Todd," she said and turned away, abandoning her sister. Still smirking, Sophie followed Melody. Patrick acted as if none of them were there.

What should I do? Jodi did not know whether she should stay or also follow the others. Wasn't she supposed to be Patrick's date? Should she say something to him? She had no idea what proper dating protocol was in such a situation.

But he is very rude. A nice guy would at least be polite, even if he didn't like me and never intended to see me again after tonight, Jodi reasoned. And it was enough of a reason for her not to care what he might think. She turned and walked away.

Melody had promised she would take her home if she wasn't having fun. But now that she was here, Jodi decided she could stick it out a little bit longer before asking her sister to drive her home. Maybe it wouldn't take Melody too long to work out whatever it was she wanted to have happen with Gill and Todd.

To pass the time, Jodi made her way to the refreshment table, selected a can of soda from an ice-filled tub, and then looked around for a place to wait it out in obscurity. Most of the chairs were taken but Jodi spied a space on the floor near a large potted plant, and went there to sit down and lean against the wall. She felt like a fool to have allowed Melody and her friends to make her up and mess with her hair. She pulled out the clips that held her hair back from her face, allowing it to fall forward again. She sipped her soda, observing the scene in front of her, and still trying to figure out what game Sophie was playing. It didn't surprise her that the girl might have a need for revenge against her own cousin. She hoped it was as simple as that and nothing more to do with Melody.

She finished the soda, and pushed away her hurt feelings. Patrick was a complete jerk and not worth enduring any suffering over his rejection of her. She quit thinking about her wounded pride, and instead amused herself watching groups of kids and trying to figure out who was putting moves on whom. But that soon got to be very boring. She had left her purse with her phone at home, and regretted it. At least on her phone she had books she could read. She closed her eyes. *I'll just sleep.* But that was impossible, for the drone of conversation too often resulted in someone raising their voice or sudden bursts of laughter, which startled her awake whenever she came close to dozing off.

She stuck it out for an hour, and decided to find Melody. She knew Todd had recently got his license. Maybe Melody would let Todd drive her home, and that would maybe give Melody the opportunity she wanted with Gill. Seemed like a good idea. She got up and began searching through the groups in the living room and into the family room and kitchen, but couldn't find them.

She found Sheryl with her boyfriend James in the kitchen, fixing something over the sink. "Do you know where Melody and Todd are?" she asked.

"Huh?" Sheryl looked over her shoulder. "Oh, I don't know. They're playing dance music down in the basement. Did you look there?"

"No, thanks." Jodi retreated, but decided to stop at the bathroom first. But the guest bathroom door was locked with the light on underneath.

"There's another one at the top of the stairs," a girl's voice called through the locked door. Jodi heard a boy's voice as well but too low to understand the words. The girl giggled.

Jodi went upstairs and at least found that bathroom empty. She went in and locked the door. After going to the bathroom, she stared at her face in the mirror. She had thought she looked pretty when her sister had finished with her and she had peered at her reflection at home. But with the scowl on her face, she now thought she looked like an ugly person with a lot of make-up on. She grabbed handfuls of tissue and wiped off as much as she could, and then washed her face.

"Hurry up!" Someone called and then knocked on the door.

"Just a minute." Jodi studied her face for another second. *Still ugly, but at least I look like me.* She turned and opened the bathroom door.

A girl who looked like she had been crying started to push past Jodi. A bedroom door down the hallway opened. The girl turned and yelled back a very derogatory expletive. Jodi stepped out of the way and the girl slammed the bathroom door shut behind her.

"Hey, is that who I think it is?" slurred a very drunk and shirtless Kirby Portman leaning in the bedroom doorway. He blinked several times, trying to focus his eyes. "Jodi? Jodi Cannon? Heeyy…." He dragged out the last word in a gravelly voice.

Walk away, Jodi told herself. But, God he was sexy looking, even drunk. The smile across his face seemed to say, 'I like what I see!' Maybe if she hadn't been rejected earlier this evening, maybe if she wasn't so bored, she might have walked away. But she hadn't found her sister and Todd, and hanging out with Kirby would help pass the time. Instead of walking away, Jodi said, "Hi, Kirby."

He slumped down to the floor with that inviting smile on his face, and leaning his head against the door frame, he held his hand out to her.

With a shrug of her shoulders, Jodi limped over and sat down on the floor bedside him. "You're pretty drunk," she stated the obvious.

"You're really cute, you know that?" He reached over and with just his fingertips, touched her cheek. "Hey, can I see your tattoo?"

"I guess." Jodi stretched her leg out and pulled back the hem of her jeans.

Kirby bent over her leg. He traced the lines of her tattoo with a finger, and then lurched forward over her ankle. For a moment, Jodi thought he was about to puke, and she started to pull her leg away. But then suddenly, she felt his lips on her skin.

He's kissing my tattoo! It seemed weird, but at the same time it sent a thrill from her ankle surging up her leg and spreading heat throughout her. She laughed and tried to pull her leg away again.

Getting himself back upright seemed to take a lot of effort. But he did, still holding onto her ankle and actually pushing his weight down for fulcrum. That kind of hurt. "Let go," Jodi cried out, still trying to pull her leg back.

Finally sitting up, Kirby released his hold and Jodi moved her leg underneath, getting onto her knees to stand up. She didn't know quite how it happened, but suddenly Kirby fell forward against her, knocking her down onto her back and then he sprawled over the top of her.

"Ouch…get off of me!"

Then his mouth was on hers, his lips pressing hard. He thrust his tongue in between her lips, moving it in a way that disgusted Jodi. One hand pushed down on her shoulder to keep her on her back and his other hand began to snake up beneath her tee shirt. She screamed a muffled scream. *No one will ever hear me!* Anger surged along with adrenaline. She bit on his tongue as hard as she could and somehow found the strength to bring her knee up to his groin and push.

Now it was Kirby who screamed, and he rolled off her. The bathroom door opened, and the girl who must have been his first victim of the evening, came out. She rushed over and helped Jodi to her feet and the two girls fled back down the stairs.

In the crowd below, the girl moved away searching for someone else. Jodi felt like she could not get enough air. She was suffocating! Trying to move as fast as she could, she lurched awkwardly to the front door and then escaped into the cool night.

Outside, she gulped in lungfuls of air. Then she rubbed her hand over and over across her mouth to remove the residue of Kirby's saliva. Going to one of the shrubs in Sophie's yard, she leaned over and spit again and again, trying to rid her mouth of the horrible taste of Kirby.

"I want to go home!" She moaned out loud. *How far is it? Can I walk home?* If she had her phone, she could have called her parents to come and get her. *What was I thinking to leave my phone at home?* It hadn't taken Melody very long to drive to Sophie's after she had picked up Todd. Maybe it wasn't too far to walk. Angry with Melody, Jodi thought it would serve her sister right to worry about her when she found her gone. She started out in the general direction of home, hoping she would come across a street sign that she recognized. "Never again! Never again!" she muttered out loud as she limped onward. Now tears came and she let them course down her cheeks and since no one was around, did not hold back her sobs.

Apparently Jodi's sense of direction served her well, for perhaps after twenty minutes or so, she came to a cross street that she knew was in her own neighborhood. Relief erased the growing fear that she had gotten lost. She was only three blocks from home. Her crying ceased and she began swiping away at her wet face.

She reached the corner of her own street when headlights coming toward her forced her to look to the side to keep from being blinded. The car slowed and Melody shouted from the open window, "Jodi! Oh, thank God!"

The car had barely come to a stop when the passenger door flung open and Todd jumped out to rush over to Jodi's side. "Are you okay?"

It was so good to see him! A friend, someone she trusted. She nodded. And then, Todd was hugging her tightly against his chest, as if now found, he did not want to lose her again.

"Get in, you guys. Let's go home," Melody said.

"Do you mind walking me home?" Jodi asked against Todd's comforting chest. She did not want to get into her sister's car and have to start explaining. Even more than that, surprisingly, she did not want Todd to let go of her.

"Go on home, Melody," Todd ordered. "I'm going to walk home with Jodi."

"No way, come on!"

"It's only a block. Go home," Todd ordered again, in a firmer tone.

"Don't be long," Melody insisted. "I'm going to wait in the car. I can't go inside alone!" She backed the car around and drove away.

When they were alone, Todd released Jodi but he kept one arm protectively over her shoulder as they started walking. "What happened?"

Jodi told him everything, including the humiliating reception from Sophie's cousin, and then the final horrible encounter with Kirby. She ended with a sardonic laugh. "So, that was my first kiss." Recalling the horrible feel, taste, and even smell of Kirby, her laugh ended in a sob.

"It's okay, you're okay now," Todd murmured to her, in the same tone he would use to soothe a frightened horse. They stopped walking and he held her again.

It didn't take long for Jodi to regain her composure. She had already cried herself out. "Thanks," she said, pulling away from him. "Tell me, what happened with you and Melody tonight?"

"We broke up," he answered and didn't sound at all broken up about it. "Actually, I was thinking it wasn't working out between us so it was a relief."

This time Jodi's laugh was genuine. "Do you mind telling me how it happened?"

"You know who Gill Overstreet is, don't you?"

"Of course." They started walking again as Todd narrated his story.

"Melody wanted to go downstairs to the basement to dance. Gill was down there and he started making moves on her. He actually stepped in front of me and began dancing with her as if I wasn't even there. Melody didn't protest and the next thing I know, he's holding her very close while they danced and it wasn't even a slow song. Then Sophie came up to me and started dancing with me. Jodi, do you think they planned all this? Because Melody saw me dancing with Sophie and she yelled at me saying it's over between us. Like, I was the one making the moves."

"Todd, I really don't know because Melody and Sophie are supposed to be enemies. Then what happened?"

"Sophie acted like she wanted to be with me for the rest of the party, but I really don't like that girl. I told Melody I was going to find you, and that's when we discovered you had left the party. Sophie's cousin started yelling at her about something and she was just laughing at him."

"Did you know I was supposed to be his blind date tonight?"

"No, you're kidding."

"Yeah, I think Sophie wanted to humiliate me for something that happened last year. That girl can sure hold onto a grudge. I wouldn't be surprised if she wanted to get back at her cousin about something as well – get double revenge."

"That sounds like Sophie, and I think her cousin is a lot like her. I wasn't around him very long, but it was long enough to figure out he's a real jerk. And I'm sorry about what happened with Kirby. While I was looking for you I saw him passed out in the hall upstairs. If

I had known…." Todd's face creased into a very dark and threatening scowl.

"Yeah, my two experiences with boys were with the two biggest creeps at the party. God, that kiss…bleh!"

They had almost reached Jodi's house. Todd stopped walking, still with his arm over her shoulders causing her to stop as well. "Jodi, I…." He turned her to face him. She looked up into his eyes to notice how he was studying her, and she was grateful for the darkness which concealed the heat rising in her face. He leaned in closer and she closed her eyes. Then she felt his soft lips touch her own - a swift kiss and then he pulled away.

Oh my, oh my! Jodi's eyes flew open, and met his still gazing intensely at her. They held onto each other with their eyes for several moments, and then Todd hugged her again. Jodi thought to herself as she willingly allowed him to hold her against his chest, *so this is what it feels like to melt!*

20 SCHOOLMASTERS

It is the horse which is undoubtedly the best and only master of the art of giving the rider a sense of feel. - Wilhelm Museler, *Riding Logic*

What a night! As Jodi collapsed in her bed and closed her eyes, her mind whirled, re-living the feeling of another's gentle lips on hers, the feel of another's heart beating against her own, a connection with another human Jodi had never experienced. *What a kiss!*

A smile still lingered on her face when Jodi awoke the next morning. Her thoughts immediately returned to the incredible finale of last night – a night that had begun with rejection and landslided down into boredom, violent molestation, and then to the final moments of rising up to the clouds when Todd kissed her.

Throughout the morning as she finished her few weekend chores before going to the stable, Jodi's mood vacillated between excited anticipation of seeing Todd and knee-trembling anxiety at the thought of facing him. Did he regret kissing her? Had he done it out of pity? Would he avoid her today? He would be here in just two hours, for Melody had promised to give them both a ride to the stable and he would walk over from his house. How should she greet him? Would there be awkwardness since he and Melody no longer were together?

The doorbell rang just as Jodi finished changing into her riding clothes. Melody was still asleep and her parents were lingering over a late breakfast in the kitchen. She rushed out of her room to be the one to answer the door. She wanted her first post-kiss encounter to be unwitnessed.

"I'll give you a ride, let Melody sleep," her father called out as she passed the kitchen.

"Thanks, Dad."

She opened the door.

"Hi," Todd greeted with his adorable lopsided grin on his face. His eyes shone.

"Hi." They both stood awkwardly, smiling at each other for a few moments. "Todd, um…hey, about last night…."

"What about last night?"

"I don't want you to feel like…I mean…." *What do I mean?* "Thank you for kissing me. It meant a lot, but I don't want you to feel obligated or let it change our friendship or…"

To her amazement and delight, Todd grabbed her wrist and pulled her outside. "Can I kiss you again?"

Dumbfounded, Jodi nodded. She closed her eyes as he leaned in. and for the second time, their lips met. This kiss lasted longer than the first, just a soft lingering before Todd pulled away and then hugged her.

Spring break over, school resumed for the final quarter of Jodi's junior year. She did not expect Todd to publicly acknowledge that he was sort of in a relationship with her. She understood the fragility of high school dynamics and how Todd's popular status could easily be shattered by dating the wrong girl. But Todd surprised her with his courage. He waited for her at the entrance doors Monday morning, and walked with her to her homeroom. He wanted to eat lunch with her, even though at their school, couples going together tended to eat lunch with their group of friends rather than each other.

"I need lunch time to get homework out of the way," Jodi said truthfully, but also to give him an easy out. "Todd, you don't have to be with me at school. I'm fine with our relationship being a secret." She smiled and gave him a conspiratorial look, hoping to make this easy for him.

"Are you embarrassed by me?" Todd asked in a teasing tone. "You don't want to be seen in public with me?"

"Right," she said laughing. "It would totally ruin my reputation."

She never ate lunch with him, and tried to discourage him from holding her hand as he walked with her to classes, but she soon gave that up. Her feelings for him intensified, that he had the courage to defy the hierarchy of their school to be with her.

Ever since Jodi asked River to help her find a suitable horse, he had been checking out horses for sale. So far, the ones in her price range with quiet manners and temperament for her level of riding skill, had all turned out to be too old with many soundness issues, or if younger, permanent lameness that their owners tried to disguise. It had been a very discouraging search and for River, often heartbreaking. Over and over he met horses that because of their kind hearts and willing natures, had been overused by various owners to the point of permanent unsoundness. These were the horses that tried to give everything their riders asked of them. These were the horses that were drugged and then entered into competitions, because they continued to perform in spite of stiffness or pain.

Only once had he found a sound horse with good manners and decent training, but really too small for Jodi. He took her to see the horse anyway. Jodi knew she could love the little gelding, but when she tried him out under saddle, his small size caused her legs to hang too far below for her to keep her calves where she needed them, and she did not feel as if she could stay in a good position on his back.

"I'll look around while I'm at Jack's place this summer," River said. "If I can't find anything on the east coast and nothing's turned up around here after I get back, I'll think about letting you buy Dune."

It discouraged Jodi to have to wait that long. She knew River wanted to keep Dune as a school horse, but she had promised if she could buy Dune, she would still let him use her for lessons.

"Dune is good for you right now," River explained. "But your riding is improving and by the end of summer, you might be ready for a horse with more scope. I'd like to see you with a horse that could perform upper level dressage because I think you will really enjoy that. Dune will try her best, but she will never be able to give you exceptional movement."

"I don't need exceptional," Jodi had declared under her breath, but River must have heard.

For her next lesson, River said, "You can ride Penny today."

"Penny…you mean Pendragon?" she asked, not quite believing what she had just heard.

"Yes, you've been doing great on Dune and I want you to compare how a different horse feels."

"You think I can handle Pendragon?"

"Yes, and I'll help you."

"Who will Todd ride today?" Jodi asked, looking over her shoulder where Todd stood, smiling.

"I'm riding Dune today," Todd answered, and Jodi realized that River and Todd had conspired this together. "I'll help you get Penny ready. Come on."

"I can't believe he is going to let me ride Pendragon," Jodi said repeatedly as they brought the big bay into the crossties. "What if I do something that will mess him up, like give him the wrong aids and get him all confused?"

"That won't happen, Jodi," Todd assured her. "That's why River is having you ride him because he is so well trained and so wise.

He will figure out what you want even if you only ask partially correct. He will train you."

"You are so lovely," Jodi murmured to the handsome bay. "I promise I will try my best and not hurt you."

Todd smiled over Pendragon's back as he pulled off the rain sheet. "You won't hurt him. Don't worry, I know you always try to do everything River tells you, and he won't let you hurt him."

"No, you're right." She bent over to pick out Pendragon's hooves with the hoof pick. When she finished with all four feet she said, "And you be good to my Dune."

"Of course, and River won't let me hurt her either."

"Are you disappointed to ride Dune today?" Jodi asked.

"No, not at all. Actually, that's part of the reason River is switching horses on us. He wants to see if I can use what I've learned riding Penny on another horse besides Fala, and Dune is very different from Fala."

"Yeah, I guess that's a true horseman, who can get the best out of any horse regardless of its talents."

"Right, a horseman like River. Have you ever seen any horse he rides look bad?"

"Never!" They laughed, which relieved some of Jodi's nervousness.

When they had Pendragon groomed and tacked up, Jodi led him to the arena, and walked him around until River arrived. He checked over the fit of the tack, and then after Jodi mounted, helped her adjust the stirrups.

"You're going to do the same things you've been doing on Dune. Start out with your warm-up stretches," River said.

"Okay." As usual, she kept the reins loose and used her legs to guide Penny away from the mounting block and onto a twenty-meter circle. She noticed how he stretched his neck forward to the bit and all it took was the merest touch with her calf to keep him on the circle's arc. She did not feel any tenseness in his muscles, even with this new rider on his back. She started to relax and began the stretches. By the time she had finished the routine, she felt much more confident that Penny was not going to get uptight with her on his back.

"You look good up there," River said, satisfied Jodi had loosened up her muscles and released much of the tension over her nervousness riding a new horse. "Shorten your reins and find the contact with his mouth…very good, keep that feel. You shouldn't need to pull back on him. He'll respond to just a squeeze of fingers. Try that now to bend his head to the outside." River watched as Jodi squeezed with her outside fingers and Pendragon yielded his head at the poll to the inside. "Good, now release and straighten."

When River asked her to trot, she immediately reacted by tensing up at the thought of trotting on such a big horse.

"Deep breath," River said, noting her nervousness. "Just squeeze on the reins for a quick second, then apply legs. Try it."

Jodi gulped in air and obeyed. To her amazement, Penny pushed up into a trot. *Yes*, she remarked to herself, *he pushed up*, for she could feel his hindquarters thrusting. The big movement startled her and she knew she must have tightened her muscles. But all Penny did was lay his ears slightly back, as if wondering, 'what is your problem?'. She forced her legs to release their vice grip, allowing her thighs and core muscles to follow his movement. Suddenly she found herself riding a horse that seemed to spring gently! His stride was bigger but so much easier to move with than on Dune.

With River coaching her through every aid, Jodi marveled at how little it took to get this big horse (taller and more muscular than Dune) to respond, and how quickly he gave those responses. Halfway through the lesson, she understood why River had put her up on Penny - to feel the difference between Dune and a horse with more talent. *This is riding dressage!* She had a few moments of regret that her beloved Dune could never achieve this level of extraordinary movement, but she did not let it inhibit the joy she was experiencing. She knew she would always love Dune and appreciate the value of what she had learned from the willing mare. But she wanted to ride this type of horse!

Todd watched Jodi's lesson as long as he could before he needed to leave to get Dune ready for his own lesson. He had not watched Jodi in a lesson for quite some time, and he was quite surprised at how good she looked up on Pendragon. Of course Penny could make any rider look good, but at the same time, he watched her trying to do everything River asked. Most of the time she was successful and was getting prompt and correct responses. He was so proud of her! After her last canter depart, he tore himself away to make sure he had adequate time to get Dune ready.

The dun mare raised her head as he opened the gate of her paddock. She quickly determined he was safe and maybe even had a carrot and she walked forward to meet him.

"Here you are," Todd greeted and gave her a bit of carrot to munch on while he placed the halter. He noted how politely she stepped up to his shoulder as he led her into the stable, never lagging behind or pulling ahead. He hadn't worked with her since before his accident and he had forgotten her perfect manners.

In the crossties, Todd removed her rain sheet and began brushing. She had half-way shed out her winter coat and the silkiness and shine of the hair surprised him. She was still not a beautiful horse, but Todd couldn't help but note how improved she looked with good nutrition, daily grooming and conditioning. Health definitely enhanced her best features and the dun color of her coat gleamed like bronze.

Dune turned her head to look at him with her one good eye, almost as if she knew what he was thinking. Todd felt such shame at how he had scorned this sweet mare and he stroked her neck now with genuine affection. She lowered her head and snorted with pleasure. He took his time brushing her, watching her reaction and lingering on the areas that caused her to stretch her neck and curl her upper lip. When he finished the grooming, he tacked her up, and led her to the arena where Jodi was now cooling out Pendragon.

"I think you can take him in now. Great riding today," River said to Jodi. Then he turned to Todd. "Let's go to the outdoor arena."

Hey, you'll be fine," Jodi whispered as she passed him.

"Thanks." Todd gave Jodi a weak smile and then turned his attention to Dune. "Okay, big girl, you take care of me and I'll take care of you, deal?" He turned and followed River outside. Since that was where the jumps and cavalletti were, he figured they were going to be part of his lesson.

Dune seemed a different horse from a year ago. *Of course she's different*, Todd realized. She's had a year of training with River, probably one of the best trainers in the country, and she's had a year of getting her muscles into shape. She was light in his hands, quick to respond to his seat and leg aids, and very willing. *This is fun!* It surprised him to discover how satisfying it was to be able to apply what he had learned riding Pendragon yet again on another horse.

"You are getting along well with her," River commented. "How do you think she compares to Penny?"

"They are different," Todd determined after thinking for a few minutes. "Penny moves bigger. You can feel his back come up beneath your seat. Dune is probably just as quick to respond to the aids, but she just can't get thrust off the way Penny can."

"Good. If you can feel that difference, you're beginning to ride like a true horseman."

Todd nodded solemnly, but his spirit soared with pride to have earned that praise from River.

"I've been working with her on flying changes. You've been doing them now on Penny. Want to try with Dune?"

"Sure!"

"Try it through a figure eight. Do you remember the aids?"

"As I approach the center of the two circles I straighten with the outside rein. When she is straight, I switch the aids. I half-halt with the new outside rein, move the outside leg slightly back and aid with the inside leg at the girth."

"Great. Go ahead now and canter on the circle to the right. For the first time, bring her to walk for a simple change but only two or three walk steps. Remember to keep her straight through the center. If the simple change goes well, then try the flying change next time around."

The simple change went well. All Todd had to do was sit deep with supporting legs approaching the center of his circle and just a quick squeeze with both reins and Dune transitioned down to walk, her hindquarters well beneath her and taking the two walk steps still connected to Todd's hands. He signaled for left lead canter to go onto the opposite loop of the figure eight and she obediently stepped up from the walk into canter on the correct lead.

"Very well done! Next time around, use the same aids but don't come all the way to walk, and then switch your aids for the change. Keep her straight through the center...great!" River exclaimed when Todd followed his directions and Dune made the flying change from left lead back to right lead correctly from her hindquarters.

This is so awesome...this mare is amazing...went through Todd's mind over and over as he and Dune completed the figure eight several times and then executed flying changes through a serpentine.

"Good enough, bring her to walk and let her stretch. Those were all very good changes. Well done, both of you. Let her know she did well."

Todd patted the mare on both sides of her neck as he murmured to her how wonderful she was.

The lesson had gone on within the usual time frame of about forty-five minutes. Todd figured they were done, but then he saw River adjusting the line of cavalletti poles for trotting.

"Shorten the reins, ask for trot and come down the line," River said, not giving Todd any time to start fretting. "No, stay balanced in the middle of her back," he directed when Todd moved up into two-point to start his circle. "Wait until one stride before the first pole to get up in two-point. Don't do anything else. Just point Dune at the line and let her do the rest."

"You got to do this for me," Todd whispered to the mare. He followed the instructions and as he completed the circle and turned Dune's head to the line, she pricked her ears, assessed the task in front of her with her one eye, and then energetically trotted down the line, picking her feet well up to clear the poles. Without changing her rhythm, she trotted away from the line, waiting for her rider to tell her what to do next. He had moved forward off her back over the poles but it seemed he had frozen in that position. As if she understood he did not know what to do, she very calmly came down to a walk and then a halt.

"Try it again," River said.

The calmness and ease with which Dune negotiated the trot poles sent the message to Todd that this was no big deal. The next time around, Todd relaxed his seat back in the saddle after completing the line and used his aids to turn Dune back around. He rode her down the line in each direction a few more times. He began to relax, and at last Dune convinced him, 'this is no big deal!'

"Good place to stop," River said. "What do you think of her now?"

"She's great!" Todd exclaimed, meaning it from the depths of his heart.

"She is fine," River agreed coming up to walk alongside as Todd cooled the mare out. "I want you to start riding her on the trails again following Tess's conditioning program. Jodi's been riding her out at walk and trot but I don't think she has the balance yet to canter up and down hills and Dune needs that now."

"I'd love to, but who will Jodi ride?"

"I talked to her about that. Jodi can still ride Dune once a week on her light day. She can also trail ride Pendragon two or three days a week. He'll behave for her and he can use the easy days.

"Oh, good, that's great then!"

"Todd," River spoke very seriously. "Take this summer to figure out what you want to do. If you want to jump again I think Dune is the horse that will help you get over your fear. It seems to me if you want to concentrate on dressage that's great. But don't convince yourself you want to ride only dressage because you're afraid to jump."

"Yeah…I…okay, I get what you're saying."

"I'm going to be gone all summer again. I think you should ride Dune in all the lessons I can give you before I leave and we'll end each lesson with cavalletti. When you can ride that line every time as relaxed as you did today, we'll add the low cross rail jump at the end. That might be enough to get you going again if you can stay relaxed over the low jump."

"Yeah, sounds like a good plan." Todd thought for a few minutes and then admitted, "I do want to jump."

"Okay, we'll see how you feel when I get back. You can also ride Pendragon. I can give you a couple more lessons on him as well, and then when Tess lines up the dressage clinics over the summer, you can ride him in those."

"You're not taking Penny with you?"

"No, just Oberon."

"Oh, great!" Todd halted Dune and dismounted. He pushed her head away as she nudged at him, and then stroked her neck, looking ahead to a summer riding two wonderful horses, plus whatever horses Tess assigned him for the trails. "When do you have to leave?"

"Right after that graduation thing I have to go to," River said with an expression of distaste.

"Yeah, that's right, and congratulations."

"Thanks, just wish I didn't have to wear that stupid cap and gown, but the school won't let you get out of marching if you want your degree."

"I'll miss you, River. And not just because you won't be around for my lessons."

"Thank you," River said softly. "I'll miss you too. I really don't want to have to be away all summer, but I do like Jack McCall. I made a promise to him, so I'm going."

On a sudden impulse, Todd added, "I'm sorry about you and Sierra. I mean…." He bit his lip, wishing he had kept his mouth shut at the dark look on River's face. But truthfully, he felt worse than ever for both River and Sierra. He possessed a new understanding of what it meant to have a special relationship with another person. He understood their loss now with more empathy.

"I know," River said, looking away. "Actually, I expect she'll be around this summer and she probably won't mind letting both you and Jodi ride Fiel once in a while. He's another horse that can teach you a lot, so you might ask her."

"Yeah, um, good idea."

"I messed up with Sierra," River suddenly confessed. "I'm jealous and stupid. Don't be like me with Jodi," he advised. "Give her space when she needs it. Let her be her own person."

"Okay." Todd stared, astounded at these words coming from River.

The night Sean proposed, Sierra stayed up until after three a.m. scrubbing her apartment and channeling her pent-up feelings into mindless work, trying to sort them out.

Down on her hands and knees mopping the kitchen floor, Sierra tried to project out of herself and look at the situation objectively as she compared Sean and River. *Sean is...well perfect. River is not.* She rubbed at a sticky spot in front of the refrigerator. *Sean understands my need to study and get top grades. River does not understand why I can't just get by.* Sierra swept her damp cloth along the ridge of the baseboards. *Sean is well read, well-educated, and interested in many things. River is only interested in horses.*

Finding no more dirt on the kitchen floor, Sierra sat back on her heels to survey the shining, spotless vinyl. "When I compare them logically, intellectually, Sean is the obvious best choice," she mumbled out loud. "But...." She stood and threw her cleaning cloth into the sink. With elbows on the counter, she supported her head in her hands, squeezing against the temples. There were all those other things. With a sigh of confusion mixed with sadness, Sierra grabbed the sink cleaner from the lower cabinet and sprinkled it throughout the sink. As she used a scrubby pad over the sink's surface, she thought about Sean's fine-textured hair that he kept in a short, trim cut. River's hair was thick, coarse, long and messy. *Oh my,* she sighed again, remembering how she used to love running her fingers through River's hair, untangling the snarls. Sean was well-built with well-developed muscles, but he was thick and soft about his middle. *He could easily get fat when he's older.* River was also well-muscled but lean and hard with a very trim waist and flat stomach. When she and River used to embrace with their bodies so close that their hip bones touched, well…they just fit perfectly together. Sean had a nice sun tan but underneath, his skin was as pale as her own. *Nothing wrong with pale skin.* But she saw in her mind an image of lying beside River, and thought how beautiful the contrast of his brown-toned skin with her own pale color.

Finished in the kitchen, Sierra moved on to the bathroom. As she passed through the living area she paused by an arrangement of mixed flowers, a bouquet that Sean had sent her at the beginning of finals week. *He is so sweet!* An earthy scent emanated from the assortment and she sniffed deeply, taking in the pleasing odor. But something about the scent recalled an olfactory memory; a mix of fall leaves, hay, horses, apples, and the unique smell of River's skin. *Oh, I do miss his smell!* She tried to identify Sean's scent, and although he never smelled bad, she couldn't distinguish anything other than his deodorant or aftershave. She shook her head and went into the bathroom.

Sierra sprayed down the walls of the shower and scrubbed the tiled floor. She scrubbed the toilet, mopped the floor, and then scoured out the sink. *Done – it's spotless!* She glanced around and then caught sight of her face in the mirror. Lines of sadness pulled down the corners of her mouth. Deep shadows hollowed her eyes. She stared at herself and thought about River's intense, dark eyes…. A sob escaped her throat. *It's been a year. Get over it!* But she dropped to the bathroom floor and sobbed over the loss of River, something she hadn't done in many months.

"You are obviously still in love with River. Are you sure River is over you?" Allison asked when Sierra called her the next day.

"How would I know? I haven't talked to him since we broke up. I'm sure he is all involved with that girl I told you about, the one he met last summer when he was doing the Jack McCall thing. She certainly could help him get over me. She's beautiful!"

Allison made a sound of disgust. "Sierra, you know better than that."

"Well, I don't know. The last time I asked Delia how River was doing she said he seemed better, but she didn't really know. He never asks about me."

"Of course he wouldn't. He's got too much foolish pride, just like you."

"Okay, okay…so what do I do?"

"You need to talk to him."

"Right, how do I do that? Call him up and say, 'River, do you still love me even though you think I cheated on you?' - something like that?"

"Not over the phone. You need to talk to him in person. Don't you think you'll have an idea how he feels if you see him face to face?"

"I just don't think I could stand it if I see hatred there."

"At least then you will know it's really over."

"It's been over a year…of course it's really over."

"Then why are we even having this conversation?" Allison asked. "Sorry…oh, Sierra, I am so sorry," she apologized when she heard Sierra gulp back a sob.

"No, I'm just a mess," Sierra said regaining control.

"Go home, Sierra. Talk to him."

Allison's advice made sense. She needed to see River one last time if things were really over between them. She just didn't know how to do it. *Burst in on him in his apartment? Come up to him when he was riding a horse so he would have to stay calm?*

Ultimately, she realized there was no chance she could ever fall in love with another man as long as her heart still wanted River. She only went out with Sean one more time, to tell him face to face she didn't want to see him anymore. It just didn't seem right to string him along.

The first year veterinary medicine courses were fortunately quite fascinating, and intrigued Sierra enough that most of the time she could push unpleasant thoughts away and concentrate on studying.

Two weeks before the end of spring quarter while Sierra was finishing up her last term papers and gearing up for finals, she received a card and a letter in the mail on the same day, the card from Laila and the letter from Tess.

With shaking fingers she opened the letter from Tess first, afraid it was bad news. She scanned the few short lines, her heart leaping at the words.

Sierra,

River graduates on June 6. I am inviting you as my guest. I know River did not send you a graduation announcement, but I also know he still loves you and really would like you to be there to see him graduate.

Tess

The trembling did not stop as Sierra fell into the chair next to the table where her roommate had left the mail. She felt dizzy suddenly, and leaned over her lap rocking herself. *Is it possible he still loves me?* She gulped in several deep breaths to calm herself, and sat up to open the card from Laila.

Inside the envelope was a formal invitation to River's commencement. Along with the invitation, Laila had placed a hand-written note.

Hi Sierra,

Please come to River's graduation. He put me in charge of the invitations so he doesn't know I'm inviting you. But I know he wants you to be there.

Please come, Laila

June 6, the weekend before finals, Sierra noted. *I could fly down Friday night and be there for the ceremony on Saturday, and fly back early Sunday morning. I will have the plane rides and most of Sunday for studying. I could do it!*

Sierra filled out the RSVP to Laila and wrote a short note to Tess. She took both letters back out to drop into the mail.

Leaning against the back wall of the crowded gymnasium, Sierra watched River walk across the platform to shake the dean's hand and receive his bachelor's degree. How handsome he looked in his dark blue cap and gown! She held her tears in check as he returned to his seat - tears of remorse but also tears of pride. A college degree, earned by the boy who once talked about dropping out of high school! No matter what happened when she faced him later, she rejoiced in this moment for what he had managed to accomplish.

When the graduates had all filed out and their friends and families began to exit behind them, Sierra also left to spend a few hours with her mother. Tess had told her they were giving River a party in the lounge at Pegasus. The party was supposed to be over by eight p.m. Sierra would drive over then to talk to River.

"I'm sorry, Mom, you cooked a wonderful dinner," Sierra said after they sat down at the kitchen table. "My stomach is too full of butterflies. I can't eat this now." She set her fork back down, unable to even put the first bite in her mouth.

"Okay, kitten, I understand. I'll just put it away and you can microwave it later if you get hungry.

"I'm going to the stable. I can visit Fiel and the other horses until all the guests leave. I just want to be there now." Sierra got up from the table, hugged her mother who kissed her on both cheeks. Then she went out and drove away.

The horses had been brought in and most had finished their evening feed by the time Sierra arrived at Pegasus. She walked down the two aisles peeking in at each horse, greeting those familiar to her and noting the ones that had arrived since she had last been here. Then she went inside Fiel's stall to feed him treats and stroke his neck. Next she visited Corazón, then the others she knew well.

I know River always checks on the horses before he goes to bed. I'll just wait for him in here, Sierra decided.

Not long after her arrival, she heard voices in the stable yard and cars driving away. Soon, River would come in through the back door. Sierra went over there now and sat down on the floor to wait. She felt nauseated, and every time she heard a car leave, not knowing if it was the last one or not, she had to lean over her lap and hug herself tightly to stop from trembling.

Long agonizing minutes had passed since the last car drove away and she heard footsteps approaching the back door. She stood, her face pale, her skin clammy, and her body still trembling.

River opened the door and stepped inside. He stopped, and they stared at each other.

"River," Sierra was the first to speak. "I need to talk to you." He stood frozen in front of her and she held her breath, afraid he would turn away and go back outside. When he finally said, "Okay," she let the air out slowly. "I…um, congratulations."

"Thanks."

Gathering all her courage she blurted out, "I want to talk about us."

Again he said, "Okay."

You're not helping me. She looked down at her hands wringing together in her nervousness, and then started in with all she planned to say. "First of all, I still love you." When she heard what sounded like River taking in a deep breath and still not turning away, it encouraged her to continue. "I blamed you for us breaking up. When you said you no longer trusted me, that really hurt. I was very angry with you and my anger made it easier to think of myself as blameless. But I've had a lot of time to think about that day and everything that happened before. I think I was kind of mad at you already because you had been acting so cold to me about not going to the dressage finals. But we were both hurting each other. You wanted my support while you rode, and I wanted your support for my need to do well on my midterms." Sierra stopped to catch her breath and gulp in a few deep breaths before admitting the hardest part.

"It's true that what you saw that day had never happened before. It's true I didn't know Sean was going to kiss me, but what I've finally admitted to myself is that I kind of wanted him to kiss me." She glanced up. She noted the startled look on his face, but she did not detect anger, or worse, hatred. Encouraged, she quickly went on, "I wanted him to kiss me because I was curious what it would be like to kiss someone else that was a nice person. And maybe deep down I wanted to show you, 'hey boyfriend, you better be nice to me because there are others out there who will be nice to me'. But whatever the reason, I was a total idiot. I am sorry. I am so very, very sorry. I love you River. I loved you then and I still love you now." She looked up again, not knowing if her world was about to crash into abysmal gloom, or ascend to the heights of joy.

River ducked his head to hide his face. Sierra could not gauge his reaction. She swallowed and moved her tongue around, trying to moisten her dry mouth. In a shaky voice she said, "I'm asking you to forgive me."

Nothing happened for several moments that lasted an eternity. Sierra was about to turn around and leave him alone, her hopes shattered.

Then, in a few long strides, River came over to her, pulled her into his arms, and hugged her so tightly against his chest it was hard for her to breathe. She felt the tremor of his shoulders.

"I love you, Sierra."

They kissed. They hugged each other tightly. They kissed again.

"You forgive me?" Sierra asked after the last passionate kiss, and burying her cheek against his chest.

"I forgive you, but you have to forgive me, too."

"What for?"

"For being such an ass."

She laughed, kissed his mouth and said, "I forgive you."

Later, lying in each other's' arms, River said, "Sierra, let's get married now."

"Tonight?" she giggled.

"Sure…no seriously, I don't want to wait any longer. We said when I graduated. So…?"

"Like how soon?"

"Right after your finals. We could elope."

"You're serious, aren't you?" She reached up to turn his face so she could look in his eyes.

"I am." He kissed her softly.

"Okay…let's do…it," she agreed, laughing and trying to answer in between him kissing her mouth. "But let's wait until you get back from Jack's and before I go back to school…early September."

21 SUMMER TRAINING

And his low head and crest, just one sharp ear bent back
For my voice, and the other pricked out on his track;
And one eye's black intelligence – ever that glance
O'er its white edge at me, his own master, askance!
And the thick heavy spume flakes which aye and anon
His fierce lips shook upwards in galloping on. - Robert Browning, *How They Brought the Good News from Ghent to Aix*

"The spur is not for decoration, River," Jack McCall said, watching River ride a red roan stallion belonging to Stone Valley Farm in a training session. "Just touch, no gouging, no pain, but the point of the spur is so much more precise than the calf of your leg. Try it."

River brought the stallion around the short side of the arena in a collected trot, and then after turning the corner, aided his mount into a half-pass by touching him with the spur. *Yes, much quicker response,* River realized as the stallion brought his hindquarters underneath, crossing his legs as he moved on a diagonal to the center of the arena.

"You see how effective that is?" Jack called out.

River straightened the stallion for two strides, then aided him for half-pass back to the rail, again touching him with the spur. At the rail he turned his head and gave Jack a nod that he understood.

"Hallelujah!" Jack cheered with one clap of his hands. "Reverse, and try that again from the other rein. At least I don't have to scold you about using spurs to go forward." He turned his attention to the other members of the team. "Spurs are to enhance the lateral aids, never to increase the speed or to go forward. Calves of your legs for forward movement. If you need more than legs, use a touch of the whip, not spurs."

The session ended with Jack finding nothing more to criticize about River's riding, but serving more as the eyes on the ground to help him school the stallion. Jack had told River he had rarely met a rider with his sensitivity as to how his horse was moving beneath him, but even the best riders benefited from eyes on the ground to help that additional fraction of what could be improved.

River agreed, and hoped he could find someone with as good an eye as Jack when he trained at home. Kate, his assistant trainer, certainly had progressed in her 'feel' of when a horse moved correctly, but she didn't always know how to correct problems she saw from the ground. Tess had a good eye for improving a horse over jumps, but not nearly as attuned to problems in flatwork. Sierra (he smiled to himself just thinking of her), noticed more and more all the time and enhanced what she was learning with reading and studying dressage videos. But she would still need years of experience to develop an eye as astute as Jack's. He suddenly thought of Jodi. *Yeah, Jodi!* He recalled some discussions with Jodi as she stood next to him while he gave lessons. She might not be an accomplished rider yet, but she already noticed more from the ground than most experienced riders. He had been quite impressed a few times when he asked what she thought, and her answers indicated she had picked up on the same faults he was about to address.

"Very good, River. I think that is enough work for him today. Any questions?" Jack asked, looking around to include those watching.

"Well, you all look very tired. Let's quit and we'll meet after dinner tonight to look at the European competitions and outline a schedule." As the team members began gathering their things Jack added, "Oh, and from now on, everyone rides wearing spurs. They are required, so I want all of you to get very comfortable using them and also wearing them but not using them."

Later at the dinner table, the discussion returned to the subject of spurs.

"I wonder how that monster star of yours is going to react to a spur," John Church commented, referring to Oberon.

"I'll wear the spurs because I have to, but I will never use them on him," River declared. He looked over at Jack when he said, "I made him a promise."

"What, not to use spurs?" Elizabeth laughed.

"When I had to put him in a double bridle I promised him if he would just take it in his mouth that I would not hurt him with the curb reins and I would never touch him with spurs."

The others at the table joined Elizabeth in laughter, except for Jack and Lisa. "Oh, come on," John said. "Are you telling us that you bargained with the monster to accept the curb bit by promising to never use spurs? And he agreed to that?"

"Something like that," River answered seriously, not at all disturbed that the others were skeptical. He kept his focus on Jack.

Jack gave him a nod, indicating he understood.

The others were used to River and Jack sometimes coming to a strange consensus concerning horses, so they weren't all that surprised that Jack seemed to have agreed with River. They laughed and talked about it among themselves, but all agreed that those two had some kind of mystical connection with horses. Lisa never laughed with the others for she had no doubts that both River and Jack communicated with horses in a way not easily explained. She had once or twice experienced such a connection herself.

When River looked her way, she smiled, letting him know that she also understood and he smiled back.

A brief glance, a smile, or a comment having to do with horses, was about the only interaction Lisa and River exchanged since returning to Jack's stable. It was not possible to step backwards to just being friends, so their relationship became one of polite teammates. River regretted his behavior of last year with Lisa, for looking back, he could see now that he had been giving her the impression there might be something between them. If he had kept things platonic, they could still be friends now. Now he bore too much guilt and Lisa still suffered too much hurt. At least she was not the type of person to hold a grudge.

As promised, after dinner Jack pulled out a list of European competitions and the team planned their summer itinerary.

Because of the three-hour time difference, River usually waited to call Sierra just as he got into bed. "We're flying to Europe in two weeks," he informed Sierra after the usual greetings filled with endearments. "Two shows in England and two in Germany."

"That is so exciting! When should I fly over?"

"It's up to you. We'll be there two months, so however long you think you can get away."

They knew Jack wanted River to compete in Europe this summer, and they had planned for Sierra to join River at least part of the time. She had always wanted to see Europe, and this was the perfect opportunity. But even more important, she could be there for River now, while she wasn't in school.

They discussed the options, and decided Sierra would fly over for his last show in England and then go with him to Germany. She would be with him then for almost a month.

That settled, River asked for all the news of Pegasus.

"Tess gave me a jumping lesson outside today on Cory," Sierra began. "He is so marvelous. I swear, River, all I have to do is point him at the jump and just stay balanced. He loves it!"

"Yeah," River agreed, thinking back nostalgically to how it felt to take a course on Corazón.

"Kate watched the lesson, and tomorrow she is going to ride Cory on the trail when I ride Felicity. I think she'll do just fine with him."

"Yeah, I watched her ride him in the arena before I left, and she did fine. Tell her it's okay with me if she wants to take him over a few outside obstacles after the trail ride."

"She'll like that. Oh, I lunged Ysbryd today, and I'll ride her on the trail tomorrow. Kate wants to know what you want her to do with Ysbryd after I leave to join you."

River had been riding his filly over the winter months, a few sessions in the arena, and then walking her out on the trails. He had asked Sierra to continue trail riding her and lunge her once or twice a week. He thought a moment and then replied, "Kate's schedule is pretty full, but if she can ride her or lunge her at least once or twice a week, that will be enough. Just ask her to make sure she gets turned out in a pasture or one of the larger paddocks."

"Okay, I will. Jodi rode Fiel today. River, she's really getting those canter transitions. Fiel doesn't move quite as big as Pendragon and can balance himself easier than Dune. I think if she rides Fiel a few more times, she'll have the ability to do as well on Penny. She's going to ride Penny on the trail the next three days, and Fiel on the flat. Then I think we'll see how she does with a flat lesson on Penny again."

"Good plan. How's Todd doing?" River had told Sierra how Todd had a fear of jumping since his accident, and even a fear of riding a horse when it spooked. Before he left, he made sure that Tess only assigned Todd conditioning rides on horses he had ridden before and that usually did not shy. He also asked Sierra to watch out for him. He did not want Todd to have another experience to set him back any further.

"He's doing okay," Sierra answered. "He rides all his assigned rides, but you know, he really only wants to ride Dune. She is such an angel! He's been consistently riding her over cavalletti, and he finally got the nerve to ask Tess to give him a jumping lesson. That's happening, let's see...this Friday. I'll be sure and watch and let you know how it goes."

"Yeah, thanks. Please don't let her push him too hard. I think he needs time and to stay safe."

"I agree. Don't worry, I'll be there."

After Sierra had given him updates on all the other horses, she said hesitantly, "One more thing. I talked to Allison this afternoon, and she thought up this plan for our wedding."

River laughed, almost to the point of choking, as Sierra described Allison's plan. "Is that really what you want to do?"

"Well, it certainly would be different and it doesn't involve any more money than what we want to spend. In fact, in a lot of ways it will be cheaper. We don't have to rent a church or anyplace like that.

"It just seems a little dramatic."

"We don't have to.do it."

"No, I don't mind," River said quickly, hearing disappointment in Sierra's voice. "I'll do whatever you want."

"Really? You'll do it?" The disappointment vanished, replaced by happy excitement. "I think it would be fun," Sierra said, "and we don't have to do anything. Allison said she'll take care of all the arrangements. We just have to show up."

"Okay," River agreed.

For several weeks now, riding Dune over the cavalletti and the small cross-rail jump no longer triggered a reaction in Todd. It became no more frightening than just working on the flat. He credited Dune with taking control of the exercise, adjusting her pace and balance to accommodate whenever she felt Todd freeze on her back. Now, he could sit deep in the approach, move into two-point as she trotted the line, stay in balance as she jumped the cross-rail, and come back into his seat at the appropriate time when she landed. He stayed focused and alert, no longer feeling the acceleration of his pulse as they approached the jump, nor freezing his muscles as Dune jumped and landed.

"You should tell Tess you're ready to try another jumping lesson," Jodi commented, watching from the rail.

Just the thought of asking Tess for a lesson caused his pulse to accelerate. *What kind of a coward have I turned into?*

"Ask her. What's she going to do, bite your head off?" Jodi persisted later the same day.

"I can wait until River gets back," Todd said defensively. *You have no idea what that woman can do.*

The look Jodi gave him, narrowing her eyes and twisting her mouth, said more than words. Shame filled him over his cowardice. *Tess is not my mother. She can't hurt me.* He repeated the thought to himself over and over as he and Jodi helped bring in the horses before going home.

"Tess is just finishing a lesson," Jodi said, very matter-of-fact as they passed the outdoor arena.

Todd took the hint. He gulped in air to quiet his nerves, and before he totally humiliated himself with his fear in front of his girlfriend, he strode over to meet Tess exiting the arena.

"What is it?" Tess greeted him with her usual curtness.

"Uh, I've been practicing that cavalletti line and I…"

"You ready to try jumping again?" Tess interrupted.

"Yeah, if…"

"I'll put you on the schedule." With that, she continued on her way, nothing more to be said.

"Whoa," Todd breathed out. *That was easy.* He rejoined Jodi who met him with a proud grin.

A week later, Todd walked Dune into the outside arena. "Okay, let's do this," Todd said to the mare. She turned her head as he snugged up the girth, to look at him with her one eye. He met that look. "You know what's coming, don't you? You're telling me it's going to be okay." He slipped his fingers beneath the girth to make sure no skin had been pinched, and then stroked her neck. "Thanks."

Sometimes, Dune started her work with stiffness in her hocks, but after several rounds of asking her to trot with her neck stretched, Todd could feel her stride become rhythmical and more buoyant. "You feeling better?" he asked. "Warmed up now?"

She snorted in answer.

Shortening the reins gently, Todd asked for more roundness, and encouraged with his legs for more impulsion. Dune 'answered' with stepping deeper underneath to push forward in her trot with more thrust. "Good girl," Todd praised. He finished her warm-up, pleased with her rhythm and balance through the transitions within the gaits, and between gaits.

"Very nice, Todd," Tess complimented as she entered the arena. "Keep that frame and let's see you execute a serpentine around that center line of jumps." She asked for a few more figures, and satisfied horse and rider had warm, flexible muscles, she directed him to the usual cavalletti line. "Great, Todd, much better than the last time. Let her have a stretch break."

As Todd gave Dune the reins, he noticed Sierra and Jodi coming up to the rail to watch. He nodded as he passed and they both gave him a thumbs up.

"All right. Start with the cavalletti, then on to the next cross-rail, round the short end and take that cross-rail oxer in the center, and finish over the next vertical in line," Tess called out.

"Okay, lady, I'm counting on you," Todd whispered. He gathered the reins, asked for trot, and headed Dune down the cavalletti. They easily finished the line and the cross-rail, for it was the same exercise they had been doing for weeks, and rode on to the next cross-rail, no higher than the one they had just jumped. Todd managed to stay balanced and in control as Dune did her job and jumped efficiently and clean. They looped around, and Todd faced Dune to the oxer. It was no higher than the previous two jumps, but had an additional rail, creating a very narrow spread. Just that extra rail suddenly loomed before Todd as twice the size as the previous jumps and his heart lurched. He felt the hesitancy in Dune's stride, as if asking, 'you sure you want to go over this?'. When Todd didn't apply rein pressure or legs to turn her away, actually froze on her back, Dune cantered on and took the jump, pacing herself to take off and land smoothly. Todd forcefully breathed out, realizing he had frozen. But now that Dune had jumped, it had been no more difficult than the first two. She was already in line for the vertical and cantering forward without hesitation, apparently having understood the course. Todd gathered his wits, moved into two-point, and stayed balanced as Dune sailed over the final jump. She cantered on, but not seeing another jump in front of her, slowed her stride, flicking her ears as if asking, 'what now?'

"You're awesome," Todd praised her, and sat deep to bring her down to trot, and then patted her neck.

"What happened at the oxer?" Tess asked, but not waiting for an answer ordered, "Do it again. Stay balanced over her back. You're doing a good job of rating her."

She's doing a good job of rating herself, Todd admitted but did not say it out loud. He repeated the course, but this time, kept himself balanced over her back, talked to her with the reins as they made the turn, and praised her as she managed each obstacle perfectly. With Dune taking care of him, he felt his fear ebbing away.

"Well done," Sierra encouraged, grinning, as he trotted past.

"Good girl, Dune," Jodi added.

The lesson continued with a few variations of the course, but all at low heights. Tess added a combination, first at two strides, and then one stride, and widened the spread of the oxer. Todd felt his heart lurch and speed up with each new obstacle, but he was able to control his fear enough to keep from freezing. He trusted Dune. All he had to do was show her the course.

Only once did he have to intervene. Tess had him round a corner to approach a low spread from the right. When Todd realized Dune galloped forward without any adjustment to her stride, he realized she had not seen the jump. He turned her head slightly to the left, and suddenly she shifted back, as if putting on the brakes. But she saw the jump, and burst forward again coming in too close, but nevertheless jumping clean. Todd fell a little forward of her motion, but had anticipated the awkward jump, and settled back quickly in balance.

"Ah ha!" Tess called out. "Good lesson there. You need to make sure she sees where she's going when turning to the right. Well done!" Tess asked him to come around the turn once again to the right, so that he could practice turning her head. Of course, the next round, Dune remembered what was coming, but Todd vowed he would pay closer attention to her blind side.

The lesson ended, and Todd led Dune back to the crossties, full of relief to have gotten through the lesson, proud of himself for facing his fears, but especially proud of Dune and grateful for how she had taken care of him.

"You know, River was right about this mare," Todd admitted to Sierra and Jodi when they joined him at the crossties. "She's special."

"She sure is!" Sierra agreed.

"Of course, you always knew that," he said, smiling at Jodi.

Todd began to look forward to jumping now on Dune. Tess gave him two more lessons in the arena, and then took him to the back field. The cross-country course raised Todd's sense of alarm, but he trusted Dune, and relying on her to take care of him, had a great lesson over a novice level course.

The next week, Tess directed him over a new course and again, Dune managed all the obstacles in her usual competent style. Todd remembered to turn her head whenever they approached an obstacle from the right. They had become a team.

"That was a training level course," Tess informed him at the end of the round.

"That was training level?" Todd asked, astounded. It had not seemed any more difficult to Dune than the novice course had been.

"Yes, except for leaving out the trickier jumps like the bank and the water. Todd, there is a schooling show next weekend. It's late for entries, but the coordinator called me yesterday. They want more training level entries, and she'll waive the late entry fee if I know anyone who wants to enter late. Want to give it a try?"

At that moment, Dune lowered her head and snorted. It seem to Todd she clearly said, 'come on, kid, we can do it'.

"Uh…okay."

"Great, I know you've galloped into water. Have you ever taken a jump in?"

"No, I haven't."

"You'll have to in the event, so let's finish up with that. Take the log pile, then the ditch, and then the center railroad ties into the water."

The ditch? Todd did not say it out loud, but his heart thumped and his stomach heaved. "Okay," he squeaked out an answer. He moved Dune off into a trot circle, trying to push the image of the looming black gap of the ditch from his mind. *Trust Dune, just trust her,* he ordered himself.

He asked for canter and turned her toward the log pile. She increased the pace to gallop and cleared the logs. He needed to make an easy loop to the left for the ditch. She would see it with her good eye. He could feel Dune assessing the distance to the ditch, galloping rhythmically but a few strides away, shortening to a comfortable take-off.

The side posts marking the ditch suddenly grew into live monsters, with glaring eyes and the ditch itself a gaping mouth, ready to swallow his horse and him whole. Todd screamed, and jerked Dune's head away, using his outside leg to turn her.

Dune's head shot up at the sudden yanking at her mouth, both from discomfort and confusion. She clearly understood she was to jump that ditch. She shook her head once, trying to regain her head, but Todd, sitting stiff on her back pulled her down to a walk. Still confused, she obediently acquiesced to this new command.

"What are you doing?" Tess shouted, striding angrily forward. "She was ready to jump!"

"I c-c-can't," Todd stuttered, his teeth chattering and uninhibited tears of shame streaming down his cheeks. "S-s-sorry, I j-j-just c-can't."

Tess's eyes opened wide in bewilderment. Something was very wrong with this kid, and if River hadn't asked her to be patient with him and give him another chance, she would have told him to put his horse away and not come back. But River had been adamant that he wanted Todd to remain at Pegasus. "Okay, okay," Tess tried to calm him down. "It's okay. Why don't you just cool her down."

"I c-can't. I n-need to…." Todd gulped in air, and leaned forward to stroke Dune's neck. "We'll jump the water," he stated. Not waiting for Tess's reaction, he moved Dune away, picked up the canter, and guided her toward the water pond. He pointed her toward the middle section of the railroad tie bank. Dune pricked her ears, brought her hindquarters underneath as she came up to the bank, and without hesitation, jumped into the water and galloped on through.

In spite of his disturbing reaction in his last lesson, Tess still wanted Todd to compete in the schooling show. They had a satisfactory dressage test and Dune had warmed up well, feeling energetic and eager for cross-country.

"You're going to do just fine," Jodi said, peering up into Todd's face. "Trust her, she'll take care of you."

In spite of all his self-talk, the steadiness of Dune, and the support of Jodi, Todd's heart flipped when the warm-up ring steward informed him he could go up to the starting box. Now his heart thumped loudly in his chest and a wave of nausea swept over him, leaving his palms moist inside his riding gloves, his mouth dry, and a heaviness in his stomach that seemed to weigh down his ability to move in the saddle. It was July and hot. Sweat trickled down the middle of his spine, and he shivered as if chilled.

"Todd?" Jodi asked, noting the sudden loss of color in his face.

With a snort and a shake of her head, Dune started to walk placidly toward the starting box. She had been here before, albeit several years ago; but she remembered this place and she seemed to know when it was her turn.

Her movement jolted Todd from his frozen state. He sucked in a few breaths and shaking his head with quiet laughter, he turned his head to smile back at Jodi, and shrugged his shoulders as if in surrender to Dune's will. "Okay, lady, you're in charge," he said to her with a stroke of her neck.

"Trust her," Jodi called out and waved. She limped away to a spot where she could watch his last few jumps of the course.

The course footing was ideal, consisting of soft dirt or leaf-strewn paths, no mud or puddles, and no dust or rocks. As Dune galloped energetically, her ears pricked in alertness, and enjoying the sponginess beneath her feet and the open air, Todd shrugged away the last of his apprehension. He did trust Dune. He knew the course for he had walked it earlier with Tess. The only ditch was a Trahkener, and something about having a thick rail across the gap changed the aspect of the jump. There was nothing coming up that should phase him, and he knew nothing would disturb his mare.

The first log jump loomed straight ahead. He felt the surge of power beneath him as Dune gathered herself and he let the motion move him up into two-point as she sailed over. He settled back as she galloped on, touching the reins to check her pace for the downhill coming up.

At the bottom of the hill, Todd showed her with a touch of the rein which section of the water he wanted her to approach. Dune jumped off the bank and galloped through with confidence, not at all disturbed over getting her feet and legs wet.

The only jump Todd really needed to take control was the next to last of the course where they took a rail fence into a corral and had to make a turn to the right to jump out. He remembered to turn Dune's head so she saw the exit fence. She snorted as if to say, 'got it', and jumped out clean. They finished the course without jumping faults or time penalties.

As he galloped Dune through the final flags and brought her gradually to trot and walk, Jodi limped forward as fast as she could, with an ear-to-ear grin. He barely had time to dismount before she hugged him in glee, but she quickly let him go, and then hugged Dune around her neck, the true star of the day.

"You are so wonderful!" she praised Dune. The mare rested her cheek against Jodi's chest, and then gratefully accepted the carrot when Jodi finally let go and offered her the treat.

A few hours later, Todd entered the arena for stadium jumping, with no more apprehension than the usual increased adrenaline from being in a competition. His mind stayed alert as he balanced over Dune, pointing her at each obstacle and then trusting her to negotiate it competently. Again, there was only one turn to the right and he remembered to turn her head so that she saw her jump. They finished stadium clean and no time penalties.

"Well done, Todd," Tess said when the final scores were posted and he found that Dune and he had placed third. The first three place winners all had clean cross-country and stadium rounds. The final placings had been determined by the dressage scores, and the point difference was very narrow.

"Is that Todd Marshall?" a woman checking the posted scores asked.

"Oh, hi Virginia." Todd turned and smiled at the instructor from Meadowood.

"How nice to see you…so, you're back at Pegasus." There was a hint of a question in her statement.

"Yeah, I am," he said.

"Hello, Virginia," Tess greeted. "How did your kids do today?"

"I only have two juniors riding today in beginner novice. Sarah placed fourth which isn't too bad for her first show."

As if on cue, Sarah popped forward from behind Virginia. "Hi, Todd," she greeted cheerfully. "Was that Dune you were riding?"

"Yeah...oh right, she came from your stable."

"I knew it was Dune!" Sarah declared looking up at Virginia.

"Oh my goodness, that really was our old mare?" Virginia looked over at Tess for confirmation, not quite sure she trusted the kids.

"Yes," Tess confirmed. "That's right, I forgot River bought her from you. What do you think of her now?" She laughed, enjoying the stunned look on Virginia's face.

"It's hard to believe. Dune always did well in the jumping, but you've done wonders with her dressage. I actually didn't recognize her." She snorted a laugh, as if a joke had been played on her. "But of course, you have River. I thought I was getting the better deal when I let him have her so cheap and got a pony club clinic out of him. You wouldn't consider selling her back, would you?" Virginia asked Tess with a hopeful twinkle in her eye.

"She actually belongs to River, but I doubt he'll let her go," Tess replied in good humor. "Todd, better go get that mare ready for your victory round."

22 A SPECIAL DAY

Wherever man has left his footprints in the long ascent from barbarism to civilization, we find the hoof-print of a horse beside it. - John Trotwood Moore

After the schooling show, Todd convinced himself he had regained his confidence. He could jump, he could event, he was back on track. He saw no reason to ever have to jump that particular ditch at home. He could manage other ditches in other courses because they were different.

"You believe you have conquered your fear?" Dr. Statton asked when Todd related in his monthly session with his psychiatrist, all that had happened at the show.

"Yeah, I couldn't have jumped again if not for Dune. She is the most amazing horse. She…" Todd proceeded to describe in detail all the positive aspects of his favorite horse.

It pleased Dr. Statton that over the past months, Todd had gradually recovered to become again the bright, enthusiastic, and happy teenage boy he had known before the accident and before his mother's death. Conquering his fear of jumping certainly had been a breakthrough in his emotional maturity. He credited him with great courage and also sweet modesty for how much he praised this horse.

He had high hopes for Todd continuing to mature into a fine young man. *Yet, I'm not sure he has come to terms with his issues over his mother. There is still something dark in his past.*

When Tess suggested he enter Dune in an upcoming rated one-day combined training event, Todd asked, "What about a dressage show?"

"Dressage?" Tess responded, saying the word as if she had no idea what it meant. "Who do you want to enter in dressage?"

"Um…"

"Do you think it would be fair to ride Pendragon at the lower levels? A horse trained all the way to grand prix? You're certainly not ready to ride anything above third level; maybe only second level." Tess actually didn't care if he rode Pendragon or that it might be unfair. People bought horses all the time trained to a higher level than they rode and competed on them. But she wanted Todd to compete in rated combined training events, hoping he would qualify for the championship, and along with Brooke and Mindy, Pegasus would send a junior team.

"I was thinking of Dune."

"That mare can jump but she is certainly not a dressage horse," Tess snorted.

With that reaction, Todd agreed to enter the one-day, not sure why he had been reluctant.

"Is it so important to compete at all?" Jodi asked when Todd later told her about Tess's reaction to his request.

"No, I guess not." Todd actually was not sure what he wanted to do as far as competitions. He didn't know why he had not wanted to enter in the one-day event, and had half-way convinced himself that he wanted to see how he would do in a dressage show.

The one-day show proved to be no more difficult for Dune than the schooling show, but the competition was stiffer. They again went clean in both stadium and cross-country, but due to her dressage score, they only placed fifth. Todd came away from that show very happy. There had been a ditch in the course, and although he froze at the approach, Dune ignored him and carried him across. *With Dune, I don't have to be afraid of ditches.*

Even so, he never attempted to take the one at home, and Tess never asked him to in his lessons.

After the last show in Europe, Jack's team members each returned to their own stables, but all were to return to Jack's farm in October for that region's championship. All his riders had scored well in the European shows, and many had placed. But the stars certainly were River and Oberon. They won three firsts and a second place, an extremely impressive accomplishment for a horse and rider unknown to the European judges.

Mrs. Galensburg had also flown to Europe and attended every one of Oberon's shows. To her delight, she had many opportunities to be interviewed and photographed as the splendid dressage star's owner. She was sure that River and Oberon would be one of the three riders to represent the U.S. Equestrian dressage team next summer. Her dream was so close to fulfillment. On returning home, she invited Tess to dinner. Tess had never seen the woman so animated or smile with such genuine pleasure.

Two days after River returned, he met Jodi coming up the hill from one of the pastures. "Can you come with me for a minute?" he asked.

"Sure." Jodi followed River into the stable yard.

A large horse van had just pulled in and parked. The driver stood and stretched out the kinks in his neck and back, as if he had been driving for a long time. When he saw River, he led the way to the back of the van, and the two of them undid the latches and lowered the ramp.

"Wait right there," River said to Jodi, a sly smile on his face.

Jodi stood near the end of the ramp and watched River disappear into the dimness of the interior. A few minutes later, he backed out a horse wearing a light sheet; a horse that sensibly set each hoof down carefully as it negotiated its way down the ramp. When it had all four feet square on the ground, the horse snorted, and whickered out a greeting, catching the scent of other horses in this new place.

"This is Maggie May," River said. The driver came over and pulled the sheet from the horse's back, revealing a dark liver chestnut coat. The horse stood well above sixteen hands, had two short white socks on the back legs and a white star in the middle of her wide forehead. "She's a Dutch warmblood mare, and if you like her, she's yours."

"Mine?" The word came out a hoarse whisper as Jodi looked into the mare's large, dark eye. Girl and mare gazed at each other, neither moving as if frozen for several moments. Then Jodi extended her hand at the same time the mare stretched her nose toward her. They touched, and for Jodi, an instant bond formed. She stepped in closer to stroke the lovely neck.

River handed her the lead rope and then helped the driver remove the shipping boots. "Walk her around to let her see the place, and then put her in the first paddock. I left it open for her.

After Jodi had settled Maggie in the paddock with a pile of grass hay, River joined her at the fence and related the mare's story. "Her owner is starting college and her parents insisted she sell the mare. She's had her since a two-year-old. She's only eight now. The girl had worked with Jack to start this mare and bring her along. She competed her this season at second level dressage, and they've done very well.

"I worked with the girl some at Jack's place, and when she heard I was looking for a horse to buy she told me she had to sell Maggie. When I told her the amount I had to spend she seemed kind of upset. I think she knew her horse would have a good home with me. Well, she talked to her parents and they finally agreed to let me buy her for twelve hundred dollars. Jodi, this mare is worth over twenty thousand!"

"You bought her for me?" Jodi exclaimed.

"If you like her. If you don't, it's no problem. I'm happy to keep her," he said very solemnly but with a twinkle in his eye and the corner of his mouth twitching.

"I love her," Jodi replied, her voice thick with emotion.

In a daze, Jodi spent the rest of the day just watching her mare, frequently going into the paddock to give her treats and stroke her neck. She stayed all day so that she was the one to bring Maggie into her new stall in the evening. Jodi wanted to be sure the mare looked content and comfortable before leaving. It was one of the happiest days of her life.

September in the northwest usually consists of sunny days and no rain, but Allison had a back-up plan just in case. Fortunately, on the chosen day, the sun shone forth with only a few amicable white clouds in the sky.

Family and friends sat in chairs arranged in rows separated by a wide aisle on a flat area of the back field of Pegasus. In front of the chairs a simple wooden platform had been constructed and adorned with pots in various sizes of sweet peas, forget-me-nots, and lavender, some of Sierra's favorite flowers. The spiritual guide chosen to officiate, waited on the center of the platform.

A trumpet blared three notes, the signal for the ceremony to commence. All eyes turned as three riders approached on dark horses at a collected canter. Corazón, the horse on the right, had his mane braided with ribbons in a muted shade of blue that matched his leg wraps and saddle pad. Pendragon, on the left, had his mane braided with lavender ribbons, and wore matching lavender leg wraps and saddle pad. Their riders, Ben Jeffers on Corazón, and Todd on Pendragon, wore white breeches, black boots, black jackets, and black helmets. Ben wore a cummerbund in blue and Todd wore one in lavender.

In the middle rode River on Oberon, his horse's mane braided with white ribbons and wearing matching white leg wraps and a white saddle pad. River wore the formal attire for upper level dressage: black Shadbelly dressage coat, white breeches, black boots and dressage hat, cream colored waistcoat, and white gloves.

All three horses came to a balanced halt to the side of the platform. Manuel, Enrique, and Jodi stepped forward to take the reins of the horses as the three riders dismounted, passed off their helmets, and stepped up onto the platform.

The trumpet player stepped back to make way for three musicians with guitar, violin, and viola. They played a lively tune as Megan, in the role of flower girl and proudly bearing Sierra's bouquet, led the way up the aisle riding on Muffin, decked out with ribbons to match the colors of the bouquet and in Megan's dress. Sierra's bridesmaids followed on foot - Allison, her high school friend Katrina, and a girl she had become close friends with at school. Kate Ramsey helped Megan down from the pony and led him away as Megan and the bridesmaids took their places on the platform.

The trumpeter played another three notes, then joined in on a lilting melody with the string musicians. Heads craned backwards, all eyes seeking the appearance of the bride. Down the hill came Fiel, his mane and tail braided with ribbons and sprigs of flowers. He wore black leg wraps and a black saddle pad that contrasted with his light color and Sierra's white dress. Sierra's mother walked alongside at Fiel's shoulder.

River's throat and chest tightened as he watched his bride approach, seeing her for the first time in her dress. He thought she was as beautiful as the most heavenly of angels, sitting regally and elegantly astride her horse. She wore a simple veil over her honey-brown hair hanging loose around her shoulders. As suited her style, her white dress had a plain bodice and a full skirt, the only adornment a trim of lace at the neck, edges of the capped sleeves, and the hem. She wore elegant white leather boots that laced up in an old-fashioned Victorian style, and white elbow-length gloves.

The musicians brought the melody to a climax as Sierra and her mother passed through the wide aisle and halted in front of the platform. River stepped off the platform and over to Fiel's side.

Pam pulled the reins over Fiel's head and handed them to River, announcing, "I give you the hand of my daughter." Pam stepped away and River lifted Sierra down from her horse. Delia Evans stepped up to lead Fiel away as River took Sierra's hand and led her up onto the platform. Megan handed off the bouquet, and River and Sierra faced the officiator.

The ceremony was short, consisting of traditional vows.

River spoke each word with deep sincerity, for he meant them with all his heart and soul. "I, River, take you, Sierra, to be my lawfully wedded wife, my constant friend, my faithful partner and my love from this day forward. In the presence of God, our family and friends, I offer you my solemn vow to be your faithful partner in sickness and in health, in good times and in bad, and in joy as well as in sorrow. I take you with all your faults and your strengths as I offer myself to you with my faults and strengths. I will help you when you need help, and I will turn to you when I need help. I choose you as the person with whom I will spend my life. I promise to love you unconditionally, to support you in your goals, to honor and respect you, to laugh with you and cry with you, and to cherish you for as long as we both shall live." His voice became hoarse and tremulous, but he managed each word clearly.

Sierra then said her vows, "I Sierra, take you, River to be my lawfully wedded husband..." She repeated the same promise, her own voice husky.

When they were pronounced husband and wife, River's and Sierra's eyes glistened as they kissed.

23 DUNE AND THE DITCH

In the outward appearance, riding should present itself as an art. Horse and rider in all movements should give the impression of two living creatures merged into one. – Alois Podhajsky, *The Complete Training of Horse and Rider*

The newlywed couple did not care that they didn't have much of a honeymoon. They already had taken a few days in Europe for tourist activities in between the shows and caring for Oberon. When River went to the Olympics next summer (nobody said 'if he went'), they would again have a little time to be tourists in a foreign country.

They spent the time remaining before Sierra returned to school, working together with the horses and some of the students. River had a lot of catching up to do and also spent hours with Kate, observing each horse in training. Kate had done her best, and the horses were all in good condition and making progress, although there was much River could see that needed improvement. But Kate had done well on her own, even more competent than last year.

The season ended, terminated after both the regional combined training and dressage championships and the national dressage finals. With River riding in a different region, Pegasus had no entries in their local dressage regional championship. But Pegasus sent an adult team and two junior riders to the regional combined training championship.

329

Sierra rode Corazón in senior intermediate to a first place win. Kate took two second places - on Prospector in senior training level, and on Jubilee in senior intermediate. Tess rode Meridian for the first time at advanced level, and took third place. Brooke and Mindy both competed at junior novice level. Brooke came in second on her horse Firefly, and Mindy on Shamrock took fifth. Todd and Dune competed at junior training level, and took a fifth place. Again the mare went clean cross-country and stadium but her dressage score put her behind the other clean horses. For Tess, it was a successful year.

With his college education completed, River settled into a new routine at Pegasus, devoting his entire day to working with horses and students. Even with Sierra away at school, River loved his new life, for he was so busy during the day, he only had time to miss her late at night. And he was so tired, that once he said goodbye to her on the phone, he fell almost instantly asleep.

Jack McCall was frequently invited to give clinics at Claremont Equestrian Center. When Jack asked River to assist him, River was more than happy to go, for it gave him time with Sierra. River also volunteered once a month to coach the pony club at Meadowood, for he took to heart Jack's views that River should use his gift to help others with their horses. At first he thought of it as a duty, but he soon looked forward to pony club day. Coaching the seven little girls and two boys, all between the ages of eight and twelve, and on their less than perfect horses and ponies, turned out to be immensely fun! Each one of those kids loved their animals devoutly. It was a joy to see how with kind treatment and proper use of aids, these animals did their very best. They would never make it to the Olympics or even national events, but both kids and animals were improving and having fun, and some of them might develop into riders capable of competing in big competitions.

It was amazing how quickly Jodi progressed with Maggie, easily working with her at first level and doing well with second and third level exercises. She loved her Maggie, but that love did not decrease her devotion to Dune. She still rode Dune on her easy trail days, and never neglected to visit Dune every day with treats.

"You want to try a dressage show with her next year?" River asked.

"If Maggie tells me she wants to, then yes," Jodi answered.

"Okay," River said with a smile. He understood what Jodi meant.

Watching Todd ride, River could see how much the boy had taken to heart the use of proper aids. He sat quietly, applying his weight and legs invisibly and using the reins softly, an extension of his hands to communicate to his mount. It was evident Todd had worked hard on all the exercises River had coached him through at the beginning of the season.

When he had returned, he had a meeting with both Tess and Kate, to go over the details of each horse and student and how they had progressed while he had been away.

"Todd has really surprised me," Tess said. "He is getting wonderful work out of Pendragon, and he's applying what he's learned to riding Dune. She almost looks like a dressage horse with him riding her." Tess laughed and added, "Almost." Then she related how the jumping lessons were going and the events he had competed in (Todd rode in two more events to earn his qualifying rides for the championship). "I guess it's okay if he never takes that ditch. I have never seen a rider react like that, and then still want to ride."

River wasn't so sure it was okay for Todd to avoid the ditch. He didn't understand what the hang-up might be, for Todd was consistently taking Dune over more difficult obstacles. That ditch was pretty straightforward, really an easy jump.

Throughout the winter months, the training schedules for the horses were as usual cut back. The only jumping now was in lessons, and the intensity kept at a non-stressful level for both horses and riders. It was a time to concentrate on refining the aids without the pressure of an upcoming show.

"What do you want to work on over the winter?" River asked Todd.

"I want to improve the sensitivity of my seat and learn quicker responses with the aids," Todd answered, his expression so solemn and his tone so sincere that River almost wanted to laugh. "I think I'd like to try a dressage show next season."

"Okay, you can keep riding Pendragon a few days a week but I want you to try those aids on other horses that aren't quite as sensitive to the aids as Penny. You've done well with Dune so, let's see…maybe I'll let you try Meridian in your next lesson."

"Awesome!" Todd's face lit up at River's suggestion.

After Meridian, River let Todd ride Felicity. It was almost as if he had never ridden her, for with his improvement in his skills, Felicity responded with energetic gaits, fluid transitions, and stayed in a rounded, upward frame. She was not at all like the horse he remembered, often resisting his hands and evading him with choppy gaits. His balanced seat, steady legs, and quiet hands seemed to communicate the message, 'I'm looking out for you, stay relaxed, pay attention'. He had the best responses from her he could ever remember, and she did not shy once. The experience cemented for Todd how important it was for the rider to stay soft and not hinder the horse's motion.

In his lessons Todd rode Pendragon, Felicity, Fiel, and every once in a while, River let him ride Corazón. Todd rode Dune out on the trails, but River was using her now to give beginner jumping lessons to some of the kids in pony club. Todd missed riding Dune as often as he used to, but trail riding her had always been the best anyway.

One rainless Saturday in November, River asked Todd, "Do you want to jump a little today?"

"Yeah, that would be great," Todd answered sincerely, pleased that the thought of jumping no longer triggered a panic attack.

"Good, you can ride Dune today."

Humming a happy tune interspersed with friendly conversation, Todd took extra care in grooming his old friend. "We'll have fun, don't you think?" he asked as he finished buckling on her bridle and led her out from the crossties. It was a very pleasant winter day with a cloud cover that kept the temperature above freezing without threatening rain - perfect riding weather.

As he stepped outside the stable entrance, expecting to head toward the outdoor arena, River beckoned him from the top of the lane. "Back field," he called out, and turned back down the hill.

Field jumping? Todd had not expected to be doing cross-country jumps. He pushed away the faint rising suspicion of what River might have planned, and led Dune down to the field and up to the mounting block.

"Walk her out to the perimeter on a loose rein, but then pick up the contact and try to get her to collect a little more at the walk."

Nodding that he understood, Todd obeyed, and once he reached the edge of the field with River following, he followed the instructions of moving her in shoulder-in to renvers at the walk, trying to keep her soft and round as she brought her hind leg underneath to move laterally.

"Good, it's hard for her, but she's really trying," River said after several attempts in both directions. "Praise her, and pick up rising trot. Lighten your hands and let her stretch and relax after that collected work."

Following River's instructions for the exercises kept Todd's mind focused on Dune's responses. After all the horses he had been riding lately, he realized how hard it was for Dune to stay round with her hindquarters engaged. She was much harder to ride, for it took a lot more effort to stay soft when she lost her balance, in spite of how hard she tried. It no longer surprised him they never received great scores for their dressage tests.

"She's trying hard. I think that's enough of that kind of work for her. Go ahead and hand gallop her in a big circle and let her stretch her neck to reward her," River called out.

"I actually understand now how jumping is so much easier for you," Todd murmured as he moved her into the faster gait and up into two-point to rest her back.

"Good, Todd," River said after Dune completed a big circle in each direction around the field. "Stay in the gallop but take her over the first log, then the coop and the stone wall. Then I want you to take her to the right and over the brush. Be sure she sees the jump when you go right."

Easy enough! Todd obeyed, enjoying the feel of Dune galloping powerfully and with obvious energy and confidence. She took each obstacle well in stride. All Todd had to do was place her in line with each jump, let her motion move him up over her neck when she arched over, and then to relax back into a soft seat in between the jumps.

I hope this works, River thought to himself, thinking now was the time to put his secret plan into action. Dune was certainly doing her best, and Todd looked confident and relaxed on her back. The ditch was in line after the brush, and Dune had just landed. He shouted out, "Keep going and jump the ditch!"

As if she understood the command, Dune pointed her ears forward, and lengthened her stride approaching the ditch, gauging the spread she needed to clear. She felt her rider tighten the hold on her bit. His muscles froze, and instead of his weight balancing with her motion, it now weighed down on her back, making it harder for her to reach with her shoulders. She shook her head, *let go*, but her rider did not understand. This had happened once before, and now the pressure at the corners of her mouth increased, asking her to stop. She threw her head up as he tried to pull her head to turn her away.

Neither Todd on her back or River watching apprehensively, could explain how Dune, always so willing and obedient, knew she needed to disobey all the messages she received from her rider. She ignored the pain on her mouth and the immobile weight on her back.

She kept her rhythm, careful in her strides, sensing she needed to make this jump smooth. She heard her rider scream as she sailed over the ditch.

Dune landed and slowed as gently as she could. River hurried over and she stepped toward him, a familiar friend, and someone she sensed could help her distraught rider.

"Todd, what is it?" River reached the mare, and stroked her neck reassuringly as he peered up into the stricken face of the boy on her back.

Tears flowed down Todd's cheeks, leaving muddy tracks. He sat like a weighted sack on his horse, his hands twisted in her thin mane. "Sh-sh-she, she p-p-put the l-l-lid down. S-s-so d-d-d-ark. C-c-can't b-b-breathe," he sobbed.

"Todd, I'm so sorry. What are you talking about? Come, get off." River reached up to touch Todd's arm to help him dismount.

Vehemently, Todd shook his head. Suddenly he overcame his frozen posture, and he leaned forward over Dune, hugging her neck, and speaking her name affectionately. Then to River's astonishment, Todd moved her off into a trot. He circled her back around and asked for canter. Then he turned her in the direction of her one eye, to face the ditch again.

Snorting in rhythm with her galloping stride, Dune thundered forward. Her rider wasn't helping much, sitting too far forward, and the reins this time loose, but at least he didn't interfere or cause her pain. She sailed over the ditch again, and galloped on.

"Absolutely incredible," Dr. Statton had exclaimed repeatedly when he met with John and Gwen Marshall after his session with Todd. He laughed good-humoredly. "A horse! After all these years of therapy sessions, it's a horse that causes the breakthrough."

It amused him that a horse taking Todd over the frightening ditch had opened up his deep consciousness to his early childhood trauma. "It's been festering down there; a memory so painful he could not remember it consciously, even though it happened again and again in his nightmares. But I think that memory started to surface when he had his accident and suffered a concussion. Then after the experience with his mother, it just needed some catalyst to erupt. I believe that ditch, when he landed in it head first and then lost consciousness, became the symbol for a trunk that his mother used to lock him in as punishment. Jumping over that ditch was the catalyst.

"We never knew. I can't tell you how many nights he would wake me with his screaming. The poor child, so obviously in terror but no idea what had happened in that nightmare. She actually locked him in a trunk?"

"Yes, Todd remembers now. Apparently that was her favorite form of punishment. He has no idea how long at any one time she kept him in that trunk, but he can remember now a few times wetting himself because he had been in there so long he could no longer hold it." Dr. Statton shook his head in pity and disgust. "It must have been hours at a time."

"If Todd could have remembered that, maybe she never would have been allowed that trial custody period. But I guess there is no point in 'if onlys' now," John Marshall remarked.

"It's going to take some more sessions to help him deal with this, but the first and most important step has been made. What's still so incredible to me is how much gratitude Todd has for that horse. We've all believed animals have been therapeutic for him, but I guess I finally understand how truly therapeutic they are. You keep Todd involved with the horses, and he's going to come out of this okay."

24 SEASON'S END, A YEAR LATER

A pony is a childhood dream. A horse is an adulthood treasure. – Rebecca Carroll

Another season over and one of the best years we've ever had, Tess thought to herself, looking over the end-of-year tally of competitions. So many surprises, well at least for her, probably not so much for River. She accepted now that he had a much better understanding of each horse's ability and also the students.

One of those surprises was that crippled girl Jodi, and her new mare. The pair had won second place in junior first level at the regional dressage championship just last weekend. *Two years ago that girl could barely even sit on a horse standing still!*

The junior and senior Pegasus teams had swept away the top ribbons at the regional combined training championship a few weeks ago. She smiled to herself as an image came to mind -River and Sierra standing together and congratulating Todd Marshall, who had won first place in junior training on Felicity. *The boy who couldn't even jump the ditch a year ago.* Tess never heard the complete story of how Todd finally managed to take the ditch here in the Pegasus field, but she knew the mare Dune had been instrumental in that happening. Well, she had to admit, she had completely underestimated Dune as well.

Pegasus Equestrian Center was certainly thriving. She sighed in contentment, fingering the most recent check from her partner, Frances Galensburg. The woman had finally realized her dream of owning an Olympic contender. River had made the US Equestrian Dressage team and had ridden Oberon to win an individual gold medal in the summer Olympics. Mrs. Galensburg's most cherished possession, prominently displayed in her home, was a photo with her as the owner of Oberon, standing next to his head, River on his back, and behind them the winning dressage score posted. Draped over the frame was the gold medal River had given her, for it meant so much more to her than it ever would to him.

Pegasus had long waiting lists for stalls, training, and lessons. Even with so many horses in training and a full schedule of lessons, River seemed very happy as the head trainer and instructor. He had told Tess adamantly, after returning home from the Olympics, that he never wanted to compete outside of their region again. Well, she supposed she would have to accept his resolve, for his reputation had been made. And who knew…another horse like Oberon who thrived with an audience might come along and just maybe….

The sound of horses whinnying, and hooves clopping into the stable let her know horses were being brought in for the evening. She shut down her computer, locked up the check and books in the file cabinet, and prepared to go home, very satisfied.

"Goodnight, sweet lady," Jodi whispered into her mare's mane, giving her one last hug.

Maggie snorted, nudged Jodi's hand but finding no more carrots, dropped her head to the pile of hay at her feet.

"You ready?" Todd Marshall came down the aisle, having just said his own goodnight to Dune, still his favorite.

"Yeah, guess we better go. I've got that early class." Jodi stepped out of the stall and latched the door. As she turned, she gasped as Todd surprised her by pulling her into his arms. "I'm so proud of both of you," he said, hugging her tight. "Your very first season, and second place!"

"Oh stop," she giggled. "It's Maggie who won, after all."

"I'm the winner," he said, nuzzling against her neck. Then he gazed into her beautiful eyes before he kissed her again.

The End

GLOSSARY OF EQUESTRIAN TERMS

Aids

Tools used to communicate with a horse. The natural aids are the seat (weight), legs, and hands of the rider. Artificial aids include whip and spurs.

Bend

A term used to describe how a horse's body curves in the direction of his movement, such as on a circle or around a corner.

Bit

The part of the bridle inserted in the horse's mouth as a means of communication or control. *Curb* – the most severe type of bit that uses leverage for control; *Pelham* – combination of a curb and snaffle bit and uses elements of both for control; the rider will have two sets of reins; *Snaffle* – direct pressure is applied to the lips, tongue, and bars of the horse's mouth; frequently it is jointed in the center; generally the mildest bit.

Canter

The third of the basic three gaits of the horse: a three beat gait in which the horse propels off of a hind leg while the other three are moving forward; on the second beat the horse touches down with the front leg on the same side and the opposite hind leg; on the final beat, the opposite front leg touches down. In this movement, the leg that touches down in the third beat is slightly ahead as well as the hind leg on the same side, which is called the lead.

Canter Pirouette

While in a collected canter, the horse executes a turn; half pirouette is 180 degrees and full pirouette is 360 degrees.

Collection

The horse shortens his stride, but the tempo does not change. The horse must bring its hindquarters underneath and carry more weight on the hind end which lightens the shoulders or front end.

Diagonal

In an arena, an imaginary line across from opposite corners.

At the posting trot, the rider rises out of the saddle when the horse's outside shoulder is forward, and sits in the saddle when the inside shoulder is forward.

Dressage

The training of a horse to develop, through standardized progressive training methods, a horse's natural athletic ability and willingness to perform and to maximize its potential as a riding horse. In dressage competitions, the horse is trained to perform precise controlled movements in response to minimal signals from the rider.

Extension

The horse lengthens its stride to the maximum length through great forward thrust and reach; the tempo or rhythm of the gait does not change.

Fédération Equestre Internationale (FEI)

International governing body for all Olympic equestrian disciplines.

Flying Lead Change

The horse changes the lead at the canter without breaking the gait.

Half-Pass

A lateral movement in which the horse moves on a diagonal; moving sideways and forward at the same time while bent slightly in the direction of movement. It differs from the leg yield in that the horse is bent in the direction of movement which requires more balance and engagement. In the leg yield, the horse is bent slightly away from the direction of movement.

Halt

The horse stops all forward movement; when performed correctly, the horse brings his hindquarters underneath and distributes his weight evenly on all four legs.

Hand

A unit of measure to determine a horse's height from the top of his withers to the ground. A hand equals 4 inches. Example: a horse that is said to be 15 -1, (fifteen hands, 1 inch) is 61 inches.

Haunches-In

See Travers

Haunches-Out

See Renvers

Inside

When riding in an arena, the side toward the center of the arena.

Lead

In the canter gait, the leading front and hind leg. In general, on a circle the correct lead is the inside lead, therefore if the horse is cantering on a circle to the right, it should canter on the right lead. Counter canter is a canter on a circle on the outside lead and is an exercise often used to help the horse learn balance at the canter.

Leg Yield

A lateral movement in which the horse moves sideways away from the rider's leg and forward at the same time, crossing his legs. The horse is fairly straight with a slight bend away from the direction of movement.

Lengthening

The horse lengthens its stride without an increase in tempo; performed at the lower levels of dressage before learning true extension of gait.

Long Rein

The reins are allowed to lengthen between the rider's hands and the bit, the rider often holding the reins at the buckle. There is often no contact with the mouth when riding with a long rein. The long rein is used to allow a horse to stretch his head down and forward and encourages relaxation.

Near

The left side of the horse.

Off

The right side of the horse.

Outside

When riding in an arena, the side toward the wall of the arena.

Passage

An advanced, collected movement at the trot in which the horse seems to pause with a moment of suspension between placing each foot on the ground; the horse almost appears to float in slow motion.

Piaffe

An elevated trot in place; an advanced movement of dressage and the ultimate in collection.

Rein Back

Walking steps backward; backing up.

Renvers (Haunches-Out)

A lateral movement in which the horse moves forward on three tracks, his shoulders on the track and the hindquarters to the outside track (in an arena with a wall, the movement is brought inside the track to allow room for the haunches out). The horse is bent in the direction of movement and the inside legs cross in front of the outside legs as he moves forward.

Shoulder-In

A lateral movement in which the horse moves forward on three tracks, his shoulders to the inside of the track and his hindquarters on the track. The horse is bent away from direction of movement and the inside legs cross in front of the outside legs as he moves forward.

Sound

A term used to describe a horse in good health without any lameness or other injuries.

Tempi Changes

The horse changes his lead at the canter every third stride (three tempi), every second stride (two tempi), or every stride (one tempi).

Training Pyramid

A guide for training the dressage horse; it begins at the base with rhythm and regularity, then moves up through relaxation, contact, impulsion, straightness, and collection at the peak of the pyramid.

Travers (Haunches-In)

A lateral movement in which the horses moves forward on three tracks, his shoulders and front legs on the track and his hindquarters to the inside of the track. The horse is bent in the direction of movement and the outside legs cross in front of the inside legs as he moves forward. The travers becomes a half-pass when the horse moves off the rail on a diagonal line.

Trot

The second of the basic three gaits of the horse; a two beat gait in which the horse moves diagonal legs in pairs such as left hind, right front together, then right hind, left front together; there is minimal head movement. The trot is the working gait of the horse.

United States Dressage Federation (USDF)

Governing body in the United States for dressage with the purpose of promoting and encouraging a high standard of accomplishment in dressage.

United States Equestrian Federation (USEF)

Regulatory organization for United States equestrian sports, formerly the American Horse Show Association.

United States Eventing Association (USEA)

Governing body in the United States for the equestrian sport of combined training or eventing.

Volte

A small circle, about six meters in diameter.

Walk

The first of the basic three gaits of the horse; a four beat gait in which the horse moves one foot at a time in sequence such as left hind, left front, right hind, right front; his head moves in rhythm with the walk.

Dressage Levels

Introductory

Training

First Level

Second Level

Third Level

Fourth Level

FEI levels:

    Prix St. Georges

    Intermediate I

    Intermediate II

    Grand Prix

Combined Training (Eventing) Levels

Beginner Novice

Novice

Training

Preliminary

Intermediate

Advanced

Age Levels

Junior – up to the age of eighteen

Young rider – age nineteen to twenty-one

Senior – over the age of twenty-one

ACKNOWLEDGMENTS

It is only through the support of my readers that this book is possible. I had only intended to write a trilogy, but with so many requests for more of Pegasus Equestrian Center, I surprised myself that there were more stories to be told. There will be one more book in the series, *The Spirit of Horses*. Thank you, everyone who kept asking.

As always, my deep gratitude goes to my husband. Dom, thank you for your willingness to read, edit, re-read, and edit some more. I know you would rather be fishing, but you have never complained. I love you.

Thank you for reading *The Courage of Horses*. If you enjoyed this story, please help other readers find this book:

Lend *The Courage of Horses* to a friend who might like it.

Leave a review on Amazon, Goodreads, or any other site of your choice. Even a line or two makes a difference and is greatly appreciated!

ABOUT THE AUTHOR

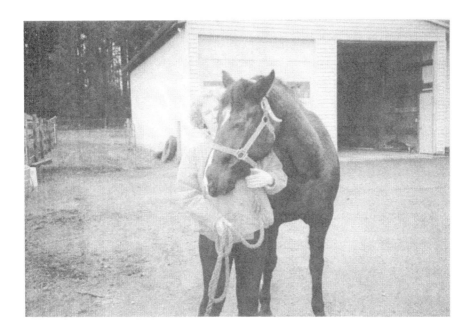

Diana Vincent's passion for horses began at the age of three when she caught her first glimpse of a horse. Ever since, she dreamed of owning her own horse, read every book about horses she could get her hands on, and finally, at age thirteen, acquired her first horse, Romeo. Since then she has owned several horses and has competed in hunter/jumper shows, eventing, and dressage. Today, Diana resides in the Pacific Northwest with her husband, and her Morgan horse, Midnight.

Diana loves to hear from readers. You may contact her at dnvncnt@hotmail.com.

CPSIA information can be obtained
at www.ICGtesting.com
Printed in the USA
FFOW03n1152040116
20093FF